DEAD SOULS

By Elsebeth Egholm and available from Headline

Three Dog Night
Dead Souls

DEAD SOULS

ELSEBETH EGHOLM

headline

First published in 2014 by
HEADLINE PUBLISHING GROUP

1

Cataloguing in Publication Data is available from the British Library

ISBN 978 0 7553 9814 0

Typeset in Granjon by Palimpsest Book Production Limited
Falkirk, Stirlingshire

Printed and bound in Great Britain by Clays Ltd, St Ives plc

Papers used by Headline are from well-managed forests
and other responsible sources

MIX
Paper from
responsible sources
FSC® C104740

HEADLINE PUBLISHING GROUP
An Hachette UK Company
338 Euston Road
London NW1 3BH

www.headline.co.uk
www.hachette.co.uk

To my mother

Author's Note

In *Dead Souls* I have – as in all my novels – used reality as the stage set while the plot and the cast are fictitious.

On this occasion I have taken a couple of extra liberties with St Mary's Abbey, the Cistercian convent on North Djurs, and the ancient Sostrup Manor House, which is run by the nuns as holiday accommodation. I have always been fascinated by the convent and the house. And as my main character, Peter, is a carpenter living in this area, nothing could have been more natural than to give him a job at the manor house and thus involve him in these mysterious events.

I would like to emphasise the following:

I have never visited the nuns, so none of the characters I describe is based on real people. Nor am I aware of any events which may have happened in the convent's recent history. I know the place only from the outside, as any ordinary, curious tourist would. The inspiration for this story was the moat, the thick walls and the idyllic yet sinister atmosphere, combined with religion.

Prologue

30 August
The Koral Strait, Kalø Bay

THE WATER WAS clear, a summer blue.

The rubber dinghy with the divers on board slowed down. Kir was sitting on the gunwale and gazing across the shimmering sea towards the ruins of Kalø Castle. It all felt unreal, as if her soul were still somewhere off the Horn of Africa. As if a Somali pirate boat might suddenly appear on the horizon and she and her colleagues would be ordered to board it and overpower the crew. Every movement required for such an operation was encoded in her body. One push of the button and the machine would be activated.

'OK. We're here. Drop the anchor.'

Her muscles tensed up under her drysuit. Her brain pumped adrenaline to her arms and legs. But her boss was no longer Captain Herman Søderberg; this time it was Commander Allan Vraa. She was no longer an elite soldier on board the *Absalon* but a mine diver on a summer mission in the Koral Strait. And she no longer had her weapon at the ready as she had in war-torn, troubled waters; she was searching the approach channel for shipping through peaceful Kalø Bay for explosives.

Allan Vraa watched a yacht sail past. It was crossing the bay a little further out. Two children on the sundeck waved to the divers in their dinghy. Kir had a flashback to the German hostages they had freed near the Somali coast. One of the boys had had hair so blond it was white, just like the boy on the deck of the yacht. His name was August, like the month that would soon be over.

I

'Watch out you don't rescue a couple of hapless tourists,' Vraa said and winked to Kir. 'It can be hard to kick the habit.'

'Can't keep a good woman down.'

He waved back to the children.

'Ready?'

She and Niklas looked at each other. This was a cushy number, clearing explosives off the seabed in Kalø Bay. They did it every three years. It wasn't long since the Royal Danish Navy divers had finished clearing up after the Occupation. Now they were looking for new munitions that might have rolled down the slope of the seabed beneath the drag of heavy barges carrying coal to Studstrup Power Station. Kir had missed out on the start of the fun. It was only two days since she had landed at Karup after her stint in Africa, which was meant to have lasted three months but had quickly turned into six. This was her first day back at work.

She adjusted her mask one last time. Then she held up a thumb and fell backwards into the water. It wasn't until the moment she hit the sea, which embraced her now with its usual chilly distance, that she became fully aware she was back in Denmark. This was, after all, where she had been born and had grown up.

The team consisted of eight divers and they worked in shifts – no diver was allowed to work at these depths for more than forty minutes every twelve hours – and they had managed to cover a fair stretch of the approach channel.

Kir was dreaming about her tuna sandwiches as she trawled the sea floor for the final ten minutes before resurfacing. She loved swimming through the water twenty metres down, watching plaice hide in the sand or meeting a codfish or an eel going about its business. Green and brown tongues of seaweed reached up from the sand and caught the rays of the sun. It was perfectly quiet. She herself was almost noiseless. Her diving equipment recycled most of the air and the bubbles passed through a bubble minimiser, which made them so tiny all she could hear was a faint hiss. The dinghy, too, was non-magnetic and low-noise so as not to trigger any lurking mines. Not that there were any mines left in Kalø Bay, but there was a huge number of artillery shells and aerial bombs and a fair amount of handgun ammunition. Divers were under instructions only to clear munitions with a total load in excess of fifty kilos. Otherwise they would be diving here forever.

Kir propelled herself forwards and her hands groped at seaweed, plants and sand. Slightly ahead of her there was a clearing as though a bomb had exploded and killed all living things, leaving behind a crater and only sand. She knew the crater well, she had been here before, but the seabed changed as the current reshaped the sand and from time to time new items were revealed.

She swam closer. There was an object lying in the sandy hollow. She had reached it now and could touch it. It felt like the corner of a wooden box or a small coffin. She dug deeper into the sand. It took time to free the box, which was indeed made of wood, but with metal fittings, a padlock and four metal corners.

Working away, she told herself it was probably nothing of any importance. Of course the box wouldn't be filled with grenades or weapons. There must be a perfectly reasonable explanation for its being here.

Once she had uncovered it, she cradled it in her arms and started her ascent. She was received by a surprised though cheerful Allan Vraa, who took the weight of the mysterious box and said:

'You are like a Labrador. You have the strangest ability to find just about anything.'

'A Labrador is a retriever,' Kir said as she squirmed on board like a whale beaching. 'It assumes that if someone has thrown an object, it's meant to fetch it back.'

'Exactly,' Allan Vraa said. 'Someone dropped this box so that you could have a chance to show off by retrieving it.'

'Whoever threw it must be very patient,' Kir said. 'I think it's been there for years.'

The box was covered with seashells and algae. It was also misshapen and looked as if only the metal was holding it together.

'I wonder what it could be.'

'Why don't we take a look?' her boss said.

'Better watch out. Could be dangerous,' she teased him as he produced a pair of bolt cutters from their kit. 'Perhaps it's infectious. An ancient virus, like in the grave of King Tut.'

'Rubbish,' Vraa said, forcing the bolt cutter handles together, and the padlock sprang open. He opened the box and both of them peered inside.

'What the hell . . . Doesn't that look like . . .'

Kir looked at the heap.

'Bones?'

'But not from an animal,' Vraa said.

Carefully, she picked one up.

'A femur?'

She examined it. The bone had yellowed with age. She could see that it had been broken and that the fracture had healed.

'What's that?'

Vraa pointed.

'A number. Thirty-one.'

She looked inside the box again.

'They're all numbered.'

'Sick bastard,' Vraa said, shaking his head. 'First, he deboned his victim and then he numbered her bones. Christ Almighty.'

'Hold your horses . . .' Kir began. 'There could be a perfectly reasonable explanation.'

Vraa glared at her belligerently.

'And what might that be?'

She fell silent. She couldn't think of anything either.

'Close the box,' her boss said. 'And call Aarhus police and tell them we've got something to cheer them up.'

4

Evening
Gjerrild Clif

Peter read the text message from Cato and jumped out of bed. The girl next to him sat up with her hair in a tangle and her make-up smeared. She pulled the duvet to cover her breasts.

'What's happened?'

He threw on some clothes.

'You've got to go!'

She looked startled, but then she slowly began to get dressed, on the brink of tears.

'You're a real douche bag, did you know that?'

Her name was Joy and he had met her at a club called Summertime. She meant nothing to him and he meant nothing to her, but neither of them had admitted it to themselves yet. The sex had been OK, but something had been missing. The most important ingredient.

'It's nothing personal. Someone's coming.'

'Your girlfriend?'

She looked upset. He knew it was a temporary feeling. Tomorrow she would be just as relieved as he was.

'I don't have a girlfriend. As you well know. Now get a move on, or . . .'

'Or what?'

There was no time for diplomacy.

'Listen. You're a nice girl. It's me.'

He stretched out his arms. 'I just haven't got time for a relationship right now, OK?'

She had her own car, thank God. Five minutes later she drove out of his life. He read the text message again. Cato said simply that his enemies were on their way. Peter had been expecting them for a long time. Now it had kicked off.

He looked at his watch. It was eleven in the evening and dusk had wreathed the cliff and the sea in darkness. He had thirty minutes, maximum.

* * *

He spent the time checking the alarm system. He took the dog with him as he made his tour and together they inspected the PIR sensors, which he had positioned one hundred metres from his cottage on the cliff. They were wired together and the cables went up to the house where they were connected to two bells and four vibrators. The sensors were the first bulwark against Rico's henchmen, who would undoubtedly arrive on noisy motorbikes with a whole arsenal of weapons, insignia and rippling muscles. There was no shortage of expressions to describe bikers, but discreet wasn't one of them.

There were six of them, Cato had said. Six men. Six avengers from Midnight Cowboys on their way from their clubhouse in Aarhus. This was the price for having killed their leader in Lisbjerg Forest earlier that winter. An unavoidable killing and one which had benefited Rico, the current leader of the gang. The court case that had followed had ended in Peter being acquitted on the grounds of self-defence, but his beef with the bikers was far from over. There was a code to be honoured. He had known that all along. He hadn't issued his guests with a printed invitation, yet he had known they would come.

After making sure that every cable was properly connected and that the system was working, he checked the second phase of his defence. Fifty metres from the house he had placed seven wireless bells at access roads and paths and various strategic places behind bushes and trees. Whenever he was at home he always carried a battery-powered remote control. On each bell he had disconnected the cable that would make it ring and replaced it with an old-fashioned light bulb, but he had carefully smashed the glass. Each bulb had then been put in a plastic bag, along with a little black powder from a screamer firework. He had put the bag inside a 1.5 litre pop bottle filled with petrol.

He checked each of the seven firebombs to make sure they hadn't been knocked over by passing animals or stolen by walkers in the area. Even though he lived on his own in the cottage on the cliff, the place attracted many wildlife enthusiasts who came to watch the birds, catch sea trout or simply enjoy the rugged North Djur landscape. But all seven bottles were exactly where he had put them. His alarm system was ready.

Back in the house with the dog, he looked at his watch again. The external inspection had taken fifteen minutes. He had fifteen minutes left. He spent them checking all the internal locks. All the chains, bolts and locks were set on all the windows and doors on the ground floor. He switched off the lights downstairs and outside. Then he went upstairs with the dog.

He was still wearing his heavy boots. Now he put on his bullet-proof vest under his camouflage jacket. He knelt down and pushed aside one of the low bookcases. His book collection had grown steadily in recent years as Manfred and he read extensively and discussed literary classics together.

He opened the secret room in the space under the sloping roof by pushing a spring lock on the right-hand corner of the hidden panel. He took out a fabric bag containing a hunting rifle which he had bought from one of Matti's connections. Peter was disqualified from owning or handling firearms, but he had regarded the purchase of the rifle as essential nevertheless. The police couldn't or wouldn't protect him. They didn't have the resources either, and he preferred to rely on himself. To that end he needed a weapon and he had chosen this rifle.

He put five cartridges in the magazine and pushed forward the bolt. He heard the click as the first cartridge slid into the chamber. He put the box of ammunition on the table. Then he picked up the night scope and attached it to the barrel. He turned off all the lights upstairs, opened the two south-facing eaves windows and left the balcony door open. This was the advantage of living in a house on the shore of the Kattegat. The enemy would not be arriving from the sea.

He positioned himself at the window overlooking the lane and waited with the rifle resting on the window sill, his senses fully alert.

The darkness had deepened. The world was at rest, but the quiet felt ominous.

Finally, he heard them. He couldn't distinguish the sound of one Harley from another and had to take Cato's word for how many there were. He tensed every muscle and leaned against the window. The dog growled from his place on the fleece in the corner.

He counted the seconds. The engine noise rose steadily. The air started to quiver.

Then the bell rang and the vibrator by the door started humming. They were one hundred metres from his cottage.

He took the remote control out of his pocket and held it at the ready. Now he could see them through the night scope. The six motorbikes calmly moved closer. Ninety metres. Eighty metres. Seventy-five metres. He had his finger on the button. At fifty metres he pressed. Puff and up went one as a spark ignited the petrol. The rider at the front was turned into a living fireball and rocked from side to side. Peter pressed the remote control again and the same thing happened. Now there were two fireballs in the summer night.

The engines came to an abrupt halt. He could hear agitated voices, but couldn't make out what was being said. However, he could see everything from the window in the glare of the fire. The four remaining bikers tried desperately to save their colleagues, rolling them around on the ground and stamping out the flames. The two bikers were screaming in pain. Then came the sound of shots. One, two, three. Half-hearted attempts to save face in a battle they had already lost. Peter responded with silence.

The two burning motorbikes lay on the ground like huge torches as the bikers put their injured friends on the pillions of the other motorbikes and fled from this accursed cliff in the back of beyond where a madman had just thwarted an attempt on his life, one man against six. Peter imagined that was how they would be thinking. They wouldn't be coming back in a hurry at any rate.

It wasn't until they had left, the fire had burned down and silence had descended over the cliff again that he lowered the rifle, closed the windows and went downstairs to feed the dog.

Next afternoon
Grenå Nursing Home

'Happy birthday, Grandad.'

Mark Bille Hansen bent over the wheelchair to deliver his message. His grandfather, who was ninety-five, grabbed his elbows with two strong hands and held him at arm's length.

'Let me see your mouth when you talk, Mark, otherwise I can't hear you.'

Mark was really too busy to celebrate the old man's birthday. Shots had been heard on Gjerrild Cliff last night and they had found two burned-out motorbikes. Everyone knew this was part of an ongoing feud between Peter Boutrup and his biker enemies, but Boutrup himself had been tight-lipped. Mark, in his capacity as Head of Grenå Police, should have been there, but now he was here because he had made a promise to his mother and she always got her way.

He repeated his congratulations to his grandfather, now with exaggerated lip movements.

'Thank you. There's no need to shout!'

'Who wants some cake?' someone called out, to Mark's enormous relief.

A trolley was wheeled in by an anonymous-looking woman who reminded Mark of a tortoise.

'Where are my ninety-five candles?' Mark's grandfather demanded.

'You've got to be joking,' Mark's mother said. 'You'd never be able to blow them out in one go.'

'Of course I can. I could blow *you* all out if I wanted to. Get out, the lot of you!'

The birthday boy waved his arms about. Mark's mother took hold of the wheelchair and pushed him to one side while the guests waited anxiously for the cake to be cut and the ceremony to be over so they could get away from this crazy old man.

Mark heard his mother trying to mollify her father.

'Come on, Dad. It's just for one day. You've been looking forward to it.'

'There's too much noise.'

'Your hearing isn't what it was.'

'I can still hear noise.'

'Please, Dad. Eat some cake.'

She gestured to Mark to fetch a plate. He cut a wedge of cake and brought it over. His grandfather grabbed it greedily and immediately set to.

Mark looked around. He liked his grandfather. And he liked the fact that he protested about his mother's fussing. He too hated birthdays, and his mother had a tendency to overdo everything. He had an idea.

'Fancy a trip outside, Grandad?'

This time he was sure his grandfather could see his lips. The old man nodded.

'Can we go to Tirstrup? To the airport?'

Mark had had in mind a walk down the long corridors of the nursing home and possibly outside into the sun just to get away from the guests and the noise and breathe in some fresh air – but what the hell. He nodded and lined up the wheelchair.

'We're just going out for a bit,' he announced to the guests, who seemed relieved. Even his mother nodded and waved. She too thought he meant a short walk around the gardens.

Instead Mark sneaked the old man down to his car and helped him into the passenger seat, folded the wheelchair and set off for Tirstrup.

'Are you going flying?' he asked his grandfather.

'No.' His grandfather seemed to be chewing on something; perhaps a bit of cake that had got stuck in his teeth. 'I just wanted to get out and feel the air on my skin.'

'And feel your hatred for the Germans?'

His grandfather chuckled. It sounded almost like sobbing.

'I want to go there to remember my comrades.'

'Men who died during the war?'

'And those who died afterwards,' his grandfather said.

He looked at Mark.

'Never underestimate them. The dead. You learn that when you grow old.'

To himself he added, almost in a whisper:

'They have a nasty habit of coming back.'

1

PETER RAN HIS hand down the new door frame in the music room, pleased with his work.

'That'll do,' he declared.

'Do? Yes, we certainly hope it will. Otherwise it's a waste of time *and* money.'

He looked up. Sister Beatrice had stopped playing and turned to him. A cheeky smile lingered at the corner of her mouth. A smile she wouldn't readily admit to and which she quickly brought under control.

'Just a figure of speech,' he said.

'From the real world, I presume?' She pointed to the tall convent window. 'Out there?'

He returned her smile. Of all the sisters, he found her the easiest to get on with. When he thought about it they had actually struck up something that bordered on friendship.

She got up and joined him. The nun's white outfit – there probably was a name for it – wrapped itself around her body, concealing generous curves no one must see, let alone think about. Her face was about to crack into a smile again. The abbess must have had a job keeping her under control when the nuns were in silent prayer. He had been told that they prayed twenty-four hours a day at the convent. Always. Night and day, at least one of them would keep the flag flying and the line open to Him upstairs.

It was a mystery how Sister Beatrice had ended up here. She was young, mid-twenties. On the whole the nuns were nowhere near as old as he had imagined and they came from all over the world. Several times he had heard their muffled laughter in the corridors and seen their eyes sparkle, but no one laughed more readily than Beatrice.

Her face revealed her every thought. It broke into all manner of expressions, ranging from giggles to profound sorrow and gentleness. Peter had had the pleasure of seeing that face several times during the summer while Rimsø Carpenters carried out repairs to the buildings that formed the St Mary's Abbey. Talking to this young German nun, who spoke perfect Danish, had been an even greater pleasure. So far they had covered every topic from faith, hope and love to a dog's delicate sense of smell and the difference between a hacksaw and a plane. There was always genuine interest in her eyes and voice. Always a fine sense of where to draw the line between the intimacy of friendship and that which went beyond. Like now, when she suddenly switched from jest to earnestness in a millisecond.

'And you caught most of them?'

'They don't take much persuading. They've no idea what freedom is.'

'They're lucky,' she said, sending him her glance which said more than the famous thousand words.

He had been telling her about this morning's events at Gjerrild: during the night some (probably well-intentioned) activists had released six thousand mink belonging to Henrik Hansen and knocked down the mink farmer's daughter when she had gone after them. Neighbours and friends had spent the night and the early morning catching the mink, but a couple of hundred were still pawloose and fancy free.

'They can't survive in the wild,' he said.

'So much for the dream of freedom.'

He wasn't sure he liked the subtext. Was she thinking about herself or him? He scrutinised her face, but it was blank. Then she changed the subject once again, a past mistress of conversation.

'It's still so peaceful out there.'

She nodded – another nod to the real world – towards the convent courtyard, which was being lashed by rain and wind from the northwest in the deepening twilight.

'Still?'

'Tonight the dead and the living will meet. If we are to believe the stories.' Something soft had crept into her voice. Her face was serious.

'In our church we celebrate All Hallows. All Saints – the thirty-first of October. But for you it's about the souls of the dead, Halloween. The living and the dead.'

'The night of dead souls?'

She nodded.

'If there's someone you're hoping to meet, you'd better keep your eyes open . . .'

A mischievous glint reappeared.

'Oh no, that's right, you don't believe in that stuff.'

She made her voice unnaturally deep and he heard himself being quoted: 'It is what it is. Everything else is superstition.'

Peter started packing up. He smiled at his toolbox as his hammer and screwdriver slotted into their places. She was the quirkiest person he had met since My, his unusual friend from the Titan Care Home days. But in a completely different way. While My was a vulnerable, wounded soul, Beatrice was a small, round apparition with dimples and a talent for cheering him up.

'Now, now,' he muttered and straightened up. 'I suppose I could make an exception and go to a meeting like that, just to be on the safe side.'

She tilted her head and gave him a penetrating look, not without a sense of triumph.

'Man is more than pure reason. He has feelings too. Do I detect a heart beating for someone you hope to meet at the cemetery at midnight?'

'Is that where it happens?'

'According to what you call superstition, yes.'

He put the last hammer in his toolbox and got up with it in his hand.

'I can always take the dog for a walk to see if anyone is dancing on the graves.'

She ran after him as he raised two fingers to his forehead to go. 'Wait. Here.'

She rummaged round at the bottom of her pocket. Taking his hand, she pressed something into his palm and closed his fingers around it.

'To be on the safe side. You need it more than I do.'

It wasn't until he came down to the courtyard with his toolbox that he looked at the object she had given him. A rosary. A string of black beads. He had seen her winding it around her fingers as she mumbled inaudibly. He wondered for a moment if it would help. Probably not, he concluded. Nevertheless, he put it carefully in his pocket.

As he did so, he spotted a figure moving across the courtyard and down behind the far end of the moat. On impulse he followed and watched the person cross the bridge over the water and head in the direction of the herb garden at the back. From the clothing, he was able to identify her as Sister Melissa, an eighteen-year-old girl, the only Dane in the convent and, as far as he had understood, a kind of trainee. That was why her outfit was a darker colour than the usual white of the Cistercian nuns. Melissa had told him she wasn't going to be a nun, but she had been attracted by the idea of a year of peace and contemplation in the convent and the abbess had granted her request.

He had observed that there was a special relationship between Beatrice and Melissa. Unspoken, but eyes could tell you so much, and Sister Melissa's in particular. The word 'devotion' crossed his mind. It was old-fashioned but appropriate. For a moment he followed Melissa with his eyes. Should he offer to help her? Fetch an umbrella from his van? Warn her that the rain would only get worse and she would get soaked because the herb garden was some distance away?

He was about to go closer when he saw another figure appear out of the twilight. A man, blurred in the rainy mist. The two of them stood together for a while. Suddenly, Sister Melissa became agitated. She waved her arms about and her head bobbed from side to side. The other person, nondescript in dark trousers and a short dark jacket, seemed calm but also intimidating. He took Melissa by the elbow and led her away. It was impossible to know whether it was against her will or not.

Peter was seized by a feeling of unease and for a moment he considered walking down to the two of them and intervening. But what was it, after all? A private meeting, or an argument? Besides, he had his policy, he reminded himself: not to get involved in other people's affairs. It was Sister Melissa's own private business who she met.

Even so, he waited until the figures had disappeared from view. Then he picked up the toolbox, went to his van and drove home to the dog.

It was late. He had checked his alarm system and already dragged his mattress onto the balcony when he remembered the rosary and what Sister Beatrice had said about the souls of the dead. He took out the rosary and slid the beads through his fingers one by one. He wasn't a man of faith. In fact, he hated religion with all his heart because other people's faiths had given him nothing but trouble. Nevertheless, he couldn't get the idea of a midnight meeting out of his mind. He could hear the voice. A girl's reedy voice with a core of obstinacy:

'I'm bloody freezing. Sodding, shitting, bollocking hell.'

My's language could be fruity when the mood took her. Her ashes had been released and he had found a site for her urn at Gjerrild Cemetery. No family members had come forward to claim her.

He looked at the dog lying on his fleece, watching him. The rain had stopped them from going out for a long walk earlier. Now, in the darkness, it had eased. He stared through the window. On the Kattegat he could see lights from a couple of vessels at anchor or crossing the sea. Otherwise it was pitch-black, but that had never bothered him or the dog.

'Come on, Kaj. Walkies?'

17

My's dog – he had inherited the Alsatian when she died – came up to him, wagging his tail and putting his big head in Peter's hand. The dog's eyes confirmed what his tail had already said.

Other people had had the same idea. Not to turn up in person, but lit candles had been placed on some of the graves, perhaps so that the dead souls would feel welcome if they happened to make an appearance.

I must be out of my mind, he thought, as the dog ran around sniffing.

What am I doing here?

Well, while he was here, he might as well have a look at her grave. Perhaps he should have lit a candle as well, but his mind had been elsewhere. He hadn't even brought flowers.

Beatrice knew nothing about My. In general, they rarely discussed personal matters. It was as if they shared a mutual respect for the choices each had made and the events which had led them to the margin of windy Denmark, on the nose of the face that formed Djursland at the edge of the blackest sea. But she knew everything about him, of course. Most people in the area did. A man who had done time for manslaughter can't avoid a certain level of notoriety.

He found her grave quickly. There was already a small candle flickering in a plastic cup. He trawled through his memories to work out who might have left it. Not many people knew of this place.

He stood for a while staring into the flame. He had chosen a natural, unpolished stone. The wording was in simple, black letters: My Johansen 30-11-1984–26-9-2010. My's life had been nowhere near as simple.

Images from their childhood danced to the rhythm of the small flame. They had grown up together at Titan Care Home where physical punishments were the order of the day. He had often thought it was the torture that broke My and turned her into what she was, but the doctors had a medical diagnosis for her. A form of autism, they said. Funny how such a small, anaemic word had been used to explain why My was like no one else in the whole world.

No one could move like My, who always wore her long coat and a woollen hat on her head with a hobbling dignity. She had a limp and could reel off crazy sentences that never finished, embroidered with puns and rhymes and plenty of curses and swearing. Her figure was elfin, her hair mousy brown and thin. Her eyes always asked questions he couldn't answer.

And now, she was up there. That was the feeling he got whenever he lay looking up at the starry sky. Perhaps he had a kind of belief after all.

Suddenly something moved on the periphery of his vision. He heard a rustling noise.

'Kaj?'

But it wasn't the dog. A figure approached him. Long coat flapping at the sides. The wind caught the hair escaping from the edges of the beanie. He blinked. My?

He was about to say her name, but he held it inside him as he watched the human figure moving closer and closer in the glow from the few flickering candles.

'I thought I would find you here,' the voice said.

'Miriam!'

'God, you look like you've seen a ghost.'

She came up to him and kissed him on the cheek, and he realised that she was very much flesh and blood.

'What are you doing here? It's the middle of the night!'

She eyed him sharply.

'It's only eleven o'clock. I thought you might want to make me some coffee. Or perhaps you've got a rendezvous?'

He shook his head and called Kaj. He looked up. It had started drizzling again.

'I hope you've got a car.'

2

He hadn't seen Miriam since the winter. In the interim he had decided he had probably seen her for the last time. Back in January, things had happened that had made him angry and had shaken his belief that they would ever speak again. And now she was sitting on his sofa with her stockinged feet tucked up underneath her and her make-up smudged from the shower they had been caught in before they reached her little tin can of a car.

'You look good,' she said to the teacup she was cradling in her hands. 'Do you miss her very much?'

'My?'

'No, I don't need to ask about her. I mean Felix.'

He shrugged. He wasn't ready to discuss Felix with her. She couldn't just waltz in after several months of silence thinking their former intimacy was still intact.

He could see that she understood. She drank her tea and hid her gaze in the steam.

'Why are you here?' he asked. 'What do you want from me?'

He was fond of Miriam, but he also had to be careful. She had already shown him once that she put money and security before friendship. But she had changed, he had to admit. There was a new earnestness to her. Her curvy figure seemed thinner, almost emaciated, but she was still attractive and sexy, and the memory of her body would always be part of him.

'I had a visitor the other day,' she said.

'Tell me something I don't know.'

Miriam and Lulu ran their own brothel in Anholtsgade in Aarhus. If they didn't have daily visitors something was wrong.

'It was a woman.'

'Piquant.'

'Stop it, Peter.'

She banged down her cup on the table. He saw that for once she wasn't wearing nail varnish. He had never seen her in jeans either. It was always corsets and short skirts with Miriam, and heels like stilts.

'Who was it?'

'My's mother.'

'What?'

'You heard me.'

'How did My's mother know where to find you?'

Now it was her turn to shrug.

'I'm in the phone book.'

'Only if you have a name.'

'I do have a name.'

My's mother. The thought was alien. Neither of them had had parents. Or at least, not parents who wanted them. Not even someone to bring them birthday presents or take them on picnics.

'What did she want?'

'Well, what do you think?'

His astonishment was replaced by anger when the truth dawned on him. He hated it when parents were suddenly overcome by remorse and the urge to pour love over their now adult children whom they had quite happily dumped on others for their entire childhood. He only had to think of his own mother. She was a journalist in Aarhus and if he let her she would be there, trying to mother him, faster than she could write a tabloid headline. Ridiculous, seeing as she had given him up at birth and hadn't seen him for almost thirty years.

'Don't tell me she was looking for her lost daughter.'

'Oh, yes, she wanted to know about My,' Miriam said. 'She wanted to track her down and tell her she had siblings. Half siblings,' she corrected herself.

'Find My? But didn't she know what happened?'

Miriam's voice went hoarse.

'Did she know that her daughter was dead and had been found hanging from a tree? No, Peter, she didn't. They don't give you that kind of information when you give up your child for adoption.'

She looked at him and collected herself. He remembered that Miriam had given birth once. A long time ago. She had told him that when she was young, she had been a drug addict and had given birth to a child who had died at birth. It still haunted her.

'I suppose there's a reason for that,' he said. 'She was no longer My's mother.' He corrected himself: 'She didn't want to be My's mother.'

Miriam rolled her eyes up to his ceiling, which needed a lick of paint.

'Listen to yourself! Aren't you on your high horse, Peter? You don't know the whole story. You've no idea what made her let My go.'

He got up and started pacing the living room. The dog lifted its head and sent him an anxious look. He was seething on the inside. There were always so many excuses for leaving children in the lurch. But it was pointless discussing this with Miriam, whose heart beat for everything from puppies to serial killers.

'Ah well, now she knows she can be on her merry way again.'

'She'd like to meet you.'

'*Me?*'

'She'd also like to see My's grave and leave some flowers.'

'Jesus wept!'

Miriam leaned forward and caught his eye. She said softly:

'And then she would like My to be transferred to a cemetery close to Aarhus where she lives.'

He knew it was inappropriate, but no other expression occurred to him to describe how he felt about that announcement:

'Over my dead body!'

3

'But couldn't she have gone . . .?'

Mark Bille Hansen suddenly found it hard to imagine where a nun would go if she were to go missing. Home? Into town? Dancing . . .? Possible scenarios appeared in his mind and not all of them could be shared with the worried abbess who had called Grenå police station.

Fortunately, it appeared that Sister Dolores, as she called herself, had a sense of humour despite her obvious concern.

'No,' she said, her voice laden with irony. 'She hasn't eloped with the gardener, she hasn't gone clubbing or joined a travelling circus, nor is she offering kisses for ten kroner on the high street because she's getting married in the morning. She's gone. Disappeared.'

'Since last night, did you say, Sister Dolores?'

How do you address an abbess? He decided to stick with Sister Dolores.

'At five in the afternoon she went to pick some herbs in the garden.'

'It was raining,' he reminded her.

She resorted to sarcasm again.

'She was wearing her water-repellent, super-nun habit. And her nun-wellies.'

He faltered and felt well and truly put in his place; the conversation was going from bad to worse:

'We're not freaks,' the voice said more patiently, as if talking to a child. 'We're human beings who have made important life decisions. But we live our daily lives like most other people. We go out into the rain to fetch herbs and we know it won't help to pray to God for five minutes' respite so we can get back inside without getting our feet wet.'

Sister Dolores sighed audibly.

'We get wet. Just like everybody else. And sometimes we catch a cold.'

'And sometimes you go missing,' Mark said.

A short pause followed, the air seeming to quiver.

'This is the first time. It has never happened before.'

Mark was reminded of the old joke about the two spinsters who had been brought up never to go outside and never to let men indoors. Until by some miracle one of them married the postman and sent the other a postcard from her honeymoon with the words: *Let the pussy cat out!*

However, it was probably not the right time to tell this joke. Sister Dolores clearly had a sense of humour, but this would be going a bit too far.

He looked at his watch. It was ten o'clock. In normal circumstances he would have given it more time – unless it was winter and minus 13° outside. Young women went missing and then they came back again, he knew that from experience. But it was clearly different with nuns.

'I'd better drop by. Is now a good time?'

'Ten minutes ago would have been better, but it'll have to do.'

Mark was familiar with the seventeenth-century convent in Sostrup. Once upon a time, the property had been owned by the Skeel family. In the Djursland of his childhood the convent had merely been part of the landscape, with its large gate and four wings with a tower and a moat, useful for playing war games. In town he had sometimes seen white-clad figures who reminded him of ghosts, but apart from that the nuns were just mysterious creatures you rarely saw or heard about.

He Googled the convent and learned that it had belonged to the Cistercian Order since 1960. In 1999 a new convent, called St Mary's Abbey, had been built a short distance south-east of the manor house.

He had never been to the convent on police business, nor had he ever imagined why he might. A couple of stolen prayer books? A sister who had overindulged on the communion wine? It was hard to imagine them at odds with their own laws or society's. They appeared to live quiet, contemplative lives, minding their own business and tending to the affairs of the convent, and they even had enough energy left over to pray for all the lost souls in the world, including his own.

As he drove his patrol car over the moat bridge and through the convent gates he couldn't help feeling a certain gratitude. There was, as far as he knew, no one else who found his miserable, diseased soul worthy of a prayer, although it was sorely in need of it.

He parked the car and got out, resolving to treat Sister Dolores and her fellow nuns with more respect than he had shown during the telephone conversation.

'Mark Bille Hansen?'

The woman who said his name walked towards him with such a light tread it was as if she was hovering. Her white habit hovered with her. Only her sturdy black shoes, sticking out from underneath the habit, seemed to be keeping her on the ground.

'This is Sister Beatrice, who has been kind enough to assist me. After all, it's not every day we have a visit from the law.'

Sister Beatrice was a totally different type to the hovering abbess. The weight of her body alone kept Beatrice's feet firmly on the ground. She had a soft, round figure, and even her nun's habit struggled to conceal her generous bosom. It looked as though she could easily smile or laugh, but at this moment she appeared tormented.

They set off across the cobbled courtyard between the red convent walls.

'Of course, we don't live here any more,' Sister Dolores said. 'Perhaps you know that we were given money for a new convent some years ago. It's round the back. The old buildings are used for courses and conferences, but we still have our herb garden down there.'

She pointed in front of her. 'That was where she went to pick herbs. Rosemary. Sister Mary was making roast lamb.'

'Sounds delicious,' he said stupidly. His dinner had been a burger from the takeaway on the corner.

'It was a Friday, so normally we'd have had fish, but it was Sister Mary's name day.'

They crossed the section of the moat which lay north of the bridge he had just driven over. Then the sisters led him down to a large, well-kept herb garden, which abounded with the kind of vegetables he always intended to eat but never managed to buy or cook. Vitamin pills had proved to be easier.

'Look. This is where she walked.'

Sister Dolores pointed to hefty shoe-prints on the ground, but it was hard to distinguish between them. There were also other shoe-prints.

'And she was alone?'

'Who else would be with her?' Sister Beatrice asked. 'We've done a headcount and we were all together indoors.'

'An outsider, perhaps? Someone attending a conference?' Mark could see his suggestion did not find favour.

'We found this,' Sister Dolores said, pointing. 'We didn't touch it, obviously.'

Perhaps even nuns watched *CSI* on TV, what did he know? Mark looked, but couldn't immediately see what she meant. Sister Beatrice pointed to some small twigs that looked like spruce.

'Rosemary,' she said. 'She must have picked it and then dropped it.'

He squatted on his haunches next to the little green sprigs and suddenly the situation felt surreal. Herbs . . . nuns . . . He was finding it hard to take this seriously. He hid his smile as he searched the grass around the spilled herbs but found nothing. Then he stood up and a glance at the faces of the two nuns made him feel ashamed. He read equal portions of horror and fear in their expressions, as if they had an insight into a world to which he had no access.

'Did anyone see Sister Melissa go down to the herbs? It was at five o'clock, you said?'

The abbess shook her head. But Sister Beatrice babbled something, then clasped her hand over her mouth.

'What was that?' he asked.

Beatrice lowered her hand.

'The carpenter left at five o'clock. Perhaps he saw something. He was in the music room putting up new door frames . . .'

'There's maintenance work going on,' Sister Dolores interjected. 'Quite a lot of jobs had piled up and we found some money to get it done.'

'What is the name of the carpentry firm?' Mark asked.

The abbess looked at Sister Beatrice.

'Now what was it?'

'Rimsø Carpenters,' Beatrice said. 'Sometimes there are two of them. Yesterday there was only one. His name's Peter.'

'Boutrup?' Mark asked.

Beatrice smiled. It was the only smile he had seen that day, but that made it all the brighter.

'Do you know him?'

He nodded.

'Yes. I know him.'

4

PETER NOTICED THE police car from a long way off and his first impulse was to turn around and drive back. He hated the police and all forms of authority with every fibre of his being.

But he had a job to do. Several door frames needed replacing, and he had also promised to look at the gutters as some sections required attention. Later it would be the turn of the roof, but that would take at least two of them. In a couple of days he and Manfred, his boss, would erect scaffolding on the north wing of the convent where several roof tiles needed replacing.

He dragged his toolbox out and slid the van door shut. He picked up the toolbox and started walking, but was stopped by a familiar voice.

'Peter!'

Mark Bille Hansen wasn't his friend, but possibly not his enemy either. He had a feeling it was Mark Bille who had managed to shelve the case of the burned-out motorbikes on the cliff back in August, which Peter regarded as a gesture of friendship.

However, his heart sank at the sight of the long-haired police officer who was approaching with the abbess while Sister Beatrice stood in the shadow of the convent wall.

'What's going on?'

The police officer held out his hand. They looked into each other's eyes. They were the same height, but Mark Bille's build was lean and tough. His face was lined, his long hair raven black. He looked more like a modern-day Native American in his boots, jeans and brown leather jacket than a Danish police officer – which was what he was.

'It seems that one of the sisters has gone missing,' Mark Bille said out of earshot of the others.

'Who?'

But Peter already knew.

'Someone called Sister Melissa, eighteen years old. She went out to collect herbs at five o'clock. About the same time that you drove home, I've been told.'

Peter only heard the other's voice as a distant echo. His whole body tingled and his bad conscience throbbed.

'Peter? I'm talking to you.'

The voice penetrated the sound barrier. Mark Bille eyeballed him. Peter nodded.

'I hear you.'

It was only a moment, but before he started telling him about yesterday's incident at the moat, the thought of saying nothing had crossed his mind. Of simply keeping to himself what he had seen. He knew he might end up being dragged into something he didn't wish to be dragged into. Besides, he felt no joy at helping the police.

'I saw her,' he said eventually. 'Someone went up to her in the rain.'

They walked down to the moat while he told Mark for the second time what he had seen and indicated the place where Melissa had met the stranger.

'And you're sure it was a man?'

'Quite sure.'

'Can you describe him in more detail?' Mark Bille asked.

Peter shook his head.

'Just ordinary. Dark jacket. Dark trousers.'

'How tall?'

'About my height, I think. Around one-eighty-five metres.'

'Broad?'

'Perhaps a bit broader. Than me, I mean . . . But it was hard to tell from a distance.'

They stood on the bridge over the moat for a while. Mark's next question hit him in the solar plexus.

'Why didn't you do something? Seeing that you had a hunch something was wrong?'

Sister Beatrice's gaze met him with the same question.

Peter closed his eyes for a brief second.

'It was nothing to do with me,' he said lamely as he heard himself reel off the world's oldest excuse.

He looked at Beatrice and felt her fear transplant itself in him.

'I'm sorry.'

'Perhaps she'll turn up,' Mark Bille said after a pause. 'Show us which way they went.'

He led them down to the place where he had observed the two of them walking and told them in as much detail as he could what he had seen. Mark Bille showed him the small bundle of rosemary and Peter squatted down on his haunches. He saw the prints and followed them. Two kinds. There were patches where the blades of grass were flattened. Something took hold of him inside, like when Kaj got a scent and followed a trail. He moved through the grass down to the furthest shore of the moat and found broken twigs and flattened grass on the way. He knew this. This was his territory: nature, the life of a hunter. He knew every birdsong, every plant, every animal. All his instincts were heightened now. He knew he was getting close to something important.

He had a feeling the others were watching him and perhaps Mark Bille was considering stopping him, so that he wouldn't ruin any evidence, but he continued to follow the trail through scrub and bushes and grass for quite a while. Then he spotted a black object lying in the damp grass close to the dark, muddy water.

He found a branch and fished it out. He carefully dangled the shoe in front of the two nuns. Everyone stared at it.

'Don't touch anything,' Mark Bille said.

Tears flowed down Sister Beatrice's cheeks. She blinked them away, in despair.

'They're hers. They're brand new.'

30

'All right then.'

Mark took out his phone and made a call. Peter knew it was to Aarhus Police when he asked to speak to Inspector Anna Bagger.

They heard him giving her a brief update and discussing the situation. Soon the police would be buzzing around the convent like bees around a flowering rosemary bush. Mark Bille was OK, but Peter had already had an encounter with the officers from the region's capital and this was not an acquaintance he wished to renew.

'We need that moat trawled from top to bottom right now,' he heard Mark Bille say. 'Can someone call the Kongsøre EOD Training Centre?'

Peter could visualise Anna Bagger's face at the other end of the line: the perfect lips pressed tightly together and the eyes with ambition written across them in flaming letters over the cool greyish blue.

'Of course I'm not sure,' Mark said. 'That's why we need to take a look . . . Yes . . . yes, probably . . . Right, that's agreed then.'

He ended the call and stood for a while staring into the moat.

'Are the divers coming?' Peter asked.

Mark made no reply. It was as if the moat was absorbing all his attention.

'She's down there,' he said at last, still staring into the black water. 'Where else would she be?'

5

SHE HAD TO be professional.

That was Kir's first thought when she saw Mark Bille talking to Allan Vraa down by the moat. His shoulder-length hair concealed his facial expression, but his body was the same: long and sinewy like a runner's, and he was wearing a leather jacket, jeans and boots. His jerky hand movements and his shuffling feet revealed his restlessness.

The police officer was clearly briefing the diving team about the assignment. A missing nun, Allan Vraa had said on the telephone when he called. This was very different from diving for munitions on a bright summer's day in Kalø Bay. But the camaraderie was the same, even though the tone was more subdued, and Kir was pleased to have been given the job. Even if it meant her confronting a man with whom, to put it mildly, she had a complicated relationship.

She greeted Mark and they exchanged a few remarks, which she knew she would turn over in her head later on when she was underwater. That was the way it always was. She did her best thinking when she was diving.

'OK. This is the situation.'

She was brought up to speed by her boss. Kir and another diver who lived locally had been called in, and there were also four divers from the EOD training centre in Kongsøre, who had come with a diving truck, dinghy and the whole range of equipment. Allan Vraa introduced her to the new colleague.

'This is John Frandsen, Frands to friends.'

He patted the new guy on the shoulder. Kir held out her hand in a friendly gesture and received a handshake as though Frands trained with hand grippers in the gym.

'And there was I thinking this was a man's job,' Frands said.

Kir hesitated. She couldn't work out whether or not he was being serious.

'Kir's the best there is,' Allan Vraa said cheerfully. 'She's just come back from the Bay of Aden, where she kicked pirate ass.'

Frands's scepticism was obvious, but Allan Vraa chose to ignore it.

'Water doesn't discriminate,' Kir said. 'Once we're down there we're all equal.'

She pointed to the moat. She was on the verge of adding that her smaller size allowed her to reach places in shipwrecks that were inaccessible to other, bigger divers. But it would have been stupid to provoke him so she kept her tone light as she said:

'Nice to meet you, Frands.'

'Likewise.'

It sounded forced. Frandsen's eyes had the exact same cold, macho expression that tended to be associated with a soldier. And his physical perfection bordered on caricature. He was almost 1.90 metres tall, with a square face and chin and thick knots of muscles in his neck.

'I expect you two to team up,' Vraa said. 'The others are doing a sweep with the sonar over on the eastern side. If you start setting up poles here, we're well on the way.'

They did as they were told without major problems or exchanges. Frands was obviously professional and knew what he was doing. It didn't take them long to arrange the poles in a tight grid on the bottom of the moat while the crew in the small dinghy rigged up the sonar and started using it.

The sonar was an effective tool for searching for underwater objects. It looked like a small torpedo and fortunately it didn't care about working in a moat filled with mud. It was lowered into the water from the stern of the black rubber dinghy and trailed along the bottom, and it could see thirty-five metres to each side. Two divers manoeuvred the dinghy and watched a computer monitor. White spots on the screen would indicate anything unusual.

After staking out the poles, Kir and Frands slipped into the water. The water level in the moat was high after the recent weeks' rain. Visibility was zero, but Kir was used to that. If there was someone on the bottom, she would find them.

She fumbled around in the mud and algae with one hand while the other held onto the line they had extended.

While she worked, she remembered the days of sunshine she had spent with her colleagues. A slice of paradise. The only surprise had been finding the box of bones. After speaking to the police, she had delivered it to the Institute of Forensic Medicine, where she had almost been ridiculed. Their verdict had been harsh and took no account of her injured feelings: it was a box of bones for educational use – the kind an anatomical institute might buy from medical equipment companies. It was probably from India and the bones came from a range of bodies rather than a single one. The forensic examiners had promised to take a closer look at the box, but at the present time their workload was too great.

Kir smiled behind her diving mask at the memory of the merciless teasing to which Allan Vraa, who had been convinced it was the work of a serial killer, had been subjected. The mood had been upbeat. Sunshine, summer and saltwater. In this atmosphere her colleagues had made her forget Africa in no time. Now, after meeting Mark Bille and this Frandsen guy, she wished she were back there hunting pirates.

She found various objects on her trawl across the bottom of the moat but left them untouched. Normally she and her colleagues salvaged all sorts of things: old oil barrels, bicycles, car tyres and so on. But time was scarce. The afternoon was on the wane, and soon darkness would close down the operation. She concentrated on one thing: finding a body. Possibly wearing a large amount of heavy, billowing fabric, which in itself would be enough to weigh it down.

Her disappointment with Mark was at the back of her mind as she worked. They had behaved professionally and greeted each other politely with Allan Vraa as their witness. Mark's words had seemed just as cold as Frandsen's eyes:

'Good that you could come at such short notice.'

She hadn't been much more welcoming herself.

'That's our job.'

He had shifted his gaze away from her.

'I hope you find her.'

She had spoken honestly:

'We will. If she's there.'

He had nodded without meeting her eyes again and had stood there staring into the black, brackish water. Then he had made his excuses, saying he needed to talk to a colleague, and left her alone. Out of the corner of her eye she had caught sight of another familiar figure, Peter Boutrup – the carpenter from the cliff with the dubious past and the big Alsatian. A strange, lonely-looking man who always seemed to be at ease in that loneliness, as though he didn't need anything or anyone. Boutrup nodded amicably to her before retreating from the moat with his hands buried in his jacket pockets. She had heard he was the last person to see Melissa alive. That thought seemed to be weighing heavily on him.

Kir turned her attention back to the assignment while the two men, Peter and Mark, flickered like phantoms somewhere in her brain. One fair and one dark. One who had served time and one who sent people to prison. One who had broken the law and one who upheld it with force. You would have thought that the police officer would be the one to exude calm. But he didn't. Peter did. The man from the cliff seemed like the rock from which his name was derived.

Kir sensed a commotion in the water behind her and Frandsen swam past like some sinister force. She forced herself to breathe calmly through her diving regulator and let the mixture of oxygen and nitrogen disperse through her body. Elements were close to her heart and she had a habit of dividing people up according to them.

If Peter was water, Mark was fire. What John Frandsen was, she hadn't yet made up her mind, but he wasn't one she liked.

Half an hour had passed when her hand felt some coarse, heavy fabric flapping in the water. A few more gropes and she touched what was unmistakably a human body. The hair was covered by cloth. She could feel the face: nose, eyes, mouth. A tongue protruding.

She signalled to Frands, lowered a weight with a length of rope attached to it so she could find the body again and rose to the surface of the brackish stream, motionless except for the movements of her own body. She trod water while pushing her diving mask up on her forehead and holding up the rope.

'I need a buoy! She's down here.'

6

I⊤ WAS NEVER enough. Nothing was ever good enough.

Shit, shit, shit!

Peter set down the toolbox. The door frame was in tatters. It was probably as ancient and decrepit as the rest of the damn place. He slammed his fist into it. How on earth had he ended up working in a convent? He, of all people, who had never believed in the existence of a God.

And even if he had, then what did that God want from him? It was something he had never been able to fathom. He did his best to live his life without being a burden on others. He also tried to be a good friend to his friends, a good colleague. However, his life seemed to have a built-in contradiction: every time he had chosen to focus on himself, he had been forced to risk everything. Every time he tried minding his own business, the outside world would come back to bite him.

He started knocking down the old door frame. The wood splintered; sharp fragments flew through the air; old paint flaked off.

It was two years since he had returned to his cottage after serving his sentence. Four years in Horsens State Prison had strength-ened his resolve to live a quiet life, just him and his dog. Look after himself. Do his job. All right, so he had enemies. And he had to take precautions or he was a dead man. But apart from that he never went near anything that smelled of illegality, prison, the slippery slope or bad decisions.

And here he was. Mixed up in something that might be a murder. Not guilty as far as the law was concerned. But – and this was the irony – guilty of having obeyed his own chosen laws.

*   *   *

An area had been cordoned off down by the moat. He had spotted Kir being briefed by her boss and had caught a smile and a nod. Her funny, pointed face and red curls usually cheered him up, but even she could not lift the heavy burden of guilt.

The police had herded people away before the divers went into action. Including him, Beatrice and Sister Dolores. Quite a long time had passed. There had been no official confirmation as yet, but there was already a rumour going round that Sister Melissa had been found at the bottom of the moat.

When he last saw her, she had been alive. He alone could have prevented her death.

Deep down, he had known she was in danger. He had known it and he had turned his back on her. He couldn't even provide a helpful description of the man she had met.

Felix had summed it up once: 'You have a namesake in the Bible. He, too, denied a friend.'

Was that really who he was? A man who denied his friends to save his own skin?

It wasn't the image he had of himself. But perhaps it was the truth.

He heard footsteps and the rustling of heavy fabric. Sister Beatrice was coming down the corridor. She was holding a rosary in her hands. Her face, so animated earlier on, was frozen.

'Peter? Are you still working?'

She came in and sat down on the piano stool. Slumped, he would have said. Her voice had also lost its melody.

'It has to be done.'

'Does it? Yes, I suppose it does.'

She sat for a while sliding the rosary between her fingers. He resumed his work, breaking down the door frame, and so barely heard what she said, but caught the meaning clearly.

'I loved her.'

He lowered his tools and looked at her.

'I loved her in every possible way. I can tell God, of course. But you're the only human being I can tell.'

She looked at him with tears in her eyes.

'I loved her and I betrayed her. And I can't tell anyone, not even the police. I can tell only you.'

Despite the gravity of the situation, he adopted a teasing tone.

'And you don't think I've got enough on my plate as it is? I betrayed her too.'

'Your betrayal was nothing compared to mine,' she insisted.

'Is this a competition?'

'I loved her. Didn't you hear what I said? She confided in me. Confidences I should have passed on. Now it's too late. Now she's dead.'

She wiped away the tears.

'If you know anything, you must tell the police,' he said.

She shook her head as she looked at him.

'It's not that simple. There are our laws and then there are society's. It's not often they collide, but sometimes it happens.'

'Do you know why anyone would want to hurt her? Do you know why she had to die?'

'Of course I don't. I can't answer either of your questions. Not with any certainty.'

She got up and went over to him and put her hand on his arm.

'We're in the same boat, you and I. God will forgive us, but can we forgive ourselves?'

Her and her God, he thought, and felt himself being sucked towards a place he didn't want to go.

'You knew her well,' he said. 'Perhaps better than anyone. There has to be a reason why it happened. Something must have happened before . . .'

Her eyes widened as her hand squeezed his arm.

'She was so frightened,' she said. 'She was so terribly, terribly frightened.'

'And you can't tell anyone else but me?'

Christ, this was going from bad to worse. He wished he was at home with the dog.

'Things spoken in confidence behind these walls can't be revealed to the world outside, least of all to a public authority,' she said. 'It's like the sanctity of confession. She begged me to keep quiet. Even if the worst should happen . . . Especially if the worst should happen,' she corrected herself.

A big part of him didn't want to hear what was coming. But another part was enticing him into a very tempting offer, if he did get involved. Forgiveness, absolution, purification of sins. A soul at peace with itself. He was badly in need of that.

'You're saying she thought someone was trying to kill her?'

'Yes, but I don't think that was what she feared most.'

She rummaged around in her pocket and pulled something out.

'More rosaries?' he said when he saw what she had in her hand. 'Isn't one enough to save my soul?'

'This is a special rosary. Melissa gave it to me. She said it was the key to everything. To her fear and the story behind it, which she never told me in its entirety. I can't give it to the police, but I can give it to you.'

For the second time in twenty-four hours she pressed a rosary into his hand. He looked at it. It was different from the first. At the end of it hung a different symbol from the one usually found on crucifixes.

'You can find out what it means. You live in the real world. You have access to information, to the internet, and you can talk to people,' she said. 'But be discreet, promise me that.'

Before he could protest, she had closed her eyes and was mumbling a prayer. She made the sign of the cross in front of his face.

'Help us, Peter. Help yourself.'

7

FRANDS NODDED BRIEFLY to Kir and they started their descent. He was holding the body bag; her hand was on the rope that went from the buoy down to Sister Melissa.

Although they weren't used to working together, they soon reached the bottom of the muddy moat. He unfolded the body bag. It was her job to manoeuvre the body inside it. Sister Melissa was lying on her stomach with her head at an odd angle. A couple of days later she would have surfaced by herself due to the gases death produces in the human body. But for now she was held down, especially by the weight of her habit.

No one knew for certain if this was a murder yet. In theory, Melissa could have chosen to jump to her death in the moat. But from what Kir had sensed, Mark Bille wasn't expecting this to be a suicide – and then there was Melissa's tongue sticking out of her mouth. Kir knew what that meant. East Jutland Police would arrive from Aarhus with a team of investigators and take over the case. Grenå Police would be relegated to somewhere Mark hated being: on the sidelines.

Perhaps she and Mark had missed their moment. She had emailed him from Africa, but his replies had dried up. And yes, he had been ill and undergone drastic treatment for cancer. But maybe it was more than that. She had heard from another source that his cancer had gone into remission after treatment. But he hadn't even bothered to tell her that.

Manoeuvring the body was difficult, even though it was weightless in the water. But after several attempts she managed to turn Sister Melissa over so she could get her arms underneath. She could immediately feel that the neck was limp in the water and the head floppy.

Frands yanked at Kir's arm. He seemed impatient and this made her nervous. She was struggling to get the body into the bag: the nun's habit spread out in the water and made the task almost impossible. In the end, she had to use more force than she had wanted to push the body inside and zip up the bag. By the time they were finally able to signal to the dinghy on the surface, tie lines to the bag and haul the body up the side, she was cursing Frands. The heavy bag was transported to the bank and they carefully let out some of the water, then Melissa was heaved onto a stretcher. Frands raised his arms in triumph and Kir despised him for his lack of respect.

'Good work,' Mark Bille said, once they were back on land.

'No, it wasn't,' she snapped. 'It went badly. I hope I didn't destroy any evidence. I had to force her inside the bag.'

'OK,' he said. 'We'll take a look.'

But she was in no mood to let him get away that easily now.

'You mean the forensic examiner will take a look. Anna Bagger will take a look. I don't suppose Grenå Police will be looking at anything in this case.'

He stroked his chin.

'We'll see about that.'

'What's happened, Mark?'

'What do you mean?'

'You know perfectly well what I mean. You're avoiding me.'

'We're here, aren't we?'

'Working, yes. But that's all.'

She had a head of steam up now. Though she often struggled to find the right words, she found them when her temper was at boiling point. Frands's attitude had been the last straw. He had assumed a proprietorial air and was busy helping to get the stretcher with the body up to the Falck ambulance, together with a Falck paramedic. Both men were tall and broad-shouldered. Why did they have to look like two action-men clones? Shit. She was always being screwed over by men.

'What happened to good manners? Such as replying to your emails?'

Mark opened and closed his mouth. Then they heard the sound of tyres on cobblestones. Mark turned his face away.

'Not now, Kir. Aarhus has just arrived.'

'If not now, then when?'

His voice betrayed no emotion.

'When the moment's right.'

'Fuck you, Mark! You're a wimp!'

She turned to leave. She didn't owe anyone anything. If Anna Bagger wanted to talk about finding the body, no doubt Frands would be happy to assist.

Nevertheless, over her shoulder, she said:

'In case they don't let you have a look, someone had tied something tight around her neck. Her head was caught in a thin loop. Just for your information.'

She drove home and was suddenly filled with self-loathing. She was thirty-two years old and pining for a police officer who wasn't interested in her. Not any longer, anyway. He had been to begin with, of that she was sure. Something had happened to him. She didn't know what, but she had to distance herself from him, and perhaps that was just as well. It was as if her love – or imagined love – was slowly but surely seeping out of her and making her see clearly: he was not the one. She had thought he was at one point, but she had been wrong.

She drove up the drive to her old summer house, which was situated outside Grenå. She had bought it when she had completed her diving training at Kongsøre and was able to get a mortgage. It was cheap, but technically speaking she wasn't supposed to live here all the year round.

She quickly moved her gear out of her old Toyota pickup and carried it into the garage, where she dismantled it, dried it and hung it up in its proper place. She was happy to admit she was a kit nerd. Everything had a place of its own and she treated her gear with

43

respect. The garage was neat and tidy. It was different in the house, where mess ruled.

When she went in, she had a shower and washed away the foul smell of brackish water. She put on the kettle and grabbed one of the bread rolls she had baked the day before – every now and then she would succumb to a domestic-goddess moment – and sat down and searched her purse for a card from an old flame she had met recently.

She was about to ring him and suggest a date when her mobile did a jig on the table.

'Kir.'

'Kir Røjel?'

'Speaking.'

'My name is Per Jarmer, Institute of Forensic Medicine. It was you who brought in a box of bones back in August, wasn't it?'

'Yes, it was. We found it in Kalø Bay, in the shipping channel, twenty metres down. Anything wrong?'

'No, I just wanted to let you know what we've found out.'

'But you've already told me. It was for educational use.'

Jarmer cleared his throat. He was the young pathologist to whom she had handed over the box on behalf of Allan Vraa and the police, as she was going to Aarhus anyway.

'That's obviously the information that was given to the police,' Jarmer said. 'But I've spoken to them and said I would contact you. It's only fair.'

'What's fair?'

There was something in the man's voice she didn't like. He gave a slight cough.

'One of my colleagues took a closer look at the bones in the box,' he said. 'We were a little rushed when they were handed in. And, on the surface, they appeared to be certified for educational use . . .'

Kir was bewildered.

'But you were all so sure.'

Per Jarmer continued.

'Only now it turns out it wasn't that straightforward. We're running some tests, but it looks as if the box didn't only contain bones for educational use, if you see what I mean . . .'

'So there were others? Where from?'

'We don't know yet. But they're not recent. Our samples say about sixty years old.'

'Sixty-year-old bones? What's so interesting about that?'

'The matter has been referred to the police.'

Such an old case. Even she knew what that meant. There was only one crime that never passed the statute of limitations.

'What did you find?' she asked.

'A broken neck.'

'Could it have been an accident?'

Jarmer cleared his throat again. More vigorously this time.

'Hardly. It's a spinous process fracture. It doesn't suggest death by natural causes.'

'So we're talking murder?'

'Looks like it.'

8

THE SUN WAS low in the sky as Peter finally drove home. When he turned off in Gjerrild and drove his van down the lane to the cliff, he gazed out at the landscape that he sometimes called his chosen sanctuary.

Out here, nature was wild and windy and didn't let just anyone in. He had chosen North Djurs for that very reason. He was a man of simple habits. Some people would call him a kind of hermit. He lived a modest, solitary life with his dog and did his work; that was it. He enjoyed nature, went for walks, followed animal trails and went hunting with his boss, even though he was no longer allowed to carry weapons. On rare occasions, a woman would visit. Felix had had an impact on him, but she had chosen a new life without him, and he understood why. The way his life was now, warring with bikers, he couldn't ask anyone to be close to him.

He reached a hilltop and looked out over the sea. The winding lane had turned into a gravel track. It terminated at the edge of the cliff, at the cottage which he had bought and done up himself. An old fisherman's cottage, painted yellow with grey half-timbering. Once he had kept a key under a white stone, so friends and acquaintances could come and go as they pleased. But that was then. Now it was alarm systems and suspicion. It wasn't how he wanted it. It was survival of the fittest.

He parked, unlocked the door to the house and let the dog out. Together they went for their usual afternoon walk along the cliff. As a rule, whenever he worked for Manfred in his workshop, the dog would go with him. But he didn't think convent life would suit the dog. It didn't suit him very much, either.

'Here, Kaj!'

He hurled a stick through the air and it landed at the foot of the cliff. The dog raced down after it. He enjoyed watching Kaj's finely tuned body in motion. He enjoyed his happiness and enthusiasm. He enjoyed his keenness to please him when he returned with his tail held high as he dropped the stick at his feet. It all helped to chase the day's events to a remote corner of his mind.

'Good boy,' he praised him. 'Clever dog.'

They didn't return to the cottage until an hour later. It was starting to get dark. A pair of headlights appeared on the lane from Gjerrild. He recognised Miriam's little piss-pot of a car. He could see there were three people inside it. He switched off the bells and the vibrators.

He was overcome by a sudden urge to flee, to jump into his car with the dog and head off into the sunset. But before he had time for anything like that, Miriam pulled up confidently in front of the cottage and she and another woman and a boy got out.

The sight of the other woman sent his stomach into a downward spin. If he had met her in the cemetery at midnight, he would genuinely have believed that My had returned. My's mother didn't have My's way of walking, but she did have her face and her elfin figure, and the indefinable quality that labels people as family. When he came closer to her, however, the family resemblance faded into the background and he saw an attractive woman, the size of Kylie Minogue, but without My's questioning eyes. Not sexy in an obvious way, but with an erotic aura of the more innocent kind.

She offered him a friendly handshake. He accepted it, but reminded himself that he hated this woman. She was one of the ghosts in his life. How often had he cursed her and his own mother to hell and beyond. There was no way she could just turn up thinking that everything was forgotten and forgiven.

'This is Peter,' Miriam said by way of introduction. To Peter, she said: 'We were just passing.'

Just passing. All the way from Aarhus to the furthest point in Djursland. He had a sharp retort on the tip of his tongue, but My's mother smiled and he recognised the supple mouth and the tiny, elegant teeth.

'I've really been looking forward to meeting you.'

He had no idea what to say. So he just nodded.

'I'm sorry,' My's mother said, as if she had forgotten something very important. 'My name is Bella. This is my son, Christian.'

Addressing the boy, she said:

'Go on then, say hello to Peter.'

She grabbed the boy by his shoulders and shoved him forwards. Christian muttered something inaudible and held out a limp hand to Peter. He had long hair with a fringe that fell at an angle in front of his eyes. He was slim, like his mother and My, but with that came the gangly movements of his age, limbs that were too long in proportion to the torso.

'How old are you, Christian?'

The mother Peter had problems with. The boy he didn't. He clearly felt just as awkward as Peter did.

'Fourteen.'

'I bet you'd rather be at home playing computer games.'

A little smile lit the boy's face.

'I'm all right.'

His eyes flitted nervously and landed on the dog. He hadn't patted it or gone near it.

'Kaj won't hurt you.'

'It's an Alsatian,' the boy said.

Bella intervened.

'He got bitten once, by an Alsatian. But Christian, this dog looks harmless enough.'

You can tell that to a frightened boy as many times as you like, but it won't make any difference, Peter thought.

'Do you like other dogs?' he asked Christian, who nodded.

'Kaj was My's dog.'

A glimmer of interest appeared on the boy's face.

'He went everywhere with her. She loved that dog. When she died, I took him in.'

Peter called the dog and Kaj contentedly lumbered over. Peter and the boy squatted down.

'Just let him sniff you. Turn your side to him, like this.'

Christian did as he was told. Raw fear burned in his eyes.

Kaj sniffed him as if his life depended on it and breathed into his hair. Christian giggled.

'It tickles.'

They sat like this for a while. Christian leaned his head into the dog, which started to whine.

'You can touch him now,' Peter said. 'He's decided you're a friend.'

'Well, I never,' Bella said. 'I wish Magnus could see this.'

'Your eldest?' Miriam asked. 'We would have had room in the car for him too.'

My's mother hesitated before saying:

'He wasn't at home.'

They exchanged a few more remarks. Peter had felt comfortable with the boy, but with the mother he felt like the victim of a conspiracy. Miriam had given him no warning. It was just like her to turn up and put him on the spot. As if the day hadn't been bad enough as it was.

He looked at Bella and his antipathy grew. He thought of My's stubborn but desperate hopes that her mother would eventually take her away from the care home. 'One day she'll turn up. Just you wait and see.' She would look so secretive and knowing that he had almost believed her. 'It's all a big mistake. One day she'll come for me.'

Miriam interrupted his train of thought.

'Right, I'm sure the two of you have plenty to talk about, and I know Bella would like to visit the cemetery. Perhaps Christian and I should take the doggy for a walk. What do you say, Kaj? Walkies?'

Kaj looked as if he couldn't believe his luck. Two walks in one day! Christian looked like the dog, perhaps thinking this was one way he could escape the trip to the cemetery.

'That sounds like a great idea, doesn't it, Christian?' Bella said. 'Getting some fresh air. And how beautiful it is here!'

The latter was addressed to Peter. Miriam grabbed his arm and pulled him aside.

'Remember: everyone deserves a chance!' she hissed between her teeth. 'She's actually very nice.'

Miriam, the boy and the dog disappeared into the twilight on the path along the cliff. My's mother – he had decided that was her name – watched them as they left. When she turned to him, her personality changed like a gobstopper going from green to blue.

'You must hate me.'

He stifled his wish to agree. She continued.

'I can see why you would. You must think I'm an evil woman. Miriam said you took care of My. She said you were like brother and sister.'

She had made a choice and handed My to strangers. He, too, had made bad decisions, especially in the last twenty-four hours. But it wasn't the same. He could have done nothing else. My's mother had had years to change her mind, but she never did.

'I know. You're thinking that I could have visited My at the care home. I could have had second thoughts and taken her home.'

He couldn't be bothered to listen to her moral qualms.

'Miriam told me earlier that you wanted to put something on the grave. We can drive to the cemetery,' he said brusquely.

She watched the three figures, who had now reached the cliff.

'I had hoped that Christian would come. But he doesn't seem particularly interested.'

Peter was with Christian on this one.

'Perhaps we should just go,' she said, still wavering. 'It's not far, is it?'

'It won't take long.'

9

MARK WATCHED AS Sara Dreyer, the pathologist, straightened up
after standing hunched over Melissa's body. A forensic examiner
would always be called to the crime scene to inspect the body.
In this case it was the bank of the moat at St Mary's Abbey where
the ambulance crew, investigators, divers and CSOs were now at
work.

Sara Dreyer held a digital thermometer in her hand.

'The body temperature is five degrees,' she said into a handheld
Dictaphone.

She turned her attention to Mark and Anna Bagger, who was
wearing wellies and a raincoat of the fancy variety.

'When did she go missing?'

'Around five yesterday afternoon,' Mark said.

Sara Dreyer shook her head sceptically.

'I don't think she's been in the water that long. Her skin would
have been more like a washerwoman's.'

Mark was familiar with the notion. When a body had been
submerged in water, the skin would wrinkle and turn white,
especially on the palms and soles of the feet.

'So how long would you say?' Anna asked.

Sara Dreyer wasn't someone who liked guesswork.

'I'll know more after the autopsy.'

Anna Bagger pulled up the sleeve of her raincoat and looked at
her watch.

'It's almost twenty-four hours since she disappeared. Are you
telling me she wasn't in the water for those twenty-four hours?'

Sara Dreyer shook her head again.

'I'm sure she wasn't.'

'Well, for how long, then?' Mark pressed.

'I can't tell you with any certainty.'

'How about without any certainty then?' Anna Bagger said.

Sara Dreyer sent them a weary look. This was the classic tug-of-war between the police's need for quick information and the pathologist's desire to back up every bit of information with science. It was also a conflict between strong personalities and glares. Anna Bagger won. The pathologist suppressed a sigh.

'Then I would estimate twelve hours, max.,' Dreyer said and snapped her bag shut with a loud click.

'So where the hell has she been in the meantime?' Mark demanded.

'Now that,' Dreyer said amicably but firmly, 'is your problem. Fortunately. But take a look at this.'

Again, she bent over the body bag which was still unzipped all the way down. It wasn't a pretty sight. The girl's face was swollen and her protruding tongue blue. There were clear marks on her throat from some kind of collar.

Sara Dreyer took Melissa's left hand and raised her arm. The movement caused the sleeve to fall back and reveal effusions around her wrist in the shape of a wide bracelet.

'It's the same with the other arm,' the pathologist said and carefully repeated the procedure to show them the blood, this time on the right arm.

'She was bound or tied,' Anna Bagger confirmed.

Sara Dreyer zipped up the body bag and Melissa's face was gone.

'I'll start the autopsy at eight o'clock on the dot tomorrow morning, so hopefully we'll soon know more,' Sara said.

The investigators from Aarhus had swarmed in shortly after Melissa's body had been discovered. They had invaded the convent like an army of ants, it seemed to Mark. Even now, this late in the evening, they were still bombarding nuns and staff and conference participants with millions of questions and he couldn't help feeling that he had been sidelined.

The area surrounding the crime scene had been cordoned off with red and white tape. It had started drizzling again, which made it more difficult for the Crime Scene Officers to search for evidence. They walked around in their white coveralls scouring the herb garden and the bank of the moat, aided by powerful lamps supplied by the Emergency Management Agency in Herning, which cast a ghostly glow over the area. Two dog handlers had also been called in. The dogs followed the trail in the grass, just as Peter Boutrup had done earlier. He was good, Mark thought, you had to give him that. Boutrup was an outdoorsman through and through. So far it didn't appear that the dogs had found anything he hadn't.

They watched as the pathologist packed up and followed the ambulance, which slowly drove off with Melissa.

'What do you think, Mark?'

Anna Bagger's boyish haircut – a new style, he had noticed – made her look even tougher and more angular than ever. Right now, she also looked focused as her gaze followed the pathologist's red car. But she still had the same soft mouth, which could blow smoke like a sailor and smile at the same time.

'What happened to that girl?'

Most people found Anna Bagger to be objective and professional, and he guessed that was true. But Mark knew another side to the murder investigator. In private she could ignite an ice cube with her sensuality. That part of their relationship was over, but she was still, he had to admit, one of the sexiest women he had ever met.

She handed him a cup of coffee without asking if he wanted any. With a delicate gesture she brushed back a lock of hair that had fallen down in front of one eye.

Mark tried to assess what she wanted from him: an honest answer, or was it just a ploy to deter him from complaining when the wheels of the investigation started turning without him?

'I think she knew her killer,' he said. 'At least well enough to walk down the garden with him, even though Boutrup said the guy grabbed her by the elbow . . . We can only speculate as to what happened next.'

'So the murder took place elsewhere?'

'Yes, probably. But we still have to look for evidence here. Both in the moat and in the area as a whole.'

'He would have had enough time to abduct and kill her and then dump her in the moat afterwards, wouldn't he?'

He nodded.

'We're talking twelve hours, give or take.'

He wanted to add that it could have been twelve hours of hell, but there was no need. From looking at Anna Bagger he could tell she was thinking the same.

Then she suddenly flipped the conversation one hundred and eighty degrees:

'We have only Peter Boutrup's word that the man was there.'

'Correct.'

'Could there be another explanation?'

Mark stared at his coffee.

'Anything's possible.'

'He's hard to read,' she said.

She had just interviewed Boutrup herself and let him go. He didn't need to remind her of that.

'You're thinking about his past,' Mark said.

She nodded. 'Once a killer . . .'

'Always a killer? Isn't that a little too simplistic?'

'Perhaps,' she said vaguely. 'But wasn't there some sort of incident last summer?'

Mark heaved a sigh. Boutrup wasn't his favourite person, but a witch hunt would merely derail the investigation.

'You know perfectly well he's got enemies. And we're not exactly lining up to protect him.'

She furrowed her brow.

'I understand he makes a very good job of that himself. I've heard rumours about a couple of human torches and burned-out motorbikes. And shootings – the man isn't legally permitted to own firearms!'

'The others did the shooting,' Mark said.

'And then there was last winter's incident.'

'He was acquitted on the grounds of self-defence,' Mark said, gritting his teeth more than he had intended. With his maverick methods and fanatical desire for freedom, Boutrup represented a source of irritation, but he wasn't a sadist who murdered young girls. 'He was set up, as you well know.'

She tilted her head to one side.

'You're protecting him.'

'Boutrup is all right. In his own way.'

She rolled her eyes.

'And what a way that is. Keep your eye on him.'

'He's not going anywhere,' Mark countered.

He meant it. Peter Boutrup had chosen the cliff and his cottage with care. He had made it his home and home was important to him. That much he had sensed about a man who had lived most of his life in institutions. His mother was a well-known journalist in Aarhus, Dicte Svendsen. It had been in the papers. She'd had him when she was a teenager and had presumed that he had been adopted, but he had ended up in a notoriously brutal home for children in Ry. Experiences like that must surely leave their mark on a man.

'So you believe him?' Anna Bagger asked.

Mark thought about it again. Boutrup could have been putting on a sideshow: inventing a man who followed Melissa and staging a false hunt for clues, then discovering a shoe he already knew would be there. In theory, he could have abducted the girl and held her in his house for twelve hours. In theory.

'Inasmuch as you can believe someone you don't know very well. But keeping an eye on him would do no harm.'

He knew he had said the latter mostly to humour her. Boutrup was different, and yes, he had been in prison for manslaughter, and of course they had to keep an eye on him. But he had already proved that he had more guts and insight than the combined forces of the East Jutland detectives and Grenå Police. Including himself.

Anna Bagger scrutinised him as she held out the palm of her hand in the rain. She called out to the Crime Scene Officers.

'Get the boys from Herning to put up the tent! This doesn't look good.'

The CSOs changed position and a couple of them walked up to the vans from the Herning agency. Shortly afterwards the tent was hauled down to the bank and erected in no time, while lamps were rigged up under the canvas. It wasn't a moment too soon. Anna Bagger nodded to Mark.

'Shall we? It's tipping down now.'

They walked together over the bridge and crossed the shiny wet cobbles in the convent courtyard. She stumbled once when her wellie slipped and he quickly grabbed her elbow. She instantly pulled her arm away.

'I'm fine.'

She straightened up.

'It's good to see you again, Mark. How are you?'

He always dreaded the question. He was asked it several times a day. People always meant well, but he had no urge to be honest, not even with her.

'Fine. Everything is as it should be.'

'And it's all gone, it's in remission?'

She must have heard, otherwise she wouldn't have asked.

'In remission, yes. They say the cancer has gone.'

She observed him carefully from the side.

'Then why aren't you jumping for joy?'

She knew him too well. He walked ahead and she followed quickly.

'Oh, but I am,' he assured her. 'But finding a young woman dead in a moat is not exactly thigh-slappingly funny, is it?'

That got the conversation back on track.

'You're bored,' she declared, hitting the bullseye. 'And now you want some action to show you're one hell of a good detective.'

'You're going to need help, Anna. This one's not for beginners.'

'And of course, you would know all about convent life, wouldn't you? Do you also have experience of celibacy?'

Her face had become alive and her eyes sparkled with mischief.

That was how manipulative she could be. Good cop, bad cop in one and the same person, but he wasn't falling for it.

'It wasn't the convent I was thinking about but Djursland. The nose of Jutland, as they call it.'

'You're saying people out here are different from the people in Aarhus or Esbjerg?'

'Oh, yes.'

They sought shelter in an archway, still holding their coffee cups.

'Enlighten me,' she said. 'What kind of place is it?'

'This is hillbilly country,' he said, because he knew the area where he had grown up well. 'The locals stick together like rice against outsiders. You need an insider to get to the bottom of this case.'

She laughed, a husky, melodic sound he remembered all too well.

'You make it sound like a Pakistani tribal area.'

He shook the rain out of his hair and rubbed the sleeve of his jacket, causing little streams of water to trickle down onto the cobblestones.

'To me it just sounds like normal provincial life,' he said.

Perhaps she was right. He knew only one province and this was it. But it could make him miss his eight years in Copenhagen so much he was almost reduced to tears.

'Please, let me at least follow the investigation,' he said. 'From the sidelines, if you insist.'

She observed him again, with another cheerful smile which she tried to hide by swallowing the last mouthful of coffee.

'OK.'

She lowered the cup and squeezed it until the plastic split. 'You can help me by coming to Aarhus tomorrow to witness the autopsy. I think I'll need all my men here.'

'Fine.'

She looked closely into his face as though testing him.

'And then I think we should search Boutrup's house tonight. You said you know the locals. If there's even the slightest possibility that the girl was at his house, we need to secure the evidence.'

She waited for a reaction, but when it failed to come, she continued:

'If you could see to that, I'd be grateful.'

She had made up her mind. He could protest, but he knew it would make no difference, so he ended up simply nodding.

'I'll get you a warrant, of course,' she said and turned her back on him.

10

'I've got an umbrella in my car,' Peter said, desperate to get away.

'I'm all right.'

My's mother peered up at him as she walked by his side through the cemetery. 'It's only drizzling.'

Drizzle. That wasn't how he would describe it. He thought about the crime scene by the convent and knew that the rain would soon wash away any evidence there was. In all the mess he was at least pleased that he had found the shoe. But even so, Anna Bagger was bound to suspect him. He had sensed her scepticism earlier when she had questioned him about the incident he had witnessed.

'It's just over there.'

She continued to walk by his side with the increasingly soggy bouquet in her arms. He led her to My's grave via a roundabout route.

'Here it is.'

He felt uncomfortable. It was like being watched by a stranger while sleeping or having a shower. This place was his private sanctuary. This was where he came when he was at odds with the world. Here and on the cliff. But he could hardly tell her that.

'It's beautiful,' she said quietly. 'What a lovely stone. Did you choose it?'

He had found the stone on the beach below the cliffs. It was probably illegal, but the stone suited My.

'I can fetch something for the flowers if you like,' was all he said.

'Thank you.'

He was glad to get away for a few minutes. When he came back, he saw her kneeling by the stone.

'Here you are.'

He gave her a special cemetery vase, which he had filled with water. She took it and pushed the pointed end into the ground in front of the stone and arranged the flowers in it. She sat for a while before getting up, soaked through now, just like him.

'You probably won't believe this, but the day I gave her up, I gave away a chunk of my heart. One day I'll tell you the story,' she said. 'And then perhaps you'll tell me about My.'

She sounded hesitant. 'Perhaps you would like to visit me at home in Elev one day and have a cup of coffee?'

He cursed her to hell and back. He had to plug the hole she was drilling in him, where compassion was seeping like rain into a holed rubber boot.

'Let's go back to the car,' he suggested.

Fortunately she complied.

'Or perhaps I might be allowed to come back one day with the children,' she said a little later when they sat, dripping wet, in the car. 'I think they would like to visit the grave.'

What was she expecting now? An invitation? Surely they could visit My's grave without involving him. But then there was her wish to have My's body moved. Fortunately, she hadn't brought the subject up and perhaps he could thwart her by showing a little more kindness. Perhaps she would finally realise that My was exactly where she was meant to be.

'You can always phone,' he said into the darkness and the rain that was drumming on the windscreen now. 'Miriam has my number.'

Miriam and Christian were sitting in Miriam's car, sheltering from the rain. The dog was by the front door under the porch. After they had said goodbye, Peter watched his three guests as they disappeared up the lane on their way home to Aarhus.

He made himself a cup of coffee, sat down on the sofa and listened to some music. Kaj came over and rested his head in Peter's lap.

'So, did you make a new friend?'

The dog looked at him. Two long walks had to be enough for

even this most indefatigable of dogs. Especially if the latter was with Miriam, who always strode out in her stilettos. Peter looked at the clock. It was only nine thirty, but the day had been crammed full of events and he felt tireder than he had for a long time.

'Beddy byes for us two boys?'

He stroked the dog and got up and Kaj followed him upstairs. It was raining so heavily that he couldn't put his mattress out on the balcony as he usually did. Instead, he opened the wide doors and lay down inside with the dog lying on his fleece and the sound of rain beating on the roof and the woodwork.

The November sky was covered with clouds and the night was as black as the water in the moat. He closed his eyes and heard two female voices swirling around in his head declaring their love for two dead young women. Girls whose deaths he could have prevented. How he had managed to play a part in both tragedies was beyond him.

He visualised the rosary with the strange symbol. What had he been thinking? Why hadn't he gone straight to Mark Bille or Anna Bagger with it and cleared his name?

He stared into the black night. He would never learn to understand people. When it came to the crunch, he was better with dogs.

11

PETER WOKE TO the bells and vibrations of his home-made alarm system and knew that someone was coming. He also knew who. His suspicion was soon confirmed by flashing lights outside the house and headlights sweeping across the windows. The dog growled from its fleece and Peter looked at the clock. It was just after ten o'clock and he had only been asleep for thirty minutes. He disconnected all the alarms. Now no alarm systems in the world would help him.

Shortly afterwards he heard banging on the door and Kaj woke up fully and barked as though he was getting paid for it. Peter wriggled out of his sleeping bag, threw some clothes on and went downstairs. A glance out of the window revealed two police cars and a van he recognised as the police's dove-blue CSO van.

Mark Bille stood in the doorway.

'I have a warrant to search your house. I hope you'll cooperate.'

Peter knew this was Anna Bagger's doing. Mark Bille was just the messenger boy.

'What's happened?'

He had to make a guess as he let them in. The dog's barking had become a growl again.

'Quiet, Kaj.'

He settled back in his basket, from where he watched the scene as white-clad CSOs started opening drawers, taking books from the bookcase and looking under all the sofa cushions. Two of the officers began checking surface areas for fingerprints with a red powder and a man wearing full breathing apparatus sprayed something on the walls. Blood, Peter thought. They're looking for the spatter of blood.

He looked away. It felt as if he was being violated and he had to restrain himself from throwing them out. Something must have happened. Could they have found something that linked Melissa's death to him? He wondered if Sister Beatrice had told them about their conversation and her relationship with Melissa.

'So much for paying your debt to society and all the other fine words you police love to indulge in!'

'Relax, Peter.'

'What are you looking for?'

He was praying they wouldn't find his weapons or ammunition under the eaves. Mark Bille raised both arms in the air. The gesture indicated a kind of resignation. Again, Peter had to remind himself that this was Anna Bagger's doing, he was sure of it. His blood boiled with rage at the detective from Aarhus.

'Why the hell would she think I have anything to do with it? I told you what I saw! I didn't keep anything back.'

'Then you have nothing to worry about.'

'I'm not worried. I'm angry. I'm an easy target and you know it.'

'I'm going to have to ask you to turn out your pockets.'

Peter shook his head.

'This is blinking insane!'

He did as he was told and emptied the contents of his pockets on the table. Mark searched through them. There was a ten-krone coin, a packet of chewing gum with two pieces left, a parking ticket and not one but two rosaries. Mark held one up.

'Get religion, did you?'

'Why? Is there some law against it?'

'Why two the same?'

'They're not the same.'

'Where did you get them?'

Mark picked up the second rosary, the one with the strange symbol.

'And what does this mean?'

'No idea. They were a gift.'

'From the convent?'

'They pay me in absolution.'

'Then let's hope it works.' Mark looked at him sceptically. 'Are they trying to recruit new members?'

The thought struck Peter that now would be a good time to tell the police about Sister Beatrice and Melissa, and about where one of the rosaries had come from. But his anger prevented him. His anger and his humiliation at being treated like a criminal. And, of course, his promise to Sister Beatrice to keep it to himself.

'Surely there's no law against that,' was all he said.

Then he decided to feed Mark at least a grain of truth.

'Sister Beatrice worries about the state of my soul. She gave them to me.'

Mark ran a finger across the symbol on the second rosary and stood for a moment as if looking inside himself. Then he put it back on the table and turned to the CSOs.

'Are you almost done?'

'We just want to take a peek upstairs.'

The white coverall was halfway up the stairs.

'Perhaps we could sit down in the meantime?'

They sat down, Mark on a chair, Peter on the sofa, but perched on the edge.

'Is it Melissa?' he asked. 'You think she was here? You think I brought her home?'

Mark made no reply, but Peter read the truth in the way his eyes went off on a wander around the room.

'Was she raped?'

'You know very well we can't tell for certain yet. The autopsy is first thing tomorrow.'

'Tortured?'

Mark Bille's face was blank.

'I didn't do it,' Peter said.

Being suspected was like being attacked by a swarm of insects. They crawled all over his body and made him feel dirty. But if they found physical evidence, at least they could eliminate him quickly. They already had his DNA profile on record. They had his fingerprints. It would be so easy.

'If you say so,' Mark Bille said with a sigh.

'Coffee?'

Peter only asked because it would give him something to do. Mark Bille nodded.

'If you're making one.'

Thirty minutes later, the CSOs had finished. They had taken prints and samples of fibres and anything they regarded as potential evidence. They hadn't found the weapons under the eaves. But they did take his computer and his phone before they left the house in convoy.

'You'll get them back as soon as we've checked them,' Mark Bille promised as he left.

'That's what I call service.'

Peter closed the door after them. He went back to bed and closed his eyes to the mess and the red powder that covered the house like a memory that refused to go away.

12

MELISSA'S AUTOPSY WAS almost as unpleasant as the examination of Peter Boutrup's house on the cliff top, where they had obviously been wasting their time.

Mark hated autopsies. He couldn't stand the stench of dead flesh, let alone the smell of someone's insides and abdominal and intestinal contents as the pathologist bared the organs and took them out en masse. Nevertheless, he had now witnessed quite a few. His eight years with the Copenhagen Homicide Squad had offered an abundance of the bodies he hated to see most of all: young men with healthy, muscular bodies and their whole lives in front of them, cut down in their prime by a stab wound or a bullet. Gang warfare, drug feuds, ethnic conflicts. But it was a fact that in their search for somewhere to belong some young people picked the wrong group. Bad judgement, yes. But in those circles gang membership gave you status, especially if you joined a gang with power and influence. It meant dealing in illegal substances, it meant unlicensed firearms and it meant a high risk of getting caught in crossfire of some kind and ultimately ending up somewhere else: on the pathologist's steel table.

The woman in front of him didn't belong to a group he had any experience of. In a way that made it much worse. He wondered if perhaps her clothing was part of it. Sister Melissa was still wearing the heavy nun's habit, and the police forensics officer and the pathologist were working together to remove it.

Mark looked away. He wasn't squeamish when it came to women and his lust had sometimes made him take risks and behave like an idiot. It was so unlike him to feel bashful in front of a young woman, but nonetheless that was how he felt.

66

Sister Melissa had chosen to wear a nun's habit and its effect on him was the same as a fabric chastity belt. Normally he loved the sight of a naked woman and even during an autopsy could be overcome by curiosity to see beautiful breasts or trimmed pubic hair, but he was conscious that he didn't want to see this woman exposed.

'The victim is an eighteen-year-old, Caucasian female,' the pathologist Sara Dreyer said to the microphone suspended from the ceiling. 'Her body exhibits normal development. Identifying features include a birthmark near her navel, which measures . . .' She took a ruler and measured, '. . . seven by three millimetres.'

The pathologist continued and identified an appendicitis scar and a second birthmark close to the right breast. Mark stared at the young body in front of him. If he ignored the severely bruised neck and the staring eyes, it was a beautiful female body, harmonious, almost luminous in its whiteness and purity. He was strangely pleased that the pathologist was a woman.

'Blood effusions on the wrists and . . . ankles. The neck has been encircled by something wide and sharp,' Sara Dreyer said. 'Such as a steel collar or something else made of metal. Lacerations of the skin as a result. The tongue is protruding and blue in colour. The face is swollen with oedema and the eyes . . .'

Sara Dreyer took a small torch and shone it into the open eyes, which Mark could see were frozen in horror mixed with shock.

'Dotted bleeding in the eyes suggests strong pressure on the airways from the metal object – whatever it was – which has also perforated the skin in places.'

Mark tried to visualise the method of killing. The evidence seemed to indicate that Melissa had been killed in a way that required time, space and a specific instrument of some sort. She hadn't just been bound and strangled with a pair of tights or a rope. Nevertheless, the divers would have to go back down. There could be other evidence down there.

He thought about Kir. He had tried to harden his feelings when they met. It was better for her and indeed better for both of them if they simply forgot about everything that had happened between them. He had made up his mind to that effect long ago. Yes, he was avoiding her. And he hadn't replied to her recent emails, but that was because he felt he had no other choice. He had nothing to offer her, he had come to realise that in the months they had been away from each other. He didn't have the energy for a relationship, it was that simple, and besides, she could do so much better.

Kir was a soldier. An elite one at that, the sort they sent to the world's trouble spots. He had read about the rescue of the hostages in the waters off Somalia, of course. It had driven him crazy wondering what her role might have been, but there was no doubt in his mind that she'd had a role. She was a killing machine, that was how she had been trained. He knew that none of the four hostage-takers had escaped from the rescue mission alive.

Kir could take care of herself. She didn't need someone who could barely keep himself upright.

'Hello, and what have we here?'

Sara Dreyer's voice brutally dismissed Kir from his thoughts. The cloth around Sister Melissa's face had now been removed and revealed an abundance of long, dark blond hair which wound round and cascaded down.

The pathologist fiddled with something in Melissa's ear.

'How strange, in such a young girl!'

She held the object up to the light.

'What is it?' Mark asked.

'A hearing aid,' Sara said and carefully put the tiny device in a metal bowl before turning Melissa's head to the other side and feeling her other ear.

'Another one,' she said, sounding surprised. 'Eighteen years old and reduced hearing in both ears.'

There was total silence in the autopsy room. Then Sara said:

'Well, it still doesn't give us the cause of death.'

She and the forensics officer took secretion samples from all external orifices with cotton buds, which were then sealed in small plastic tubes. The officer also took blood samples from the victim's arm and placed the small tubes, neatly labelled, into a container. Mark was pleased to see the work was done with care and as much respect for the deceased as was possible in the circumstances.

At length, after a silence, the pathologist said:

'OK, Melissa. Please forgive us, but I'm going to have to take a look at your insides.'

Three hours later, Mark left the Institute of Forensic Medicine at Skejby Hospital, turned on the satnav and drove to an address he had found on the internet, in a suburb called Brabrand. As he drove, on a sudden impulse, he rang the number he had also scribbled down and made a quick appointment.

The girl who welcomed him in the doorway couldn't have been much more than twenty. She was wearing a short black PVC miniskirt and her stomach was solarium-brown with a piercing in her belly button. A see-through crop top revealed the outline of a minimalist lace bra. She reeked of cheap perfume.

'Laila?'

She opened the door.

'Come in.'

He entered through a bright hallway with several pairs of shoes in a tidy line. He noticed there were also children's shoes.

'Through here.'

She took his arm and guided him through a cosy living room, which extended into a kitchen, and onwards to a room that was utterly different from the ones he had just seen. The bed was covered with something that looked like a sea of blood, but which turned out to be distressed velvet. The walls had been painted black and were decorated with framed erotic posters and in several places incense sticks were burning in small porcelain holders, emitting a spicy fragrance of warmer, more sensual skies.

'What would you like?'

'Whatever's easy.'

She pushed him down on the bed. On the bedside table there was a bowl of condoms in various colours. She picked it up and offered it to him as if it was a bowl of sweets.

'I don't think . . .'

'Those are the rules.'

'Yes, but I still don't think . . .'

He wasn't good at this. Not any more.

She started to unbutton his shirt professionally and caress his chest. Images from the autopsy crowded his mind. The saw cutting through the chest. The ribs being severed and removed one by one. How fragile the human frame is, he had thought. The bones which are there to protect us can break so easily.

In the end when the organs had been examined and removed, the face had been peeled off as if it were a Halloween latex mask. All of a sudden Sister Melissa was a bloody, unrecognisable lump of bared muscle, tendons, bones and teeth. A zombie grinning up at him.

'Relax. It'll be all right.'

Laila cooed with fake concern. He pushed her out of the way with more force than he had intended.

'It's no good. I've made a mistake. I'm sorry.'

'There's no need to get violent,' she gasped and fell onto the bed.

Mark was soaked in sweat. What if she called the police?

'I'm sorry, I didn't mean to . . .'

Before she could make any demands, he reached for his back pocket, fished out 500 kroner and threw the notes on the blood-red bedspread. Then he stumbled out of the door.

It wasn't until he was in his car and had calmed down again that he called Anna Bagger, who picked up the phone at first ring.

'Yes, Mark?'

'She was garrotted. Do you know what that means?'

'Of course I do. Don't you think I watch films about hired killers?'

'Hired killers? In Djursland?'

'You said yourself it's hillbilly country. Everything happens under the surface.'

'But garrotting, being bound to a chair and all that?'

'We've never seen that before,' she admitted. 'Not in this country.'

'There would have been a spike on the metal collar. It pushed against her neck from behind and broke her spine,' he explained.

The scan had revealed the latter.

'She definitely wasn't killed near the moat,' Anna Bagger stated. 'He's hidden her somewhere. You didn't find anything at Boutrup's, I gather?'

'Nope. He didn't do it. Waste of time.'

'Oh well, it was worth a try.'

He wasn't so sure about that. Boutrup wasn't someone he would like as his enemy.

She said:

'There's still the area by the moat. Why don't you ask your diving chum what she thinks our chances are of finding anything?'

13

'You should complain to the ombudsman,' Manfred said. 'Or whatever he's called.'

'It's no use. Best to forget about it.'

Peter balanced on a ledge as he took the aluminium pole which Manfred passed to him. It weighed almost nothing. That was the beauty of erecting scaffolding. It was as fast as building a house of cards, but was much more stable. In no time at all you were ten metres above the ground, whence all the problems of the world seemed small and insignificant.

'Wait. I just need to slot it in.'

He used a little extra force to make both ends of the pole go into the appropriate clamps.

He had only told Manfred about his house being searched because otherwise he would have heard about it from another source. He wasn't trying to involve his boss in anything, but his anger at the police intrusion still rankled. His anger plus the humiliation of always being treated like a suspect.

He made sure the pole was firmly in place. Manfred climbed up to the third level – he was a small, nimble man who could balance like an acrobat. He sat down on the plank-work next to Peter and looked down into the convent courtyard where the Rimsø Carpenters lorry was parked with the rest of the scaffolding in pieces on the back, like a game of spillikins. Then he scrutinised Peter.

'Are you OK?'

This was Manfred's way of letting him know that he had detected a change. Peter had glanced at himself in the mirror and seen the haunted, anxious expression on his face and the grey colour it had taken on.

'It's a horrible thought that I was part of it,' he mumbled.

Once he had digested his run-in with the police, it was Melissa's death that had been foremost in his mind. He had been awake all night thinking about her and what he had seen. Not until the morning, when the rain eased off, had he dragged the mattress out onto the balcony and finally fallen into a deep, confusing sleep, which had done him no good at all.

'It isn't your fault,' Manfred said. 'You couldn't have known what was going to happen. You couldn't have known that man was going to kill her.'

'From where I was standing, I knew.'

'No, you didn't,' Manfred said. 'It's just how you feel now. With the benefit of hindsight. It's not logical.'

Manfred looked at him.

'And you're normally a pretty logical guy. So relax.'

Peter was tempted to say that the search and the murder of Sister Melissa were not the only things weighing on his mind. The rosary with the strange symbol on the end was eating away at him too.

'Why don't you come over to ours for dinner tonight?' Manfred said. 'Jutta is cooking chilli con carne. Bring the dog, that'll give the kids something to look forward to.'

Later, when they broke for lunch, Peter made his excuses and went looking for Sister Beatrice. He didn't find her, but he did find the abbess busy trying to catch a bird that had strayed through a window into the dining room.

'Poor wee creature. It's dazed. Oh, goodness, it's you, is it?'

She sank down on a chair.

'Perhaps you could help me, Peter?'

He smiled at the sight of the blanket she was holding to her chest.

'Well, chasing after it won't work. It's not a burglar.'

She shook her head.

'I know nothing about birds.'

She looked at him. He recognised his own wan expression from the mirror.

'I barely understand human beings.'

'I was telling myself the same only last night.'

She put down the blanket on a chair beside her and stroked the checked pattern.

'It wasn't your fault. If it was your fault, then it was certainly our fault too. Nobody really noticed her going. We were all busy with our own thoughts.'

She said it again as if to establish it as fact:

'It wasn't your fault.'

'I believe opinion is divided on that.'

She opened her mouth to say something, but he held up a hand.

'And please don't try to fob me off with your God.'

She smiled like a young girl caught kissing her friend's boyfriend.

The bird had settled in a corner of the room and was pressing itself against the wall. It was a swallow. Its plumage shone, black and midnight blue. Peter could see how fast its heart was beating.

He went over and squatted down on his haunches near to it. It looked up at him with black, blinking eyes filled with fear. He reached out for the bird and held it in his cupped hands. He felt tiny sharp claws against his skin as he carried it to the open window.

'Fly up to God, Little Bird,' the abbess mumbled as he released it.

'And fly away home? I thought that was for ladybirds?'

Sister Dolores smiled.

'*Whatever*, as they say in the outside world.'

She heaved a deep sigh.

'We had exchanged so many letters, Sister Melissa and I. She was fascinated by our life here. Within the walls, as she used to call it, like the Henri Nathansen play. She thought it sounded so safe. She so passionately wanted to experience convent life.'

She looked at him.

'It was unusual, of course, for such a young girl, and a Dane at that. She was never going to become a nun, but she was at a point in her life when she needed safety and a regulated life. That was how she put it.'

'And I expect she had a strong faith?'

'Mm, perhaps.' She picked at the fabric of her habit. 'That was her private business. But she begged and pleaded to come here. Just for one year, she said, so we knew right from the start that her time here would come to an end.'

She looked at him.

'And so it did. A brutal, premature end.'

A place of safety, he thought as he returned to the scaffolding where Manfred had already started work after the lunch break. But was that really why Sister Melissa had come to the convent: because she was scared and she believed she would be safe behind its thick walls?

It could have been a young girl's logic based, perhaps, on some romantic notion of what life was like at a place like St Mary's. No one would think to look for her here, she might have thought. No one who wanted to harm her would be able to get a toe inside such a place of sanctity.

14

KIR KNEW THE car pulling up in her drive all too well.

She had just finished her workout and had stowed the mat in the garage. With a towel around her neck, patches of sweat on her T-shirt and her hair piled up in a messy heap with a clip, she didn't feel at her most attractive. She felt Mark's expressionless eyes on her, looking her up and down.

'Busy?'

'Just my usual workout,' she said, holding the door open so he could at least step inside.

'And what can I do for you?'

She was perfectly aware that she was not making things easy for him, but yesterday's rejection still stung. She had no intention of letting him off lightly.

'I've come straight from the autopsy.'

She sniffed the air.

'Strange, you smell of perfume.'

He blushed. Bullseye! He reeked of hooker a mile off, she thought, and retreated behind her dining-room table, nodding to indicate that he could sit down on the furthest chair.

'We'd like to resume the search in and around the moat.'

'For the murder weapon?'

He shook his head.

'She wasn't killed there. But to be on the safe side, we need to go through that moat with a fine-tooth comb, so to speak. It's all we've got to go on right now.'

'Anything specific in mind?'

'Not really. Mobile, credit card, condom . . .'

'Surely that's likely to be on the bank, if there is anything?'

'True,' he conceded. 'But . . .'

'You're grasping at straws?'

He made no reply. She hadn't been able to get a good look at the body. The Falck crew had quickly moved it inside the ambulance, and only the pathologist and the police had had access.

'So all you've found is Melissa and her shoe?'

'Yep.'

She got up and filled the kettle with water. She was starving and needed something in her stomach or she would start to feel sick.

'Coffee?'

She made the offer purely out of politeness.

'Er . . . Perhaps I had better . . .'

She turned around.

'Come on, make up your mind.'

'Well, OK, yes, please.'

'Bread roll?'

She halved a home-made roll. She had baked the remains of the dough this morning, and the smell drowned his hooker's perfume, almost.

'I don't think . . .'

'Yes or no?'

'Yes, please. Christ, you don't take any prisoners, do you?' he sighed.

'That's how you get when someone screws you over,' she said with her back to him and turned around with the bread knife in her hand. 'Correction: that's how I get.'

He grinned and held up two palms.

'As long as you don't slice me in half with that knife, I guess we'll be all right.'

She looked at the knife.

'Hm. If I were you, I'd watch . . .'

'Please, Kir.'

He lowered his hands. 'I'm sorry, I've been such an idiot.'

'What am I supposed to make of that?' she asked, still holding the knife. 'That you're sorry and that you know you've been an idiot? Or that you're sorry you've been an idiot?'

'Aren't we just splitting hairs now?'

'Only an attempt to clarify: are you an idiot who is sorry, or are you just an idiot?'

He threw up his arms.

'All of it, I guess. Christ, you're hard work!'

He looked her in the eye.

'Can we bury the hatchet and be nice to each other? And please, cut those rolls and put the damn knife away.'

'Bury the hatchet? No explanation?'

She kept the knife at her side. He gulped. She could see it was hard for him, and she felt sorry for him, almost.

'I can't cope with anything right now,' he said, sounding deflated. 'Or anyone . . .'

Finally, she lowered the knife.

'A truce? Is that what you want?'

Immediately she wished she had picked a better word. But her life choices had left their mark and her vocabulary didn't come from glossy psychology magazines.

'If you like.'

'Just friends?'

He nodded.

'I can't have a girlfriend. I'm no good right now.'

'Why not?'

'Because I can barely function, after the illness. I can't get anything right.'

'Except your job?'

He nodded. 'Except my job.'

She buttered the rolls and forced the slicer through the cheese.

'Is that the best you can do?' she asked.

'I'm afraid so.'

She put the bread rolls on a plate, made two mugs of coffee and put everything on the table. Then she rubbed her palms on her tracksuit bottoms and offered him her hand across the table.

'OK, deal. Just friends.'

He looked a little surprised, as if she had accepted his offer too quickly. Perhaps he had hoped for more resistance. He took her hand.

'Deal!'

'Now eat.'

She was well aware he'd had his eye on the bread rolls on the cooling rack from the moment he'd arrived. He grinned and tucked in like someone who hadn't seen food for days.

'So what's this murder weapon you're hoping to find somewhere?'

'A garrotte.'

The hand with the bread roll stopped just before it reached her mouth.

'Why a garrotte?'

'She'd been strapped to something,' he said. 'And a spike had been pressed into the back of her neck to break her spine. Apparently that's a tell-tale sign that someone has been garrotted.'

She took a bite and munched for a while.

'How weird.'

'What is?'

She shook her head.

'It's probably nothing . . . But I found a box of bones, late last summer. Out in Kalø Bay, in the shipping channel.'

She told him about the incident and the phone call from Jarmer, while he wolfed another bread roll and washed it down with coffee.

'Someone must be investigating that case,' she said.

He nodded.

'But they're probably not working flat out to get a result,' he said, and got up. 'I'll speak to Anna about it. It definitely sounds like something we need to take a look at.'

'But it's sixty years ago,' said Kir, walking him to the door. 'It's highly unlikely to be related to Melissa's murder.'

'You're probably right. See you at the moat?'

She nodded and looked at her watch.

'I'll be there in forty-five minutes.'

Privately, she thought that finding a body was one thing, but if the murder weapon wasn't in the moat, what exactly *were* they looking for?

Could there be anything else in the stagnant, brackish water?

15

Jutta's chilli con carne was famous all across Djursland. Or, if it wasn't, it ought to have been. It was strong without being too fiery, suitably spicy with fresh chillies, and it had been simmering on the stove all day. Jutta served it with cold beer and Peter discovered to his surprise that he was still hungry after his first helping.

'There you are. Can't risk you fading away,' Jutta said and piled another steaming mound onto his plate. 'That'll put the colour back in your cheeks!'

The children giggled at the sweat streaming down his face, as always happened when he ate spicy food. He gave seven-year-old Joachim a light punch.

'Mind your own business, you cheeky monkey.'

'I'm not a monkey,' the boy grinned, spluttering rice everywhere.

'Yes, you are, you wriggle like a monkey!'

The boy practically doubled up laughing. His sister, four-year-old Mie, joined in, with chilli all around her mouth, a milder version than the hot dish the adults were eating.

'OK, that's enough,' Manfred shouted and banged the table with his fist in mock anger, making the beer bottle wobble. Jutta caught it before it fell.

'You're just as bad as the kids,' she said.

'You chose me,' Manfred smiled sheepishly.

'OK, kids. If you've had enough to eat, off you go,' said Jutta.

'Yes, go outside and play with the chainsaw,' Manfred added and playfully smacked his daughter's bottom as she passed him on her way to Kaj, who was lying down on a rug.

A measure of peace descended and Peter leaned back holding his beer, grateful that Manfred had embraced him into the heart of the family. It did him good to have his thoughts distracted by the children, the food and the company, and he felt his problems recede and melt away.

They finished eating and helped to clear the debris. Later, while Jutta made coffee, Manfred set out the chessboard on the coffee table.

'Did you actually know Melissa?' Manfred asked when they were well into their game and Peter was on the defensive.

'Only superficially,' Peter said. 'I know Sister Beatrice better.'

Manfred took his bishop.

'So you don't know who her mother is?'

Peter looked at him.

'I think you're trying to put me off my game here.'

He took Manfred's pawn with his rook.

'So who is her mother?'

'Alice Brask. Name mean anything to you?'

'Nope. But it sounds as if it ought to.'

'Check,' Manfred said, taking the queen with his knight.

Peter leaned back with his hands folded behind his head. He could see that he had already lost, and it wasn't the first time.

'OK, who is she?'

They finished playing and Manfred checkmated him as expected. He, too, leaned back from the chessboard.

'A journalist from *FrokostBladet*. One sharp sister. Writes mostly about health and consumer issues.'

'A sharp reporter whose daughter is a nun? That's what I call teenage rebellion.'

Peter thought about his own mother, who was a crime reporter for *FrokostBladet*'s rival. The nearest he came to her these days was on the rare occasions he saw the newspaper and was confronted with her photograph above the byline for one of her articles. It wasn't so much hostility between them; it was more like patient anticipation. One day they would meet again, they both knew they would.

82

'Yes, it's a bit more radical than becoming a carpenter,' Manfred conceded.

He tipped the pieces off the chessboard, folded it over and started putting pawns, bishops, rooks and knights into the box.

'Just for your info, in case you didn't know, she's run campaigns on everything from dangerous chemicals in toys to the risk of getting brain tumours from mobile phones.'

'I thought that myth was busted long ago,' Peter said.

'Alice Brask is one of the last believers,' Manfred said. 'She says she has evidence from various pieces of research that underline the risk.'

'Poor Melissa. It can't have been much fun having a mum who wants teenagers to stop using their mobiles,' Peter said. 'That must have given her street cred among her friends.'

'Yeah, I bet.' Manfred closed the chess set with a click. 'But perhaps you should take a look at her blog. Alice Brask has already written about the murder of her daughter and she mentions you.'

'*Me?*'

Manfred put the set back on the shelf under the coffee table.

'Not by name. Just something along the lines of "a carpenter saw Melissa talking to a man".'

Peter stood up. This was all getting too much for him. He had enough enemies as it was. Would he now be hung out to dry in his role as a witness?

Manfred went out of the room and came back with a laptop.

'Here. Take it. You need all the help you can get.'

Peter protested, but Manfred ignored him.

'I've just bought an iPad. I can use that until you get your own computer back.'

He winked at Peter.

'You can start by checking out Alice Brask.'

Peter gave in. Once Manfred had made up his mind he was unstoppable, and it was true that Peter needed internet access.

'And you'll want to get yourself a new mobile,' Manfred said. 'So people can get hold of you.'

Peter nodded. Neither of them was particularly good at saying thank you; it was implicit in the nod and their friendship as a whole. He looked around him.

'Right, where did the monkeys go? Two of them have to say goodnight to me.'

When he got home, he looked up Alice Brask on the internet and soon found her blog. Manfred had been right. Besides expressing her views on everything from the use of depilatory creams to the dangers of eating meat, there was also an update on the murder of her daughter. Her item was framed in black. It was illustrated with a photograph of a smiling Melissa – in her normal clothes – and entitled 'My beloved Melissa RIP'.

The text was brief and precise, like the style of the homepage, but even so emotions filtered through:

I have previously written about the pointless violence in our society and the fear it creates. I have written about young people going into town for a night out, finding themselves caught up in an unprovoked attack, and about parents who are woken up the next morning by a phone call telling them their child is in intensive care. I have argued for moderation and sought to avoid panic. It is important that young people are given the freedom to decide where they go and who they see. We can't keep them on a leash.

My daughter made a decision, which I didn't agree with, but which I supported because it was her wish. She wanted to try living as a nun in a convent, if only for some months. Melissa had faith. I don't. But I had hoped she would find herself in the process. And I believed that, if nothing else, she would be safe from the unprovoked violence every parent fears.

She wasn't. Yesterday she was reported missing from St Mary's Abbey, where for five months she had lived the life she had begged to have. Later that afternoon she was found dead in the convent moat. She had been, as the phrase goes, 'the victim of a crime'.

No thick walls, no faith and no prayers were able to protect Melissa. The question is now if anyone – be it higher forces or those of law and order – has the ability or the desire to hold the perpetrator to account.

Peter read on. A little further down he found the information Manfred had mentioned:

A carpenter working at the convent yesterday saw Melissa with a man by the moat. Whether the witness was able to provide a detailed description of the killer, I can't share with you on these pages. But if you have seen or heard anything and if you feel you're banging your head against a brick wall with the police, I am always happy to accept information here on my blog.

16

LISE WERGE PULLED the handbrake and leaned back in her seat to brace herself for a visit to her mother's.

She had driven from Grenå to Sostrup with a growing sense that she would rather be anywhere else. But it was no use. There were some obligations in life you couldn't escape, if you wanted to be able to look yourself in the eye. One of them was visiting your old mother, even if it was hard.

She sat for a moment taking in the view, with the engine still running, as if she wanted to have the option of a quick getaway. The house she hated more than anything else in the world stood in front of her. It was called 'The Woodland Snail' and, as its name suggested, was situated near a forest. It was a two-storey red-brick house with a dark, sinister basement that had always terrified her.

The story went that Lise's grandfather had built it with his own hands when he came back from the war in southern Europe in 1939. For every brick he cemented in place, he buried some of the horrors of war, and when the house was finished at last, he was a new man: strong, bristling with energy and ready to set up his own business and provide for his family. From then on, he never said a single word about what he had seen.

He had died long ago, before Lise was born, so she had never met him. What she knew of him came from her mother, who had idolised him and particularly admired his strength, both physical and mental.

'Don't ever let yourself be intimidated,' he had said, lifting her mother aloft, all the way to the ceiling. 'In our family we don't take any crap, remember that.'

In our family. It was a phrase he had been fond of. It was always followed by some statement about how their particular family was different from everyone else. It was also a phrase her mother liked to use.

Lise had spent most of her childhood wishing the opposite: that they were just like other people. Later it had become her life's mission: to be utterly ordinary.

At length she switched off the engine, got out and slammed the door, suppressing her feelings of unease. The forest had always seemed like a carnivorous plant to her and the house a helpless insect. There were always branches swatting at the windows, birds building nests under the roof and creepy crawlies finding their way through every nook and cranny.

At this moment gusts of autumn wind were tearing at the tree tops and leaves were spiralling to the ground like kamikaze planes. Heavy clouds had gathered since the morning, threatening to burst open and make another concerted effort to submerge the house, which stood in a dip with a brook close by. Only a few hundred metres from here, separated by a single farm, was St Mary's Abbey.

Lise was always reminded of the gingerbread house in the Hansel and Gretel story whenever she saw her childhood home. She had yet to decide who the witch in the story was, and that was something she really preferred not to think about.

She looked at her watch. It was early. Her mother was probably still having breakfast. But she had decided she had better look in on her in view of the drama that had taken place nearby. Old Alma might be one tough old lady, but elderly people tended to get nervous very easily and Lise took her role as next-of-kin seriously. At the age of forty-nine it was just one of the many roles she had assumed. She was also a care assistant at Grenå Nursing Home. And then there was the role of grieving widow of Jens Erik, who had died from cancer two years ago. Her role as mother, however, was not one at which she excelled. She was well aware that she had never played it to anything other than lukewarm reviews. A performance level that ran in the family.

* * *

Her mother, however, didn't seem bothered by the previous day's events at the convent. Quite the opposite, it struck Lise, seeing her mother sitting in the open-plan kitchen munching a slice of toast, her nose buried in the newspaper and her glasses perched on the tip of her nose. Fortunately, at the age of eighty-six, her mother was still lucid. And physically she had never had much to complain about. She was a strong, vigorous woman in every sense. That was what the doctor had said when Lise had had to call him one night last year when inexplicable stomach pains had overcome the old lady. Gallstones was the verdict. They were crushed with laser treatment and Alma was able to return to her Woodland Snail, defiant, it seemed to Lise, bordering on exultant.

'I bet you hadn't expected that,' she gloated. And indeed, Lise had not. In fact, she had almost been hoping for another outcome.

After the gallstones it was as if the devil had got into the old woman and she had started bossing people around even more. Most recently she had decided she would dictate her memoirs to Lise. It was remarkable how she always knew exactly what Lise should be doing in her spare time. Like now, when she lowered the newspaper and looked at her with a glance that never doubted her own fine qualities.

'So it's to be today, is it?'

'What is, Mum?'

Lise pulled out a chair and sat down.

'My memoirs, of course. Didn't you bring your tape recorder?'

Lise had hoped that project had been forgotten. Damn. She opened her bag and took out the cakes instead.

'Raspberry slices. Freshly baked.'

Her mother rejected the offer with a wave of her hand.

'I've just eaten. Go home and fetch a tape recorder.'

'But Mum . . .'

The tape recorder was in the car. She had brought it just in case, but had hoped Alma had forgotten their agreement.

'Terrible business about the dead nun,' she tried.

Again her mother rejected the notion with a wave of her hand.

'Why should nuns be spared? So someone killed her. It happens to young girls sometimes. When you have lived as long as I have, you know it's one of life's risks.'

She glared sharply at Lise.

'After all, killing an old woman like me doesn't present much of a challenge. Nor much in the way of satisfaction.'

'Satisfaction?'

'It's their innocence that is killed, don't you see? It's the only thing that makes any sense.'

Without warning Lise started sweating all over. Surely her GP would have to prescribe her hormone pills now. She couldn't believe how stingy doctors had become with HRT patches.

'You read too many crime novels, you do,' she said, and got up. 'I'll just see if that tape recorder might have found its way into the car somehow.'

She preferred her mother's boring memories to her musings about murder. It was a bizarre hobby her mother had developed in recent years – she had started consuming crime novels at the rate of at least three a week. Reading was, of course, a fairly innocent pastime, but Lise was of the opinion that Alma's imagination did not benefit from all the gore and the exotic ways in which the victims in these stories were bumped off. Perhaps there were bats in the belfry after all.

She went outside, took the tape recorder from the glove compartment and returned with it.

'Would you believe it? It was there all along!'

Her mother's gaze from behind the spectacles shone with scepticism. She buttered herself another slice of white bread.

'What a surprise,' she said. 'It was probably your subconscious that made you put it in the car.'

She bit off a large chunk of her bread, which was now spread with blueberry jam.

'Or perhaps you did it in your sleep. Is it on?'

Lise checked the voice-activated device and pressed *Record*.

'It is now.'

Her mother swallowed her food and washed it down with coffee.

She half-closed her eyes, watching Lise under heavy eyelids, and Lise was reminded of an ancient tortoise, with leathery skin and growths and a thick neck, which could retract its head under the carapace or peer out bravely if necessary. Beauty wasn't a feature that had ever troubled her family.

'There are families with talents,' Alma began. 'Families with certain talents that run in the blood, that are passed on from generation to generation.'

Lise shifted on her chair and poured herself a cup of black coffee.

The next sentence tasted almost as bitter as the coffee:

'Some families have a talent for playing music,' Alma continued. 'Others for baking or cooking or gardening.'

The old woman's voice suddenly grew stronger and fuller, as if she was in a courtroom trying to convince a judge. She opened her eyes fully and looked at Lise and through the façade she always tried to maintain.

'In our family we have a very special talent . . .'

17

'DID YOU KNOW that Melissa's mother was a journalist?'

Peter was spending the morning repairing a window in the large convent kitchen. Sister Beatrice had decided to keep him company and was currently kneading bread dough. She sat erect on a chair with a ceramic bowl in her lap. A thin layer of flour was sent up the sides of the bowl every time she ground the palm of her hand into the dough.

'Yes, why?'

Peter was putting new sills on the casement window, having first removed a couple of the old ones.

'Oh, nothing. It was just a strange combination: a journalist with a daughter who wants to be a nun.'

'I don't think Melissa found it strange.'

'But her mother wasn't crazy about her decision?'

'Are mothers ever?'

He guessed not. Peter carried on working. It was ten o'clock and at eleven Manfred would turn up and they could start replacing the roof tiles.

'What was she so scared of?'

Sister Beatrice paused for a fraction of a second, then carried on pounding the dough.

'I don't know.'

'But she must have said something. There must have been something specific to cause the fear.'

She stopped and looked at him, a trace of flour on her cheek.

'Someone threatened her. To begin with, she thought it was a joke.'

'To begin with? When was that?'

Beatrice squirmed on her chair and turned the bowl in her lap. In her face Peter could see respect for past promises struggling with a determination to solve the murder. She breathed rapidly.

'It started when she turned ten. On her birthday.'

Peter stopped sanding the sill.

'But she was just a child!'

'From then on it happened every year,' Beatrice said. 'I think she thought each time would be the last – until she turned fifteen and realised it would never stop.'

'What kind of threats?'

Beatrice had recommenced kneading the dough. But it was as if she no longer put any thought or effort into her task.

'When she first told me, I didn't really believe her. I thought – as she had originally – that it was a coincidence.'

She looked up. The flour fell from her cheek and was lost in the white of her habit.

'The first time, someone put a dead bird in her school bag. Melissa thought some of the children at school were bullying her, the ones she didn't get on with. She didn't tell anyone.'

'And the following year?'

Beatrice shook her head.

'I can't remember the sequence exactly. But there was a cat disembowelled and left on the drive.'

She looked at Peter.

'It was Melissa's cat. It was ginger and its name was Mons.'

'You said something about threats. Were there any letters?'

'Not for the first two years. But the third year she found a note in her lunchbox along with a rotten mackerel. It was a warning. If she told anyone, her family would be harmed.'

'And her family is?'

'Single mother – the journalist – and there's a younger brother called Jonas. She was especially afraid for him. And she knew her mother would just go straight to the police and the papers with the story and broadcast it to the world. She couldn't run that risk. She was a cautious girl.'

'Were there more notes after that?'

Beatrice nodded.

'From then on, there was a note every year. Always on her birthday.'

'What happened to the notes?'

'I don't know. She didn't say. But I imagine she destroyed them.'

'They could be evidence,' he said.

'I don't think she thought along those lines. She was just trying to protect herself and her family.'

'She could have gone to the police.'

Beatrice's voice suddenly sounded both weary and obstinate:

'I've already told you. She was scared something would happen to her family. You've heard about abused children, that's exactly why they don't tell. In that sense Melissa was being abused.'

'And then she got the idea of going to a convent?'

Beatrice's eyes moistened. She put down the bowl and pulled a handkerchief from a deep pocket, then clutched it in her hands on her lap.

'She had a friend online. She persuaded her. Melissa thought the convent was a place of safety, but she was still scared.'

'With good reason, evidently.'

'Yes, with good reason.'

Her answer was filled with regret.

'How did she get the rosary?'

'She was attacked last year, on her eighteenth birthday.'

Peter positioned himself so that he could see her face, which reflected her fluctuating emotions: concern, uncertainty and grief.

'What happened then?'

Beatrice's hands wrung the handkerchief. Her eyes grew round and big and seemed to fill her whole face.

'He was waiting for her when she came back from school. There was no one else in the house. He was hiding in the carport and pulled her inside when she got off her bicycle. Melissa had her keys in her hand as she was in the process of locking it up. She jammed a key into his face and he ran off.'

'And the rosary?'

'It was left behind in the carport after he had gone. She thought he might have lost it in the heat of the moment.'

'Did she see him?'

Beatrice shook her head and got up. She found a tea towel in a drawer, spread it over the dough in the ceramic bowl and set it aside.

'Not properly. It was dark, November.'

'And she didn't describe him to you in any way? Height, weight, that kind of thing?'

'All she wanted to do was forget him.'

She added: 'Have you found out anything? About the rosary, I mean?'

He shook his head. Not just to signal no, but because the whole thing was a mess. She picked up on it instantly.

'You will help me, won't you, Peter? You won't let down a friend?'

'A friend who is putting pressure on me, who promises absolution in a dream world in return for breaking the law in the real one?' He shook his head. 'I still think you should go to the police with what you know.'

She pursed her lips. He recognised her stubborn expression and knew he would get nowhere. He told her about the police coming to his house and his futile search on the internet for something that resembled the symbol on the rosary.

'I've been trying, Beatrice. But I'm not getting anywhere.'

'You must be patient,' she said.

'I must be potty,' he said.

The rain had eased now and the sun peeked out from behind the clouds. Manfred was already on the top section of the scaffolding, busily replacing a couple of roof tiles, when Peter arrived in the convent courtyard.

He cupped his hands around his mouth and called out.

'Thanks for last night.'

Manfred gave him a quick wave.

Peter was about to start climbing when the scaffolding started to sway.

'Watch out!' he shouted and Manfred tried to counter the movement by stepping from side to side on the top. Peter did a quick mental calculation. It was eight metres to the top. He couldn't climb it; he would only topple the scaffolding. All he could do was wait.

'Get out of the way . . . Keep well clear . . .'

The composure in Manfred's voice was surreal. Peter watched him. There was no time to get help. Could he catch him if he fell?

The moment froze in time. It was as if the scaffolding had gone completely still, as if the swaying had stopped, but it was only an illusion.

Then he heard an ominous creaking sound like a ship's mast before it snaps. Peter tried to find a position which would allow him to catch Manfred. But suddenly everything, metal poles and planking, came tumbling down on top of him, and Manfred's small body, which had climbed so many roof ridges, followed in its wake.

'Nooooo!'

Peter's scream was interrupted when a pole hit him and knocked him flat. It took a minute before his hearing and sight returned. Something warm dripped from his face and he tasted blood as the world spun around him.

'Manfred!'

Peter heard groaning from somewhere under the collapsed scaffolding and started crawling on his hands and knees, struggling to get his bearings. He tossed the wreckage aside as he groped his way forward.

'Where are you?'

'Here, Peter. I'm trapped.'

'Lie still. I'm coming!'

Peter worked like a madman to clear a path until he heard Manfred's familiar voice, still calm and measured, but barely audible, nearby.

'Lie still, was that what you said?'

Muted laughter.

'That's the only bloody thing I can do.'

Peter heard Manfred groaning, then he said:

'I can't feel my legs.'

The world jolted into place once more and Peter could see everything clearly again. Manfred was lying under a section of the scaffolding and looked up at him with shiny eyes. Peter was dripping blood onto his friend but was unable to tear himself away. He took off his jacket, scrunched it up and put it under Manfred's neck, and then got to work on removing the boards and poles.

'It'll be all right. Help's on its way.'

He stopped. Manfred had his eyes closed now. His face was the colour of the clouds in the sky.

'We'll soon be hunting in the forest again with the dog.'

Manfred's arm reached out and patted Peter's sleeve.

18

'THE INVESTIGATION INTO the box of bones is being handled by Oluf Jensen in Aarhus. He's retiring in the spring,' Anna Bagger said.

Mark Bille felt frustrated. That combination did not bode well for the investigation.

Anna Bagger's silk blouse flashed icy blue as she went up to the board and placed two round magnets on a photo of Melissa's mother.

'This lady is something of a nut job.'

She tapped a knuckle on the picture of Alice Brask, an attractive woman with short dark hair, flawless skin and a classic face with high cheekbones. Her smile was distant.

'Martin and I visited her yesterday,' Anna Bagger said. 'An ice queen, if you ask me.'

Women were often harder on other women than men were, Mark thought. Anna wasn't exactly like a hot water bottle herself, what with her cool colours – blond hair and shades of blue, which she always wore – and her private, slightly awkward personality.

'Anyway, we'll save it until everyone's here,' she said.

'Have you spoken to Oluf Jensen?' Mark asked.

Anna Bagger studied the board again, from where a smiling Melissa – her mother on the edge of the photo – looked down at them. The autopsy photographs had been put up next to the smiling girl. What a macabre line of business they were in.

'I've had other things on my mind. Why don't you contact him?'

He assumed this was her way of telling him he could take over that line of enquiry. He also assumed it was because she didn't regard it as important. A sixty-year-old skeleton with a broken spine wouldn't exactly make an ambitious detective lick her lips. Even if a crime lay behind it, Anna Bagger would score more points both with the public and her superiors if she could tie up Melissa's killing – uncover the motive, obtain a confession and deliver a case that would stand up in court. Anyone who had killed sixty years ago was likely to be rotting away in a nursing home or be dead themselves. Where was the fun in that?

'OK, I will.'

'If you can find the time, that is,' she said, tucking a stray lock of hair away from her face. 'I mean, you've still got your own shop to run.'

He knew she had a habit of speaking in code. This was her way of telling him not to get carried away. She was the head of the investigation and he was the local plod whose job was to catch burglars and muggers and help old ladies cross the road. Who cared if he had more than eight years of experience with the Copenhagen Homicide Squad and was probably better qualified to lead an investigation than she was?

'Don't worry, I will.'

He hesitated. 'But don't you think there might be something in this old case?'

She sat with one buttock on the corner of the table and one leg dangling in the air.

'It can hardly be the same killer. Or perhaps you disagree?'

Did he? Or was he just so desperate to prove himself that he was clutching at straws, because work was all he had left?

He walked over to the window and opened it to air the room before the meeting.

'It's an unusual way of killing someone.'

'And we're definitely talking about garrotting, are we? What if it's just your old-fashioned broken neck?'

'Not according to Sara Dreyer. The broken spinous process is apparently a unique feature of garrotting.'

'It sounds rather far-fetched to me,' she said.

'I agree it's not the same killer,' Mark said. 'But it's the same MO. Melissa also has a fractured spinous process, as you can see from the autopsy report.'

She nodded to indicate that he should continue with his train of thought.

'It could be a coincidence. Or it could be a trigger.'

Even he could hear the connection sounded strained. A murder in the present inspired by a sixty-year-old crime?

Her lack of reaction spoke volumes. He looked away and out of the window. The car park was starting to fill up as her team arrived. Once again Grenå Police Station would provide the setting for a murder investigation. It was only last winter they had fought for space when Anna Bagger and her team had made this station their HQ. This was what happened when there was an unexplained death in the area. Aarhus would come in and take charge while the five local police officers and two receptionists had to huddle together.

'Morning, all!'

Martin Nielsen was the first to appear in what had become a de facto incident room. He was quickly followed by the other detectives and eventually the whole team had gathered. Chairs clattered, jackets were peeled off, people chatted like kids before a lesson. Thermos flasks of coffee were brought in and put on a trolley with the attendant cups, sugar and milk.

Mark took a seat, but didn't feel he really belonged. Anna Bagger opened the meeting.

'Melissa. Let's sum up what we have.'

'We have a body and we know how she was killed,' said Kim Svensson, who had red hair and was new and keen and whom Mark had met once before. 'We have an approximate time of death and the place where the body was found.'

'But we don't have the murder weapon,' Martin Nielsen interjected.

'We won't find that in the moat,' Mark said.

'But there might be something down there of use,' Anna Bagger said and looked questioningly at Mark.

'The divers will try again today,' he confirmed.

Anna Bagger cleared her throat:

'Who have we talked to?'

'Boutrup,' Martin Nielsen said. 'And the abbess and all the sisters. And the staff and the conference guests. No one was of any help other than to provide a fuller picture of Melissa.'

'Do we have a list of staff and guests?'

Martin Nielsen produced two pieces of paper and handed them to her.

'ScanRapport, an IT company with ten employees, was having a meeting at five o'clock when Melissa disappeared. Everyone attended. Another company, a chain of shoe shops called Healthy Feet, were holding a course for fifteen employees, but they all spent the after-noon sightseeing locally and didn't return until six o'clock.'

He nodded to the papers. 'The rest is in there.'

Anna Bagger skimmed the list, then put it down.

'We've drawn a blank on Boutrup for the time being,' she concluded. 'And we can presume the nuns are telling the truth, can we?'

'God's servants on Earth,' Nielsen said, scratching his chin. 'No, I don't suppose we can.'

'But do we have reason to think that they might know more than they're letting on?'

'Not at the moment.'

Anna Bagger paused in front of the blackboard and chewed her lip. Then she folded her arms across her chest and started pacing up and down.

'I think we need to bear in mind that the sisters might have their own agenda. The reputation of the convent, for one. And the fact that they serve other masters, I mean the Vatican.'

She pointed to the ceiling. 'And Him upstairs.'

'Are you saying they might be lying to protect their own interests?' Mark asked.

Anna Bagger splayed her hands. For a moment Mark had a vision of her standing in a church blessing her flock.

'I'm not saying that they're lying. But if it was a choice between following their own internal religious rules and following society's, I honestly don't know which they would choose.'

Everyone seemed to be mulling that one over in the ensuing silence.

'Right,' Anna Bagger said. 'Melissa. What kind of victim are we dealing with?'

'That depends on who you ask,' Martin Nielsen said. 'According to her mother she was hard to get to know, secretive. She had her own ideas and she didn't share them with others.'

'Or not with her mother, at any rate,' Anna Bagger said. 'Alice was complaining about that.'

'Perhaps she should ask herself why. After all, she is a journalist,' Pia Thorsen said. 'She has a blog.'

'And the day after her daughter was murdered, she wrote about the investigation, thank you, yes, I know.' Anna Bagger sipped her coffee with an expression of distaste.

Pia Thorsen made another attempt.

'For every action there is an equal and opposite reaction. Newton's Third Law. If your mother is a battleaxe who sticks her nose into other people's business, it makes sense that her daughter will be cautious and private.'

'What about friends and outside contacts?'

'She cut them all off when she joined the convent,' Martin Nielsen said. 'For the same reason, she hadn't seen her mother or brother for six months.'

Anna Bagger nodded. This was information she already had.

'She's difficult to get a handle on, our do-gooder Alice.'

Her gaze swept the room and landed on Mark.

'Mark, why don't you try some of your down-home charm? Seeing as you're going to Aarhus anyway to talk to Oluf Jensen . . .'

Mark didn't know whether to be flattered or not. She waved her hand in circles:

'You're the local policeman. Remember, you're not involved in the investigation. You're just there to say you're sorry for her loss, check if she's OK, was there anything important she might have remembered, blah blah blah . . .'

She was warming to her own brilliant idea and pointed a finger with frosted nail varnish at Mark.

'She's fifty-one. She's vain. She's good-looking.'

There was a knock on the door. Jens Jepsen, a local police officer, popped his head round. His gaze landed on Mark.

'There's been an accident at the convent.'

The words vibrated in the air before their significance dawned on Mark. *Kir!* It was his first thought and it washed over him with the force of a tsunami. She must have had an accident while she was diving in the moat . . . Her oxygen tank had exploded . . .

'Some scaffolding collapsed,' Jepsen said. 'One person is in hospital.'

Relief raised Mark from his chair. Boutrup. A shame, of course. But rather him than Kir. He couldn't control his thoughts.

'Kir Røjel called. She was at the convent when it happened. She thinks we ought to take a look.'

19

JUTTA WITHOUT MANFRED was like a junkie without junk.

Dishevelled and in torment, she was chain-smoking outside the hospital entrance. She had asked Peter to get her some cigarettes and a lighter from the kiosk, although she had quit smoking five years ago.

'You might as well go home,' she said.

Her face was drained of colour. Her eyes, which at first had darted everywhere, had eventually calmed down, but it was the ominous calm of someone who knew that the worst was yet to come.

She pulled the leather jacket tighter around her and blew smoke out of the corner of her mouth.

'There's nothing they can do right now, they say. My sister will be here soon.'

She tried to look positive, but failed miserably.

'My mother has promised to look after the kids. And the dog.'

'Otherwise I'll be . . .' Peter tried.

Jutta smiled a mirthless smile.

'You've got work to do. I know that's what Manfred would say . . . That you should take over and get the job done.'

She flicked ash and it flew all over the place.

'Work is piling up.'

He could hear Manfred's voice in her, but couldn't think of work. Why Manfred? A man with two small children and a young, insecure wife. Why not Peter? It would be more logical. And it would have spared him the guilt that was accumulating on top of all the other baggage he was dragging around. Manfred had spotted that straightaway, of course.

'It was just bad luck it was me,' he had said as he lay waiting for the ambulance. 'It could have been you. It's no one's fault. You know that, don't you? Shit happens. That's life.'

Peter had nodded, of course. But they both knew it wasn't quite as straightforward as that. And now he was standing here with Jutta. 'He'll be fine.'

He said it as much for his own sake as for hers. 'He'll be all right again.'

'Of course he will.'

She sniffed. He didn't know what to do with himself. He patted his back pocket to make sure his wallet was still there. It was a habit from a time when this was far from a matter of course.

'Do you want a cup of coffee?'

She nodded and removed a stray strand of tobacco from her tongue with her cigarette hand. Again, some ash flew off into the autumn wind.

He went inside and hurried down the corridor looking for a vending machine. On his way he passed patients, relatives and staff in various permutations while the events of the last few hours went round and round in his head. Manfred's composure when the ambulance arrived and the medics stretchered him into the back. His quiet banter with the Falck crew. And then the silence after they had obviously decided to give him a sedative. The arrival at the hospital where white coats and green scrubs had surged around them and where one staff member had tried to get Peter to sit down so that he could have a look at the cut on his forehead. The scene Peter had caused when he had refused to leave Manfred and the fuss he had made when they took his best friend away. And Jutta hadn't even arrived yet. Their insistence that it was best to get started as soon as possible and his embarrassing behaviour when he had accused them of being vultures and hypocrites, people who lived off the misfortunes of others.

'What would you lot do with yourselves if we didn't fall off scaffolding, eh? You'd be out of a bloody job, wouldn't you?'

To his surprise no one had seemed annoyed or responded with

anything other than quiet, cheerful remarks to the effect that, of course, they spent every waking hour hoping people would fall off ladders, scaffolding and down staircases.

'Sometimes we even go so far as giving them a helping hand to be sure there's always plenty for us to do,' one of them said.

Miriam had rung in the middle of it all. He had forwarded the number of his new mobile to those contacts he could remember by heart. Miriam wasn't top on his list of people he was pleased to hear from, but nevertheless he told her what had happened. She managed to talk him down:

'They're just doing their job, Peter,' she had said. 'It's not their fault Manfred got hurt.'

She had an irritating habit of always putting things into perspective when he least needed it, he thought. He found a vending machine and inserted some coins.

Again, he reviewed the last couple of working days in his head. Manfred and he were always careful when they erected scaffolding. Neither of them cut corners; they trusted each other. But he had been distracted while they were working, absorbed by the dredging of the moat, by My's mother and her bizarre arrival, the killing of Sister Melissa and Beatrice's subsequent revelations. He had felt the rosary weighing heavily in his pocket while he clicked aluminium poles into their clamps and tested their strength every time he laid out boards for a new platform. Had they remembered to lock the castors? He was absolutely sure he had. Besides, they always checked each other's work at the end. So how could it have happened? There was no wind of any significance in the convent courtyard. Everything had been quiet and peaceful.

He touched his forehead. Once Jutta had arrived, they had persuaded him to go to casualty for some stitches. Seven in total. The doctor had also shone a light into his eyes and said he might have suffered mild concussion. Fortunately it wasn't serious enough for the hospital to offer him a bed, so he was discharged with instructions to go home and rest and take paracetamol if the pain got worse.

When he returned with the coffee, there was no sign of Jutta. A nurse told him she had been called in to see the doctor, so he sat down and waited and ended up drinking both her coffee and his own before she returned, solemn yet composed. And, if possible, even paler.

'They're doing some tests, but he still has no sensation in his legs,' she said. She flopped down onto a chair but immediately jumped up again. 'They say that the fall could have paralysed him temporarily. But he might also be . . .'

She gulped. Tears filled her eyes, which were already red.

'He may never get better.'

'How long before they know?'

'They can't say.'

Her voice was paper-thin. 'It varies.'

His mobile rang just as he was about to get up and give her a hug. It seemed stupid to answer it, but even more idiotic to let it ring. Jutta stared pointedly at his pocket.

'Just answer it,' she said at length, close to hysteria.

He quickly hauled it from his pocket and went down the corridor. He gave vent to his irritation when he saw who it was and barked:

'Yes?'

'Peter,' Mark Bille Hansen said.

'Now what? Don't tell me you want to confiscate this phone as well? This is bordering on harassment.'

'I'm not confiscating anything. We're at the convent. The scaffolding.'

'I'll clear it up.'

'Kir has found something. We're waiting for a forensic report.'

Forensic report. Alarm bells started ringing. The hospital staff's jokey comments about giving a helping hand zoomed back like a boomerang.

'From a superficial examination we can see saw marks on the metal,' the police officer said.

20

THIRTY MINUTES LATER he saw with his own eyes what Mark Bille meant. The scaffolding was still lying in a heap in the convent courtyard. The difference now was that the CSOs had drawn white chalk circles and were busy bagging up the poles that had been sawn through.

'What's happening, Peter? This doesn't look like a message from your biker gang friends . . .'

Mark Bille squatted down and pointed to the saw marks.

'No.'

He looked up and sideways at Peter.

'So who is it? Have you made some new enemies?'

Mark got up while Peter reviewed potential candidates.

'Come on. Help me out here.'

Mark Bille was all right, but the rest of the police force could pack up and move to Greenland as far as Peter was concerned.

'You have a leak,' he concluded. 'As a result, someone tried to kill me.'

'That's a serious accusation. Would you care to elaborate?'

'Someone told Alice Brask, Melissa's mother, that a carpenter saw something that afternoon. She posted it on her blog.'

'So you're saying one of our police officers talked?'

'Who else?'

'And someone read that blog and decided you were going to have an accident?'

Peter looked at the collapsed scaffolding. He could still hear it crashing down and see Manfred's body falling through the air.

'Not someone. The perp, to use a technical expression.'

He continued:

'The perp can read. He has a computer, but that's not all. He's a narcissist. He follows Alice Brask's blog to see how she refers to him. And he exploits every piece of information to sabotage your investigation.'

'Including killing witnesses?'

'Why not? He's on a roll.'

His anger followed him until he left the convent soon afterwards to drive to the cemetery. It was late in the afternoon and the sun hung low in the sky. The bouquet on My's grave looked like someone had flattened it with a steam roller. He felt like picking it up and hurling it away.

He stuffed his hands into the pockets of his work trousers as he stared at the grave. He imagined the worms inexorably munching away under the ground. Just as they were working their way through human remains, his anger was eating its way through him. If he didn't do something soon, he would end up a hollow shell with his insides rotted away.

He scuffed the gravel with the tip of his shoe. There was still humidity in the air and the ground was sticky and dark.

Things had changed. Melissa's death had affected so many things, including his relationship with the convent and with Beatrice. But worst of all, he could have lost his best friend, and Jutta might have lost her husband and her children their father.

Even when the ambulance had taken them to the hospital, it hadn't crossed his mind that it could be anything other than an accident. But the evidence was clear: it was sabotage.

He didn't doubt for one second that the sabotage had been meant for him. His enemies were out to get him, only this time they weren't Rico's foot soldiers. He was certain Melissa's murderer was behind it. His logic was that if the witness was gone, the perpetrator couldn't be identified.

That was what had happened. And Manfred had paid the price, possibly with his mobility. Manfred was an innocent bystander. An ordinary man with a family and a job who had made the mistake of choosing an ex-convict and albatross as his employee and friend.

Peter wandered around the cemetery for a while, then left and drove home in the late afternoon. The clouds had disappeared and the setting sun cast low rays across the fields, where the winter seedlings shone a luminous green. Beyond them the Kattegat sparkled metallically and the waves were silver-crested as he drove home along the familiar narrow lanes leading to Gjerrild Cliff.

For a long time now he had said that revenge was not for him. Revenge was for amateurs, for people who couldn't think of a better way to fill their lives.

Not that he was short of things to avenge in his life, if he had to look. And once upon a time, thoughts of revenge had filled most of it. He and Cato, his old pal from the care home, had had big plans in that respect. The thought and talk of revenge had been the adhesive that bound them together in those days. Anyone they had ever met, who had failed them, would one day experience revenge served cold. Everyone – sadistic care home managers, powerless caseworkers, corrupt doctors and callous parents – would get a taste. It gave them a strange sense of satisfaction to imagine how they would do it.

Cato had never strayed from that course. But Peter had changed. Four years in Horsens State Prison had taught him that revenge was a waste of time. Taking revenge never made anyone happy. He only had to look at the other inmates. Many were inside because they had wanted to avenge something. Bikers taking an eye for an eye and a tooth for a tooth; men who had murdered out of jealousy and in a blood rush; financial disagreements that had been avenged with stabbings and physical violence. It was all on display in Horsens. And it was not a pretty sight.

After his release he had sworn that a thirst for revenge would not be allowed to ruin his life. He had decided, if not to forgive, then at least to let bygones be bygones and forget.

But now everything had changed. Someone had taken Melissa's

life and possibly ruined Manfred's. Someone was after him. He didn't want revenge but something akin to it. He wanted this person held to account and confronted with their actions. And yes, the temptation to close his hands around the neck of the guilty person and pay him back in the same coin was enormous, because he didn't believe for one second that the police could get them justice.

He had to find the someone who was trying to destroy his and others' lives. An alarm system was no longer enough.

He had reached the pig farm and had just driven past the large silo when a car sounded its horn at him. In his rear-view mirror he saw a small red Chevrolet hopping along the road My's mother was hooting and waving to him from inside the car.

He stopped and saw her get out and approach him. She was wearing jeans and a soft, light-coloured sweater. He rolled down his window.

'You've been to the cemetery,' she said.

He just nodded. Here, in his private part of the world, her eagerness irritated him.

'And you're back in Djursland,' he said. 'That was quick.'

It sounded rude, but he didn't care. It was a shit day and her presence didn't make it any better.

Her face fell.

'You're annoyed with me.'

He didn't disagree.

'I understand, but I promise you I only want what's best. I just wanted . . .'

'It's a free country,' he said, less angry now. 'You can come and go as you please.'

She bit her lip. Her hair fell over her shoulder and at that moment the sun caught it and it shone almost golden.

'I've baked a cake. I thought you might like to make some coffee . . .'

He searched for an excuse to say no, but his hesitation allowed her an opening:

'I heard about what happened to that girl, Melissa. How awful.'

He just nodded.

'And then I realised that I actually know her, from a long time ago . . .'

'You do?'

She backtracked.

'Well, no, not really . . . But I did know her mother. We were practically neighbours. Then the family moved to Randers . . . Anyway, I'm just wittering on. So how about that coffee?'

He nodded.

'OK.'

The eagerness had returned to her voice.

'Deal. I'll just follow you, shall I?'

21

'I'M MAKING A list of missing persons reported at that time. It's going to take a couple of days, as you will appreciate.'

Oluf Jensen didn't appear to be quite as inefficient as Mark had feared. He might be close to retirement, but the eyes behind the spectacles were alert and he had a touch of the old-fashioned detective about him: thorough and conscientious to a T, as he sat there in his corduroy jacket behind the desk at Aarhus Police Station. His teeth were crooked and yellow as if they had gripped a pipe for decades and sucked nicotine into the enamel. His hair was longish and curly without a hint of grey in the ash blond. He looked more like an academic than a police officer.

'How far are you casting the net?' Mark asked.

'Across all of Denmark. But focusing on East Jutland and Djursland in particular, of course.'

'Perhaps I can help,' Mark offered. 'I know the area. Families here tend to stay put within a radius of ten kilometres.'

Oluf Jensen flicked through some papers.

'I would welcome your help. I am a bit trussless here, if I may put it like that.'

'Trussless?'

The investigator wafted his hand as if swatting a fly. His eyes glinted.

'No support. A feeble attempt at humour. My colleagues ignore me.'

The krone dropped with an audible clunk.

'Ah, support as in back-up. . .'

Oluf Jensen looked at him over the rim of his spectacles with a certain amount of forbearance. 'Nasty business, those two murders,' he said. 'But also intriguing, of course.'

'Same MO, you mean? Separated by so many years.'

Mark still felt a little wrong-footed. Oluf Jensen nodded.

'Stirs the imagination, eh, a riddle stretching across so many decades?'

'And a garrotte,' Mark said. 'It belongs to the past rather than the present.'

Oluf Jensen winked behind his glasses.

'I agree. The garrotte – if that is what we're talking about – was originally a Spanish invention.'

The garrotte could originate from Timbuktoo as far as Mark cared, but Oluf Jensen had clearly looked into the matter. You probably had time to do that sort of thing when you weren't trying to run a police station and keep a team of out-of-town detectives happy.

'The garrotte was Spain's answer to Madame la Guillotine, a device for executing prisoners. You were sat on an upright wooden chair and a metal band was placed around your neck and tightened from the back with a screw. You were strangled by the metal band while a metal spike was forced into your neck and broke your spine.'

As he spoke, Oluf Jensen tried to demonstrate the executioner's technique. Mark broke into a sweat at the mere thought of it.

'Jesus Christ! I'd prefer a bullet – or a full salvo,' he said.

He had always thought that death by strangulation was the worst way to die. He had been terrified that his cancer would spread to his lungs and slowly deprive him of oxygen. Not that he had ever told anyone that.

'If their aim is good, yes,' Oluf Jensen said, not without a certain macabre delight. 'But the garrotte was actually a reliable method of killing.'

'Please tell me it's no longer legal?'

'Not any more, no. But it wasn't outlawed in Spain until the early 1970s, when they abolished the death penalty.'

'Melissa Brask was fixed to a chair. How about our friend in the bone box? Did the same thing happen to him?'

'Unfortunately, the forensic examiners can't tell us that.'

'But surely it can't be the same person? Who carried out both killings, I mean?'

Oluf Jensen leaned back in his chair and looked at Mark.

'In theory, everything is possible. But if the forensic anthropologists are right and the bones are from around 1950, we would be talking about a killer who would be in his mid-seventies, at least.'

'Even so, there must be a certain margin for error, perhaps in our favour?'

'Nevertheless . . .'

Oluf Jensen took a black ink pen and started drawing on a piece of paper. A few swift strokes and a rigid, high-backed chair appeared. A few more and a girl was sitting on the chair with a metal band around her neck. The band was tightened by a man standing behind her, turning a screw.

'A little hobby of mine,' the detective muttered. 'It comes in handy.'

He sketched a second device. A metal band with a pointed object attached and a stick as a handle.

'It's called a Catalan garrotte when there's a spike on it,' Oluf Jensen said in a serene voice.

He looked up at Mark.

'It's quite an effective way to kill people. It's still used in some places, as far as I know.'

'I thought you just said it was forbidden now?'

'Officially, yes. But there are certain military situations where it has been used. Undercover work, as it's known.'

'Where?'

'In the Foreign Legion, they say . . . As I said, it's a silent mode of execution. If it's carried out correctly.'

Oluf Jensen added a few more squiggles.

'But we can probably ignore that possibility in this case, don't you think?'

Again there was a glint of good humour behind the glasses. Mark nodded. He knew he should never eliminate anything or anyone, but it was hard to imagine the Foreign Legion striking in Djursland in the present or in the past.

'If it's around 1950,' he said, 'that makes it a few years after the war had ended. Could it have anything to do with the war?'

For the first time, Oluf Jensen looked at him as though he were a star pupil and not the class dunce, too dim to understand anything.

'Go back only five years and you have liquidations during the final phase of the war. In the last few months before the Germans capitulated, around four hundred people – informers, if you will – were killed without a trial.'

'So our victim could be one of them?'

More squiggles on the paper.

'Now, there's still the issue of the MO. Most liquidations were carried out by the Danish Resistance movement. They used guns.'

'But if they wanted to avoid noise?'

'I believe silencers had been invented back then. But yes. It's a possibility. We'll know more when we get the list.'

Mark anticipated quite a workload if they had to check four hundred names plus miscellaneous enquiries. Anna Bagger had made a smart move. He would be kept busy for weeks and thus out of her investigation.

'Perhaps we could request more help,' he suggested. 'To go through that list, I mean.'

Oluf Jensen got up.

'Resources, my good man. They don't drop out of the sky and certainly not at this station.'

The detective held the door open for him and they went down the corridor together.

'Let's be honest,' Oluf Jensen said before they parted. 'It would take a miracle. Both to get more manpower allocated to this case and for us to have a breakthrough. I'll be in touch when the list arrives. Meanwhile, why don't you scout around locally for stories from those days . . . See what crawls out of the provincial woodwork.'

Mark wasn't normally a man who believed in miracles. Nonetheless, he left the police station with a dash of optimism. He didn't believe in miracles, that was true, but nor was he ready to dismiss them out of hand. He was, after all – as far as he was aware – one himself.

22

'WHAT A LOVELY house!'

Peter tried to put himself in Bella's shoes and in a flash he saw what she saw:

An ascetic bachelor home with white walls, sparsely furnished and no superfluous ornaments on the window sills or shelves, but a bookcase laden with books arranged alphabetically. Fortunately, he'd tidied up after the police visit.

There were scrubbed, pale wooden floors, white-washed ceilings and unframed paintings on the walls, most with the same motif: the countryside and the sea right outside the door. The simple life translated from prison cell to freedom.

'Take a seat. I'll make some coffee.'

While he was in the kitchen, he could hear her wandering about. He knew she was stopping in front of each painting and reading his signature. He knew she was trying to get to know him and he was pleased he had taken down the other paintings long ago. He always painted in series: the same subject over and over again. The tree outside Titan Care Home, consumed by flames on canvas more times than he could count.

He brought in the coffee and mugs.

'So tell me about Melissa's mother.'

She turned around.

'You paint well. But why do you always paint the same scene?'

'There are shades of difference.'

As in real life, he thought, and nodded towards the window.

'It changes all the time.'

The light, the wind and the clouds were better at mixing colours than he was with his palette. He felt that the pictures displayed his shortcomings.

'I just paint what I see.'

She seemed to accept this explanation. He had no wish to tell her that he was unable to hold any more than this one view inside him. The cliff and the sea were overwhelming to a person who had stared at four cell walls for the same number of years.

'Are they for sale? I might want to buy one.'

He could do with the money, but he didn't like the idea of it. You didn't trade with your enemies – or perhaps you did. Wasn't that exactly what he was about to do now?

'They're not for sale.'

'Isn't everything?'

There was a teasing tone to her voice. She had brought with her a Føtex plastic bag. Now she took out a cake dish, put it on the coffee table and removed the tea towel. 'Voilà! Dream cake.'

For a while they were busy with the rituals of pouring coffee and serving cake. Then he told her about the scaffolding accident and Manfred. He intended to use it as leverage to find out something about Melissa's mother. And, as expected, Bella's eyes widened.

'And you think it happened because Alice wrote about you in her blog?'

She made it sound implausible, so he replied by just staring at her and drinking his coffee.

'You look like My,' he blurted out. 'And yet you don't.'

'Tell me about her.'

He had to give her something, so he told her about the day when five-year-old My had turned up at the care home. He had been eight at the time.

'She couldn't cope,' he said, and could see he was twisting the knife inside her with every word. He persisted:

'So she started living in a fantasy world. She told herself that her mum would come back and fetch her.'

'Oh, my God . . .'

Bella put down her cup and raised a hand to her throat. He didn't look at her as he continued:

'You've probably read about the home. There were punishments. My couldn't take them. She became increasingly weird.'

'It was recommended to us. My husband . . . He had heard so many good things about Titan,' Bella said.

'Then he must have had selective hearing.'

'Perhaps he did . . .'

'And taken a perverse pleasure in other people's misfortunes.'

She shook her head.

'No, no, he wasn't like that. But, yes, he was the one who thought we couldn't have My living with us. Her diagnosis, you know . . . She was perfectly normal, the first few years, but suddenly she changed.'

'You're talking about her autism?'

'That's what the doctors called it.'

Bella nursed her mug of coffee. 'My husband wasn't My's father, you see. I didn't meet him until after My had had the vaccination.'

'What vaccination?'

'The MMR jab. A kind of triple cocktail. Anders was convinced that was what had given My autism. There was so much uncertainty around those vaccinations.'

She must be using that as an excuse, decided Peter, who knew nothing about such things.

'And Anders didn't want an autistic child? What a charmer, I must say.'

Peter set down his mug. What was it about women who let others decide their children's fates? His own mother had done the same. The now super-confident journalist Dicte Svendsen had once been a young, insecure mother, who had let herself be swayed by other people's opinions. It wasn't a truth she liked being confronted with, and it was one of the reasons they didn't see each other. Her behaviour had imitated Bella's: a little bit of external pressure, and hey presto, the kids were handed over to strangers without anyone checking whether they were all right.

'I was very young,' Bella said. 'I was sixteen when I had My. I couldn't handle a child, let alone an autistic child. Anders was ten years older than me.'

'And ten years more stupid.'

He saw Bella wince. He continued:

'My, however, wasn't stupid. On many occasions she was smarter than all of us put together.'

Bella sat with a small smile playing around her mouth.

'My knew she was different,' he said. 'All she wanted was to be like everyone else.'

They sat for a while in silence. Then Bella said:

'I asked for it. It hurts, of course, but it's necessary.'

'Why now?' he wanted to know.

She looked down at the table.

'My husband. We got divorced last year. I'm trying to pick up the pieces of my life and look at them with fresh eyes. Starting over, I believe they call it.'

She met his gaze.

'Anders is a good man, but a little old-fashioned. He's an army man. He likes order, and yes . . . discipline. But he isn't evil.'

'They're the worst,' he said. 'The ones who aren't evil and do everything with the best of intentions.'

She squirmed, but he didn't care if this was hard for her. It was up to him to make it hard.

'What about Alice Brask? Tell me something about her.'

'I know her from Elev. We lived in the same street as Alice and our children went to the same nursery and later school.'

'What was your relationship with her?'

She thought about it for a little while.

'I respected her . . . She knew so much about all sorts of things.'

Then, apropos of nothing, she said:

'My son, Magnus, has gone. He's run away. He's eighteen.'

She gripped his arm.

'There's something about you, Peter. You had a way with My.'

Her eyes had taken on the fervent expression of someone who has faith.

'You can find him, if you want.'

Her voice was intense. Her body trembled so much that he could feel the vibrations.

'I know that must sound strange. But everything is connected: My, the divorce, the past. Even Alice Brask fits in somewhere, only I just can't see where for the moment.'

Peter's head was spinning. What was her agenda? He wasn't a hero who made it his mission to save other people's children. Why him?

'What do the police say?'

'Nothing.'

She grabbed his arm a second time.

'It's a family matter. He hasn't been abducted or murdered. He's eighteen. He's just run off. Here.'

She rummaged around her bag and produced a photograph. He looked at it. It was like being hit by a stun gun and for a moment he felt numb. He knew perfectly well that she was manipulating him. But it was working. The inner worms started gnawing again when he saw the boy who looked so much like his half-sister that they could have been twins. Hopelessly vulnerable, dreamy and puckish, My was staring straight at him.

'Please, Peter,' Bella pleaded in her most poignant voice with eyes that trusted him as My's had done. 'You have so many contacts. Miriam says you helped my daughter. You must help me to find him.'

23

SABOTAGE.

Kir had turned the word over in her head as she left the moat and her colleagues behind and headed for the harbour after yet another unsuccessful dive. Peter Boutrup had been angry. She could tell from his closed expression and the jerky way he moved as if he was struggling to keep everything together. But in the middle of it all, he had also expressed his gratitude. Just with a nod and a brief thank you for spotting the saw marks on the poles. There was respect in that nod and the hint of a smile in his otherwise solemn, battered face.

She didn't know why his face pursued her. Now, all the way down to the harbour, which she loved early in the morning and at all times of the year. In the summer, the warm mist would make the decks of the fishing boats and the tarmac on the quay steam. In hard winters, the snow would brighten everything up and ice would form on planking and in sheltered corners.

Today the light hung low across the Kattegat and deepened the colours of the ships. A storm had been forecast, but for the time being the sun was out and the clouds were staying away. The search in the moat had been suspended the previous day, following the commotion of the scaffolding accident. Today the team had picked up where they left off, two divers going down at a time. Even in such shallow waters they needed their breaks, and right now she had some free time while she waited to be called back.

She drove her red pickup down to the mole where the dinghies were straining at their moorings. There was always some obstinate angler who would defy a bad forecast and get up at the crack of dawn. She had a hundred kroner in her pocket. The thought of a couple of juicy plaice – and a dinner with Mark Bille, who might have news about the box of bones – had prompted her to drive down here.

'Hi, Karl. Have you got something for me?'

Karl was the father of one of her old school friends. He had taken early retirement and now had time to focus on what really mattered after a lifetime of working in a machine works.

He shook his head.

'I haven't been out.'

He nodded his head backwards to the other dinghies with outboard motors.

'I think Jokke has. Try him.'

Karl winked at her. 'Besides, he always lowers his prices for lady customers.'

'Are you calling me a lady, Karl?'

Kir looked down at herself. She was wearing her usual outfit: jeans, desert-coloured Gore-Tex boots and a green army jacket zipped right up to her neck. Was it any wonder men didn't find her attractive?

'Of course you're a lady, Kir.' Karl stroked his chin. 'You can't change that, no matter how many layers of clothing you put on.'

She carried on down the jetty. Quite a few people had come out to tinker with their boats. There was some activity over by the fishing cutters. She could see a Falck emergency vehicle parked over there and hear loud voices.

'What's all that about?'

Jokke followed her gaze. He was in his forties but had retired on a disability pension due to his bad back. Now he stood in his boat easing wriggling fish out of the net and into a white bucket.

'Damned if I know.'

He spat across the gunwale.

She pulled the note out of her pocket.

'How many can I have for a hundred?'

'About ten of the good 'uns, I reckon.'

'And you'd gut them for me at that price?'

'You drive a hard bargain.'

But he agreed. He skilfully gutted the plaice and chopped off their heads, throwing the fish waste to the gulls.

While she waited, she watched the commotion on the quay where the cutters were moored. Then she put the bag of fish in her car and strolled over to see what they were doing. She knew most people at the harbour, and the boats. The Falck vehicle was parked in front of Jens Bådsmand's cutter and now she could see a diver swimming around at the aft end.

Jens and his son Simon were standing with their hands buried in their pockets, chatting to one of the other fishermen and a Falck man in a blue overall and fluorescent vest. Simon's friend, Nils, was watching everything with curiosity.

'Do you need any help?'

Kir addressed Jens and his son. Jens wiped his nose on the sleeve of his jumper and shook his head.

'Not now that I've paid for Falck membership. It's part of the insurance. Otherwise I'd have called you, Kir, don't you worry.'

'What's the problem?'

'There's something stuck in the propeller. It won't do what I want it to do.'

'And you're about to head out?'

He nodded and put a hand on Simon's shoulder.

'The boy has to learn some time, doesn't he?'

'The forecast is bad.'

Jens Bådsmand dismissed this with a wave of his hand.

'One forecast is good, another crap. What are you going to believe? My bones tell me it'll be fine.'

It was like that with fishermen. They were used to reading the weather.

'So, Simon, no more school for you?'

The boy nodded. He had acne and was a few kilos overweight, just like his father.

'He left school this summer,' his father answered for him. 'So if he wants to learn the trade, now's the time.'

Jens Bådsmand was a skilled fisherman and his vessel, the *Marie af Grenå*, was one of the best maintained boats in the harbour.

'But he might go on to further education later,' Jens said. Simon nodded again. 'Then he can study marine biology and tell us about all the fish we're not allowed to catch.' Jens playfully took a swipe at his son, who ducked with a grin.

'And how about you, Nils?' Kir asked his friend, who had been at school with Simon. She knew them both. 'Are you going fishing today as well?'

Nils shook his head and looked annoyed.

'I've got to go to work.'

'Where?'

'Supermarket. Kvickly. But I'd rather be out fishing.'

'What's that you've got there, Kasper?' Jens called out.

The diver had surfaced from the water with a mass of net in his arms. He yanked off his mask. Kir had never seen him before, but even so there was something familiar about him. He nodded to her as if he knew who she was. Cold eyes met hers.

'Some pound net had got caught in the propeller.'

He started to come up. The other Falck man stood ready to help. When the diver was finally out, he stood dripping water as he peeled off his equipment. He coldly looked Kir up and down.

'So you're the fearless diver from the Bay of Aden?'

It was said sarcastically. 'You know my brother, I believe,' he added.

Of course. Now she saw the resemblance.

'Do you mean Frands? One of the mine divers?'

That was all she needed. A clone of the very tiresome Frands. The Falck diver raked a hand through his wet hair in an affirmative movement.

'What a coincidence,' Kir said. 'Have you just joined Falck? I thought I knew most of their people.'

She tried to ignore his threatening demeanour. He stood with his legs astride and a little too close to her.

'Do I look like a new guy?'

There was a hint of contempt in his voice. She had no idea why.

'Your brother and I worked together at the convent, but I guess you've already heard?'

He nodded and water flew everywhere.

'I've also heard the search in the moat has been called off,' he said.

'Has it?'

Kir felt out of the loop. He widened his legs even further and his eyes narrowed.

'A woman who's a mine diver,' he said, staring at her. 'How many officers do you have to bed to get that far?'

She stared back, caught by surprise, and her jaw dropped. For a few seconds there was only silence and the sense that the bystanders were holding their breath. Someone must have pissed in his porridge, she thought, or his brother's. Perhaps Frands had applied to serve on the *Absalon* and been turned down – what did she know?

She forced herself to smile sweetly.

'You and your brother have got a lot in common. You both seem to suffer from insecurity and . . .'

He grinned and furrowed his brow at the same time. It made him look like a snarling predator.

'You're a flash in the pan, Kir Røjel. Everyone knows you're screwing your boss and that police officer. Otherwise you'd never have got to the Bay of Aden or been given that job in the moat.'

'. . . a fear of women,' she said, quivering on the inside. 'My guess is an overbearing mother and potty training issues. Couldn't you sit straight or did you have to share with your brother?'

She turned on her heel. Her remark was neither witty nor clever, but she had a strong hunch it was close to the truth.

When she came home she threw the fish in the fridge and called Mark.

'Why don't I know you called off the search?'

'You'd have to ask Allan Vraa about that,' Mark said.

That was the last thing she wanted to do right now. Kasper Frandsen's accusations – lies though they were – sat in her like barbs.

'It's a question of resources,' Mark explained. 'And we can't claim we're looking for the murder weapon. Melissa wasn't killed near the moat; she was taken to another location first.'

Talking about the case helped. The diver from the harbour faded into the background.

'But why? If all he wanted to do was kill her, why not just strangle her there and then and chuck her in the water?'

'He had a plan,' Mark said. 'He knew exactly what he wanted. And it involved time alone with the victim.'

'Torture?'

'Mental torture, obviously. Physical? The garrotte in itself is an instrument of torture. That girl went through hell.'

There was silence for a moment. Then Mark said:

'What do you know about what went on during the war around here?'

It was something of a leap, but she was happy to follow his train of thought, away from the murder and her run-in with Frandsen's brother.

'Quite a lot as it happens,' she admitted.

'You do?'

He sounded surprised.

'It's something I'm interested in. Also because we hunt around for old munitions in the Koral Strait from time to time.'

'The Koral Strait? That sounds more like Australia than Djursland,' he said.

'It's by the shipping channel through Kalø Bay. That's where I found the box of bones.'

'It's possible that the bones are from the post-war years.'

Of course, Kir thought. It made sense.

'Are you still there?' he asked after a pause.

'Yep.'

She remembered the bag in the fridge.

'I'm going to fry some fresh plaice tonight. If you come over, I'll tell you about some local history from those days.'

'Don't forget our truce.'

'You can stick that where the sun don't shine.'

She ended the call and knew he would come. He would keep his distance. She knew that, too. But she had begun to think this might be OK.

24

AN *ARMY* MAN. That was the word that had got him thinking about a possible solution to the rosary mystery. Bella had told him her ex-husband was an *army* man.

Peter rang Matti. He was his closest connection to anything army-related. Matti and he shared a history that went back to their childhood, but the most recent chapter was that Matti had turned up as a prison officer when Peter was in Horsens. The prison service and the army appeared to have something in common, certainly plenty of uniforms and symbols.

Peter described the rosary.

'It looks like an ordinary rosary with a crucifix hanging from it – except this is not a crucifix.'

'So what is hanging from it?'

He looked at the rosary, holding it up to the light while standing with the mobile in his hand.

'Well, I guess it is a crucifix of sorts, but on top of it there's a crown, and behind the crown there are three things that look like something from a historical film about war – you know the sort of thing I mean?'

'Go on.'

'There's an old-fashioned gun – it must be a muzzle loader – one of those weapons the beefeaters in the Tower of London walk around with – and a crossbow . . .'

'That beefeater thing? Something like a pike or a halibut?' Matti prompted.

'A fish?' Peter queried.

'No. A halberd,' Matti corrected himself.

'Ah yes, that's it. A musket, a halberd and a crossbow.'

He could practically hear Matti scratching his head.

'And you've looked it up on the internet?'

'The problem is I don't know what I'm looking for. Do you have any ideas?'

After further consideration Matti decided that he hadn't.

'But perhaps a military historian might know.'

Matti didn't happen to know any military historians, of course, but he did know a guy in Ebeltoft, who once upon a time had been a commando and was now running rehabilitation programmes for ex-offenders.

'The two have a lot in common,' Matti yawned down the phone. 'It's all shut up and do as you're told. Which is what you want when you get out of prison.'

It most certainly wasn't what Peter had wanted when he had been given back his freedom. No one would tell him to shut up and do as he was told ever again. But that was another matter.

He got the guy's name and phone number. After talking to Jutta – Manfred's condition was still unchanged – he started ringing round to find a replacement for Manfred and another carpenter, so that they could keep on top of the jobs in the order book. Then he took the dog for a walk, went to work and grafted until the afternoon, when he drove to Ebeltoft.

It was a place to start, he thought as he drove. A tiny flap he might be able to lift to get a glimpse of the mystery he had got himself mixed up in: Melissa, Manfred, and now Bella's missing son. He hadn't promised to find him, but the link to Alice Brask touched a nerve somewhere. Everything was connected, Bella had said. But why would a runaway boy and a murdered nun have anything in common just because they used to play together as children?

Bella was a canny manipulator, he had discovered. And now she had succeeded in drawing him in and getting him to agree.

The name of the commando was Sigurd Banner and he trained ex-offenders in a wooded area with a brook near a summer house development behind Ebeltoft. It was getting dark and thick clouds were gathering above them as Peter drove into the yard. He could just make out some barracks and an assault course with red wooden obstacles, which looked like the kind of thing you saw on TV. There were obstacles to be surmounted using your arms, there were ditches to cross, posts to climb, barriers, rafts, ropes, streams and a climbing wall, which wasn't for the fainthearted. He counted seven people in grey tracksuits doing the training, including two girls with swinging ponytails and bouncing breasts.

A man who had to be Sigge himself – that was the name Matti had used – was standing with a whistle around his neck shouting out words of encouragement to the hard-working participants.

'Shift your ass, Sonja! Come on, folks. You can do it!'

Sigge was the desert rat incarnate with bulging biceps and bull neck. He was wearing full camouflage gear.

Matti had obviously kept his word and warned Sigge, because he held up his hand in greeting and spread five fingers when he saw Peter.

'Five minutes. We just want to finish the circuit,' he called out in a commando voice.

Peter signalled that he would wait. He sat down on a tree stump and looked on as the participants sweated and strained in front of him. It was clear that the exercise was about teamwork. Helping one another was what gave good results. Until the whistle sounded and the participants collapsed in a heap.

Sigge clapped his hands and praised them.

'Well done! In for a shower now and get changed. Chop-chop!'

Most of them ran inside the barracks. Sigge came over and shook hands with Peter.

'Matti called. He said you had a puzzle for me.'

He winked, and wrinkles from a life spent outdoors gathered around his eye.

'I can't resist a good puzzle, so fire away.'

Peter took the rosary out of his pocket.

'It's this symbol here at the end.'

Sigge took the rosary and scrutinised it. For a moment, he seemed lost to the world.

'Here. I've made a sketch.'

Peter took out a piece of paper and handed it to Sigge, who took it and studied the drawing. He looked up, clearly fascinated by the puzzle.

'Can I hold on to it for a couple of days?'

'Of course.'

Sigge waved the paper. 'It's definitely a military symbol, but I need to do some more digging.'

He folded the drawing neatly and put it in his pocket.

'I'll call you as soon as I've got something. Now, please excuse me. I've got to go and keep an eye on the miscreants.'

Peter watched him as he crossed the exercise circuit with long, confident strides, his arms down by his sides. So much had happened recently, all of it shit, and he felt he was being forced into a direction he didn't want to go. But, for the first time in days, he finally felt as if he was making some headway. This was going to pay off.

His good mood lasted all the way home to the cliff, where he turned off the engine and got out of the car in the dark.

He sensed a shadow behind him and heard the crunch of boots on gravel, then an arm grabbed him around his neck and squeezed. It took only a few seconds for his body to hark back to the days when being assaulted was an everyday occurrence. His brain slipped into autopilot as he wriggled out of the grip and launched a kick into the ribs of his attacker – a man, and a big one at that – followed by an upper cut which audibly crunched into the man's jaw and produced a grunt. But this guy was no pushover and a knee into Peter's crotch left him doubled up on the gravel. He reached out for the man's leg, but let go when a kick to his kidney made him see a cartoon-style moon and stars. Again he reached out and this time managed to drag the man down with him. They rolled around in the gravel, and he got hold of a fleshy face and pressed his fingers into the man's eyes. Then he felt hands around his neck and thoughts of Melissa's encounter with the garrotte made him sweat and fight extra hard. But not for long. Another knee to the groin and a punch to his kidney region sent him into a darkness blacker than the one they were already in.

'That'll teach you not to poke your nose into other people's business,' the stranger's voice said.

Before he lost consciousness, he was vaguely aware of the man searching his pockets. The last thing he heard was the dog barking inside the house and a car starting up and driving away from the cliff.

25

LISE WERGE WAS waiting.

To pass the time, she pulled a newspaper out of her handbag. There were stories about the dead girl at the convent and a scaffolding accident at the same place. A man was in hospital. His condition was no longer critical, but between the lines the article hinted that his life was as good as ruined.

She put the newspaper to one side. She didn't like the sneaking sense of uncertainty that could suddenly steal over her. Not for the first time in the last few days, she wished she had married Claude, moved to France with him and started a new life there.

But Claude's patience had run out and she had ended up with Jens Erik and a house in Veggerslev close to her family. It was the biggest mistake of her life.

She heard a lock click and the door opened. Lone entered wearing jeans and a navy blue, close-fitting jacket; she was petite and shapely with a trim waist and attractive pert breasts. Lone was one of the lucky few in the family who had escaped a turkey neck and saggy skin. She looked more like the board member of a major company than a prisoner.

'Hi, Sis!'

Lise got up and they hugged each other. Lone's gold earring scratched her cheek. She sat down on the sofa next to Lise and took both her hands in hers.

'How nice of you to come.'

A visit to Lone in prison was a stark contrast to visiting her mother. The latter was pure duty. The former was usually a pleasure. The fact that her sister, who was younger by two years, had killed her husband didn't diminish the pleasure. Laust had been an asshole. Of course, that didn't make it right to get him senselessly drunk and hold a pillow over his head, but there were mitigating circumstances. And blood was thicker than water, as her mother always pointed out. However, this didn't prevent the unpleasant newspaper articles having a lingering effect on Lise and complicating the visit.

'How exciting! And what have you brought me today?'

Intelligent eyes scanned the presents Lise had spread across the table: magazines and books. Lone's thirst for knowledge knew no bounds. While in prison she had already taken a bachelor's degree in law and was well on her way to a master's. The other presents – the novels – were just to pass the time.

'No sweets or chocolate?'

'You always say you can't have them, that you're watching your figure.'

The smile made her face even prettier.

'Then it has to be true, if I said so myself.'

Lone sifted through the books on the table, her small hands rapidly examining the treasures. Gold glittered on every finger.

'Yum, nice easy reading,' she said, looking at Lise with a mischievous smile. 'Buy two get one free?'

'Something like that,' Lise admitted. 'I can't afford to keep you in leather-bound first editions.'

'Føtex?'

'Bilka. They practically give them away with the groceries.'

Lone studied the titles and nodded her approval. She chuckled with contentment from somewhere deep in her throat, and Lise knew that she had hit the bullseye with her purchases. It was a good starting point for the real reason for her visit.

'Mum sends her love.'

'How is she?'

'She's getting old.'

'She'll never grow old. She's a sly one, she is.'

Lone was already absorbed in the first chapter of a Norwegian family saga. She turned the crisp pages.

'She has decided to dictate our family history to me,' Lise said.

Lone looked up from the book and slapped it against her thigh with a loud laugh.

'I thought it was my job to write a portrait of the family. We managed over one hundred pages . . .'

Lise picked up a book as well and flicked through it randomly. The paper was cheap and the cover flimsy, but so what? It was the contents that mattered when you were rotting inside these walls and you had only your imagination.

'Are you saying there's already a draft?'

'Of course.'

'Where?'

'Hmm. Let me see . . .'

Lone adopted her secretive smile as she pretended to be interested in the blurb on one of the books in the pile.

'I wonder if I can remember?'

'Lone!'

Lone adjusted her hair. She had always been vain. She smiled, and suddenly Lise wondered if loving your family was in fact that healthy. It had never happened before, but now she looked at Lone's hands and saw them squeezing the life out of another human being. A bastard, admittedly. But still a human being.

'Perhaps it's in the attic in the Woodland Snail. After all, it was some years ago, and we never finished it.'

'Why not?'

Lise regretted her question immediately.

'Yes, why do you think?'

The reply was caustic. An awkward silence ensued until Lone said:

'Well, at least coffee doesn't make you fat. Shall I go and get some?'

Suddenly Lise couldn't stand the thought of eating or drinking away from home. She braced herself, produced the newspaper and placed it in front of Lone.

'Have you read what happened at St Mary's?'

Lone didn't even glance at the newspaper. She looked Lise in the eye until Lise dropped her gaze.

'Of course,' Lone said eventually. 'A terrible business.'

A terrible business. The words buzzed round Lise's head and gave her a headache.

'Do you know something, Lone?'

To her irritation, she could only manage a whisper. Lone's lips pursed into a thin line and her face changed with lightning speed. This was another side to her sister. Terrifying, all-consuming evil.

'And what would that be?'

Her tone threatened a confrontation now.

'I don't know . . . I can't ask around, but . . .'

'But what, sweetheart?'

Lise steeled herself.

'Is he out? Is Simon out?'

Lone shook her head. She examined her nails and twirled a lock of hair around a finger.

'I haven't heard anything. Forget about it. It's so many years ago.'

It worked every time. Lise felt deflated and her brief appearance as the confident sister was over.

Lone folded up the newspaper and stuffed it in the bin. Again she put on her usual smile and patted Lise's hand, which was lying limply in her lap.

'There! Now we'll say no more about it, will we?'

26

PETER WOKE TO the sound of the dog whining and its snout examining him all over. A paw gently scratched his sleeve. Then he heard a voice and felt hands the size of shovels slap his face from side to side.

'Wake up! Peter!'

Searing pain shot through his body and collected in an explosion in his head. If only whoever it was would go away and leave him be. If only he wasn't so bloody cold.

'Peter, for Christ's sake! Come on!'

It took forever before he could open his eyes just a fraction. But through the crack, he saw a figure crouching over him with a knobbly head, a badly patched-up cleft palate and eyes that were studying him.

'Bronco?'

The giant's face cracked into a familiar smile.

'So he didn't beat your brains out after all!'

'Who?'

Bronco shook his head and blew out his cheeks. Water from his hair dripped down onto Peter's face. He registered that it was raining. In fact, it was tipping down.

'No idea. I found you a moment ago. I had a job for you but couldn't reach you on your mobile.'

'I've got a new one. What about Kaj?'

'He was going crazy. He could see you lying out here. I found the key in your pocket and let him out.' A memory shot through Peter, followed immediately by a tumble of questions.

He had returned from Ebeltoft and someone had been waiting

for him in the darkness. Who? Did it have anything to do with the killings, or was it just his old enemies ambushing him? How long had he been lying here?

He tried to struggle onto his elbows but had to give up and slumped back. It was wet underneath him, he could feel that now. The gravel drive had turned into mud. And it was windy too. Then again, a storm had been forecast.

'Here. Hold on. We'll get you inside.'

Fortunately, Bronco wasn't the type to call the police or an ambulance. Nor was he the sort to ask any questions. The giant slipped his arms under Peter and stood up effortlessly. The dog skipped around them as Peter was carried inside the house. Bronco laid him down on the sofa as carefully as if he had been a trained nurse and Peter was a sick slip of a child.

'Right. Let's get those wet clothes off you.'

Bronco started pulling shoes and socks off Peter, who tried to resist.

'Don't. I can do it myself,' he groaned.

'No, you bloody can't,' Bronco grunted. 'Not in your state.'

It was futile. Bronco, who was a carpenter and sawed wood with bulging muscles, had other talents as well. In no time at all the wet clothes lay in a pile on the floor and Peter was dressed in a black tracksuit. The dog watched with interest.

'Not a peep from you,' Peter mumbled, pointing at Kaj, who lay down with his head on his paws and what looked suspiciously like a grin.

'What the hell have you gone and got yourself mixed up in this time?' Bronco said. 'First the scaffolding and now this.'

'At least he didn't get inside the house,' Peter said, remembering the unfamiliar voice and the warning.

'I wonder what he wanted.'

Yes, what did he want? Then it came crashing down on him. Of course!

'Hand me that pile.'

Bronco handed him the wet clothes. Peter searched every pocket.

'It's gone.'

'What is?'

'The rosary . . .'

'What are you talking about? Have you turned to religion?'

Peter leaned back on the cushions and looked up at the ceiling.

'It's a long story.'

The mobile rang in his jacket pocket. Yet again, Bronco had to hand him a wet garment. Peter dug out the mobile.

'Good evening, it's Sigge.'

Peter suppressed a groan, but not for long, and he couldn't help swearing whenever a sharp pain bored into his kidney.

'Are you all right?' Sigurd Banner said.

What kind of parallel universe was he living in? He was being nursed by a gigantic carpenter with hands the size of sledgehammers and now a commando was expressing concern about his well-being.

'I'm all right,' he declared and struggled up into a sitting position. 'Go on.'

'It turned out to be quite straightforward,' Sigge said. 'It's the Legion's flag.'

'The Foreign Legion?'

'Not the French one. Spanish.'

'I had no idea there was a Spanish Foreign Legion.'

'Very few people do,' Sigge said. 'And they stopped recruiting foreigners in 1984. Nevertheless, today they have approximately six thousand legionnaires. Some are stationed in old Spanish colonies. Others take part in modern wars: Afghanistan and Iraq. Their HQ is on the holiday island of Fuerteventura.'

'OK . . .'

Peter had no idea how to respond to the information. Sigge continued.

'At the time of Franco their motto was *"Viva la muerte"* – Long live death. They're well known for worshipping death as a romantic ideal.'

Peter was about to ask if that didn't apply to most soldiers, but held his tongue. Sigge clearly knew what he was talking about.

'So they exhibit death-defying courage then?'

'They don't fear death. But that doesn't mean that they're foolhardy, either. They're some of the most highly trained soldiers in the world. Elite troops, just like Danish commandos.'

He paused.

'Whatever you're mixed up in, let me give you some good advice: be very careful! These guys are no pussy cats.'

Later, when Bronco had fallen asleep in an armchair and the dog had settled down on the rug by the sofa, the Spanish motto flitted around in his brain. *Viva la muerte*. He was sure he had seen or heard about it before, but he couldn't place where. Eventually he fell into a painful sleep and dreamt that a giant of a man was beating him to pulp over and over again.

27

'I JUST WANT you to know that I'm better at doing this than cooking.'

Kir grabbed the laptop and flopped down next to Mark. After the failure of her overcooked plaice it was about time she demonstrated her skills in other areas.

'You're saying that the bones are from the post-war period?'

'We can't know for certain,' Mark said. 'But it's likely. The latest is that they're now looking for a DNA match so they can identify the body.'

She clicked and could feel him edging away from her and craning his neck to see the screen. Neither of them had mentioned their truce.

'I told you about the Koral Strait.'

She clicked and a naval chart appeared.

'Here. This is where the shipping channel to Kalø Bay is at its narrowest. Just after the war up to forty thousand tons of aerial bombs and other munitions were dumped here. Quite a lot of it came from Tirstrup Airport, which had been built by the Germans using Danish labour.'

She looked at him and then turned her attention back to the screen.

'Later, in order to transport fuel to Studstrup Power Station, the Danes had to dredge the channel. That was in the 1960s. A German company got the contract, together with the Danish Navy. The Danes subsequently realised they could handle the job themselves so they fired the Germans. And take a look at this.'

She clicked and a picture appeared. It was one of her favourite photographs. It was in black-and-white and showed a huge column of water in the bay, obviously following an underwater explosion. In the foreground a ferry sailed on as if nothing had happened.

'It was sabotage, 1969. A German diver was pissed off at having been sacked and wanted to get his own back on his company. He detonated a bomb. It left a massive hollow in the sea bed four metres deep and around twenty-five by sixty metres wide.'

She looked at Mark.

'Now, this might not mean anything, but I found the box of bones right in the middle of the hollow.'

Mark stared at the photograph.

'So what you're telling me is that the box hadn't been there for all those years, but that it was dumped there by someone who knew where the hollow was and knew it would be buried even deeper?'

She shrugged.

'Perhaps. Incidentally, civilians are forbidden from entering that area. But that doesn't stop people from fishing illegally or diving down to the wrecks which are also in the channel.'

'So the box could have been kept somewhere else for many years.'

'Some years. At least until 1969.'

He leaned back in the sofa, but she could see that she had fired his imagination.

'So it's someone who knows the waters around Djursland. The shipping channel. The Koral Strait, or whatever you call it . . .'

'Sounds about right.'

'Someone hid a box of bones, possibly at home in a shed. Suddenly it became necessary to get rid of it. Perhaps someone got suspicious, about a crime that took place many years ago.'

'Perhaps . . .'

She produced more photos. It was a combination of work and pleasure for her, and she wanted him as her ally.

'Possible motive for killing at the time,' she said. 'Tirstrup Airport.'

'My grandfather worked there during the war.'

'Half of Djursland did,' Kir said. 'Is he still alive?'

'He's in a nursing home. He turned ninety-five back in August.'

She clicked and found more black-and-white photos from the

Occupation: men with shovels and diggers, men with horse and carts, men in ditches.

'Danish workers were given the choice between building the airport or collecting unemployment benefit, which they couldn't live on. A number of Danish construction companies offered to work for the Germans.'

Mark followed her train of thought.

'I'm guessing their popularity dipped when the war was over.'

She shook her head.

'The construction companies had had no scruples about raking it in during the war. Collaborators were up to all sorts of fraud and fiddles. So after 1945 there were three to four thousand workers who were not very happy. They turned their anger on Danish traitors.'

'Liquidations,' he stated. 'Payback time.'

She clicked again and more old photos appeared.

'The airport wasn't for harmless passenger planes. Look here.'

'What's that?'

Mark nearly broke his neck trying to see. 'A plane on top of another plane?'

She was in her element now. He should see the collection of model war planes and ships she kept in crates in her garage. She had assembled them herself and glued and furnished them with historically accurate stickers: symbols from that period. Not to mention all the World War II books in two layers on her bookcase.

'It's called a *"Vater und Sohn"* – a father and son. It was part of a secret German project that went under the codename of Beethoven. It's a so-called Mistel plane.'

He looked at her, open-mouthed. Even she could hear the nerdy enthusiasm in her voice.

'A Mistel plane consists of a two-engine bomb-carrying drone with a fighter plane mounted on struts on top. The fighter plane flies to the target on the drone, the cockpit of which is replaced with an elephant bomb, as it was known.'

'Is that its trunk there?'

Mark pointed to the photograph. The lower plane did indeed have a very long nose.

'That nose forms part of an explosive charge of 3.6 tonnes. The Brits were terrified that the German project would be successful. As a result, they bombed Tirstrup Airport repeatedly. An elephant mine could blow its way through eighteen metres of solid steel, it could destroy practically anything. This is what they were making in Tirstrup.'

'And this is the kind of thing you dive for in the Koral Strait?'

She nodded.

'And possibly it was one like this that exploded that day in 1969?'

They sat for a while digesting the food and the topic they had just discussed.

'You said you were going to get a list, of people who had gone missing towards the end of the war and in its aftermath?'

He nodded.

'Oluf Jensen is going to get it.'

'I wonder how many locals we're talking about,' she said. 'I wonder if it's even possible to identify the victim.'

'The forensic anthropologists are working hard at it,' he said. 'And don't forget there was a fracture to the femur that had healed, which could prove very helpful to us.'

Kir clicked and the old photos were gone. Her screensaver was an underwater photograph of a dive near a hole in the ice with blues and greens and whites and a cold sun. Mark continued:

'I think they're a bit embarrassed about their initial mistake, so they're trying extra hard to come up with some usable DNA.'

She packed away the computer.

'I knew you could find DNA in water. But after so many years?'

'They're not looking for ordinary DNA. It's known as mitochondria or mtDNA,' said Mark, who had spoken to the forensic examiner. 'It's the kind you find in mummies, for example. That was how they identified the murdered family of the Russian Tsar when they found their bodies. MtDNA can't be passed on from men to their children, so you need to get hold of a female descendant. The Tsar's family shared mtDNA with Lord Mountbatten, because both he and the Tsar's family had inherited it from Queen Victoria.'

'Do you think our bone-man is related to Queen Victoria?' Kir asked.

'I doubt it.'

He got up. It was getting late and they were both tired. For a moment she searched for the attraction between them, and it was as if he was doing the same. But then she remembered the smell of hooker and the truce, and he possibly remembered something completely different, and the professional side won.

'But if we link a name on the list to some mtDNA, we can reckon it'll be among the mothers in the family that we'll find it . . . Thanks for dinner. I'd better be off.'

'You should come diving one day,' she said.

He smiled.

'Have you ever found one of those elephant mines?'

'Yep.'

'And have you helped to detonate it?'

She nodded.

'Now off you go, cop. It's time for me to turn in.'

28

Alice Brask, Melissa's mother, lived in a residential area of Randers.

The houses had obviously been built in the 1960s and the 1970s. Some had been renovated with new glossy black roof tiles and zinc-framed gables. Other owners had apparently used the house's equity in the first half of the so-called Noughties to build conservatories, orangeries or extensions of various kinds, while the rest of the house was left to rot with loose roof tiles, dubious woodwork and punctured double-glazing.

At the end of the cul-de-sac was a small, yellow-brick house with a wooden porch and west-facing garden. Not in any way ostentatious, but nicely maintained. Outside, in the carport, was a burgundy Ford Fiesta.

The weather hadn't improved much. Rain was falling steadily and the wind was howling, so the rain from the west looked like fluttering curtains. Peter had heard on the car radio about all the problems the autumn gales had caused. Several basements had already flooded; a car had driven into the harbour in Aarhus; a fishing boat was in distress somewhere off the island of Læsø and a major rescue operation was underway.

He winced as he parked and got out further up from the house. He had woken up in pain to see a note from Bronco saying he had gone to work. There was coffee in the thermos flask. He had forced down a cup of the tar-like substance, as well as two painkillers and a bowl of porridge. Then he had opened the laptop, read Alice Brask's blog and seen that she was constantly updating it with everything she knew – or believed she knew – about the investigation into Melissa's death. The story about the scaffolding accident was also there:

> Attempt to eliminate witness? A worker from a local carpentry firm today met with a serious accident . . . The unfortunate is a colleague of the man who told the police what he had seen by the moat on the day that Melissa was killed. Coincidence? You can only guess, but rumour has it that the police are treating the accident as suspicious . . .

Blah blah blah. Where the hell did she get her information from? And so quickly?

Peter felt like hurling Manfred's computer out of the window. Instead, he shut it down after making a note of Alice Brask's address. It was time for him to have a chat with the grieving mother.

And now here he was, in the pouring rain. Feeling as if he wanted to enter a house and strangle a woman he had never met, who had just lost her daughter.

He plunged his hands into his pockets just to keep them under control. Then he heard a door open and a woman dashed out and got into the Fiesta. He glimpsed a dark raincoat and a pair of smart, neon-coloured wellingtons before the door was slammed and the Fiesta reversed out of the carport.

Disappointment was no more than a fleeting emotion. He automatically got back into his van and followed the burgundy car, keeping a reasonable distance between them without losing sight of Alice as she drove off towards the centre of Randers. He didn't know the town well, but it couldn't possibly be as illogically planned as Aarhus, where he always had to keep a wary eye open for one-way streets. Once he nearly lost sight of the Fiesta when it turned off quickly and headed for an area of very short, narrow streets. The traffic was heavy. People had clearly opted to take their cars in the bad weather, and he had to nip in and out as best he could while the rain streamed down the gutters and tyres sprayed it back up onto the windscreen.

The burgundy car indicated and slipped into a parking space between a van and a Mercedes. He quickly tried to get his bearings but had to park illegally, far too near a corner, to make sure he had a hope of seeing where Alice was going.

He took the risk, slammed the door shut and followed her at a distance, wishing he had brought something to ward off the rain. Instead, he put up his collar and sploshed through the drenched streets. She was in a hurry. Every now and then she would glance at her watch. He guessed she had arranged to meet someone.

Then she turned around and looked down the street as if searching for someone and Peter had the clear sensation that she had seen him. He nearly slipped into a doorway but then, fortunately, she continued on her way. And almost before he had time to realise, she stepped inside a café called Klostercaféen.

He stopped at a discreet distance. Should he go after her? Had she seen him? And what was he actually doing, following a woman just because she had written something in her blog?

He slowly strolled past the café and felt like an idiot. Cafés were for women who drank lattes and gossiped about boyfriends, husbands and fashion. He would stick out like a sore thumb.

But there were lots of people inside the large L-shaped room. He saw Alice Brask wrestle off her coat and sit down at a vacant table. Her date was apparently even later than she was.

Without a moment's reflection he pushed open the door and entered while she was busy draping her coat over the back of her chair. He headed for the opposite end of the room and thus avoided her gaze. From this relatively secure position he told himself he had a complete overview of the place. And when he found a newspaper on a rack and ordered an espresso, without her turning around, he started to feel very pleased with himself. She had no idea, it was obvious. He could do a star turn in a spy film if someone made him an offer. He poured sugar in his espresso, leaned back and opened the newspaper.

The bell above the door jingled. Another customer entered. An umbrella was shaken. Hair nudged into place. A woman in high heels sashayed into the café in the direction of Alice Brask's table. Peter nearly choked on his coffee. Miriam!

She scanned the room while making a beeline for the journalist at the end of the room. He instinctively hid his face behind the newspaper. She hesitated, noticeably. Then she appeared to make up her mind that the coast was clear, went over and held out her hand to Melissa's mother.

29

POLICE OFFICERS HATED rain. Not only was it unpleasant to move about in drenched clothes and wet conditions, it also washed away evidence. Rain made their work more difficult and could ultimately decide whether or not a case would stand up in court.

And that was what it was all about. Did they have a suspect? Could they build a case? Was there something tangible to give to the prosecutor?

This was why the mood was at rock bottom when Anna Bagger's team met that morning. Mark couldn't only see it. He could smell it. It hung over the detectives like a damp cloth. Defeat. It hadn't helped that he had just aired a slightly crazy theory about bombs and post-war scores being settled. Anna Bagger might just as well have patted him on the head as if he were a little boy with a toy car when she dismissed his account about the meeting with Oluf Jensen and Kir's information with a wave of her hand.

'As long as we have no concrete evidence, I'd like to focus on the Melissa case.'

One detective after another gave their input and contributed to the depression. They were pursuing nothing but dead ends.

Melissa's friends, schoolmates and teachers had been interviewed without anything to show for their efforts. A picture was starting to appear of a reticent girl who spent a lot of time alone and had her own ideas about the ways of the world – ideas more suited to the world of the convent than outside its walls. The only possible leads now seemed to be the girl's computer and her mobile from the days when she lived a more normal life. Neither of them had so far proved to contain anything of significance, but forensic examinations were still ongoing.

'Mark? Did you find the time to speak to Alice Brask?' Anna Bagger asked with a weary look.

'She wasn't at home when I stopped by. I can try again, if you like.'

'After this meeting, possibly?'

It was an order rather than a request. 'Your box of bones isn't going anywhere,' she added.

He didn't agree entirely, but he merely nodded.

'The scaffolding accident,' Anna said. 'What do we know about it?'

'The CSOs confirmed that the metal poles had been cut with a hacksaw,' Martin Nielsen said. 'But there is no other evidence. Potential fingerprints were washed off by the rain, and no one appears to have seen anything.'

'When was the scaffolding put up?'

'The day before the accident,' Martin Nielsen said. 'The sabotage could have been carried out at night.'

'The question is whether it has anything to do with Melissa's murder,' Anna Bagger said. 'Manfred Kaster hasn't been on our radar in that respect, but Peter Boutrup has. I thought our theory was that the accident was meant for him?'

There was nodding and affirmative muttering all around.

'You've spoken to Peter, Mark. What's your impression?'

'That he was shocked and angry,' Mark said. 'As I would be if my best friend became a cripple because I'd been named as a witness in a murder case.'

'Named?'

'Alice Brask,' Pia Thorsen said. 'Her blog. She must get her information from somewhere.'

A strange silence descended over the officers. Who had leaked information? Anna Bagger broke the silence:

'Number one: let's not forget that Boutrup is a man with enemies. There's last winter's events and the burned-out motorbikes in August. In theory, the scaffolding could be the handiwork of the biker gang and might have nothing to do with the murder of Melissa. Number two: other people apart from us know that Peter Boutrup is a witness. The nuns, for example. And perhaps the divers, depending on what we've told them.'

Her gaze landed on Mark, who looked at his watch. He had wanted to be a part of the team and the investigation, but as of now he was desperate to get out. He didn't like Anna Bagger's insinuations, and besides, he had an important appointment, but not one he felt like sharing with her. She was resentful enough as it was.

He made his excuses as soon as possible, promised to have a talk with Alice Brask later the same day, and then put the ruins of the investigation behind him.

He half-ran through the rain to get to his car and drove to the other end of town. A few minutes later he pushed open the glass door to the nursing home and stepped out of the rain, but stopped abruptly. The smell alone was enough to send him straight back out. There was a sterile smell of hospital and it filled him with unease, and he had to force himself to stand still.

Children and old people were far from his speciality, he was happy to admit that. He wasn't good with anyone weak. He knew why. It was his deep-rooted fear of becoming dependent on others, and he had come dangerously close.

'Can I help you?'

The woman wore a blue smock and seemed friendly in a busy sort of way.

'I'm here to visit my grandfather, Hans Mortensen. I called earlier.'

She went over to a counter and looked at a computer screen.

'Mark Bille Hansen?'

'That's me. We met at his birthday party in August.'

'Lise Werge.'

She held out her hand. His unease continued as she accompanied him down the corridor to his grandfather's room.

'He's been a bit lethargic today,' she warned him. 'But he's fine apart from that.'

'Does that mean his memory is still OK?'

Mark hadn't seen his grandfather since the birthday.

'Oh yes. He's got a memory like an elephant.'

She glanced at him as she walked alongside him. She was sturdy and had short legs, but her eyes were striking and they distracted the observer from her looks, which she could have been luckier with. He estimated her to be in her mid-fifties. One of those anonymous women men never really saw or thought much about. But then again . . . There was something vigilant about her, as if she noticed everything about him, Mark thought.

'Here we are.'

She knocked on the door and opened it.

'Hans . . . Your grandson has come to see you . . .'

She looked at Mark, who repeated his full name again.

'Mark,' was all she said.

The man in the wheelchair was watching an old-fashioned television mounted on the wall: TV2 News. He reached out and switched it off and then turned to them and Mark saw a lucidity in the blue eyes and good humour in the curve of his mouth. His body had crumbled pitifully, but his hands suggested what the rest of him had once been: strong, muscular and capable of hard work.

'Hello, Mark. It's been a while.'

Mark felt rebuked.

'But then why enter the ante-chamber of death, if you can avoid it?' his grandfather said.

Lise Werge cleared her throat.

'You two have a nice chat and I'll bring you some coffee and biscuits.'

She withdrew and left them alone. His grandfather followed her with his eyes.

'She's nice enough. But she has secrets . . .'

He looked at Mark and gestured that he could sit down on the chair opposite. 'Then again, don't we all?'

Mark pulled out the chair and sat down. He unbuttoned his jacket, feeling hot. He looked at the old boy with the sharp eyes and remembered their day trip to Tirstrup. His grandfather had insisted on getting out of the car and going in his wheelchair in the blustery conditions to remember his dead comrades.

He had loved seeing his grandfather outside, his hair flapping in the wind, but now he was back here, in the ante-chamber of death, as the old man himself called it. Was this the fate that awaited Mark himself one day? Rotting in a nursing home while his body slowly gave up and his thoughts kept churning around as incessantly as always?

'You look a bit wan,' the old man said. 'Open a window, if you like. A draught never did anyone any harm.'

'I'm a police officer, Grandad. You remember that, don't you?'

Mark got up and opened the window a crack.

'Of course. I'm not totally senile yet.'

The old man smiled wryly. 'I imagine you're here on police business, aren't you? Though I can't imagine how a geriatric like me can help you.'

Mark caught himself wishing he had got to know his grandfather better. But he had lived in Copenhagen for many years, and in the year he had spent here in Grenå his illness and work had taken up all his energy.

'You told me about Tirstrup Airport during the war. I need to know more.'

The old man's face darkened.

'Bastards.'

'The Germans again?'

Hans Mortensen chuckled.

'Them too, of course. But our own were much worse. Collaborators, who got rich at other people's expense. There were workers who had to provide for large families. One man had eleven kids at home. If we didn't accept the jobs at the airport, they took everything from us – support, social help.'

His hand tightened into a fist on the table.

'We were forced labour. Slave labour for the Germans.'

'What kind of work was it?'

'Clearing trees to begin with. It was a plantation before and the whole lot was expropriated by the Germans. Then there was the landing strip. Later we had to dig underground hangars where they could keep the German planes, so they couldn't be seen from the air. We dug up enormous mounds of earth deep into the trees, along the south side of Grenåvej.'

'But the British still found them?'

A big grin spread across the old man's face, wreathing it in a countless number of creases.

'Damn right they did! I saw it with my own eyes.'

'What happened?' Mark asked.

'Some massive explosions, that's what happened,' his grandfather said. 'Later, the farmer next door said his thatched roof had literally jumped a couple of metres. At first people thought the Brits had hit some underground fuel tanks, but it turned out a bloody elephant mine had exploded. Boom!'

He was gripped now, Mark could see. The light switch in his eyes was fully on and his brain was obviously engaged. It was sixty-six years ago, but Hans Mortensen was back at Tirstrup Airport with his comrades the day the Brits came.

'It was one Wednesday in February. 1945. There were a few of us digging, another underground hangar, when we heard the air-raid alarm. We heard shooting. Then we saw planes flying low across the area, just above the treetops, with their machine guns strafing the ground. We legged it into the forest and hid behind the earth-works, from where we could see horses bolting in all directions, still harnessed to carts and with men on top. I ran over to help one who had been thrown off. He thought he was trapped under his own cart, but it had flown through the air and landed on top of the horse in a ditch.'

The old man's head nodded at the memory. His hands were trembling.

'The Germans had anti-aircraft guns everywhere. Bullets were whistling around us. But the Brits had flown in below the radar and caught the Germans with their pants down.'

His body shook in a mixture of coughing and glee.

'They even managed to take out one of those bloody father and son planes.'

'A Mistel plane?'

Mark's grandfather nodded and appeared to be chewing some mucus that he had brought up.

'Yes, that was their name. Mistels. Bastards, they were. The plane caught fire and exploded. None of us could hear a thing for days afterwards.'

His eyes met Mark's.

'That was the end. After that, it all fell apart. The workers sabotaged production. We didn't turn up; we just let it all go to hell. We knew the end was coming.'

'What about old scores? Liquidations? After all, you knew the people who made money from collaborating with the Germans.'

His eyes wandered. Mark knew he had pushed too hard.

'I wouldn't know anything about that,' the old man said.

'Perhaps someone you know would remember?' Mark suggested. 'Or someone you used to know?'

The silence lasted. It was as if the man in the wheelchair had fallen asleep. Mark resisted the impulse to glance at his watch but was saved when Lise Werge came in with a trolley.

'Coffee and biscuits for you. Just help yourselves.'

The old man's head jerked. Then, looking out of the window where the rain was still lashing down, in a burst of indignation, he said:

'Someone had to pay, didn't they? The others took care of that.'

'Who had to pay?' Mark asked. 'What were their names?'

The old man flung up a hand.

'Look it up in a history book.'

30

PETER DROVE IN a red mist. The incident at the café was still eating at him and his faith in the world. Miriam, of all people. Miriam, in whom – being the idiot that he was – he had confided about everything that had happened since Melissa's death. Miriam, who had waltzed in with My's mother, who had given him good advice after Manfred's fall. Miriam, who purred in ecstasy when he caressed her and came in an explosion when his fingers found her innermost core. Only it had been a while since he had done that. Felix had arrived on the scene and he had lost interest. And so Miriam had taken her revenge. Of course he had known it all along, but it was hard to admit that their friendship had foundered.

Her car was parked below the flat in Anholtsgade where she and Lulu had their massage parlour. How often had he come here for an hour of peace and quiet and relaxed companionship? He had been here with My and Kaj. Here he had thrown off his mental rucksack and enjoyed the atmosphere of easy-going sensuality; here he had sought refuge when the world threatened to push him over the edge.

He had thought they were friends. But you couldn't be friends with a hooker; experience should have taught him that long ago.

He took the stairs in long strides. He knocked, but then pushed open the door. The chain was on. It rattled when he shook the door handle.

'I'm coming!'

She was wearing high heels and the red corset cinched her waist. The leather skirt was short and revealed black suspenders and stocking tops. She was expecting customers.

Her eyes widened.

'Peter!'

She removed the chain and he roughly pushed his way past her.

'Come on in, why don't you?' she called out after him.

'I saw you! In Randers one hour ago!'

He found it hard to control his voice. She bundled him into the living room where Kaj had so often spread out on the carpet by the coffee table and enjoyed a false sense of family.

'Sit down. I'll get you a drink.'

'I don't want a drink.'

'Fine, but I do.'

She disappeared and quickly returned with two glasses and a bottle of sparkling wine.

'Look at the state of you! You look like a stray dog.'

She inspected him and poured him a glass despite his protests.

'Who beat you up?'

Once he would have welcomed the concern in her voice, but he wasn't falling for it this time.

'Surely you already know.'

'Me?'

'Me,' he sneered in a high-pitched voice. 'That's what happens when you go running to the press. It gives people ideas: why not knock the shit out of XYZ?'

'I didn't go running to the press.'

'So what do you call meeting the journalist who constantly blogs about me? *A local carpenter saw a man at the moat* . . . Blah blah . . .'

'But I met her to tell her to stop!'

'You did *what*?'

Miriam sipped her drink. She was sitting up straight with her knees together. Always a lady. Never vulgar despite the provocative outfit that came with the job.

He leaned forward, towards her. He was aware it might seem threatening and in fact she did jerk back.

'*What* did you just say?'

She got up with the glass in her hand.

'Calm down, will you?'

She paced up and down. 'I can explain. That is, if you're interested in anything other than your own preconceived ideas.'

She sat down again. A finger with a long red nail ran around the rim of the glass. She sighed.

'Perhaps I should start somewhere else.'

He didn't say anything, but his rage continued to simmer. She got up again and went over to a shelf where her and Lulu's private photographs were displayed in silver frames. There weren't many, but those there were told the story of the life they had ultimately chosen to live.

Miriam took the photograph of My and Kaj and looked at it with her head tilted. Half-turned to him, she said:

'OK. It was a lie, about My and the grave. We made it up to get you on board.'

'A lie? How was it a lie?'

'Well, I suppose in time it became a kind of truth, but . . .'

She turned round fully with the photograph in her hands.

'Bella came here to find work. As people do from time to time when they're hard up.'

Of course that did happen. Some women turned to the world's oldest profession as a temporary solution to earn money.

'I didn't know her. She didn't know me or Lulu.'

She held out a palm. 'It was a coincidence. We weren't the first place she tried.'

He had never believed in coincidences. The very suggestion made him sceptical.

'I spotted the family resemblance immediately.' She returned the photograph to its place. 'It was obvious. I just wanted her to leave, but then she noticed the photograph, and . . .'

Miriam slumped back down onto the sofa with her arms down by her sides as if she had suffered a defeat.

'Bella could see it too. Her face went all white and I had to let her sit down.'

Miriam swallowed. She drank a little more wine, but it didn't appear to be to her taste and she returned the glass to the table.

'Then I told her about My and she broke down totally, right here on the sofa.'

Miriam's eyes took on the dark shadow that sometimes came when she got involved with other people. Which she did only with great reluctance because, as she always said, it usually gave her nothing but trouble.

'And you told her about me?'

He could hear his menacing tone. He had yet to be convinced.

'About you, yes. And then it was as if she saw hope. I could tell from looking at her, the way she sat up and composed herself.'

Miriam looked at him, hesitant.

'I'm sorry, Peter. Sorry that we lied to you. But she told me about the divorce and how her older son, Magnus, had disappeared. She was desperate . . .'

The pieces started falling into place. Two women with a scheme. Two women who had used My for their own advantage.

'I wanted to help her. She couldn't go to the police. Magnus is eighteen and there was no suggestion of a crime. After all, he had taken his rucksack with him.'

Her hand closed around the glass again, but she let it remain where it was.

'I could think of only one person who could find him for her.'

Miriam looked him in the eye.

'And so you concocted that story about My? The reality is she doesn't give a toss about My.'

He had to struggle not to let his anger boil over.

'My, whose only crime was to be born to a calculating bitch of a mother and fall into the hands of a naive hooker whose heart bleeds for children and dogs.'

'That's not how it is, Peter.'

She said it so quietly that he barely heard, which only made him turn up the volume.

'So how is it then? Can you tell me that?'

'After the divorce, Bella wanted to reach a stage where she could go out and find My. She had no idea that My was dead. But

Magnus took priority . . . She was scared it was to do with a drug debt . . .'

Again she spoke so quietly he could barely hear. Even so, the words echoed in his head. A drug debt. That was why he was useful. That was why they hadn't battered down the police doors.

'If the boy's a drug addict, perhaps you should ask yourself why,' he said.

She reached for his sleeve. He pulled away.

'You're too hard on her, Peter. It was her husband who made her give up My. Now he has left her. My is dead. Her son has disappeared.'

She grabbed him again and this time she didn't let go.

'If you think she ought to be punished, then that's exactly what's happening to her now.'

She sent him a determined look:

'Talk to her. Give her another chance.'

'Don't you think I have enough trouble as it is?'

She nodded.

'Yes. But you're the type who can handle it.'

'And Bella isn't?'

Miriam's eyes softened.

'In a way she's like My. She might be "normal", whatever that is, but she's fragile, Peter. And she's scared.'

'And what about Alice Brask?'

Miriam picked up the glass again and this time she took a decent swig before she put it down.

'I contacted her. I read her blog and didn't like what I found about you. I asked her to meet me and told her I had something she would find interesting.'

'And then you gave her Bella's story?'

She shook her head, avoiding his gaze, and stared into the glass where the bubbles continued to rise in an endless stream. Miriam, who was so private and whom he would never get to know fully. Miriam from the nice family who had cut her off when they learned how she earned her money.

'I gave her mine.'

31

A TRUCE. MISTEL planes. Liquidations.

Kir grunted the words at every push-up. Exercise was her friend. Pain and effort washed through her body and made her forget there were other ways to use it – exhilarating, sensual ways which could send her into ecstasy, and which she missed.

This wasn't ecstasy. Far from it. It was an anaesthetic and she knew it. It was one way of surviving and one way of being physical. The only option available to her right now.

Elephant bombs. The Koral Strait. Father and son. Collaborators.

After the abortive dream of love, she and Mark were at least engrossed in the case. They were both convinced the bones in the box had a significance for the here and now. In this way they were united on something, which the world around them didn't seem to understand. At any rate, not Anna Bagger.

She flopped back on the mat in the garage where she kept her weights and her workout equipment. This was her den. It was also where her diving equipment hung from dedicated pegs or was stored on shelves in colour-coded boxes. The boat on the trailer took up quite a lot of room and there was no space for the car, which was always parked on the drive in front of the summer house.

Her mobile rang and she groaned as she stretched to reach it from the edge of the table. Sweat dripped down on it as she held it to her ear.

'Kir here.'

'You all right?'

'Allan! Where are you?'

Her boss's voice sang down the telephone. In the background she could hear helicopter rotors and people shouting to each other over the noise.

Adrenaline surged through her and her body tensed in anticipation.

'Kongsøre. We've just come back. But now we're heading your way.'

'What's happened?'

'SOK is requesting assistance with a fishing vessel that has gone down in the Kattegat, off the coast of Læsø. It's a high risk operation, Kir. There's no time to rig up a diving ship.'

'Count me in!'

She had nothing to lose. No family. No children. Not even a boyfriend. If anyone was prepared to run the risk, it would be her. And he knew it.

'OK. We'll pick you up en route. Grenå harbour in twenty-five minutes?'

'Fine. What's she called?'

She had a sudden premonition.

'What? Hang on . . .'

The signal quality was poor. In the seconds that passed she thought about the chubby, spotty boy with the hopeful expression in his eyes. A boy who had just left school with his whole life in front of him.

'*Marie af Grenå*,' Allan Vraa shouted.

The premonition formed a knot in her stomach. Jens Bådsmand and his son. Two good people lost in a storm. It was a cruel reminder of nature's power.

'Another fisherman saw her disappear from the radar south-east of Læsø,' Allan Vraa continued. 'They barely had time to radio Mayday. He dropped a buoy over the position, so SOK quickly called off the search.'

'And they found no one on the surface?'

'Nope. We're pretty sure the crew went down with the vessel, but there have been some protests that the search was called off too quickly. Some people think that if they were wearing life vests, the crew could have survived longer in the water than the time SOK spent searching. That's why SOK contacted us. Quite simply, we're going out to save their asses.'

'And there was a crew of two?'

'Father and son, as far as we've been told. Anyone you know?'

She swallowed, but then pushed her feelings aside and let pragmatism take over.

'Jens Bådsmand and his son, Simon, aged fifteen. I chatted to them in the harbour only yesterday. We talked about the weather . . .'

There were no lives to be saved. And yet speed was of the essence.

She gathered her equipment and quickly drove down to the harbour and joined the five mine divers in the helicopter when it landed on the quay. She knew them all, including Frands, who nodded coolly. She considered mentioning her encounter with his brother, but the noise was so loud that she could only talk to Allan Vraa, who was sitting closest to her.

They took off and soon there was only water as far as the eye could see. The waves had calmed down, but a fresh storm had been forecast. They had to hurry.

'What's the position?'

Allan Vraa showed her on a computer screen.

'Forty-five metres down. It's not easy,' he shouted over the noise.

Not easy, no. The regulations stated that below thirty metres there had to be a pressure chamber on the diving ship in case of an emergency. Allan Vraa had requested one of the navy's larger ships kitted out as a diving vessel with a pressure chamber and equipment suitable for deep diving, but SOK, the navy's operative command, had urged the divers to hurry. From their point of view this was all about putting a prompt stop to the mounting criticism, especially from colleagues of the lost fishermen. There hadn't been time to prepare the diving ship properly, but they had arranged for a pressure chamber to be made ready at the naval station in Frederikshavn and a doctor and chamber operators to be put on standby. If a diver got the bends, they could soon be transported by helicopter to northern Jutland.

'The whole thing stinks, but we have to make the best of it,' Allan

Vraa called out. He tried to get everyone's attention by leaning forward and making eye contact with each of them in turn. 'Watch out for ropes or nets. We dive in pairs. One diver searches the wreckage; the other stays clear so they can come to the aid of the first. Each team is down for five minutes: the first team locates the wreckage; the second finds the bodies and creates a safe passage to them; the third team tries to recover them. Got it?'

They nodded and each of them gave him the thumbs-up. Five minutes. Was that enough time to recover the bodies of Jens Bådsmand and Simon?

'Let's hope it's pretty accessible,' Niklas said. 'But we should expect the wheelhouse to be facing downwards.'

'We'll see,' Kir said. 'Hope we can locate her.'

'Visibility is poor after the storm,' Allan said. 'As we would expect. You say you know them, Kir? You spoke to them down at the harbour?'

'There was something caught in a prop.'

'Any connection, do you think?'

Kir didn't think so.

'They got it sorted. Some pound net had got entangled, but Jens had cover with Falck. Otherwise he might have called me . . . or so he said . . .'

They were interrupted by the pilot's voice over the intercom. They had reached the position. Kir looked down at the metallic blue sea beneath the helicopter. Foam crests rose with rhythmic regularity like a musical note setting off oscillating sound waves. Below, there was a marine vessel whose colour practically matched the water it was bobbing up and down on.

'Kir! You go first!'

Allan Vraa called out the sequence of the divers being lowered to the deck. She clicked the buckle on the seat belt and stepped into the harness. Less than a minute later she was suspended from a wire above an apparently endless ocean.

32

THE BLACK GOLF GTI was a battered older model, but still fast for all that. Peter watched it corner, tyres squealing, and continue down the road in the residential area as if the devil himself were clinging to the bonnet. He automatically clocked the registration plate. It was a by-product of living a life when he was constantly on the lookout for his enemies.

He drove up in his van until he spotted number 11. Bella's house in Elev was a typical 1980s red-brick house with small windows, neat angles and a privet hedge around the garden. A small car was parked in the carport. There were also a couple of bicycles. One of them had been knocked over by the wind.

He was about to ring the bell, then discovered that the door was open, and he carefully pushed it.

'Bella?'

There was no reply so he took a couple of steps into the hallway.

'Bella?'

She was definitely at home. It was late in the afternoon, her car was outside, the door was open. Or perhaps she was in the garden – although the weather wasn't encouraging, even if the rain had eased – or visiting a neighbour. But a vague foreboding that something was amiss made him continue through the house while calling out her name. Fragile was how Miriam had described her, and he too had sensed it and allowed himself to be swept along on a wave of sympathy. But Bella was and always would be a liar. He had to keep that in mind. A desperate mother, a fragile woman, but still a liar.

'Who is it?'

The voice was delicate, as if it was about to break.

'It's me. Peter.'

He walked in the direction of the sound. She was sitting in the kitchen, curled up in a corner on the checked linoleum floor. There was fear in the stare she sent him. Blood was dripping onto the floor from her left hand, which she held awkwardly in her lap. He quickly knelt down beside her and his anger evaporated.

'What happened?'

She was crying. Tears and mascara formed trails down her cheeks. She held up a hand like a child wanting it to be kissed better, and images of My danced inside his head.

'He was going to snap off my finger.'

Now the voice broke into a sob.

'He had bolt cutters.'

Peter carefully lifted her hand. Bella's index finger hung down limply and the skin was broken.

'Can you move it?'

She could, just about.

'Come on.'

He tried pulling her to her feet, but she stayed where she was.

'I'm taking you to casualty.'

She shook her head vehemently.

'Leave me alone. It's fine.'

'It's not fine. Your finger's broken.'

He looked at her. He realised he couldn't shift her, so he squatted down next to her.

'Was it the guy in the black Golf?'

She sniffled a yes.

'Who was he?'

But he knew the answer before he had even asked the question and its implications hit him like a karate kick. A drug debt. Penalty interest. Miriam had been very clever. He could see it all now: *Just give Peter a call. He's in with biker gangs, he'll talk to them . . .*

'They call him Gumbo,' Bella whispered. 'I don't know what his real name is . . .'

She looked up, despair written all over her face.

'He says Magnus owed him ten thousand kroner but now his debt is twenty thousand because Magnus hasn't stumped up.'

He watched her. Miriam had turned her down as a potential employee, but sitting here pressed against the kitchen cupboard, scared witless by a lousy debt collector, she still had a faintly erotic aura about her, from the way she trembled to the eyes that drew his in.

'Where can I find Gumbo?'

She sniffled again.

'He sells drugs – cola, they call it – outside the *gymnasium*. One of Magnus's friends got into trouble and his father forked out fifteen thousand kroner, but I never thought it would happen to Magnus.'

'What is it with Magnus, Bella? Where is he?'

'I don't know. You were going to find him.'

'Magnus ran away because he owed money, didn't he?'

A sob burst out of her.

'It's the only explanation I can think of.'

'Why didn't you and Miriam tell me that in the first place? Why hide behind that story about My?'

She pulled her knees up under her chin, then ran one hand over her hair and moistened her lips. He could see they were cracked, as if she had been chewing them.

'My was always a part of it. Part of me. When I saw that photo at Miriam's, I had no doubt that fate had led me to her.'

'The same fate that told you to abandon My?'

He had been manipulated. They had lied to him. He was entitled to react.

'I was a bad mother, I admit it. What more do you want me to say?'

She bowed her head and gave a heavy sigh. He got up.

'Do you have a first-aid kit? We should at least try to bandage that finger.'

'In the cupboard above the cooker,' she said.

He looked around. On the walls there were photographs of children and a couple of framed posters emblazoned with glib slogans: one against wearing furs, another about saving whales. There was also a kind of certificate stating that Bella owned X number of rain-forest hectares. Easier to save the world than your own children, it seemed.

'What do you want from me?' he asked. 'Do you want me to find Magnus, is that it?'

She stared down at the floor.

'I told you. The police won't help.'

'You haven't even told them, have you?'

She shook her head. Hair fell down and covered her face.

'Stirring things up only makes them worse. You know what it's like . . .'

And he did. In theory you were supposed to go to the police, but experience told him that no authority could protect you when it came down to it. You had to do everything yourself. That was what real life was like.

He spotted a red first-aid box in the cupboard and found a roll of bandages and some iodine. There was also a small pair of scissors. Once again he knelt down next to Bella, dabbed iodine on the injury and bandaged her finger tightly.

'He sends me a card every now and then,' Bella said.

'What kind of card?'

Peter cut the bandage and attached the end with surgical tape.

'A postcard.'

He got up to return the first-aid box to the cupboard. Christ, this was just fantastic. A boy goes missing and sends his mother postcards.

'*Wish you were here, send more money?* That kind of thing?' he asked over his shoulder.

She struggled to her feet and waved her finger in the air.

'Thanks for this.'

Her voice was slightly more under control now. She went into the living room next door and he followed. She opened a drawer and gave him three postcards.

'From different places in the country,' she said, which he could see from the postmarks. 'No texts or emails. Nothing that can be traced.'

'Good old-fashioned snail mail.'

He read them. They were all brief but affectionate.

I'm all right. Don't look for me. Love, Magnus.'

I love you. Kisses, Magnus.'

The final one was more disturbing:

I have to do this. Trust me. Love, Magnus.'

The handwriting was immature but consistent. Same slope, same angles and loops. A young man's uncertain penmanship, and yet that same young man had made a deliberate decision to leave his home and his family.

'And you're absolutely sure that it's his handwriting?'

'I'm not stupid.'

He looked at her, wondering. The trails down her cheeks had dried, making her look pitiful and lonely. She took the postcards and was about to put them away. He couldn't restrain himself; he reached out and took them back.

He turned them over.

'Can I keep them?'

She nodded.

'Was he scared? Could you tell from the way he was acting?'

She closed the drawer with a shove of her hip.

'How do you know with teenagers? What's going on inside their heads, I mean. I had no idea he was unhappy.'

'What sort of interests has he got?'

She smiled thinly.

'Being outdoors. Scouts. He's not a big lad, but he wanted to be a tough adventurer.'

Drugs and the outdoor life. Peter couldn't make it add up.

'So he would be able to handle himself outdoors? What about equipment?'

'He took some with him. A tent and a rucksack.'

Peter remembered that Miriam had said something about a rucksack.

'And you're sure he isn't with his dad?'

She nodded emphatically, her arms crossed and her lips compressed.

'Absolutely sure. Magnus hates his dad.'

She returned to the living room and rummaged around in the drawer again. When she came back, she handed him a photograph of Magnus. It was the same picture she had shown him before, only in a smaller format.

'I know. You haven't promised to look for him.'

She held up the photograph.

'But there's no harm in you having this, should you stumble over something.'

He took it, thinking the first thing he would stumble over would be the guy with the battered black Golf GTI.

33

THE ROPE FROM the buoy down to the wreck seemed to go on forever. The first two divers had followed it for a long time and had still not got all the way down before their five minutes were up and they had to resurface without having located the wreck. The next two – Frands and a man called Kim – refused to dive because they thought it was too dangerous. Allan Vraa couldn't object to that. The mission had proved to be riskier than even he had thought.

'Kir?'

Kir stared across the waves, which were bordering on stormy. The rubber dinghy bobbed merrily underneath them. The sea was black. It was as if the flecked crests were being quickly swallowed up and sucked down into an endless black hole. Getting down wasn't the problem. But if the waves worsened, getting the divers back up to the rubber dinghy might prove impossible.

She looked at her boss.

'If you say no, we'll call it off,' Allan said.

It wasn't a threat; he was simply stating a fact. He would understand if she didn't want to. Again she looked at the sea where the *Marie af Grenå* had disappeared. She imagined Jens and Simon lying down there and couldn't bear the thought of a sunken grave for a spotty young man who had been dreaming about the future that lay before him.

She nodded.

'Let's get to work.'

'It's pitch-black down there,' Allan said, hauling the buoy up onto the dinghy. 'We have to pull on this rope to the anchor until it's taut to avoid wasting too much time. What would you rather do: locate or recover?'

'Locate.'

'Then you dive first.'

She nodded. They succeeded in pulling the rope taut and she fell backwards into the waves with an air line and was swallowed up by the agitated sea. As she sank towards the bottom, her inner screen flickered with images of two men, one restless and one calm: Mark and Peter. They had stood side by side in the convent courtyard examining the vandalised scaffolding while she watched them. One dark, one blond.

She could feel the pressure rising as she descended. It pressed against her ears and nose and throat and hissed inside her head. But she forgot all about it when she picked out the contours of a wreck on the seabed.

The *Marie af Grenå* was lying on her side. Kir attached the line for Allan Vraa to follow. Time was short, but visibility was poor and it was hard for her to find her bearings.

She found the wheelhouse and looked inside, as best she could. She thought she saw something orange inside. That might mean one, or perhaps both, fishermen were inside the boat. Orange was the colour of the overalls that most fishermen wore.

She tried to force open the door to the wheelhouse. When she finally succeeded, her time was nearly up. Kir reached in an arm and felt around. Two pairs of legs; she had been right. But she could see something else now. A bundle in the furthest corner. She wanted to examine it, but the clock was ticking.

A jerk on the line from above was confirmation. She had to make her ascent.

She took a risk and eased her way into the wheelhouse. She wanted to reach across the two bodies to feel the bundle, but her diving tanks got caught on something; for a moment she was stuck and she fought with her panic. Black lightning flashed through her brain. She gasped inside her mouthpiece until she had her mind under control. Easy now. Remember to breathe in and out.

There was another jerk from above. Allan Vraa was getting impatient.

She wriggled. First one way, then the other. Nothing happened. Seconds passed. Drastic measures were called for. She took a chance and pushed hard. Whatever was holding her would either have her trapped or it would break.

The jerk sent her flying into the cabin. She was free. She reached over and found the bundle in the corner. Some boxes must have shifted. Otherwise whoever was there would have been invisible. She could feel legs and arms and a head.

Kir tried to move the bodies, but they were wedged fast. She took her knife and cut at the ropes that had caught on her a moment before. And then it happened. She touched a body, it came away and she found herself held in a tight embrace from which she could not escape. Lifeless arms swayed in the water around her; a face came close to hers; a dead body pressed itself against her in an obscene advance. She pushed the bundle away and wanted to shout, but she couldn't break free from the intimate contact.

She received the Morse signal through the line, which told her she had to rise NOW and no later. But the tug felt very distant.

She mumbled *I'm coming, I'm coming*. But soon afterwards there was another tug.

All right. I'm on my way.

Time was now an endless dimension. Something of which there was an abundance. Her head was buzzing and Allan Vraa's jerking of the line felt like a threat. The sea embraced her. Her thoughts bubbled inside her head with a pleasurable lightness, as if she had drunk champagne. The dead body let go and she propelled herself forward as her ears filled with sweet music.

Then the music turned sinister and images of her family appeared: her father who had never accepted her decisions in life. Her brothers, Red and Tomas, who had proved such a terrible disappointment. Her mother with her nervous fidgeting and her small, compact body. She hadn't seen them for a long time. The core, the very heart of her family had proved to be rotten. Could you avoid being contaminated by the corruption and evil if you had grown up with it?

This was something she had battled with ever since the events of last winter. She was one of them. Was she fundamentally rotten? Was that the reason she swam around all alone through her life? Maybe she should just let herself be carried away by the current and swallowed up by the sea.

Her head was spinning and ached from the pressure.

'What the hell do you think you're doing, Kir?'

Allan Vraa's voice came from the heavy clouds passing across the sky above her. She felt nothing. She wasn't aware that she had been pulled on board. She wasn't even aware that she had lost consciousness and she didn't hear herself say:

'Three dead bodies.'

Nor was she aware that she was being ferried back to the navy vessel, hoisted up to the helicopter and flown to Frederikshavn.

34

MARK HADN'T TELEPHONED in advance. However, Alice Brask looked as if she had been expecting visitors when she opened the door. Her face was flawless and her skin obviously well looked after – apparently without the help of make-up. Narrow eyebrows rose in perfect arches and her smile seemed obligingly professional. She reminded him of the doctor at Rigshospitalet who had diagnosed his cancer and told him with a self-assured smile and sympathetic but remote gestures that his prospects were bleak.

'I just came to proffer my condolences,' Mark said after he had introduced himself.

This was enough for sesame to open and she invited him in, which allowed him to have a good look at her from the back:

A simple, long-sleeved and tight-fitting T-shirt with a hint of a bra. Well-fitting Replay jeans and a fashionable studded belt. Leather pumps with heels that made her hips sway. Her hair was short and a sharp contrast to Melissa's flowing brown locks. In fact, it was hard to detect any family resemblance, except possibly the skin, which was pale, almost milky white.

'Do sit down.'

He turned down an offer of coffee and took a seat on the black leather sofa. The house was spotless in every respect, just like its owner. Montana bookcases, Piet Hein dining table and Jacobsen's Ant chairs. He recognised the design from the stolen property room at the police station. There was a pile of newspapers on the coffee table. He could make out photographs of Melissa and the convent and guessed that Alice Brask followed everything that was said or written about the case, on the Net, the television, the radio and in the press.

'Did you know Melissa?' Alice Brask said, taking a seat in an armchair opposite.

'No, but I've heard a lot about her. The nuns were very fond of her. They're in deep shock.'

She shook a cigarette out of a packet of Prince Light lying on the table. He wouldn't have put her down as a smoker. And indeed the smell of smoke inside the house was very faint.

'An old habit that has resurfaced,' she said, passing the packet. He refused.

'No coffee, no fags.'

She lit a cigarette and blew out the smoke with sensual movements of her lips.

'So what does a policeman do for fun?'

He shrugged.

'Find the company of charming women and indulge in a little bit of passive smoking?'

Her eyes narrowed as she sized him up. He might have overstepped the mark. After all, she was a mother who had lost her child rather than a date to flirt with, and upon closer inspection he could see that the make-up failed to conceal the dark rims under her eyes and the tiredness in them.

'What about the funeral?' he continued quickly. 'I expect it'll be a relief to get that over with.'

She nodded and placed a hand behind her neck and moved her head in circles. She made the movements look graceful.

'Her body will be released today. The funeral is on Saturday. I'll put the time in my blog, as you might have seen.'

'Are you sure that's . . .'

'Wise?'

She raised her eyebrows. In reality it was probably the blog that was stopping her from collapsing in a heap of grief, he mused.

'You're risking a large turnout.'

'That's not a risk,' she said with an edge to her voice. 'It's what I'm hoping for.'

Her resolve was clear in the way she flicked ash into the Georg Jensen ashtray.

'I have many . . . followers, let's call them that. People who read and comment on my blog. People who think the way I do, who are critical of the system and the authorities telling us what to do as if we were little robots.'

Mark got the sense this was a line she was reeling off for the hundredth time. She came across as an authority figure herself, someone who liked influencing other people's actions. He had read her blog. She was a woman of many opinions and her disciples seemed devoted to her. Their blogs certainly suggested as much.

He held up his hands in defence.

'It's your decision, of course. I'm sure most people would only want to express their support and sympathy.'

Except the killer, he thought. He was sure that whoever had killed Melissa also read the blog. But no doubt she was well aware of that. Perhaps she even felt it was a way of communicating with the killer. He decided not to broach the subject and risk antagonising her.

'As you know,' he said, lowering his voice, 'I'm not a part of the investigation, but I was asked to be present at the Institute of Forensics . . .'

This information clearly had an effect. Her cigarette hand froze somewhere between her mouth and the ashtray. Her face stiffened.

'You were present at her autopsy?'

The last word had to be forced out.

'Yes. Sara Dreyer is very skilled,' he hastened to add. 'It was performed with dignity.'

What must it be like to receive images on your retina of your child's body, sliced open? This was beyond his imagination.

Her hand stirred and she took a drag on her cigarette.

'Why do I need to know about that?'

He cleared his throat.

'We're wondering about something: Melissa's hearing aids . . .'

The reaction came far too quickly and too fiercely:

'What have they got to do with anything?'

Her eyes narrowed again. It was as if an invisible partition had shot up between the two of them. Half of his brain raced to come up with something with which to reassure her while the other half wondered what raw nerve he had hit.

'I was wondering if her hearing might have been a factor. Maybe she didn't hear her attacker . . .'

'Nonsense. That carpenter saw them meet and speak,' she said.

'No offence, but that's confidential information.'

The cigarette was squashed in the ashtray. She got up. It was quite clearly time for him to leave.

'I'm her mother. I'm also a journalist, and I have my sources. I'm convinced the police work more effectively when the press is snapping at their heels.'

He, too, got up. This had not gone well.

'The carpenter's scaffolding was sabotaged. You wrote about that as well. An innocent man is lying paralysed in hospital.'

'I know. I wrote it in my blog. You're probably wondering why at the police station. You think I deliberately risk other people's lives. But I'm of the firm opinion that getting things out into the open will help the investigation. Covering up the truth never leads to anything good.'

She was good at turning everything to her own advantage, Mark thought as he retreated towards the front door. He would hate to be a part of this woman's life. You would risk being sacrificed to some cause which in her eyes was greater than normal consideration for others. Had Melissa felt the same? Had she fought to have an ordinary, loving relationship with her mother instead of clashing over her sacred principles and being cudgelled over the head with them?

He thought about the pallid young girl on the pathologist's steel trolley. He was starting to understand why a girl like Melissa would seek refuge behind thick convent walls.

He turned in the doorway before leaving.

'I came here to express my condolences, that was all.'

A conciliatory expression stole over her face and the tightness around her mouth softened slightly.

'That's all right. I'm used to being alone with my ideas and points of view.'

'I don't think you're alone,' he said. 'And I'm sure your fans would be disappointed if you stopped writing your blog.'

She smiled and all of a sudden she was beautiful. Her eyes glowed, clear and strong.

'Thank you for saying that. And for coming.'

They shook hands. Her handshake was persuasive, just like most of her behaviour. After he had walked down the steps he turned around again.

'Melissa's hearing. Was it congenital?'

She shook her head.

'It was the result of an illness when she was seven.'

He clicked the remote to unlock the car.

'What illness?'

'Measles.'

She closed the door behind him.

35

THE STUDENTS HAD long since started filing out through the glass doors of Risskov Gymnasium. Individually or in clusters, chatting, they headed for their bicycles and cars, to freedom, their bags slung over their shoulders. The wind howled and took hold of the girls' hair and their flapping coats, which were soon buttoned up tightly. The lucky ones with hoods pulled them up to ward off the rain, which was pelting down once again.

Peter sheltered by the van in the car park fingering the wire in his pocket.. He scanned the scene. He had spotted the black Golf under a tree parked on the road. He didn't know what Gumbo looked like, but identifying him proved to be an easy matter. The dealer was lurking around the corner at the exit to the car park. He was wearing a shearling cowboy waistcoat and a thick red-checked shirt and looked like a lost Canadian lumberjack. He had a bushy moustache. The rest of his beard was dark stubble and his hair was cut so close to the scalp you could see the folds of flesh in his neck. A boy went up to him. They huddled together and spoke softly, while other students gave them a wide berth.

The two of them then sheltered inside a lean-to and carried on with what they were doing. It was almost impossible to see, but Peter was convinced that some goods were exchanging hands. Then the young boy strode on with a spring in his step and his hood pulled up.

Perhaps three minutes passed, then another customer came by and Gumbo repeated the choreography from before. There was grinning and nodding and a matey punch on the back with a fist.

Peter looked around. The stream of students had started to ease. He made up his mind to go and, unseen, jogged to the road and

Gumbo's car. He took the wire out of his pocket and bent one end of it into a hook. Then he coaxed the wire down behind the window seal on the driver's side and kept wriggling it until he heard a click and the lock opened. He unlocked the back door and slipped inside. He locked both the driver's door and the back door from inside and kept well down so that he could not be seen.

The Golf was as battered inside as out. The seats were worn, the foam padding protruded and there were black cigarette marks on the ceiling and burn marks everywhere. The ashtray was overflowing and the stench of tobacco and sweat was unbearable. Scattered on the floor and seats were fast food containers and empty Coke cans.

Soon afterwards he heard footsteps and the click of locks being opened with a remote key. He held his breath, forced himself down on the foul-smelling seat and got foam rubber up his nose. Gumbo opened the door. The entire car sank as around 100 kilos plumped down onto the driver's seat. Gumbo reached for his seat belt and inserted the buckle. Peter sat up, careful not to make any noise. In one swift movement he flipped the wire over the man's head and pulled it back against the neck rest.

'Don't move.'

Gumbo gurgled in protest. His hands shot up and tried to loosen the wire, but Peter tightened it even more.

'Hands on the steering wheel.'

Gumbo's hands fluttered vaguely in the air for a couple of seconds before landing on the steering wheel.

'OK. Drive.'

'Wh . . .?'

The question came out as a wheeze.

'Home. You've just invited me to coffee and biscuits. I can hardly restrain my excitement.'

Gumbo fumbled with the key. In the mirror Peter could see his eyes darting around the car, hunting for a way out.

'Forget it. You've already lost.'

Starting the engine and tentatively joining the traffic, the dealer appeared to agree.

'I know where you live, so no funny stuff.'

This was a lie, but spoken with sufficient authority for it to have the required effect. Gumbo groaned. Peter slackened the wire a little. They drove down Skejbyvej, on towards Vejlby Centervej and onto Grenåvej. Finally Gumbo turned down a rural lane and pulled up outside an old red-brick house which, in appearance and state of maintenance, resembled the car.

'Open the glove compartment.'

Gumbo did as he was told. Peter could see the man's hand shaking. In the glove compartment there was a gun, a pair of bolt cutters and a roll of gaffer tape.

'Pick up the gun with two fingers and pass it to me.'

To be on the safe side, Peter jerked the wire tight. A whimpering protest erupted from the man's throat.

'No tricks.'

The fingers pinched the gun and passed it backwards. Peter took the weapon and pressed the barrel against Gumbo's neck.

'Now the bolt cutters and the tape.'

Gumbo fumbled for the tool and the roll of gaffer tape. Peter grabbed them and stuffed them into his jacket pocket. Then he whipped the wire from Gumbo's neck, opened the rear door and stepped out onto the damp gravel, pointing the gun at the man in the front.

'Out!'

Gumbo obeyed, and Peter floored him with one kick from behind. He sat down on him and forced his knees into Gumbo's back while twisting his arms behind him and quickly tying steel wire tightly around his wrists. Then he forced Gumbo to stand up.

'The key?'

'In the car.'

Still pointing the gun at the man, Peter snatched the key from the ignition. He pushed Gumbo towards the entrance to the house, unlocked the door and shoved him inside.

It was a very small, dilapidated cottage. Everywhere there were overflowing ashtrays, porn magazines, free newspapers, pizza boxes and empty cans. It reeked of fetid air and stale sweat.

Peter shoved Gumbo into a chair and heard the sound of a beer can being crushed under the man's weight. Then he took the roll of gaffer tape and taped the dealer's legs to the chair, one after the other. Afterwards he wrapped tape around Gumbo's chest so that man and chair became inseparable.

He took the bolt cutters out of his pocket and put them on the table between them. Gumbo stared at the bolt cutters. Sweat poured from his forehead and down his face. His eyes rolled in panic.

'OK,' Peter said amicably. 'Time for you and me to have a nice little chat.'

36

LISE WERGE CLUNG to the edge of the lifeboat. The sea was rough. Behind her the fire roared on the burning ship. Around her passengers from the ship were sinking beneath the waves. A woman clutching a child reached out to her with a pleading gesture for her to take the child. Lise stared at the baby. She saw a small, wet bundle and a lock of dark hair sticking out. The child's cry rent the air. Lise looked away.

She felt a push as she lay there in the icy water. Someone was trying to force her to release her grip. It was the man from the restaurant. She had seen him drinking beer in the bar. He had a beer gut and wore a checked shirt and a jacket which was far too tight. Now he was fighting for his life in the water. If he could have pushed her away and climbed into the lifeboat himself, he would have done so. But she fought him off. She kicked and punched and bit. Eventually he gave up. She saw him sink with a sigh. Then she pulled herself up and landed on top of the others in the boat. She was so cold and wet that she could barely feel her body.

She woke up soaked in sweat and with a throat that rasped like a man's unshaven cheek. For a moment she just lay there staring, aware she was somewhere between dreaming and wakefulness. She still had the baby's cry in her ear when it mutated into the ringing of her alarm clock.

It was five o'clock in the afternoon. Her nap was over and that was just as well.

She got up and showered to rinse off the sweat. The *Scandinavian*

Star had been the lowest point in her life. She had been to Oslo to visit a friend who was working there. It was 1990. She was young and in love and busy planning her move to France. The future had looked bright and she had been lying awake in her cabin and relishing being alive when she heard shouts from the corridors. There was a fire on board.

Afterwards, when it was all over, she realised how lucky she had been. Most of the passengers on the lower decks had succumbed to toxic fumes from the ship's ceiling panels. People died as they lay in their cabins. After thirty seconds of smoke inhalation you lost consciousness. Three minutes and you were dead.

Lise had staggered out into the corridor in her nightdress and followed the stream of people heading for the lifeboats. Everything was chaos. The panic-stricken crew had no idea what they were supposed to be doing. They issued contradictory orders and so it was every man for himself.

She could clearly remember the moment when her grandfather's motto suddenly went through her head: 'In this family we don't take any crap.'

It was like winning the jackpot on a one-arm bandit, the sound of coins spilling out in the form of a crystal-clear truth: she was not going to accept dying.

It was that truth which had kept her going that night in the lifeboat. Yes, she had pushed others out of the way to save herself. Yes, she had averted her face from the crying child. She had done the only thing there was to do: she had survived.

'Have you had another nightmare?'

Her mother knew her too well. Lise wished she hadn't agreed to look in on her today, but she was working nights and had promised to turn up at six p.m. exactly and continue working on the family history. Besides, she had a bone to pick with her mother.

'It's nothing.'

She placed the tape recorder on the kitchen table in the middle of the bread, butter and cheese. Her mother was already busy sating her boundless appetite. Slice after slice disappeared between her lips, washed down with mouthfuls of black coffee.

'You've always been a softie,' Alma said as she munched. 'There was nothing else you could do, you know that. You did the right thing.'

'Yes, Mum.'

Her mother reached out and grabbed her wrist hard. It was so rare for them to touch that Lise jumped.

'Don't you humour me.'

Lise wriggled free.

'Moral scruples are the devil's work,' Alma continued, and broke off another chunk of bread and dipped it in her coffee. 'The road to hell is paved with guilty consciences.'

Lise said nothing. She had heard it all before. Alma's head stuck up slightly from under her carapace. The tortoise looked at her.

'Be proud that you come from a family that doesn't allow itself to be dictated to.'

Lise found her voice.

'A family of murderers and collaborators?'

But it took more than that to provoke her mother. She smiled at the coffee cup before draining it and immediately pouring more pitch-black liquid into it.

'A family that knows how to survive and doesn't allow itself to be bossed around – not by rules and regulations, nor by people's folly or any other idiocies.'

Lise thought her mother was going to grab her wrist again so she flinched when the cardigan-clad arm shot out. But it was for the butter dish. She held it with a firm grip. The knife went in and she buttered the white bread with great precision, all the way round the corners.

'I went to see Lone yesterday.'

The knife froze in the air.

'You could have taken me along.'

'It was a spur of the moment thing,' she lied. 'I got off work early. I told her about your project of dictating the family history to me.'

Alma said nothing. When it suited her, she would pretend she could hear nothing and knew nothing. The knife started buttering again.

'Lone said there is already a version. She said you dictated it to her. Is that true?'

Her mother nodded while her jaws chomped on a mouthful of white bread.

'So why do we have to do it again?' Lise demanded. 'Why repeat it when we've already got the story – where, incidentally?'

Her mother sat in silence for a while. Then she said:

'It does you good to have it laid on thick.'

'Having it forced down my throat, you mean?'

Alma shrugged.

'Call it what you like. Besides, we never finished.'

'Because Lone killed Laust?'

Another shrug.

'He was a moron.'

Lise couldn't disagree. Nevertheless, a protest welled up in her.

'You don't kill other people just because they're idiots.'

'No,' her mother said. 'Most people don't. They just put up with it.'

She packed away the butter and the cheese with emphatic movements.

'Most people get what they deserve.'

37

PETER TOOK OUT the photograph of Magnus and held it in front of Gumbo's eyes.

'Do you know this guy?'

Gumbo nodded.

'Did he owe you money?'

The sweat trickled down the man's face. His head shook a no, followed by a nodded yes.

'Yes or no?'

'We had a deal.'

His voice was hoarse with nerves.

Peter opened the gun and made sure it was loaded. He pointed it at Gumbo, who stared back, wide-eyed. His body squirmed in the chair, but to no avail.

'Didn't your mother ever teach you it's not nice to threaten people?'

Gumbo just stared at him.

'You went to see Magnus's mother.'

The eyes blinked. The mouth opened, but Peter cut him off.

'You won't ever do that again, have you got me? Or else I will personally chop your bollocks off and force you to eat them.'

Gumbo nodded and looked nervously first at the gun, then at Peter. As if to emphasise his willingness to cooperate, he nodded once more.

'Good, I'm glad we've got that sorted out,' Peter said. 'Then there's Magnus. What did he buy from you that meant he ended up owing you twenty thousand kroner?'

Gumbo paled. Peter took aim and smiled with his finger on the trigger.

'He bought some coke for his friend. He often did that.'

'Without paying?'

'He paid.'

'So what was the twenty thousand about?'

Gumbo squirmed again, making the tape crackle.

'My silence,' he mumbled.

'What?'

'I promised to keep my mouth shut about something I'd seen, know what I mean?'

Peter tried to hide his surprise.

'And what had you seen?'

'I saw him with a girl one evening,' the dealer said, in a voice that came out too quickly from sheer terror. 'It was in the gardens behind the school. It was obvious they didn't want to be seen together.'

'What were they doing?'

Peter was completely baffled. Magnus and a girl. How could that be worth money to anyone?

'Just sitting close together.'

'Doing what?'

'Talking.'

'Who was the girl?'

'It was that . . .'

Gumbo nodded towards the pile of free newspapers on the tiled table. Peter picked up one of them. Melissa's face was all over the front page. He held it up.

'This one?'

'Yes. She was murdered. Strangled, I think.'

Peter lowered the newspaper and hefted the gun. He got up and pressed the muzzle against Gumbo's temple and the stench of urine hit his nostrils as the man's bladder opened.

'What was your original deal?'

'One thousand.'

'One thousand kroner for you not to tell anyone that you had seen him and Melissa together?'

Gumbo nodded.

'And then you spied a chance to raise the price to twenty thousand when the girl was found dead?'

'I knew that Magnus had gone missing. I just put two and two together,' Gumbo mumbled.

'And you used these to make your point?'

Peter picked up the bolt cutters and weighed them in his hand while still holding the gun in the other. He got up again and stood opposite Gumbo, who was shaking like a dog.

'Or perhaps you just wanted to check they worked?'

He pulled the man's body forward, grabbed hold of his hand, forced his right forefinger into the jaws of the bolt cutters and closed them.

'Did you tell Magnus's mother what the debt was about?'

'Yes. But she already knew.'

'From you?'

'Yeees, fuuuck that hurts!'

His howling sounded like a fire alarm, but Peter knew that no one could hear them and maintained the pressure.

'So it wasn't the first time you'd been to see her?'

'No . . . Jeeeesus Christ . . .'

'Who are you working for?'

The lie was expelled in a gasp:

'No one.'

'Funny, I was sure I recognised your methods from somewhere.'

Peter squeezed the bolt cutter even harder and heard the bone crunch.

'Rico,' Gumbo cried out, confirming Peter's suspicion. He swore under his breath. As if he didn't have enough problems, he was now doing his best to create even more conflict with the Midnight Cowboys than he already had. The biker gang controlled the East Jutland drugs market. They had their hangers-on and their supporters among small-time dealers like Gumbo. It wouldn't be long before Rico learned that the man from the cliff had been causing trouble on his turf. So he might as well try to turn it to his own advantage.

'I know Rico well,' Peter said, squeezing harder. 'Give him my regards and tell him to deal with me from now on. Not Magnus.'

He released the bolt cutters. The finger hung limply from Gumbo's hand. Peter pushed him back in the chair. The man's head flopped down and he was close to passing out from the pain.

'And not his mother, got that?'

No reaction. Peter placed the bolt cutters under Gumbo's chin and pushed his head up. The eyes rolled around in their sockets before disappearing under his eyelids. Saliva and mucus bubbled from his mouth and nose. Finally he made flickering eye contact.

'My name is Peter. Say it.'

'P . . . e . . . ter,' came the feeble response.

'Do we have a deal?'

The man nodded.

'Then say it.'

Gumbo's face was drained of blood and he had stopped sweating. He looked like someone on his last legs. He had several stabs at forming the words with his lips before he was able to squeeze them out, almost inaudibly:

'We . . . have . . . a . . . deal.'

Again, the eyes went walkabout and the man's head flopped the way it had when Peter removed the bolt cutters. He reached for the keys lying on the table.

'Good. I'm going to borrow your car to get back to town.'

He got up and dangled the car keys in front of Gumbo, who didn't seem to notice.

'You'll find it where you left it. We'll have to do the coffee bit some other time.'

38

'I was stupid. Unprofessional.'

'Shhh.'

Mark stroked her hand.

'Anyway, you have better things to do than sit here. You, of all people, must surely hate hospitals.'

Kir felt embarrassed. She had never been so embarrassed in all her life. She had no idea what had come over her, but she had definitely been affected by the pressure and had been as light-headed as if she had drunk champagne. She had felt invincible. Which could be fatal for a diver.

'They put me in the pressure chamber. I showed symptoms of the bends.'

She hated saying the word. Hated that she hadn't shown better discipline.

'But you were right,' he said. 'You acted on your instinct and you were right. The *Marie af Grenå* had an important cargo, which we probably weren't supposed to know about.'

'A stowaway?'

'A dead stowaway.'

'Of course he was dead. They all were.'

'But this one was dead from the start.'

'I don't understand . . .'

She stared at him.

'What do you mean, Mark?'

The operation had been interrupted after her dive. But the following day Allan Vraa had gone down with Niklas and salvaged the three bodies. The third one, the unexpected stowaway, turned out to be the body of Simon's friend, Nils.

She knew from looking at Mark that he was wondering how much he could tell her. It irritated her.

'Come on, out with it!'

'Nils had been garrotted.'

'You're kidding?'

But she could see from his face that it was true. Nils Toftegaard, son of Hans Toftegaard, who was the brother of one of her old school friends. Nils, who had wanted to be a fisherman, but had got a job in Kvickly.

'We think he was killed in the same place and in the same way as Melissa. Later his body was hidden behind crates and coils of rope on the fishing boat.'

The killer must have known that the *Marie af Grenå* was going to sea. The body would go on a trip, but it would also return home. Unless . . .

'The Falck diver,' she said.

'Who?'

'Kasper Frandsen. He's the brother of one of the mine divers. He was down by the harbour diving around Jens Bådsmand's boat, freeing the propeller of pound net.'

'And?'

That was it, of course. It was obvious. She *had* seen him before, not just his brother.

'I believe he was also one of the Falck men who collected Melissa's body.'

'That could be a coincidence. All part of his job.'

'It still seems too much of a coincidence to me,' she insisted.

Mark looked dubious, but she could see he was following her train of thought. It was well known that certain killers got off on appearing close to the crime scene and watching the police at work. There were even cases where killers had been interviewed on TV. The TV stations loved replaying such footage once an arrest had been made. However, this mostly happened when there was a sexual motive for the crime. She remembered a case from England where a school caretaker had turned out to be the killer of two girls he had persuaded to come to his home, where he had drowned them in his bath tub. He had been very keen to talk to TV reporters.

'OK, we'd better check him out,' Mark said.

'He could have put Nils on the boat during the night,' she said.

'But why? What's his motive?'

'What's *anyone*'s motive?'

Four people had been killed in the space of a few days, but the victims were very different. Melissa and Nils were roughly the same age. Was that the link? But then there was Jens Bådsmand and Simon, who was also a teenager. Why did they have to die? Or were they just collateral damage?

'Perhaps the boat was sabotaged,' she said. 'Remember the scaffolding. Perhaps someone tampered with it.'

'That happens all the time,' Mark grunted.

'No, it doesn't. But it might be what happened here,' she said. 'We may never know. No one is going to raise a boat lying at a depth of forty-five metres. Unless you dived down and . . .'

'Forget it,' said Mark, who had read her mind. 'That's police work. You focus on getting better.'

'I *am* better and I'm bored here. You, of all people, should know that.'

He looked as if he did. She pointed to a cupboard in the corner.

'Please would you get my clothes?'

He got up and passed her the clothes with a suspicious look.

'Now what?'

'Turn around, cop.'

She sat upright in the bed and pulled off the hospital gown. She hated it. Hated the sensation of the fabric against her skin, the smell of institution and detergent.

'You can't just . . .'

'Turn around, I said.'

He did as he was told. She felt much more comfortable when she had her jeans and jumper on. In a matter of seconds she had packed her few possessions.

He glanced at his watch, still with his back to her.

'I've got a meeting shortly, Kir. I can't just . . .'

'Where?'

'At the police station. With Oluf Jensen.'

She finished tying her shoelaces.

'OK. Please would you drop me at the railway station? I've just discharged myself.'

39

BELLA APPEARED TO have recovered after the previous day's encounter with Gumbo's bolt cutters, but she looked like someone who feared Peter's anger even more. Her eyes flitted around the room looking for something to hold on to and her hands were constantly on the move. Her body language exuded defensiveness.

'You knew Magnus was meeting Melissa. Why didn't you tell me?'

Bella wrung out the dishcloths and wiped the kitchen table in long, orderly sweeps.

'I told you it was all connected,' she muttered. 'Alice Brask. Melissa. Magnus's disappearance. I kept nothing from you.'

She kept her eyes on her work.

'Connected? That's the biggest understatement in the world. Your son is in contact with a girl. He disappears and the girl turns up dead. Murdered. Have you any idea how that looks?'

Nervously, she nudged some hair away from her face with her wrist.

'Magnus is no killer.'

'I'm sure the mother of the Boston Strangler said the same thing.'

She tidied the dishcloth away and wiped her hands on her apron with her forefinger, still bandaged, sticking out. She eyed Peter. And then she went into the living room.

'Magnus was scared,' she said over her shoulder. 'You say Melissa was scared too. That makes two scared teenagers, one of whom is now dead.'

'What was he scared of?'

She rummaged around in the drawer of an old-fashioned dresser, then took out a note.

'I should probably have given this to you sooner.'

He took it and read the handwritten message:
'There's a debt to be paid. It's due soon.'
Bella looked at him with resignation.
'I found it scrunched up in one of his drawers. Obviously, I searched his room when he disappeared.'
Peter held up the note.
'And this isn't Gumbo's handwriting?'
She gave a short laugh.
'Everyone knows that Gumbo can't read or write. The man's as thick as a plank, but handy with a pair of bolt cutters.'
She shook her head.
'I asked him about it. He went mental. I think that was why he broke my finger . . . I provoked him and said I didn't think he could use bolt cutters, either.'
'So Magnus has another enemy, apart from Gumbo?'
She nodded.
'The same one as Melissa?'
'Perhaps. I'm not sure.'
'And you really have no idea who it might be?'
She looked angry now. A vertical furrow appeared between her brows and she narrowed her eyes.
'Of course I don't know who it is. I would have told you.'
Would she? It sounded convincing, but he didn't trust her. She was beautiful and fragile and she appealed to his protective instinct, but she had lied to him, more than once.
'You have to go to the police.'
Her face hardened in defiance. It was My to a T when she had her mind set on something.
'I daren't.'
He understood that well enough. In debt to a brutal debt collector, a son on the run, exposed and alone – any pursuer would quickly get the scent, just like a hunting dog would smell an injured animal.
'So what do you want?'
She put her hand on his arm. He resisted but was drawn in by her eyes, which were filled with fear.

'The same as before. For you to find Magnus and bring him back to me.'

He was stupid, he was well aware of that. But somewhere out there a young boy needed his help. It wasn't Magnus's fault that he had an impossible liar for a mother. And it wasn't his fault that someone had killed Melissa and might now be looking for him. That was how it was, Peter thought. Magnus was a victim, just like Melissa had been – but why? What was the link between two people who had only known each other as children? Could it be fear, of a common enemy?

He mulled it over as he left Bella shortly afterwards with a few tips as to where Magnus might have gone. The postcards sent a clear message. The boy was continually on the move. Bella told him he had been a boy scout and that for some time now he had given guitar lessons for cash, so he must have some money.

Survival shelters were a good bet, Peter reckoned. A boy scout would know how to camp out in such places, even in a windy, rainy November. He would know how to survive, just as Peter had known when he'd left prison. Out in the open. That was where he belonged. And he had known it as surely as the sky was high and blue, and that the trees lost their leaves in the autumn and grew new ones in the spring. He knew what it was like to be Magnus, to trust only animals and nature rather than people.

He spent the day searching in and around all the shelters he could find in areas where Bella had told him Magnus had been with his scout troop. He ended up at the Super Best supermarket near the shelter in Mollerup Forest by Vejlby. Here he bought three tubs of potato salad, three packets of sausages, some coleslaw, dog treats and a six-pack of beer. At the till he produced a photo of Magnus, but the girl barely glanced at it before shaking her head.

Afterwards he bought an Othello layer cake at the bakery and showed the photo to the lady behind the counter. She took her time, but also ended up returning it to him.

'So many people come here, you know,' she said.

On the way out he saw a noticeboard where people advertised items for sale or pinned up missing cat posters. The idea of adding a missing boy poster seemed absurd. However, he considered the possibility as he drove home to the cliff top and his dog.

40

'THE GOOD NEWS is that the pathologists have found mitochondrial DNA in one of the vertebrae.'

Oluf Jensen waved the report in front of Mark's nose. They were in his office again. This time Mark could actually smell the smoke from the pipe which the detective almost certainly kept hidden in his desk drawer.

'Who knows, we might be able to identify our bone man after all. In theory,' Jensen said cheerfully.

'In theory,' Mark said. 'But where do we start looking?'

'Aye, there's the rub. Where to look?'

A raised index finger – Oluf Jensen must have been a senior teacher in his former life – was held up in the smoky air. Mark thought he was going to suffocate.

'Do you mind if I open a window?'

Oluf Jensen stared at him, as if Mark had announced he was about to remove his trousers. Then he waved again, now with his whole hand.

'Please yourself.'

Mark got up, pushed open the window and inhaled a big lungful of fresh city air. He lingered by the window sill.

'What about the list of missing persons from the post-war show-downs with collaborators? Have you made any progress there?'

The detective nodded, spun around in his chair and launched himself at his computer with effortless expertise.

'It's not complete yet.'

He peered at Mark over the rim of his glasses. 'And it never will be. But we have some local names to follow up. If I may ask you to be patient . . .'

Mark waited while his colleague opened a file and printed a copy for each of them.

'Take a look at this.'

Oluf Jensen handed Mark a sheet of A4 paper. There were four names on the list. Each one was followed by a few explanatory lines.

'Bear in mind that these are people who went missing and remain unaccounted for in the period from January 1945 to January 1946,' Oluf Jensen explained with a gravity that suggested he intended to test Mark on all the names later. 'Most were found, remember. Some with a bullet in the brain or another part of their anatomy.'

'Do we have a list of their names as well?' Mark asked.

Oluf Jensen returned to his computer.

'Of course. There are twelve from the Djursland area. But none of them could be our bone man.'

Nonetheless, he printed that list as well and handed it to Mark.

'The more I think about it, the more I believe it must have been a local murder, irrespective of whether it was motivated by a post-war score to be settled or something purely personal.'

Mark nodded.

'Agreed.'

He felt slightly less like a student and more like a colleague when he repeated what Kir had told him about the Koral Strait and the elephant mine that had detonated in the 1960s when the channel was being cleared.

'Interesting,' Oluf Jensen conceded. 'If the box has only lain there for twenty years or so, where were the bones being kept in the meantime? Could they have been buried somewhere – in a garden, perhaps – or stored in a basement?'

His eyes sparkled behind his spectacles. Mark could see the ardour of a bloodhound and he felt a momentary kinship between them.

'And why would someone suddenly get an urge to dispose of them by sailing to an area which technically speaking is prohibited?'

Mark ran his eye down the first list. He didn't recognise any of the names, even though he was Djursland born and bred.

'Are they all collaborators or what?'

'It's probably not that simple,' Oluf Jensen said. 'At least one man was a Resistance fighter who disappeared without trace. I would assume there must have been some tit for tat murders.'

Mark read out loud:

1. Kurt Falk, contractor, born 1899, reported missing from his home on 27 April 1945. Never been seen since. Kurt Falk supplied concrete components for the construction of Tirstrup Airport as a subcontractor to a larger company, AK Cement A/S.

2. Allan Holme-Olsen, pipefitter and Resistance fighter. Born 1910. Reported missing on 1 May 1945. Worked on the construction of Tirstrup Airport from 1943 to 1945.

3. Herbert Kolding, born 1906, a shopkeeper from Grenå. Allegedly abducted from his home by members of the Resistance in March 1945. Rumour had it that Herbert Kolding was an informant. He was never found. No one has been held accountable for his disappearance.

4. Tage Juel Larsen, a builder from Ebeltoft, born 1902. Is alleged to have supplied building materials and expertise to the Germans. Disappeared from his home in April 1945 and has never been seen since.

Mark looked up with the paper in his hand.

'I don't recognise the names, but I'll try to track down some relatives of these four men. It would be the obvious place to start, given we're talking about Djursland.'

Oluf Jensen started doodling on his own copy of the list, as was his wont. Soon each name had its own symbol: the contractor – a lorry, the Resistance fighter – a gun, the shopkeeper – a bag of flour and the bricklayer – a trowel.

'Sounds like you know the place well?'

The question came as dripping mortar was added to the trowel.

Far too well, Mark thought.

'I'm Grenå born and bred.'

Oluf Jensen finally tore himself away from his artwork and put down his pen.

'Remember, it has to be the maternal line. You need to get hold of one or more of the people from the female bloodline. Then we'll take blood samples and see what we get.'

Mark felt a light tingle run through his body. It was his equivalent to the twinkle he'd seen earlier in Oluf Jensen's eyes. He recognised the first clear phase of the pursuit, when you finally found a toehold that might in the end prove to be strong enough for the uphill struggle that the solving of a murder case always constituted. Sometimes it was up a vertical cliff face with one hand on first one jutting overhang and then another, projections you had never imagined could exist when you started your ascent.

'Just imagine if we were to find a match,' he said.

Oluf Jensen nodded.

'Then we really would have something to go on.'

41

'DINNER'S READY!'

As Peter had expected, chaos reigned in Manfred and Jutta's house. No dinner preparations had been made, the place was a mess, Jutta's unwashed hair stuck to her scalp and her clothes hung off her as if she hadn't eaten for days. But her eyes gleamed:

'He moved a foot! He's going to be all right, Peter. I think he's going to recover.'

She fell around his neck as if it had been he who had brought the good news. The kids came running in from the paddock, snot running from their noses and mud on their trousers, and they almost knocked him over, and King, the family's dachshund, eagerly sniffed his trouser leg. Kaj settled down in dignified isolation on the sofa rug and observed the scene.

Peter placed the Super Best shopping bags on the kitchen table and started unpacking.

'This is going to be a gourmet meal,' he promised the children.

'What's goormay?'

'It's when something tastes nice. Where do you keep the ketchup?'

They knew exactly where to find the mustard and the ketchup. Their eyes shone and their voices were happy, and for a brief interlude Peter savoured the family's warm embrace.

'Get me a frying pan, will you, kids?'

They rummaged through the contents of the kitchen cupboard, knocking over some pots and pans before they found what they were looking for.

'Daddy's coming home again,' Joachim exclaimed. 'He can wiggle his toe.'

'His whole foot,' his sister corrected him.

'His whole leg,' Joachim called out.

'He can fly!'

'He certainly can,' Peter said. 'I saw it with my own eyes.'

'Through the air?'

'Where else, you monkey?'

'I am not a monkey!'

'Yes, you are, you squirm like a monkey,' Peter said and tickled the boy under the ribs as he always did. 'I've never seen anything like it.'

They exploded with laughter. It was as if the seriousness of the last few days had finally become too much for them and had been shattered by their pent-up joy.

Jutta went to have a shower and soon returned in fresh jeans and a soft jumper with her hair fanning out across her back. There was colour in her cheeks again.

'This is so nice of you, Peter, it really is.'

She had green eyes, he only realised this now. Jutta's special qualities were not the kind you noticed straightaway. He had known her for years, and to begin with, she had just been a skinny, shy, pale girl who was in Manfred's shadow. But the new situation had changed her, he thought. She'd had to step into the limelight for a while. She took up more room now than she had ever done and he saw that she was beautiful in a very special way, with her sparkling eyes and dark red hair against her fine skin.

They ate, and they all ate well. Grateful for this moment, Peter pushed his plate away and let the good news sink in. Manfred would make a full recovery. The doctors had said that once he regained sensation in his legs, progress could be very quick indeed. Soon Manfred would be climbing roof ridges and going hunting. Once more he would be the man in his family, play with his kids and tease them until they fell over laughing. And he would return and love Jutta as she deserved to be loved.

Peter drank his beer and watched the horseplay between her and the kids as if all the worries of the world hadn't been weighing them down only a short time ago. As if the sword of destiny hadn't just missed them by a whisker.

It was like looking at a near-perfect photograph. Families were like that. But take away one component and an otherwise perfect picture was suddenly distorted. It could be hard to see what was missing. In this case it was obviously Manfred, it was easy. In others, the problem was more subtle and the surface happiness was like one of those pictures where you had to search to find five mistakes.

Where were the mistakes in Bella's family? Why had Magnus decided to leave? And why was no one to know that he was meeting Melissa?

He saw the children teasing their mother, saw the way her eyes beamed as she watched their game with the mustard and tomato sauce. There wasn't a trace of any underlying anxieties in Jutta. His thoughts slipped effortlessly from her to Kir. There was something about both their personalities that made them stand out from so many other people. Honesty was a good guess. Neither Jutta nor Kir appeared to have hidden agendas. That was the difference between them and Bella.

He decided to head home after a couple of hours; they protested, but he could see that they were all exhausted.

'Everything's going to be all right,' Jutta said with a gentle goodbye hug. 'Soon you'll be playing chess again, Manfred will win and I'll cook chilli con carne.'

He waved to them and sounded the horn, and Kaj stuck his head out of the window.

Once home, he took out the photograph of Magnus, made ten copies and inserted the caption:

'Have you seen Magnus? He has left home and his family misses him terribly . . .'

He added his own mobile number. Bella wasn't like Jutta or Kir. He didn't trust her.

42

'I HOPE YOU'LL be patient with me. I'm not very fast.'

Kir did hamstring stretches against a tree. Her old flame, a former Falck diver called Morten, did the same. He was the man she had almost called the first day she had dived into the moat. They knew each other, not from diving but from the gym. Once, on a night out, there had been the potential for an affair, but nothing had ever really come of it, quite possibly because Morten had been a married man in those days. Years later, a friend had told her that he had got divorced. Morten himself had recently told her that his disabled daughter had died, so he had put his house up for sale and moved into Grenå for a fresh start.

'Your life has just been saved in a pressure chamber and now you're whingeing about not being able to run fast. I think you need to get a better perspective on life.'

If only he knew how much more perspective she had acquired recently. She had told him about the body in the moat and the fishing cutter with the three dead bodies. She had also told him a little about the box of bones. But she hadn't told him about her truce with Mark, the indirect reason that they were out for a run together now. Something needed to happen in her life. Morten was one possibility. So she had called and suggested an early-morning run through Polderev Plantation, followed by brunch at her house. It had taken him all of two seconds to say yes.

They started running alongside each other. Morten was a fairly big guy but he wasn't particularly fast, and she had no trouble keeping up with him, even though her body still felt woozy.

'So what was it you wanted to know?'

He was already panting. He had quit his diving job long ago and was now working as a doorman at a club called Summertime by Grenå harbour. The rest of the time he worked for Falck as a driver, as well as doing other casual jobs.

'One of your colleagues, or former colleagues – Kasper Frandsen. Does that name ring a bell?'

'Of course, Kasper. Funny guy.'

Kir snorted with derision.

'Funny isn't quite the word I would have used to describe him.'

Morten grinned in her direction. The sweat was already pouring from his face.

'So you've met him?'

'That's one way of putting it.'

She told him briefly about her scene with Frandsen at the harbour.

'That sounds like him. They call him Mr Hyde.'

'Oh, why's that?'

'He has one hell of a temper. I've been on the receiving end of it myself a couple of times.'

'What else do you know about him?'

'He's in the middle of a divorce from what I hear. He used to live with his wife and children somewhere in Grenå. I don't know where he lives now.'

Mr Hyde. The diver's face appeared in Kir's mind as she ran.

So how many officers do you have to bed . . .

It struck her there had been a cruel quality to his expression when he had stood there, legs astride in front of her, small, sharp eyes squinting at her through narrow cracks. Cold and calculating, as if he was sizing her up to see how he could get the better of her.

Her legs felt tired. The fatigue spread to the rest of her body, but she doggedly kept running. She had to focus and be objective, not panic and then draw hasty conclusions. Kasper Frandsen was an unpleasant so-and-so, and his colleagues called him Mr Hyde, the other side of Dr Jekyll. His job as a Falck diver meant he moved around like a hunter. If it was human game the man was after, he certainly had the opportunity – to throw his prey into a moat which he would later help to search, for example. It was perfect. In fact, he was a textbook example of a serial killer. And that was the problem. The fit was too neat and she had already taken a dislike to him.

'So what's this about Kasper?' Morten asked, jumping over a puddle with a lumpen elegance. 'Why are you so interested in him?'

'Oh, no reason.'

They ran the route they had agreed. With half a kilometre to go to her house, she accelerated:

'Loser makes coffee!'

They had just poured Morten's coffee into the cups when she heard a crunch of tyres rolling across her drive and raised her head. She looked out and saw a police car, and suddenly wished Morten wasn't there. But there was no time to hide him in a closet or shove him out the back, and she was forced to open the door to Mark.

'Have you got a visitor?'

It sounded more like an accusation than a question.

'Is there a law against that?'

His face darkened.

'It's eight o'clock in the morning.'

'And?'

'So was this a visitor who stayed the night?'

She couldn't help laughing. She spoke quietly so that Morten wouldn't hear her:

'Christ, what a way to put it! Why don't you just ask me outright if I had sex with him?'

'Did you?'

'So what if I did? How is that any of your business?'

She jabbed him in the chest.

'The truce was your idea, remember?'

He swallowed. He had turned even darker than usual and his eyes were hard and black.

'Well, you could have been a little more discreet.'

'This is my house, in case you'd forgotten.'

She doubled up with laughter. This added to his irritation, she saw. She opened the door wide.

'Why don't you come inside and meet the competition,' she spluttered. 'His name's Morten.'

Mark hesitated, clearly at a loss. She felt a tinge of sadness. He touched something in her, but the strong attraction had gone. He seemed somehow adrift, and she was no longer in love with him. She wasn't in love with Morten, either, but perhaps he was a way to move on.

'Come inside, you numptie,' she said to Mark. 'He's just a colleague. We've been for a run.'

She pushed him into the living room, where Morten leapt to his feet and held out his hand while quickly gulping down his food. Kir rustled up another cup of coffee.

'Any news?'

Mark drank his coffee as fast as he could. He was obviously not at ease in Morten's company. Kir wondered if it might have something to do with the fact that Morten was fairly muscular. Whereas Mark was the skinny, feline type, Morten was a bear.

Mark finally stood up and produced a piece of paper from his pocket.

'I've brought you the list we were talking about.'

'OK, thank you. Can I read it?'

Mark nodded but with a warning glance at Morten, who jumped up.

'I'd better be off.'

Kir protested, though without much conviction.

'Let's do this again some time.'

'Absolutely.'

Morten looked as if he wanted to give her a hug, but was afraid to. Big hands hung helplessly from the end of his arms, spread outwards. Kir reached up and planted an innocent kiss on his cheek.

'See you.'

'Let's do this again some time,' Mark mimicked when Morten had gone. 'What kind of a ruminant was he, then?'

'You're jealous.'

'Am I hell. But he didn't seem to have two brain cells to choose from.'

He followed her back into the living room. 'You deserve better.'

She turned around and he almost bumped into her.

'You, perhaps?'

'I didn't say that.'

He flopped down on her sofa. She poured more coffee and unfolded the list.

'I just wanted to see if any of these names rang a bell.'

43

THE CHILDREN WERE wearing snowsuits in every colour imaginable. They squealed with delight as they slithered down the short slide and laughed their heads off when a heavier child on the seesaw sent them high into the air.

They swarmed around the playground like noisy and colourful mini-astronauts, and for a moment, Peter paused to breathe in their joy and their pluck.

Watching them was like the hours with Jutta and the children: a welcome injection of normality. He had spent the morning driving around with his home-made missing person posters and stuck them up on various noticeboards in strategically chosen supermarkets. That in itself was an absurd action on top of a week of incidents that had whirled him around in a centrifuge of murder, accidents and misery.

After his efforts to locate Magnus, he had made for Elev, passing the nursery on his way. On impulse, he had stopped the car and got out.

The sight of the children was balm to his soul. They didn't know how lucky they were, he thought. It was a case of picking the right number in the lottery, and these children had clearly come out of it very well.

'Can I help you?'

One of the nursery teachers approached him. He had been looking at her as well, possibly not quite as discreetly as he ought to have. She was pretty in a very Danish way: she had blond plaits and freckles and dark brows, which as of this moment were indicating disapproval. It dawned on him what she must have been thinking.

Being a man in the company of children was not as easy as it had been only decades ago.

'I . . .'

He hadn't prepared anything, and suddenly it was as if every possible explanation could be misinterpreted.

'Are you looking for someone?'

He nodded.

'I was wondering whether there was anyone who had worked here for many years . . .'

'Why?'

She was on her guard. She had already taken against him, but he knew that behind the stern expression there were smiles and dimples. He had seen it just now when she was playing with the children.

'I'm looking for a young man called Magnus,' he said. 'He's eighteen years old, but he used to go to this nursery. He's gone missing . . .'

And I believe it has something to do with his childhood. That was what he was thinking, but he couldn't make himself say it out loud. She would either laugh herself silly or tell him to go to hell.

As it was, she stood there for a moment, her expression changing from distrust to normal reflection.

'You want to talk about a boy who used to come here, what . . . twelve – thirteen years ago?'

He essayed an apologetic smile.

'I know it might sound a bit odd . . .'

'Are you family? His father? If he's gone missing, surely you should report it to the police?'

He liked the fact that she was so logical. In fact, he liked her, full stop. She was protecting her children, that much was clear. And justifiably, in case he was a paedophile planning to abduct a child.

'His mother has asked me to lend a hand . . . The police aren't involved. He's eighteen and we think he's just hiding somewhere.'

She scrutinised him while she weighed up the matter. Then she appeared to decide he was worth a shot.

'You'd better come with me.'

She accompanied him inside the nursery, where small shoes and bags and coats had their allocated places on shelves and pegs in a range of colours, through a room cluttered with toys where moulded plastic chairs were arranged in a circle as if there had just been an important round-the-table discussion.

She knocked on an office door, which was ajar. There was a nameplate: Annelise McPherson. Obviously married to a Scot, he thought.

'Annelise?'

'Yes, come in.'

Behind a desk and a computer sat a curvaceous middle-aged woman with her hair up in an artistic heap. She smiled.

'Yes, Hanne?'

'This is . . .'

'Peter Boutrup.'

'Peter Boutrup. He . . . He's looking for a boy who used to attend this nursery . . .'

'Oh yes?'

The woman called Annelise furrowed her brows and looked almost as sceptical as her younger colleague. Peter decided to turn on the charm.

'It was just a spur of the moment thing.'

He flung out an arm in what he hoped was an apologetic gesture. 'I was passing and saw the children playing outside and I already knew Magnus used to attend this nursery . . . Bella told me.'

'Bella? Bella Albertsen? I remember her well.'

He nodded.

'Magnus was a lovely little boy. Did you say you were looking for him?'

'He's been gone three weeks. I know he's eighteen, so he's entitled to do whatever he likes. But his mother . . . Well, you know, mothers and sons . . . She's really worried.'

'I can imagine.'

The nursery teacher signalled that she was leaving. Annelise nodded for him to sit down and he pulled up a chair. This wasn't the boring office of a business manager with expensive art on the walls. Children's drawings were plastered everywhere. Everything seemed colourful and cheerful and underpinned with a hint of sensible educational values. The children were holding hands and playing together. There was a wide spectrum of skin colours and everyone was happy.

The thought crossed Peter's mind that this was a perfect representation of an imperfect world. This taught children from an early age how to depict a fantasy or a half-truth. He was no different. He had once done the same.

'Magnus,' Annelise said. 'He was a bit of a paradox. He never wanted to come indoors when he was told to. But at the same time, he was delicate – physically, I mean.'

'But not mentally?'

'Oh, no. He had a will of iron. He was a little survivor.'

Peter hoped that was still the case.

'I was wondering if anything from the past might have influenced his actions today . . . He seems to be running away from something.'

He hoped she would see it as an open-ended question. She sighed.

'Bella was a good mother, but she was also easily influenced and she didn't always have the best advisers.'

She touched the pile of greying hair lightly as if to make sure the hair slide was still in place.

'But it's difficult to be a parent and make the right decisions, isn't it?'

'Are you thinking of anything in particular?'

She brushed a stray lock behind her ear and allowed herself a little time before replying.

'It's like all other aspects of life, I suppose: the leaders set the pace. And then there are those who follow without ever asking too many questions . . .'

'The others?'

Annelise McPherson rocked her head from side to side, as if weighing up the pros and cons. 'It could have affected a small boy, who knows . . .'

Peter was frustrated but didn't press her for anything more concrete. Perhaps she sensed his frustration because she stopped herself almost halfway through the sentence as if it hadn't occurred to her until now that she was talking to a total stranger.

She shook her head.

'Perhaps you should discuss this with Bella. After all, you know her.'

44

THE HOUSE STOOD in the middle of the forest, half-swallowed up by encroaching nature. Its name was 'The Woodland Snail'. It had been an imposing building once, he could see that. But decay and – Mark guessed – a shortage of money had allowed moss to spread across the roof, branches of trees to press against windows and gables and for weeds to flourish. The overall impression was sinister and dark, like an alluring gingerbread house in a fairy tale.

After he had rung the doorbell it took a while before someone called from inside.

'Who is it?'

It was a voice that said *Go away and don't come back*. Mark adopted his friendliest tone:

'Mark Bille Hansen, Grenå Police.'

The door was opened a crack. A security chain separated him from an old woman who reminded him of a tortoise with her small, half-hidden eyes, short neck and numerous wrinkles in an almost square face. Her body could only be guessed at. It bulged in every conceivable, and inconceivable, place and she had tried to hide it under a dark dress and a woollen jumper.

'Police?'

He nodded.

'Do you have any ID?'

He was surprised, but produced his warrant card and showed it to her.

'Please may I come in?'

She didn't move from the spot. Her eyes, filled with mistrust, measured him from head to foot.

'What's this about?'

Mark had to count to ten in order not to lose his patience. What was wrong with people these days? They watched too many thrillers on TV and behaved as if they had fifteen bodies buried in the back garden.

'It's about your father, ma'am.'

He was on first-name terms with the abbess, but this woman was like a fairy-tale witch. Better address her as ma'am, so as not to provoke her, he decided.

'What about him?'

'Perhaps it would be best if I could come inside?'

The old woman peered up at him from under heavy eyelids.

'If you tell me what this is about I'll be the judge of that.'

'Kurt Falk. He was reported missing just after the war. We've found skeletal remains from that time and we're investigating to see if they match any living relatives.'

She didn't seem keen, but after further scrutiny of both him and his warrant card, she removed the chain and opened the door. He followed her into an old kitchen where a newspaper lay open on the kitchen table. A half-done crossword puzzle. There was also a pencil.

'Sit down.'

He did as he was told. She plonked herself down heavily on the chair opposite him and sank into her vast body. It was hard to know whether she was looking at him or not, but he had a sneaking feeling that every centimetre of him was being subjected to close inspection.

'I know it's many years ago now, but perhaps you can tell me a little bit about the circumstances of your father's disappearance.'

Had she fallen asleep? Her eyes were closed and her neck had retracted deeper into her dress so that her body and face had become one, or so it seemed. Then she said:

'Where did you find the bones?'

There was something about the question or the way she had asked it which made Mark hesitate as to how much she ought to know.

'It's a long story.'

'I've got plenty of time.'

'I'm afraid I can't go into detail,' he said. 'But perhaps you have a job remembering things from those days?'

She was stung by the remark, as he'd intended.

'There's nothing wrong with my memory.'

He was absolutely sure there wasn't. She looked like the kind of person who never forgot if someone had moved the sugar bowl or stepped on the Persian carpet wearing muddy shoes.

'You were fifteen years old in 1945. Were you at home?'

She nodded to herself.

'Of course, I lived here.'

'Here?'

Her head emerged from the carapace as she looked around and waved an all-encompassing hand. 'This is my childhood home. My father built the house himself.'

'And you have lived here all your life?'

'No.'

It was obvious she was waiting for his next question, but he held back. If she could play the long game, so could he.

'Alfred and I moved in when my mother died in 1967,' she said after a lengthy pause in which she'd had time to put on her glasses and fill in some squares of her crossword.

'Alfred? Your husband?'

'My late husband, yes. He died soon afterwards.'

She drummed her fingers on the table. Her nails were long and grubby. Her eyes peered at him from under her eyelids and they were not friendly.

'Men tend to die early, don't they?'

He cleared his throat. She appeared to be mulling over a difficult clue in her crossword.

'What happened that day in 1945?'

'Livestock,' she muttered.

'I beg your pardon . . .'

'Six letters. Fifth one is an L.'

He leaned forward.

'And it starts with a C,' he said. '*Cherry red* is cerise.'

'So it is . . . The doorbell went one day and there they were.'

'Did you know them?'

Another pause. Mark pointed.

'*Empty*, eight letters, is *deserted*.'

She filled in the squares. The pencil was pressed hard against the paper.

'There were two men. We didn't know them. They had guns. The bastards took him in their car.'

'Cattle,' Mark said.

'What?'

'Livestock.'

He pointed again. She put down the pencil.

'They shot him.'

'But his body was never found.'

'Those bones,' she said. 'Was that man shot too?'

She was sharp, he thought. A little too sharp.

'We don't know for certain yet. To begin with, we're trying to get the body identified.'

'After all those years?'

'We've found DNA. Genetic material.'

'I know what DNA is. I'm not an idiot.'

Not very likeable, either. She was acting as if she was guilty of a crime, but Mark couldn't imagine what an eighty-year-old lady could possibly have to hide.

'Is there any family left on your paternal grandmother's side? That might help us to identify him.'

'Not that I know of,' she said, writing *CATTLE* in the squares. 'And you can go now. My daughter will be here shortly.'

As he left the drive, he nearly crashed into a red car coming towards the house. He hastily swerved to avoid losing his wing mirror. In the driver's seat he caught a glimpse of a familiar face: the care assistant who had brought him and his grandfather coffee and biscuits.

45

PETER NOTICED THE red pickup after finishing work at the convent, when he stopped off in Voldby to fill up his van with diesel.

Kir was hidden behind a pillar. She glanced up from putting in petrol and her smile of recognition reminded him of something.

'I've been meaning to call you,' he said. 'To thank you.'

She looked confused.

'For spotting that the scaffolding had been tampered with.'

'Oh, that.'

She had finished now and shook the last drops from the nozzle.

'Someone would have noticed it eventually anyway. The police or the forensics officers, for instance.'

He was tempted to say the police and their forensics officers could go screw themselves. She pushed the nozzle into the pump and clicked the petrol cap in place.

'Shit!'

She held up her hands and took a step backwards. 'How do you avoid getting diesel all over yourself?'

She was about to wipe her hands on her trousers, which were camouflages with several pockets.

'Hang on.'

He pulled some paper towels out of a dispenser and handed them to her. He watched her clumsily wiping the diesel off her hands, a dimpled smile in the offing, and he suddenly felt something click between them. They were both soldiers of sorts coping with unique circumstances. She had a brother in prison and another hospitalised after an encounter with a girl gang. Her parents had favoured their useless sons and never noticed their daughter. He had a mother who hadn't wanted him and a half-sister he had sporadic but friendly contact with. He regarded himself as marginally better off than Kir.

'How's Tomas?' he asked.

He knew that Kir had been fond of her younger brother, even though he had turned out to be a violent psychopath.

'He's still in a coma.'

She hesitated. 'It's probably for the best.'

'Do you ever visit him?'

She nodded.

'Somebody has to. Mum and Dad don't and Red isn't able to.'

She looked uneasy, but also a little relieved.

'Thanks for asking. My family isn't the most popular on the planet.'

He smiled.

'You didn't pick them. This is something I know a bit about.'

'Ah, that's right. Do you ever see your mother?'

'No. I'm probably not as brave as you.'

She blushed slightly. Not because of his words, he guessed, but because he had winked at her.

'Haven't you got a sister as well?'

'Rose. My half-sister. She's twenty-four.'

The thought of Rose made him feel warm inside. He had only met her twice, but the kinship seemed real and at times they would chat on Facebook. A fact their shared mother loathed. She preferred to handle the relationship between her two children herself.

'I've heard about what happened near Læsø the other day,' he said cautiously.

'What have you heard?'

She looked guarded.

'That a diver got the bends.'

'That was me.'

She chuckled, almost apologetically, and scraped the tarmac with her foot.

'I did something really daft. I stayed down too long thinking I was in control.'

He hadn't thought of her as someone who could lose control. She must have had a reason.

'I ended up in the pressure chamber in Frederikshavn.'

'How are you now?' he asked.

Her face split into a smile. The dimples were very clear now. She was an odd girl, red hair and freckles, flat as a board with a straight back like a boy's. And yet feminine enough to walk around in camouflage trousers and heavy boots and still make a sexy impression.

'Fit as a fiddle,' she declared. 'Feeling a bit low, though.'

She grew serious again. 'I've just visited a mother up here' – she swung an arm to indicate the direction – 'to express my sympathy at the loss of her seventeen-year-old son.'

'That's young.'

She nodded.

'I knew him. I know the whole family. Nils's mother was my old teacher.'

'That must be difficult,' Peter said. 'Did you recover his body?'

She shook her head.

'My colleagues did. Along with the other two. But Nils was a surprise. He wasn't meant to be on board at all.'

She eyed him assessingly.

'OK, I'm about to tell you something which might not be made public for a few days, but he was killed in exactly the same way as Melissa.'

The following pause was eloquent. Then she broke it.

'Two teenagers. A boy and a girl. Weird, isn't it?'

Peter nodded.

'Very.'

'What's even weirder is that I found a box of old bones in Kalø Bay late last summer,' she said with a slight shake of her head. 'The guy in the box had been killed in just the same way: garrotted.'

'Garrotted?'

'It's an old method of execution, from Spain.'

She looked as if she was about to say something else, but swallowed her words. After all, she was close to the police and of course she had heard that they had searched his home.

Then she brightened up again.

'I'd been meaning to get in touch with you. I've got an old summer house in need of repair. I've saved up some money.'

She looked hesitant.

'But perhaps my timing is bad, now that Manfred is in hospital . . .'

'I can stop by one of these days,' he suggested. 'Manfred's on the mend. They say he can wiggle his foot.'

Her face lit up, then it darkened. She was too good for that police officer who didn't seem to be so keen on her any more, he thought. She deserved better.

'All right then, see you, perhaps.'

She gave him her number, got into her pickup and drove off with a cheery wave. He stood for a moment watching the car as it left, then put diesel in his van, feeling strangely abandoned. He pulled himself together and pushed his Dankort into the card machine.

Melissa and Magnus. And now this Nils. What was his story? Peter wondered if his family had also lived in Elev, and if he had known the other two.

The digits on the fuel pump blurred in front of his eyes as he filled up.

Kir had said that Nils's mother used to teach at Grenå School, where Kir had also been a pupil. It didn't suggest an immediate link with Elev, but that didn't mean there wasn't one.

He drove home to the cliff and used Manfred's computer to search the Net. On Yellow Pages he found two teachers living in Voldby. One was a man, Henrik Hermansen. The other was a woman called Anni Toftegaard – Nils's mother.

Three young people. Two of them killed in the same way and the third on the run. It couldn't be a coincidence.

He took a break and put the kettle on for coffee. Then he fetched his easel and paints and let his thoughts freewheel while he mixed colours and worked on a picture of the grey sea by the cliff, with seagulls circling low and two fishermen in waders fishing for sea trout.

Bella was right. The motifs he chose were limited and the colours were muted. But it was here in this narrow band of colours, which matched the life he lived, that he started to calm down. His muscles began to loosen their grip on his bones. His mind let go of its familiar orbits and soared to places he didn't normally go.

Melissa was dead. Nils was dead. His only chance was to find Magnus and speak to him, but his search had yet to produce a result. Bella was the wrong person to ask. She only gave him half-answers, even though she desperately wanted him to find her son. Bella – sweet, naive and feminine Bella – wasn't quite so naive after all. Otherwise she would never have gone to Miriam and survived Gumbo's visit without falling completely apart. He sensed that Bella had something to hide. If he wanted to know something about Magnus, it would have to be without her help.

Bella clearly hadn't had an inkling that Melissa and Magnus were in contact until Gumbo had told her. The computer had almost certainly been their lifeline. Melissa's computer was definitely in police hands, but not Magnus's. However, he wouldn't be able to access it without asking Bella.

Peter cleaned his brushes and stopped painting. He switched on Manfred's computer, went onto Facebook and searched for Magnus Albertsen. There were five different Magnus Albertsens, none with a photograph matching that of Bella's son, but there was something else. One of the Magnuses had taken a photograph of a campfire and used it as his profile picture. Peter took a chance and wrote a message:

Hi, Magnus. If you read this, I want you to know that I knew Melissa. It was me who saw the man she met outside the convent on the day she died. I know you were friends. Nils Toftegaard is dead.
I really want to help. Hope you will answer this.
Peter

He sat for a long time hoping for an answer. But it was like waiting for a voice from the grave. Nothing came and eventually he logged out and took the dog for a walk. On his return he dragged the mattress and fleece onto the balcony and they went to sleep.

46

'OK,' Anna Bagger said to the team plus Mark. 'Nils Toftegaard. What do we know?'

The board had been filled with more photographs. A young man with dark hair and dark eyebrows in a pale face stared at them. A matching photograph of a dead Nils Toftegaard hung beside it. The only similarity was the size of the two pictures. It was hard to see it was the same person. The dead boy's face was swollen and clearly marked by the brutal garrotting and the subsequent sojourn forty-five metres below the sea. It wasn't a pretty sight.

The detectives presented the results of their enquiries, one after the other. Mark listened to their descriptions of a bright, well-liked young man who achieved good grades and who, after finishing the ninth class, had hoped to go on to the *gymnasium*. The family couldn't afford other possibilities, so Nils had got a job in Kvickly to scrape together some money and get some work experience. Yes, he very much wanted to be a fisherman. The sea had attracted him, as it had done so many local lads, and his friend's father was a fisherman. On the day of his disappearance they had been down at the harbour watching the Falck divers free the propeller. Afterwards Nils had gone to work at Kvickly in Grenå, right next to the old cotton mill. He had left work when the supermarket shut at seven that evening and cycled home to Voldby. Since then no one had seen him.

'The big question is: what's the link between the two victims? Any suggestions?'

No one had any ideas. The two teenagers had grown up in different locations in East Jutland: Melissa in Elev near Aarhus;

Nils in Voldby where his mother was a teacher and his father ran an organic farm.

They debated how to proceed and allocated tasks. The lives of Nils and his family had to be gone through with a toothcomb, as always happened in murder cases. Neighbours, workmates at Kvickly, school friends and relatives had already been interviewed without any result. It was and remained a mystery where Nils had been during the twenty-four hours from the time he left Kvickly to when he was found dead in the wheelhouse of the *Marie af Grenå*.

Mark listened and made polite noises but refrained from mentioning the bones in the box and his work with Oluf Jensen. It would merely cause irritation and be viewed as an attempt to shift the focus away from more urgent matters.

In the end he slipped out, got in his car and drove to the nursing home. This time he went straight to his grandfather's room.

As before, the TV was on, but the old man looked lost in a world of his own.

'Oh, so it's you, is it?'

He muttered these words after Mark had knocked and opened the door. But he didn't add anything.

Mark sat down on a chair opposite him anyway.

'How are you, Grandad?'

His eyes were fierce.

'How do you think I am? It's a boring life being dumped here.'

'But they treat you all right, don't they?'

The old man nodded.

'As long as you do what you're told.'

Mark chuckled.

'And you don't always?'

A hand clutched the edge of the table – an aged hand with liver spots and more wrinkles than Mark could count. But it was strong, and as it held the table, the knuckles were white.

'So what do you want today?'

Mark was pleased his grandfather went straight to the point. In his childhood he had been a distant figure. His grandmother had been the centre of the family. Sometimes it was a curse the way women dominated in matters of relations, as if they had a monopoly on deep emotions. Everyone else had to tiptoe around them in the background like shadows.

He took out a list of names.

'I've tracked down the names of some local people who went missing right after the war,' he said. 'I'll tell you what this is all about first, though.'

He told him about the box and its contents.

'Today modern science gives us the opportunity to identify these bones,' he said by way of heavy-footed explanation, but it was unnecessary. It was clear his grandfather understood.

'We can't be sure the man in the box is one of the people on the list, but then again it's a possibility since these men have never been found.'

His grandfather flapped his fingers as if summoning someone.

'Show me that list. That's what you're here for, isn't it?'

'Yes,' Mark said. 'I was thinking . . .'

The old man tossed his head.

'Give it here!'

Mark reached into his pocket.

'My glasses.'

Mark looked around.

'On my bed.'

He took them from the bedside table where they lay on top of a newspaper. His grandfather put them on and ran his eyes down the list. His hands holding the sheet of paper trembled slightly.

'Harrumph.'

His grandfather emitted a variety of noises in the seconds it took him to read the names. Mark tried to interpret them. Then the old man said:

'Allan was all right. A good chum.'

'You worked together at Tirstrup?'

His grandfather nodded.

'He was forced into it, just like me. He was young and had a wife and baby to support.'

'Did you know he was a member of the Resistance?'

Mark's grandfather shrugged.

'No one knew anything for certain in those days. It was better that way.'

'Was he capable of killing, do you think?'

'We all are, if we have to.'

'But could he have been involved in liquidating collaborators?'

'I wouldn't know anything about that.'

'Do you know what he was doing at the end of the war?'

Mark asked as gently as he could. His grandfather glared at him.

'It wasn't some bloody game. Not for any of us. A few chaps had the guts to do what had to be done. If Allan was one of them, then you and I owe him a debt of gratitude.'

His eyes ran up and down the list again.

'Falk!'

The name was uttered with obvious contempt. 'Now there's someone who deserved to die.'

'Why?'

'Why? Can't you guess?'

'Did Allan do it?'

The old man started to shake. It took Mark a couple of seconds to realise that he was chortling quietly to himself.

'Kurt Falk. They called him the Cardinal. If anyone ever knew how to look after himself and his own, it was him. He made a packet from selling out.'

'Why the Cardinal?'

The heavy shoulders heaved and sank.

'I don't know. I think he might have been to Spain, but that was before my time.'

Mark wanted to ask more questions, but there was a knock at the door and the woman he had seen recently popped her head round it. Old Alma's daughter. She had come to the house in the forest when he was leaving.

'Do you want some coffee, Hans? Oh, sorry, I didn't realise you had a visitor.'

Mark stared at the woman and remembered her name: Lise Werge.

Afterwards, when he had left the nursing home without catching a glimpse of her, he remembered what his grandfather had said about her the first time: that she was a woman with secrets.

47

PETER HAD WOKEN with a burning desire and a name that drew patterns on the open sky above him.

Bella. Bella. Bella.

It was like a tumble drier with a jammed start switch. He knew she was playing on his weakness for My and damsels in distress in general. Nevertheless, he couldn't forget about her, no matter what he did. Even if he stood on his head whistling the national anthem, she was still suckered to the inside of his brain. He wasn't in love, he knew that much. It was a more dangerous cocktail: anger, the urge to protect, desire, all rolled into one.

He would think he had everything under control and then the image of her mouth would appear, supple and red as if she had been wearing lipstick and had wiped it off. She pleaded, she begged, she had no inhibitions. She drew him closer. His mind resisted, but his body went its own way.

He went to work at the convent and was well into his working day when it struck him: 20,000 kroner was far too much money for knowing about Melissa and Magnus's friendship. Gumbo must have had something on Bella herself. But what?

He deliberated for another couple of hours. During the lunch break his realisation grew so compelling that he left the work to Bronco and his brother, and drove to Gumbo's hovel in Lystrup. He couldn't talk to Bella. She would lie and look at him with tears in her eyes. With Gumbo he was on home ground.

There was no sign of life when he got there. Gumbo's battered old car was parked in a muddy puddle in front of the house. He touched the bonnet: stone cold. He opened the passenger door and

rummaged around in the glove compartment. The gun fitted nicely
into his hand. He pointed it downwards and concealed it behind his
body as he tiptoed around and cautiously looked through the
windows. For a moment, he thought the chaos looked the same as
the last time. There was a difference, though. He could see that now.
The drawers were open, and the furniture had been slashed.
Everything had been spilled onto the floor. Someone had been there
before him.

He pushed open the front door. It was unlocked and swung on
squealing hinges. The stench was unbearable but indeterminate:
pungent and sweet, bitter and acrid and nauseating, all at the same
time. He breathed through his mouth and disconnected his olfactory
senses as best he could.

'Gumbo?'

He shouted the name into the pigsty of fast-food leftovers and
empty cans and bottles. But there was no reply.

He kicked a pile of pizza boxes on the floor and they went flying.
There were still marks on the chair from the gaffer tape. Someone
had been here and freed the man, but possibly not for a better fate.

Peter fought his way through the mess and found a bedroom that
looked like a junkie's final resting place. And, as he had half-expected,
there was Gumbo, stretched out on the bed, swimming in his own
body fluids which had soaked into the mattress like some foul-
smelling soup. He was naked and his hands and feet had been tied
with gaffer tape to the corners of the bed. Someone had amused
themselves by doing exactly what Peter himself had threatened to
do: only a pool of blood remained where the dead man's genitals
had been. The killer had stuffed Gumbo's prick and balls into his
mouth, down his throat, possibly choking him in the process. Around
his mouth, where bits protruded, Gumbo's face was blood-red, as if
he had eaten raw steak and followed it up with a whole bottle of
tomato sauce. Lumps of yellow vomit were splattered across his chest
and bed and mixed with the red. Gumbo's expression was one of
sheer terror: his eyes were wide with fear, his face contorted as
though he had met the very devil himself, which possibly he had.

235

Peter suppressed the nausea in his throat and touched the body. It was almost as cold as the car bonnet had been, but the blood had yet to congeal. It couldn't have been long since Rico and his henchmen had been here. That was how it must have been: Rico had sussed that one of his debt collectors was running a little business on the side. He couldn't allow that, so Gumbo had to die, preferably in a manner that would send a message to everyone that no one went behind the boss's back and got away with it scot-free.

Peter cast a final glance at the dead man. Trying not to think about what Rico and his men would do if they came back and found him, he left Gumbo to his fate and started looking around. They had been searching for something. They had upended every item of furniture, lifted carpets, pulled out drawers and knocked over anything that moved. He went from room to room. Desperation had sent them around the whole house in much the same way. Which could mean only one thing: they hadn't found what they were after.

For a long time Peter surveyed the battlefield of wrecked furniture and junkie detritus. There couldn't be anything here – not after Rico's treatment, which made the police's ransacking methods resemble a Sunday stroll. So where? Gumbo wasn't the brightest man on the planet, but perhaps he'd had a flash of inspiration.

Peter scanned the living room, but there couldn't have been a single square centimetre that had not been examined. His gaze then floated out of the window and landed on the dealer's car. He remembered the cut-up seats and the smell of alcohol, vomit and tobacco while he had been lying in wait on the back seat. He also remembered that when the police raided his home, they had failed to inspect his van. Obviously it hadn't crossed their minds.

He left the house, went out and opened the car door. He stuck his hand into the many cracks in the seat, but found nothing apart from springs and chunks of foam. He got out again and opened the boot. That, too, was filled with junk. He tossed out a pile of pizza boxes and beer cans, pulled up the floor and had a look underneath. There was no spare tyre. In its place, however, was a black cardboard box. He lifted it out, got into his own car and opened it. It appeared Gumbo had a sideline as a photographer, because there was a pile of photographs in a folder. Peter flicked through them. The figures in the pictures were all dressed in black and wore hoodies and held baseball bats or other weapons in their hands. At first he didn't understand what or who it was. Then he recognised a face. Bella. Leaving her own front door in the darkness with what looked like a pair of bolt cutters in her hand. There were others, too. He recognised a photograph of Alice Brask cradling a baseball bat. Inside the box there was also a little black book, in which Gumbo – who, according to Bella, couldn't read or write – had laboriously entered initials and numbers in a simple and straightforward statement of his accounts.

Peter sat for a while with the box on his lap, fully aware that he was risking his life by staying here. Rico's henchmen could return at any minute.

But what was this all about? How could Gumbo blackmail women who behaved like this? Obviously they were activists of some kind. But what kind? There were no banners, no slogans, there was nothing tangible. Yet there were photographs of car number plates and of figures dressed in black milling around. And there was a date: 30 October. Perhaps this was an important piece of information, because one thing was certain: none of these women had wanted these photographs to be made public. The entries in the little black book proved that: they had all paid for Gumbo's silence.

48

THE CARDINAL. SHE had heard the name being exchanged between the old man and his grandson when she was eavesdropping outside.

Lise Werge felt her temperature rising. Another hot flush. The doctor would have to make a decision about HRT soon.

'Here we go, Hans. Brace yourself.'

She bent forward with the showerhead in her hand and checked the temperature of the water. Unlike her own temperature, which had already resulted in sweat breaking out on her back, the water was a touch cold. She adjusted it and splashed warmer water on the old man's shoulders and saw it run down his torso and into his groin. He sat naked on the plastic bench in the middle of the bathroom. It took two carers to wash him.

'Right, Hans. Nice to have a proper shower, isn't it?'

It was her colleague who asked. Hanne was so gentle and good, and she had probably never had a single wicked thought in her life. Hanne would never dream of spraying very cold or very hot water over an old man just because he had touched a sore spot.

Lise was tempted to direct a jet of cold water right into the man's face and ask him what he knew about the Cardinal, but she didn't dare. And anyway, what was the point? What was required was not a crass, vindictive act but a cool, measured approach towards a man she should be able to wind around her finger.

'It's all right,' the old man said, looking as if he hated every minute of it.

Lise understood him all too well. She had often thought she would rather kill herself than end up here at the nursing home where she worked.

Not that it was any worse than other places, but a dignified life was not what she would call it. It was storage, no more, no less. In style, but even so.

They washed Hans, dried him and got him dressed. Then they helped each other move him into his wheelchair with the hoist.

'Right, Hans. That's better, isn't it?'

Lise pushed him down to the communal lounge, where the others were sitting in their wheelchairs.

She knelt down in front of him.

'What's this I hear, Hans? Did you really use to work in Tirstrup during the war?'

The old man glowered at her. 'Why do you want to know?'

She felt skewered by his eyes even though they bore the marks of age and a life lived.

'It's exciting for those of us who never experienced it ourselves,' she lied. 'And Mark's a police officer, is that right?'

She chose a light tone of voice, as though being a police officer was the finest career imaginable. She had seen Mark driving away from her mother's house yesterday, and when she entered the kitchen she had, for once, been met by a shaken Alma. Not physically, of course – she had her nose buried in her crossword – but mentally. Her voice had quivered and her hand trembled as it held the pencil.

'They've found some bones,' she had said. 'They're asking for DNA samples. He wouldn't tell me where they found them.'

Alma had grabbed her sleeve.

'I have to know where, do you hear?'

Lise looked at the old man in the wheelchair. How much did he know? How much did she herself really know? Most of it was gleaned from conspiratorial silences and her hunches. Unlike Lone, she had never belonged to the inner circle.

'A police officer,' she repeated. 'How wonderful!'

'What's so wonderful about that?' Hans said, skewering her with his gaze once more.

She gulped. It was all about getting him started. Once Hans got going there was no shutting him up.

239

'Do you think it's true they've found some old bones from the war? I've heard some rumours.'

The old man's lips moved silently. She got up for some coffee and a slice of cake while she waited for him to thaw.

'There you are, Hans. Kringle, just the way you like it. And black coffee, isn't that right?'

He slurped his coffee and scowled at her.

'They've found a box containing some bones in the Koral Strait,' he said. 'They think the bones belong to the Cardinal.'

'The Cardinal?' she asked innocently. 'Who's that?'

He slurped his coffee again.

'A real bastard, he was. Pure evil. The devil incarnate.'

Suddenly he leaned forward and grabbed her wrist.

'He always wore a rosary around his neck. Ha! As if God was on his side.'

She had always known it was only a question of time before old scores were settled. She was a part of those scores whether she liked it or not.

The old man's hand drew her closer. She could smell his breath and felt a fine spray of saliva over her face as he said:

'So, what's your secret? I know you're hiding a secret!'

49

'WHAT HAPPENED TO Nils?'

The Facebook message appeared on the screen. Magnus had replied.

Peter's heart started to pound. He was out there. He was alive. Now it was a question of being careful. Building trust so that Magnus would agree to meet him.

He described Kir's account of the diving operation and wrote a summary of everything he knew about that side of the case. The other side, about Gumbo and Bella and the mysterious photographs, he kept to himself.

Soon afterwards he could see that Magnus had accepted his friendship.

'How do you know Nils?' Peter wrote. But nothing more came from Magnus. The connection, or the hope of it, died.

Frustrated, he sat back, glaring at the screen. Then he checked the list of Magnus's friends while his head buzzed with ideas. Most murders were not committed at random, that much he knew about police work. The killer was usually someone known to the victim. It could be a close relative, a parent or a son or a daughter. But it could also be someone different and more remote. Someone who lived on the margins.

Magnus had 205 friends. Peter clicked his way through them. He found Melissa and Nils and lots of other people, apparently of the same age. There were not many adults. Those there were appeared to be family. Bella didn't feature. Then again, which eighteen-year-old would want to be friends with their mother on Facebook? But fourteen-year-old Christian was there – Christian who had been afraid of Kaj, but who had overcome his fear.

Peter sent Christian a friend request and attached a photograph of Kaj.

He took a break from the computer and made himself a cup of coffee. It was mid-afternoon. The sight, and not least, the smell of Gumbo's dead body hadn't left him, even though he had taken a lengthy shower. He had also bought a SIM card and tipped the police off about the murder. But he had taken the liberty of removing the black cardboard box. He had to ask himself what it meant and how the photos of Bella and the other women could be relevant to the cases of the dead teenagers. Who were these women – how did they know each other?

After the coffee he took the dog out onto the cliff and let it frolic around. Then he returned to the computer. There was still nothing from Magnus. But his younger brother Christian had welcomed him into his Facebook universe.

Christian had more friends than Magnus. One of them was Anni Toftegaard, Nils's mother. Another was Alice Brask. A third was Bella.

The mothers! He took Gumbo's photographs, flicked through them and sat thinking long and hard. He had asked Magnus how he knew Nils, but had not received a reply. Now Christian had given him the answer without realising. There was a connection, which went right back. The children knew each other through their mothers – the mothers who dressed in black and carried out raids under cover of darkness.

He remembered what the head of the nursery had said about Bella, that she hadn't always had the best advisers. Was her circle of friends downright dangerous? What exactly were they doing? Perhaps he could link Gumbo's photographs to something more tangible.

He clicked onto Alice Brask's blog and read it from start to finish, but found no mention of the names Bella or Anni Toftegaard.

However, the blog was filled with opinions for and against all sorts of things. Against nitrogen emissions in agriculture, lengthy transportation of animals, breeding animals for fur, tree felling, even against wind farms, and generally against any initiative made by higher authorities with consequences for ordinary citizens.

It all made a great deal of sense but was expressed in such a sanctimonious tone that Peter was not tempted to join their flock.

Some people, though, loved being part of a group, especially when a leader emerged for them to unite behind. That was all well and good, but who was to say whether the leader always led them in the right direction? Even Alice Brask could be wrong or go too far.

If a woman like Alice Brask decided to set up a network, which wasn't just about exchanging opinions and attitudes, it could go terribly wrong, Peter thought.

He checked to see if Magnus had replied. He hadn't, so he switched the computer off.

Peter had hoped to access *FrokostBladet*'s archive, but unfortunately it wasn't online yet. He made a couple of calls and arranged a time for him to look through old newspapers on site. Then he fed the dog, took the car and drove to Aarhus, where the newspaper's concrete bunker was located in a suburb near Skanderborgvej.

At reception he paid for access to the archive. From then on it was plain sailing, and soon he was seated with coffee and cake and a screen while a helpful assistant kindly explained to him how to search for names, headlines and subjects.

He typed in the name of Alice Brask, and up they came, her articles and contributions to the newspaper with dates all the way back to the 1990s. The topics were very similar to what he had seen on her blog, but here they were explored in greater depth.

He quickly skimmed through them. There were plenty of topics. But if he was going to link Bella and Anni Toftegaard to Alice Brask, perhaps he shouldn't be looking in the articles. So he changed tack and tried with letters to the editor, columns and commentaries. There were numerous letters to the editor, both for and against Alice Brask's opinions. Some were nothing less than hate-filled. He printed a few, then kept searching. Finally, he found a letter from 2005, which was signed by a number of writers.

'Ban fur farming' was the headline and it was accompanied by a photograph of a mink in a cage, which immediately produced in his brain a series of flashbacks of all the mink that had escaped from Henrik Hansen's farm.

He read the letter, which logically and objectively outlined the conditions under which animals were bred in captivity. The signatories were able to document mistreatment and neglect, causing the animals to suffer, bite one another and themselves, and generally have miserable lives. There were also photographs and they were not for the fainthearted. The animals suffered, of that there was no doubt.

'We must put a stop to this kind of abuse in Denmark,' the letter concluded. There were five signatories. In addition to Alice Brask, who was the main signatory, there were the names of Bella and Anni Toftegaard, together with two other women, someone called Ulla Vang and a Ketty Nimb. Peter took out the black book. The initials matched. There was both a UV and a KN in Gumbo's accounts, just as there was also an AT.

He printed the letter and sat reading it and rereading it. He remembered the posters on the wall in Bella's kitchen. Bella and Anni were, together with Alice Brask, part of an animal welfare network, it seemed. Gumbo's photographs proved they might have done more than simply write about it. It seemed extreme to link this kind of action with killing teenagers, but one thing was certain: it was one way of making enemies. He knew of at least one man who would happily have seen women like these strung up from the nearest tree.

50

Kir lounged in bed. Her energy levels still hadn't returned to normal after the perilous dive and her body was struggling. Waves of exhaustion continued to wash over her, even though she'd had an hour's nap, a rare thing for her, and it irritated her beyond belief. She stared at the posters on her walls. Where others might have chosen more peaceful subjects, she had put up framed photographs of various types of mine and instructions about how to defuse them. She usually loved lying here, letting her eyes wander from one to the other, knowing that this was her job: preventing explosions.

Now there had been an explosion in her life. Her misjudgement of the dive off Læsø and the discovery of Nils as an unexpected additional passenger sat deep within her, throbbing. And in the wake of that, she thought about the incident in the harbour and her encounter with Kasper Frandsen. Mr Hyde, the man with the irascible temper. The colleague who had just got divorced.

She hadn't heard anything from Mark about how seriously the police were taking her suspicions. But the question kept rumbling around her head: was it him? Had he somehow managed to sabotage the fishing boat when he dived down to remove the net from the propeller? Perhaps he had lured Nils into meeting him somewhere after he had finished work at Kvickly. He could have killed him and clandestinely driven him back to the *Marie af Grenå* and concealed the body on board, knowing full well that Jens Bådsmand was planning to go to sea and that the boat would go down with the crew *and* the stowaway. And he might also have killed Melissa. He could have placed her body in the moat, only to turn up later in the Falck vehicle and drive away with her corpse.

She sat upright in bed and swung her legs out and into a pair of down-at-heel trainers. OK. In the clear light of day, it sounded a bit far-fetched – even to her. But then again, many of the murders that had been carried out over the years sounded improbable. Murder was often theatrical; a murder could be staged down to the last detail. It had happened before. But in Grenå?

She dragged herself into the kitchen, where she made some coffee and a cheese on rye bread sandwich. It took only a few calls to get an address in Veggerslev and ten minutes later she was out of the door with a bag over her shoulder, half a *smørrebrød* in one hand and her car keys in the other.

There was no harm in taking a look.

The house was on a bend, a small bungalow with a garage. There was a wooden fence adjoining the neighbours on both sides, and a dishevelled beech hedge obscured the view of the road. A white Volvo van was parked in the drive.

Kir pulled over fifty metres from the bend, so she had a good view of the area. She looked at her watch. It was one thirty. Now what?

She was reminded of some TV series where police officers staked out people's houses for hours and ended up falling asleep just when the action was about to kick off, with a mug of coffee and doughnuts from a nearby diner on their lap.

She might have to wait for an eternity or things might move fast. But she prepared herself for a long wait. Officially she was still on sick leave.

She switched on the radio and thought about her encounter with Peter Boutrup at the petrol station, smiling as she recalled how she had blushed when he had winked at her. Damn! She had never been able to control her blushes. It was a lifelong source of irritation, yet for some reason she felt happy about it.

She leaned back in her seat and turned up the volume when the local news came on: Fishermen were angry at SOK because of its slow response to the accident in the Kattegat, a fire in a silo on the harbour had nearly cost one man his life and a young man had been saved by a friend when he fell asleep on the railway tracks in Grenå after a night's drinking.

The time was now half past two and she was starting to doze off out of sheer boredom when she heard a car door slam in the drive. Soon afterwards an engine started and the white Volvo reversed out.

She quickly started the pickup and drove after the Volvo. She gripped the steering wheel tightly, peering ahead to see if she was following the right car. Somewhere at the back of her mind lurked the question, what was she actually hoping to achieve, but she ignored it. This was pure instinct. But it was strong. She was convinced Kasper Frandsen was guilty.

The roads were narrow and the Volvo was moving fast. Soon they had left the villages behind them: Dalstrup, Villersø, Enslev. They were driving towards Grenå, first down Kanalvej, then Mellemstrupvej. Here, they turned off down Bavnehøjvej and into the residential area in the north-western part of the town. The Volvo stopped outside a house in Jasminvej and this time she saw Kasper Frandsen's powerful frame as he slid the van door shut and walked up the garden path with familiar ease.

Another long wait ensued. She kept an eye on her watch. An hour and three quarters had passed when she decided to get out and take a look around. She walked up to the Volvo and looked in through a window, but there was nothing of any interest inside. Only a jumper on the passenger seat, otherwise nothing. She tried the handle gently, but of course the car was locked.

Then she heard voices, loud and agitated. Was that a woman screaming? It sounded as if something was being knocked over.

When she heard the door open, the sound of angry footsteps down the garden path and a man's voice, she pressed herself against the corner of the hedge. Some of the words seemed almost to quiver in the air:

'Stupid bitch! I'll kill you one of these bloody days!'

The door was slammed with a loud bang. Kasper Frandsen stormed past Kir but didn't notice her in his agitation. Shortly afterwards she heard him open the door to the Volvo, get in and speed off down the road.

Holding her breath, Kir remained pressed into the hedge for some minutes. Then she pulled herself together, went back to her pickup, got in and assessed the situation. Decision made, she returned to the house and rang the bell.

'Who is it?'

The voice sounded muffled on the other side of the door.

'Kirstine Røjel. I just wanted to . . .'

The door was opened and a woman looked out through the crack.

'Who are you?'

The words in the woman's mouth sounded slurred. And no wonder. An ugly bruise was starting to spread across the left-hand side of her face. Soon she wouldn't be able to see out of that eye.

Kir improvised:

'I was just passing and I heard a rumpus and wanted to see if I could help?'

'No, thanks.'

The woman was about to close the door, but Kir pushed against it in as friendly a manner as she could muster.

'Funny, you look like someone in need of help.'

'I . . .'

The woman didn't have the strength to push the door to. She staggered. Unbidden, Kir entered and grabbed the woman's arm.

'Here, let me help you. You shouldn't be on your own.'

Perhaps it was the military voice that did it, or perhaps the woman had just reached rock bottom. She moaned softly. Kir locked the door behind them and manoeuvred her into a well-lit living room. Now she could also see marks on the woman's throat where Kasper Frandsen had tried to strangle her. She thought about Melissa.

'What's your name?'

'Jeanette.'

'Why did he hit you, Jeanette?'

Kir stroked the woman's hair. She was shaking. Kir took a blanket from the sofa and put it around her slender shoulders. She was not much more than a girl, she thought. Twenty-five, maximum. Bleached blond hair with black roots hung in clumps around her swollen face. Her hands flapped helplessly.

'I'd kill for a cigarette.'

'I can get them for you.'

There was a tiny shake of the head and a grimace.

'I've quit.'

'How about something to drink? A cup of tea?'

'In the kitchen,' she said, sounding resigned.

Kir found what she was looking for in a neat, retro kitchen and put on the kettle. She brought in a mug of tea; Jeanette warmed her hands on it and sat for a long time inhaling the steam.

'Is he your ex?'

Jeanette nodded.

'You could take out a restraining order.'

She looked horrified.

'We can't get the police involved. He'll lose his job.'

'Surely that's not your problem? You *are* divorced, aren't you?'

'Yes, but he would go mental. As it is now, I can handle it. He doesn't come here very often. Only when he needs to let off steam about something.'

'So you've volunteered to be his punch bag?'

Kir could hear her own patronising manner and regretted it. And indeed the woman sent her a look, a reminder of just how easy it was to judge others.

'Rather me than the kids,' she said.

51

PEACE AND QUIET had descended once more upon Henrik Hansen's mink farm, which lay squashed in between two pig farms on the flat, windy terrain between the cliff and Gjerrild village. Row upon row of squat covered cages had made the farm's characteristic architecture something of a landmark, so whenever anyone asked for directions in the area they were told: 'Just drive straight towards the sea and then turn right by the mink farm . . .'

If the animals happened to value that kind of thing, they had a great view of the Kattegat, not unlike the panorama from Peter's cottage. Now they had also had a taste of freedom. It was hard to believe that only one week had passed since he and the other neighbours had helped Henrik Hansen to recapture the little creatures.

'Peter! Is that you?'

The mink farmer had a shotgun broken over his arm when he appeared from the feedhouse, the gravel crunching under his high rubber boots. He was a short, compact man with a fiery temper and hard eyes that brooked no opposition. A cap was pressed down over his forehead and temporarily hid his facial expression. Peter nodded at the weapon and held up his palms.

'Are you expecting visitors?'

'You can never be too careful. A man must be prepared to defend his property.'

They looked at each other and Henrik Hansen's face took on an embarrassed expression. They both knew what he was thinking: it was just such an act that had put Peter behind bars when uninvited visitors had forced their way into his property and shot his dog.

Henrik took out the cartridges, clicked the barrel into place and rested the gun against the wall.

'How's Ida?'

'Nice of you to ask.' The mink farmer looked tormented. 'It's the injury to her head that worries me.'

Henrik took off his cap and twisted it in his hands.

'That poor girl will never be herself again,' he said. 'No matter what the doctors say.'

Peter thought about Manfred.

'How about a cup of coffee? I think Hanne has left a flask in the kitchen.'

They went through the utility room, which was filled with filthy work clothes and footwear. Henrik's hunting dog – a Small Munsterlander – lay in a basket and gave short wags of its tail to warn them away. Four puppies were sucking at its teats. They were five weeks old.

'Why don't you get yourself a proper hunting dog?' Henrik asked.

'Are you offering me a special deal?'

Henrik kicked off his boots. Peter was about to follow suit, but Henrik's arm stopped him. 'No need. You haven't been out in the mud.'

Peter squatted down and chatted calmly to the dog, which appeared to be reassured.

'I'll give you a pup for free, as a thank you. It's good to know your neighbours are there for you when you need them.'

Peter got up and they walked from the utility room into the kitchen, where a flask was indeed hissing away.

'Have a seat.'

Henrik produced a couple of cups and poured coffee for them. Peter thought about the night when Manfred had called to tell him the mink had escaped, as part of a neighbourhood network. Everybody came to help and by dawn they had captured most of the animals. The mink had no idea what to do with their liberty and were running around the cages in confusion, hoping to find their way back to their food. They wouldn't survive in the wild.

He didn't have strong feelings about fur farming. He didn't like seeing the little creatures in captivity, but neither did he feel any bleeding-heart sentimentality for cute little furry animals, as long as they were being treated properly in their cages. He thought about the photographs he had seen in the newspaper and shuddered.

'Have they found out who did it?'

Henrik sat down, slurped his coffee and snorted.

'As if they could be bothered to waste time on this. They've got enough on their plate as it is.'

The two killings hung in the air between them.

'But how about Ida? That was a violent assault, wasn't it? Surely they take that kind of thing seriously?'

They. Peter wondered briefly at their use of language. As if the word *police* was something you didn't want to get too close to, as if they lived in a police state. But that was how it was in the country from his experience. The authorities were the Devil's Spawn, and he found it hard to disagree. Most people were of the opinion that not much good would come from getting the police mixed up in anything. People settled things among themselves. He wondered if that applied to Henrik Hansen. Would he turn vigilante on anyone who hurt his livelihood?

'They say they're looking into it,' Henrik said. 'But what do they know?'

He gestured with a hand. 'They've only been here once, and to my knowledge, they didn't even look at the graffiti those fatheads left behind.'

Peter remembered that the activists had spray-painted slogans on every available surface – 'Ban fur farming', 'Free the animals' – that kind of thing.

'What do they call themselves?'

Henrik Hansen spat out the name:

'The Animal Welfare League!'

'And you have no idea who's behind it? Locals, or outsiders?'

'It was planned down to the last detail. And there must have been a lot of them, or they wouldn't have had time to open all the cages.

I'm guessing they were outsiders, but they must have had some help from someone on the inside.'

Henrik glanced sideways at Peter and turned the coffee cup in his hands. 'Ida was on to them. She'd done some digging in the tree-hugger community. It's only three years since the last attack.'

'I didn't know that. Are you hoping that Ida will take over the farm one day?'

Henrik Hansen shrugged.

'She's twenty-five now. She's studying business and corporate finance, so that's where her interests lie. But back then she was absolutely furious. The whole family was.'

'So what did she do?'

'You've got to remember that she was young. It was probably foolish and I should have stopped her, but she tried single-handedly to infiltrate various groups.'

Peter scrutinised Hansen, whose gaze darted uneasily from the checked PVC cloth to the thermos flask and to the window, where he could see the rows of cages and just about make out the mink twisting and turning behind the wire mesh.

'Did she get anywhere?'

Henrik Hansen nodded.

'Enough for her to gain the trust of a few of them. By email, of course. I don't think they ever actually met.'

'And perhaps the others found out? Was that why Ida was given such a beating?'

Henrik Hansen heaved a long sigh over his coffee cup.

'It's tempting to think so. If they had worked out who Ida really was.'

'How did the attack occur?'

The mink farmer looked at his hands; they were calloused and had the kind of permanently dirty fingernails you get from working outdoors, no matter how much you scrub them.

'She was just lying there when I came out. In between two rows of cages. Someone had hit her with something hard – a torch, the

253

police think – and cracked open her skull. There was blood all over the place.'

The rest was history. Peter knew it well because he himself had turned up half an hour later.

'Who were they? Has Ida said anything?'

'Women.'

'Really?'

Peter's pulse shifted into a higher gear. He thought about the date in Gumbo's photographs: 30 October. It was the day they had recaptured the mink. The day before Melissa disappeared.

Henrik Hansen nodded.

'It seems to be some sort of all-woman network.'

'Young?'

'Not all of them.'

'And you don't have any names?'

Henrik Hansen shook his head. Then he looked across his coffee cup at Peter.

'Why are you suddenly so interested in this, Peter? It's not like you've got any gripes against them.'

There was the semblance of a warning in his voice, like the dog when it had wagged its tail at him earlier. Peter had his answer ready.

'Manfred fell from some scaffolding. You've heard about that, have you?'

Henrik nodded, now with some understanding in his eyes.

'Do you reckon there's a link?'

Peter shrugged.

'Manfred was one of the first to help you recapture the mink, wasn't he?'

'Yes, I called him. After what happened three years ago, the neighbourhood network was his idea. Do you really think that . . . Those bitches . . .'

'I can't be sure, Henrik. But Manfred's my friend. I would do anything to protect him.'

He must have touched a nerve because Henrik Hansen gripped his cup so hard the coffee slopped over.

'Yes, that's how it is with friends. You would do anything.'
'Perhaps I could talk to Ida?'
'I'll tell her to give you a buzz.'

The whole thing seemed absurd and out of proportion, but people had been killed for handfuls of change, so why not this?

As he drove off, Peter reflected that Henrik Hansen was right. You could never tell. Maybe a middle-aged woman was playing animal rights Superwoman in her spare time and along with other fanatics got a kick out of breaking open mink cages.

But then maybe an angry mink farmer might hit on the idea of avenging an attack on his daughter by subjecting the Superwoman's daughter to some rough treatment, or any sons and daughters of activists who came near his home and property.

Absurd, improbable. Of course. To those on the outside.

But when he reviewed the events of the last week, there seemed to be a sudden logic to it.

52

'AND YOU'RE GETTING enough sleep?'

Mark was tempted to roll his eyes, but stopped himself. When did he ever get enough sleep? It was a long time since he'd had an uninterrupted night and the previous one had been no different from the rest. He had woken up feeling feverish and with an almost infinite hatred of a body that would no longer do what he wanted.

'That's not the problem,' he said to the doctor who sat with her nose buried in his medical records. How many people had access to them? How many people could open them and read about his pathetic condition, and then gloat? There it was, written in black and white – he was a mere shell of a man who was not up to anything.

'So what is the problem?'

The female doctor didn't exactly exude empathy. But then again he could hardly expect it. He had ranted and raved at her so often out of sheer frustration with the lousy scan results and she probably hadn't forgotten that. The scans were fine now, but another problem had arisen. One she clearly knew, but appeared to have forgotten or derived a certain satisfaction by asking him to describe.

'I can't get an erection.'

He was well aware that he stated this as if it were a personal death threat to her. And she duly arched her eyebrows and looked at him and then at the computer screen behind which she was ensconced.

'Oh, yes,' she said. 'So it says.'

He guessed she was somewhere in her late thirties. She was also blonde and attractive in that cool, confident way he used to be able to match and even play up to. But at this moment all he wanted to do was slip away.

256

'And how does this manifest itself?'

If he hadn't already been sitting down, this question might well have forced him to take a seat. His anger began to seethe. *How the hell do you think, woman*, a voice inside him said, which he quickly suppressed. There was no point making an enemy of his doctor.

'As a lack of desire? Or as a purely mechanical problem?'

Seriously, was she asking him if he ever felt the desire to have sex? How could he explain to her that he felt an enormous desire to feel the desire? That his lack of desire burned holes in him as big as the ones made by his service pistol on the silhouette targets at the shooting range?

He thought about the fiasco with the hooker after Melissa's autopsy. About her thighs and her lips. About the panic which had spread through him, like the nauseating incense that had filled her room.

'Lack of desire,' he mumbled.

The doctor looked at her medical records again.

'There doesn't seem to be any physical explanation for impotence,' she said, liberating the word he hated most in the whole world. More than cancer. Or a dismissal from the force. More than an icy rejection from Anna Bagger or an ultimatum from Kir. Death would be preferable. And yet here he was.

'I'm tempted to conclude the problem is up there.'

She pointed to his head. 'But then again I'm not a sexologist,' she added.

'No.'

'How about Viagra?'

'How about it?'

'It might be worth a try . . .'

He bet her husband was a virile consultant whose dong was as hard as a pestle and who wielded it with the precision of a scalpel. Mark hated him.

'Perhaps.'

She took that as a yes and wrote a prescription and he knew he ought to have been grateful. This wasn't even her department. She was an oncologist and this was simply a routine check-up. She could have passed him up through the system.

She looked at him with something akin to tenderness as she handed him the prescription.

'And there are absolutely no situations where it returns? Where you feel . . . stirrings?'

He thought about Kir and sitting close to her on the sofa. Looking at her computer screen and talking about Mistel planes and elephant bombs. He thought about the warmth he felt inside and the stirrings, yes, there had been stirrings. But he didn't trust anything, least of all his body. It had let him down time after time. It was one big double-crosser and he was damned if he was going to take the initiative only to fail. He had done that once too often.

'Nothing significant,' he said.

The doctor rose to signal that the appointment was over.

'Try to relax a bit more,' she advised him. 'You have to get used to the fact that you're not about to die. The thought of having to live can also be scary,' she said with a wink. 'Take it easy and let the others catch criminals, if you can.'

Take it easy. If only she knew that work was the only thing that was keeping him going. And that the thought of succeeding at least in police matters was like a balm to an open sore. If he couldn't get no satisfaction, as it were, he at least wanted the satisfaction of seeing his work appreciated – in the eyes of Anna Bagger, despite her scepticism regarding the bones in the box, and in the eyes of Kir, despite her moron of a running partner.

Mark staggered out through the hospital door and felt like kicking the legs away from under an old man who was hobbling along with a Zimmer frame. But fifteen minutes later, when he pulled up in front of a house in Åbyhøj, he had calmed down. He even felt ready to confront a period of Danish history which he had never given much thought to before.

He rang the bell and a woman opened. She looked like an old lady in miniature, elegant and slim but tiny. Her eyes were friendly, analytical and very lively. Her hair was dyed a dark colour and lay like a curly cap against her head.

'Hello. Mark Bille Hansen. I called earlier.'

She held out her hand and opened the door wide.

'I'm so excited,' she said and ushered him into a comfortable living room. 'I barely slept a wink last night.'

It was the typical home of an old lady, with embroidered cushions and high-backed Rococo furniture and an old bureau. She told him to take a seat on the two-seater sofa. Set out on the table already were delicate porcelain cups decorated with a floral design and a silver thermos flask. There was also a bowl of peppermint chocolates wrapped in green paper.

She took down a framed photograph from the bureau and went over to him with it.

'He was a handsome man, wasn't he?'

It was their wedding photo. The bride was wearing a white dress down to her calves. The pleated fabric around her hips was held together by a wide ribbon.

Mark nodded. Allan Holme-Olsen was wearing a dark suit that strained against his broad shoulders. He was only twenty years old but was already a big man with a thick neck and a strong jaw. There was something steely, resolute and at the same time tender about him as he stood there gazing down at his bride. She was petite and slim, but with an abundance of life in her eyes, and a chin that jutted out stubbornly. It wasn't difficult to recognise her, even though more than sixty years had passed.

'He was the love of my life,' said Marianne Holme-Olsen, who was now a widow and lived alone in sheltered accommodation.

'But times were hard. The war was hard for everyone, especially a newly married couple with a baby. Allan hated working for the Germans, but he didn't have any choice.'

She got up and fetched a photo album.

'You wanted to know if I had any photos from the Tirstrup years. I couldn't find very many.'

Nevertheless, there were some.

'Here he is on a tractor. And here. That's the Resistance group. There were three of them.' She looked at Mark. 'This one was taken right after the war had ended.'

The three men stood shoulder to shoulder. They wore threadbare suits and looked like overgrown schoolboys. Allan was in the middle. Something in Mark reacted when he recognised the man to the far right. He turned over the picture, and there he saw the names of the three men.

Marianne Holme-Olsen pointed to another photograph.

'Here they are digging ditches in Tirstrup.'

Mark cleared his throat.

'Please can I borrow the album for a couple of days?'

'I don't suppose that would do any harm.'

The words came hesitantly as if she found it hard to let go of the past. She ran a finger across the edge of one of the stiff pages.

'And you're saying his skeleton is in a box?' she asked, and added, 'I mean, if it is him.'

Mark told her about the box, this time in more detail than over the telephone.

'Did Allan ever break his leg?'

'He got trapped under a horse-drawn cart when he was young. He limped on one leg.'

'That increases the likelihood that it's him. Our man in the box had a healed fracture of the right femur.'

He saw her eyes glow and her cheeks flush.

'It would be good to lay him to rest,' she sighed. 'It's been so many years and of course I knew his disappearance was related to the war. But knowing where he is . . . having a grave to visit . . .'

Her voice wavered: 'It would mean so much for me to have closure, before my time comes.'

Mark nodded.

'Of course. Is there any family left on his mother's side?'

'Why do you ask?'

'So we can get a DNA sample.'

'There's his cousin's daughter, Lillian. I can give you her number. Help yourself to some coffee and a chocolate in the meantime.'

She got up and returned with a dog-eared address book, its pages loose. Mark poured coffee from the thermos flask and unwrapped a mint chocolate. After some searching she eventually found the information.

'If we get a blood sample from Lillian, we can hopefully give you some certainty.'

She sipped her coffee and carefully replaced the cup on the saucer.

'That will be very strange but also a relief.'

Mark cleared his throat.

'Do you know if he knew a man they called the Cardinal?'

She closed her eyes as if sifting through her memories, but quickly opened them again.

'Do you mean Kurt Falk?'

She looked down at the black-and-white photographs. A thin parchment-like sheet separated each stiff cardboard page.

'Allan never said anything, but many of us believed that he and his colleagues killed the Cardinal after the war.'

'What do you know about Kurt Falk?'

She flicked randomly through the album.

'He was high on the list of those collaborators who had it coming to them.'

'Allan disappeared,' Mark said. 'What happened to the other members of his group?'

She shook her head and sat for a while staring vacantly ahead.

'I only know that one of them disappeared as well.'

She pointed. 'Allan thought the Cardinal was behind it.'

'Behind it in what way?'

Her eyes widened.

'They said the Cardinal disposed of his own enemies.'

'You mean he killed them?'

She nodded.

'It was something to do with his time in Spain, during the Spanish Civil War. It was common knowledge that he'd had a very secret job, reporting directly to the General.'

'The General?'

'Franco.'

Mark swallowed. Of course. It was obvious now. The Cardinal hadn't joined the Republican side, that would have been very unlike him. He had worked for the Nationalists and the army, who would hold the country in its dictatorial grip right up until the 1970s. The Cardinal. The Church's and the army's man. The new rulers' guard dog.

'So what was his job?' he asked.

A note of horror entered her voice.

'Now this might just be an old wives' tale. But Allan and his friends used to say that he had been an executioner for the Falangists, Franco's men.'

53

IT WAS LATE by the time Peter finally got home. After his visit to the mink farm he had gone to work at the convent and then over to see Jutta and the children, who were able to update him on Manfred's progress.

Jutta's eyes shone with a glow that evoked memories in him of another pair of eyes, another woman who had come back to life after a confrontation with death: Felix, who had brought him back to the land of the living by making him love again.

Where was she now?

He took the dog onto the cliff top in the moonlight and under the stars, which glittered and sparkled, some with great intensity, some less. The memory of Felix was starting to fade, he was aware of that. She had opened the world inside him and it was a brighter place now. But they'd both had to move on with their lives; that had been on the cards from the start. He thought about Kir and her crinkly smile. She and Mark Bille had had something for a while, but perhaps not any more? There might be a chance for him, if he dared.

He looked up at the sky, at Sister Beatrice's God, who might or might not be up there. You couldn't trust him, either in love or in war. He was tempted to conclude that this God knew nothing about human beings; otherwise, why take the young ones? Why let their parents raise them in the expectation and belief that they would perpetuate life on earth, only to extinguish that hope? It made no sense.

Before he went to bed, he logged onto Manfred's computer. There was still nothing from Magnus; he must have taken fright. Perhaps he thought his enemy was watching him in cyberspace. As far as Peter could see, there had been no activity on his profile. But he discovered something else. By scrolling down the list of Magnus's friends, he found a Victor Nimb and an Ea-Louise Vang. The names were too rare for them to be a coincidence. Victor and Ea-Louise had to be the son and daughter of Ketty Nimb and Ulla Vang respectively, who had both been co-signatories to the 2005 letter which Bella, Anni Toftegaard and Alice Brask had also signed as contributors.

He leaned back in his chair as everything clicked into place: this wasn't just about Magnus and Melissa and Nils. This was a network of teenagers whose mothers were friends, and possibly animal activists as well. They didn't live within physical proximity of each other, but they clearly had something in common. Perhaps their mothers had held meetings and dragged their kids along. Melissa, Magnus and Nils. And now also Victor and Ea-Louise.

According to Beatrice, Melissa had been receiving threats and unsavoury approaches since she was ten years old. He wondered if that had happened to the others. Was the note threatening Magnus from the same person? Perhaps they were all – just like Melissa – trying to deal with the threats in silence so as to protect their families. Did the mothers even know their children were being put under pressure?

Peter thought about Bella and concluded that they didn't. Until Gumbo had turned up, Bella clearly had no idea what Magnus was afraid of. She lived in a world of her own – a world she was committed to changing for the better: from stopping mink farming and agricultural pesticides to preventing the extinction of the whales. Bella wore blinkers the size of dinner plates when it came to Magnus. Were all the mothers like that? Was this a story about how children lived in one world while the mothers lived in another? Peter was tempted to think so. But where did that leave the fathers?

Melissa was dead. Magnus had run away. Nils was dead.

Peter didn't know why someone out there would want to kill the teenagers. But one thing was certain: Magnus had made a wise decision when he ran away and went into hiding. Perhaps he had also tried to persuade the others to string along. Perhaps he had tried to persuade Melissa and Victor and Ea-Louise to join him. Because he had been right. Whether this was about their mothers or about themselves, they were all in mortal danger.

He sat for a long time staring at the screen. He thought about calling Mark Bille. But what good had it done him when he volunteered the information that he had seen Melissa's murderer that day by the moat? He had found himself under attack and his house had been searched. Besides, there were his other enemies to bear in mind. They were still out there somewhere, no matter how many alarm systems he had. He had to be prepared for a backlash after his treatment of Gumbo. The question was, when and how?

He laced his fingers behind his head. The cursor kept flashing, black on white, with an almost hypnotic effect.

Going to the police with his information wasn't an option for him. He had a criminal record. Anna Bagger would probably be licking her lips if she could bang him up.

Meanwhile, the real killer could eliminate his victims, one by one.

Peter looked at his watch. It was eleven o'clock. He was bone weary and his body was still sore after the run-in with the guy outside his cottage and the collapse of the scaffolding. An assault and an accident. The rosary. The Legion. Bella and Gumbo. How was it all connected?

He blinked, but his exhaustion was too great. His eyes started to close. He did one final search on the Net and found two addresses in Aarhus, one for Ulla Vang, who was a *gymnasium* teacher and lived in Hasle, and one for Ketty Nimb, who was a nurse and lived in Tilst. Then he settled down on the balcony with the dog by his side.

Before he fell asleep, he made a mental note to call Kir soon and take a look at her house. Perhaps she would invite him in for coffee.

Now what was it she had talked about? Something about old bones and garrotting, and a Spanish method of execution . . .

He fell into a restless sleep with the dog close to him and the stars above covered by clouds while three words pounded inside his head: *'Viva la Muerte, Viva la Muerte.'*

Long live death.

54

KIR WENT OUT with Morten for another run.

It was a pleasure to have him plodding alongside her in the morning air, heavy and stable and reliable.

This was how it should be, she thought, as they cut a corner and temporarily found themselves on the verge. Her life could have panned out like this if she had made slightly different choices. A life with Morten?

In theory it could have been them. In theory they could have shared a life.

All of this, though, was only a sign that she missed someone to share her life with. She was thirty-two years old. She was a mine diver, but she was also a woman and she very much wanted a family. Mark had opted for a truce. Peter wasn't interested; otherwise he would probably have called about her summer house. So what was so wrong in shining her spotlight on someone else?

The only problem was that she wasn't in love with Morten. Perhaps she was no longer in love with Mark, either. She barely knew what she was, except restless.

'You're one hell of a runner,' Morten laughed as he panted at her side. 'I guess I'm making the coffee yet again.'

'Are you sure you haven't just become very slow?'

'Slow? Who, me?'

She was aware that he put in every ounce of strength he had. And, for a couple of seconds, they were neck and neck before she left him standing, but then she throttled back to enjoy their companionship. Her fitness was starting to return after her session in the pressure chamber and she could feel she had to make a conscious effort not to humiliate him totally. He wasn't in bad shape, she thought, but it was a different class to her speed and stamina. She couldn't match him in terms of muscles. And he attacked the hills in Polderev Plantation with the obduracy of a tank on a battlefield. He wasn't the type to quit, he was something else. He was the type she could trust.

'Did you know that Kasper beats his ex?'

'No. Who told you that?'

'She did.'

It felt a bit embarrassing to have to admit that she had performed her own stake-out with no back-up. But she had to share the story with someone. Mark was nowhere to be found – he was probably hunting down potential family members of the guy in the bone box – and Morten knew Kasper Frandsen, who was gradually becoming her prime suspect. Besides, she had plans for Morten.

'I can't say that I'm surprised,' he wheezed alongside her. 'But should you really be going around spying on people like that? If he can beat her up, he can also beat others up.'

She was touched by his concern.

'I can take care of myself,' she said. 'Besides, Jeanette is my new best friend. I'm visiting her again today.'

'Watch your back, Kir. Don't get involved in other people's private business,' Morten warned. 'And you know what they say: battered wives always go back to their husbands.'

'He's a bastard.'

'What else has he done? Apart from irritating you professionally and beating up his ex?'

'I think it's him,' she said as they crossed the road and continued down towards her summer house. 'I need to know more about him. But I think he's the killer.'

They had reached her home. As per their agreement, Morten started making coffee. He brewed it in silence, then he turned to her.

'These are very serious accusations, Kir.'

'I know. I haven't told anyone else. For now it's between you and me.'

'But, for Christ's sake . . . the man might be a fool. But a killer?'

Morten pressed the plunger of the cafetière as he said the word. 'Now that's a totally different thing. Do you have any evidence at all?'

She held his eyes. He was nice and she liked him. But, in common with most people, he just wanted to think the best of others. Only she had learned the opposite. She had learned there was rarely smoke without fire and it paid off to follow your gut instinct, at least to some extent.

'I need to know what other secrets he's hiding.'

Morten was a practical man.

'How exactly are you going to do that?'

'I have to get inside his house.'

He rolled his eyes at the ceiling in exasperation.

'Just listen to yourself, Kir! You can't just break into people's homes. It's a criminal offence, woman!'

'Of course it is.'

'Why don't you ask your police friend? Can't he get a – what's it called?'

'A warrant?'

She sipped her coffee. 'It won't work. There's not enough evidence. No judge would ever grant a warrant because some mine diver had a vague hunch and because the guy beat up his ex.'

'So what are you going to do?'

She weighed up the pros and cons. She had told him as much as she thought she could without compromising the case, but only because she had needed his help. She had made up her mind after going to Jeanette's house, where her suspicions had been confirmed when Frandsen's ex-wife had held a hand over her bruised neck after the attempted strangulation.

'He loves taking it right to the limit, and when we have sex,' she had said and looked at Kir with terror in her eyes. 'I've passed out several times after he has handcuffed me and tightened that sodding neck ring.'

From that moment Kir had been itching to put paid to Kasper Frandsen's activities. She still was.

'I need to know when he isn't going to be there,' she said to Morten. 'Two hours is all I need. Plus someone who'll ring me if he unexpectedly decides to return home.'

'Return? Where from?'

Caution had crept into Morten's voice. She couldn't blame him.

'From an evening out with an old mate, who rings up and suggests they go for a beer,' she said.

He held up both hands in a defensive gesture.

'Forget it!'

'Please.'

He shook his head.

'This is not going to happen.'

'You won't get into any trouble, Morten. If anything goes wrong, on my head be it. All you have to do is call Kasper and say: "Hi, I saw you in the street the other day and wondered if you fancied going for a beer . . ." How hard can that be?'

'You're out of your bloody mind, Kir. Crazy.'

'OK, so I'm crazy. But help me. Just this once.'

He began to laugh. That was better. A sign that he was softening. She put her hand on his arm and gave him the best doe-eyed look she could muster.

'This is important to me, Morten.'

She saw doubt and resistance and something she couldn't fathom in his gaze.

'OK,' he said. 'On your head be it.'

55

'MARK BILLE HANSEN,' the chemist called out.

She was young and looked stern in a sexy way, with horn-rimmed glasses, a bob and a serious face. The white coat gave her an authority which, under more private circumstances and in another life, would have made him want to tear it off her.

For now he restricted himself to shuffling up to the counter with his jacket collar pulled up and his hands in his pockets. He had deliberately avoided the chemist in Grenå where everyone knew who he was. Here, at Store Torv in Aarhus, he had some degree of anonymity. Or at least he had until they shouted out his name.

'Viagra!' said the woman who looked more like a girl. She was around twenty-five, he guessed. Did she even know what the little blue pills were for?

It appeared she did. She leaned over the counter towards him – slim waist, small, shapely breasts and a low-cut T-shirt under her coat – and opened the packet very carefully with a lot of rustling. Slowly. She had well-manicured nails, not too long, with a neutral polish. She was a girl who wanted to be taken seriously. A diamond solitaire ring flashed on her finger.

'Have you taken them before?'

Her voice blared out as if from a megaphone. He should have said yes, but he was too slow; of its own accord, his head shook from side to side.

'No.'

It was a mistake, of course, which he realised immediately. She launched into a lengthy explanation and at a decibel level that suggested she considered him to be hard of hearing. He became acutely conscious of the other customers in the chemist's. When he entered there had been only a few. Now the place had filled up and they stood close behind him. He was sweating. The young woman's mouth was going twenty to the dozen and words were pouring out that he barely registered. Until she finally folded the leaflet, slipped it back inside the packet, closed it and dropped it into a bag. He paid for it with his Dankort card.

'Good luck with it all,' she called out after him as he left.

Thirty minutes later, but still feeling dazed, he knocked on the door to Oluf Jensen's office at Aarhus police station.

'Do come in, Mark.'

Mark was half-expecting his colleague's X-ray vision to penetrate the chemist's bag and exclaim with the same voice of authority as the assistant at the chemist's:

'Viagra! Have you taken them before?'

But instead Oluf Jensen said:

'I'm so glad you're here!'

He looked like a prospector on the trail of gold. His eyes sparkled with excitement. He leaned across the desk with his whole body, his hands fluttering in the air, obviously missing a pipe stem and a bowl of tobacco to cling onto.

'I've got IT on the job,' he said to Mark.

'Doing what?'

'More background research, looking at old police reports and newspaper articles. My nose . . .'

He rubbed his nose with his thumb and forefinger. 'My nose tells me we're on the right track.'

He tilted his head to one side and looked at Mark.

'We've been too rigid in our thinking. Because we have an approximate dating of the bones, we've been concentrating on the years following the war.'

He flung out his hand.

'Now that might have seemed an obvious place to start, in the light of all the scores being settled in the post-war period.'

'Are you saying we have to go even further back?'

Mark had lost perspective of time. He found it hard enough to keep a perspective of his own life.

'Of course. It was you who gave me the idea,' Oluf Jensen said.

Did he? As they had agreed, Mark had contacted Oluf Jensen every day. He had also called him to report on his meeting with Marianne Holme-Olsen. And, yes, she had mentioned the rumours about the Cardinal, as he was known. But Mark hadn't taken them very seriously. Perhaps he had been too focused on the photographs she had lent him, which he had studied all night until his eyes closed from exhaustion. And on the meeting with the doctor and the prescription she had given him.

'You told me about the Cardinal,' Oluf Jensen said. 'A Kurt Falk . . .'

'Yes, he doesn't sound like someone you'd want to meet at night down a dark alleyway . . .'

'. . . working for Franco during the Spanish Civil War, according to the rumours.'

'Yes, that's the point. Just rumours.'

'But surely there must be a way to verify them. You said his daughter was fairly uncooperative?'

'Very.'

Mark had a flashback of the old woman with her crossword on the greasy kitchen cloth. Her tortoise neck and tiny, peering eyes.

'Perhaps another family member would be more helpful?' Oluf Jensen suggested.

'There is a granddaughter,' Mark said tentatively as he remembered his grandfather saying: *She's nice enough. But she has secrets.*

'Why don't you try to get in touch with her? Find out what she knows about her family history? Who knows, you might get a lucky break.'

'Possibly . . .'

The words buzzed around in his head. Now what was it Marianne Holme-Olsen had said about the rumour that the Cardinal had been an executioner?

273

'The garrotte,' he said. 'It was still used in those days, wasn't it? If he was an executioner, then he must have used one.'

Oluf Jensen nodded. Mark continued. The Viagra and the old photographs vanished from his mind.

'He would have known how it worked, inside out.'

'He was a skilled craftsman,' Oluf Jensen added.

His colleague had started doodling, as he invariably did: a horizontal board; a vertical one. A matchstick man on a hard seat. Arms and legs shackled. An iron ring around the man's neck and a clamp at the back which could be tightened to force the spike into the victim's neck.

'He could have brought it home with him from Spain,' Mark said.

'It would have been something of a monster to transport up through Europe,' his colleague said.

Oluf Jensen drew the executioner. Another matchstick man. This one had a firm grip on the clamp. Mark could almost visualise the scene. He could smell the fear and the panic. He could feel the iron ring tightening and see the arms and legs jerking.

He met his colleague's intent gaze. Oluf Jensen was the executioner who kept tightening the clamp until the insight finally came:

'He could have built one himself,' Mark said.

56

TIME WAS RUNNING out.

Peter's thoughts were running riot as he drove towards Aarhus in his van.

It was already too late for Melissa and Nils. Magnus was on the run. Finding the other two whose mothers had signed the letter to the editor was now a matter of life and death.

Ulla Vang lived in a residential suburb of Hasle. She and her husband both taught at Aarhus Statsgymnasium in Fenrisvej.

Ketty Nimb lived in Tilst in an old farmhouse in dire need of a loving hand. She was divorced and worked as a nurse at Skejby Hospital.

Peter located the houses of both women and subsequently worked out where their children were likely to go to school. Ea-Louise Vang probably went to the Statsgymnasium where her parents worked, Victor Nimb perhaps to Langkjær Gymnasium. Peter decided to start in Hasle. Outside the main entrance to the school some girls told him which class Ea-Louise was in. They gave him directions to the classroom. After wandering up and down some corridors and asking a few more questions, he finally found it. But when he asked about Ea-Louise, a girl with curly hair shook her head.

'She hasn't been to school for a couple of days.'

'Is she ill?'

The girl shrugged.

'It's hard for her to skive off. Especially with her parents.'

She said this with sympathy in her voice.

'So she really is ill?'

'Might be. But why don't you ask Ulla? She would know. She's just coming . . .'

Peter looked up. Before he had time to say anything, the girl called out to the teacher just entering the classroom:

'Hi, Ulla! There's a guy here looking for Ea-Louise.'

They looked at each other for a split second. Enough time for Peter to register a woman who could have been beautiful, if it hadn't been for her ashen face and taut features which signalled a state bordering on panic. She was thin and looked as if she was cold; perhaps that was why she had buttoned a long black cardigan all the way up to her neck. Her hand shot up to the top button at the mention of Ea-Louise's name.

'She's been gone since the day before yesterday,' Ulla Vang said as they sat in the head teacher's office a few minutes later, after Peter had explained his connection with Bella.

Jens Vang had joined them. He was an athletic man in his forties. Peter could visualise him with a football whistle in his mouth, holding up a red card.

'We're going out of our minds with worry,' Jens said.

'Why haven't you contacted the police?'

Ulla Vang's eyes flitted nervously. Her explanation sounded like an echo of Bella's.

'The girl *is* eighteen. Besides, she's sent us a postcard.'

Her eyes clung to Peter's for reassurance. Jens Vang took her hand.

'They make their own decisions at that age,' he said.

'We were hoping it was just a phase,' Ulla said, freeing herself from her husband's hand. 'Normally she's a responsible girl. Mature for her age.'

'Ea-Louise knows Bella's son, Magnus,' Peter said. 'Could she be with him?'

The parents looked at each other. They clearly knew nothing. Peter decided to try another approach.

'Melissa's dead. Nils Toftegaard is dead.'

Ulla Vang looked like a corpse in a sitting position. She nodded vacantly.

'We heard. It's awful. But . . .'

'Has it occurred to you that these killings might be connected?'

They looked at each other. A horizontal frown appeared on Jens Vang's forehead.

'But Nils drowned. This is completely different. And the others . . . They didn't really know each other . . .'

'They're all friends on Facebook.'

Ulla dismissed the suggestion.

'So many of them are. That doesn't necessarily mean that they're friends in real life.'

Jens shook his head. 'It must be a coincidence.'

'Nils didn't drown,' said Peter, knowing he was breaking every rule now. But, as he sat there in the head teacher's office, the truth finally dawned on him: he was the only one who knew of the link between the teenagers. No one else, neither their parents nor the police, had joined the dots yet.

'Nils was garrotted. Exactly like Melissa.'

A few seconds passed. Peter looked at their faces and he saw the change. Anger in the husband. A ferment of emotions in his wife.

He produced the letter to the editor from his pocket and unfolded it on the table. They stared at it, confusion written all over their faces.

'I could be wrong, but this is what I think,' Peter said. 'When you wrote this, you pissed someone off big time.'

He tapped his fingers lightly on the paper. 'But I don't think you stopped at writing letters.'

He looked at Ulla, whose face went scarlet. Jens also looked at her. Peter stuck his hand in his jacket pocket. One by one, he produced Gumbo's photographs and spread them over the table in front of them.

'Ulla?' her husband said. 'What's all this about?'

She said nothing but sat with her lips pressed together, staring into space. Peter continued:

'At some point, you went from word to deed. Am I right?'
No reaction.

'Words were no longer enough, didn't really get the point across. Your letter was printed, but it didn't change anything. Then Alice Brask had an idea. Time to go to the barricades. Time to go out and fight, rather than just sit behind a computer. Am I right?'

Ulla Vang opened her mouth but no words came out. She cleared her throat and tried to find her voice. There was defensiveness in her eyes, Peter could see. Protest, even. And when she finally spoke, there was no sign of regret.

'Who do you think you are?' she said. 'You come here and slander us with half-lies and half-truths. What gives you the right to do that? Are you a police officer?'

'Ulla!'

Her husband put his hand on hers again. She shook it off.

'Ea-Louise just left. She'll come back. She's mature and sensible. Don't you dare come here and try to frighten us.'

'You planned and executed raids on mink farms and shops selling furs,' Peter said. 'You went beyond the law. You hurt someone's business. You made enemies.'

'Is this true, Ulla?'

Her husband was looking more and more confused.

'You sneaked out during the night in your black clothing and opened mink cages and sprayed slogans and beat a girl half to death.'

'Ulla! Say something!' Jens Vang was practically shouting.

She snarled into his face.

'So? This has got nothing to do with anything else! We only do what we think is right.'

'But you can't . . .'

Jens Vang's face contorted in anger. His eyes welled up. 'That Brask cow,' he said. 'I knew she was bad news from the start.'

His wife stared at him as if he hadn't understood a thing.

'What would you know about fighting for what you believe, about the feeling of making a difference? The only place you do anything heroic is on the football pitch.'

Jens Vang threw his arms in the air.

'Heroic? Making a difference? Tell me, have you gone completely mad? There's a difference between expressing your opinions and breaking the law. Hasn't that occurred to you?'

'Animals are suffering!'

'They may well be. But there are other ways. Pressure. Demos . . .'

He pointed to the letter to the editor: 'The pen is mightier than the sword. Democratic methods!'

He was starting to sound more and more desperate. She glowered at him.

'But it doesn't bloody work. Democracy is a pile of overrated shit! It doesn't get you anywhere.'

Jens Vang looked stunned, as if he had been the victim of a dirty tackle.

'Nevertheless . . .' he finally stuttered. 'You still have to try. Otherwise you're no better than them.'

He asked quietly: 'Is it true that you beat up a girl?'

'It was her own fault. She was a spy,' Ulla Vang said in an agitated voice. 'She was trying to infiltrate us!'

Peter observed the quarrel for a little while. This wasn't helping him at all. It wasn't helping anyone.

He got up and left.

57

THE DEVIL INCARNATE.

Lise Werge let herself into the Woodland Snail. It was one o'clock in the afternoon and her mother was having a midday nap. This was her strict routine. You could set your watch by Alma's snoring. She heard it the moment she stepped inside.

The Devil incarnate was how old Hans, the police officer's grandfather, had referred to the Cardinal. What did that make her – second-generation Devil's Spawn? What and where you come from – how much did that really mean? Were you forever imprinted with the same stamp as your fathers and ancestors, or did it stop at some point? Did the line quite simply come to an end, so that you could be liberated?

Old Hans had had no doubts. She could still feel his grip on her wrist and smell his breath by her face:

So what's your secret?

If he only knew.

She tiptoed through the kitchen where a newspaper lay open at the crossword and a solitary coffee cup was left behind after the morning ritual. She looked in the bread bin. Her mother's vast appetite had made deep inroads into the loaf Lise had brought the day before. Much too deep. But Alma never had visitors. At least, not the kind other people had.

Lise slumped on her mother's chair and flicked randomly through the newspaper. Then she got up and walked through the house, touching the heavy furniture as if it could tell her the truth; she glanced at the countless knick-knacks placed on window sills and shelves, her heels sinking into the soft carpet. She opened the curtains in an attempt to entice the light inside, but to her it seemed just as dark, as though the sun couldn't really find its way in. Dark and heavy and oppressive, like the memories rumbling around deep inside her.

She went to the staircase. There was a portrait of her grandfather on the wall. The resemblance between her mother and herself had always frightened her. The tortoise neck was thick and short. The face square and creased, even in this picture, which was supposedly from his youth. But the most disturbing feature was the eyes. They looked out at her, cold and penetrating. They were her mother's eyes when she told her off. They were her own eyes when no one was looking. When she washed old Hans and felt a deep urge to scald him with the shower.

She started climbing the stairs. It was ages since she had been on the first floor. A cleaner came every now and then, but most of the time her mother coped on her own. No one was allowed upstairs. Nor was anyone allowed access to the basement. Mere mortals were allowed on the ground floor only; all other areas were strictly out of bounds.

But today Lise decided to ignore the rules. Her heart was pounding. She felt she was just what she used to be; a little girl snooping in places where she was not allowed. An inquisitive little girl who knew nothing about the evils of this world.

That had soon changed.

She opened the doors to each of the three bedrooms. But they were empty and the made-up beds stood ready, awaiting new guests like a Hotel of Evil.

Then she caught sight of a hatch to the attic and remembered what Lone had said. That the last draft was up there. The history which Alma had dictated, first to Lone and then to Lise. The story she hated and feared.

There was a ladder to the attic. She climbed up and then stopped for a moment while making up her mind. Down below, she could still hear Alma's snores, vibrating through the house.

She flipped aside the hatch and clambered inside. Her eyes had to acclimatise to the light seeping in through the cracks.

Then she saw the furniture: a mattress, a small table and a chair.

Her skin tingled with fear. There was a crust of bread and some cheese on the table. There was also a knife. And something else.

She looked around, into the darkness. She wanted to utter a name but it got stuck in her throat. She walked across to the table. On it lay an old exercise book like the ones they'd had in school. It was open. She recognised Lone's handwriting. She looked around furtively. Then she stuffed the exercise book down the waistband of her skirt and buttoned her cardigan over it.

For a long time she stood there holding her breath, expecting to hear something. A rustle. A cough. Something. But nothing came. He wasn't there.

She climbed down the ladder and closed the hatch. Then she went downstairs and sat in the kitchen until her mother appeared.

'What are you doing here?'

Alma was far from pleased. She sniffed the air. Lise was annoyed with herself for putting on perfume that morning. Her mother had a very acute sense of smell. Now her nostrils were flared like a dog's. Alma walked from the kitchen into the living room and saw the open curtains. Lise followed her as she walked to the stairs, stopped and looked up.

'You've been upstairs.'

'Yes, Mum.'

'Where else have you been?'

'In the attic.'

Alma spun around. She was agile for her age and size. An arm shot out. Lise took a step backwards. She looked at her mother, whom she hated. Like she hated all of her accursed family because it was such a big part of her and because she couldn't escape it.

'He's out. You're hiding him. You've been hiding him all this time.'

'Nonsense!'

Alma pushed her out of the way and waddled back to her kitchen. Lise followed her.

'Why haven't I been told? I have a right to know. He's dangerous!'

'I can control him,' her mother said without turning.

'Where is he? It was him, wasn't it?'

'Him? What do you mean?'

'The girl in the moat.'

Alma shook her head.

'Rubbish. He wouldn't hurt a fly.'

'Where is he?'

'Not here.'

'Then where?'

There was no reply. Her mother's face had closed. She sat down and stared at her crossword. The body withdrew into itself.

Lise had only one ace left to play. She felt impotent, but she had to play it.

'I know where they found those bones,' she said.

Her mother was like a stone which had suddenly come to life. Everything about her started to move. The head shot out of its tortoise carapace and stretched on the neck towards her. The hands lowered the newspaper. The heavy body leaned across the table.

'Where?'

For once Lise resisted the pressure. For once she disobeyed an order and responded with an unyielding stare.

'First you tell me where he is.'

'I don't know. He has somewhere else.'

'Where?'

'With a friend, I think.'

'Did he escape?'

Alma looked at her with a thinly veiled smile of triumph.

'They let him out. The doctors think he's cured.'

Cured. The word reverberated inside Lise's head. It bounced from wall to wall inside her skull, giving her an instant headache.

'He'll never be cured. He's just faking it,' she said.

'Where did they find those bones?'

'In a box at the bottom of the Koral Strait. By Kalø Bay.'

Her mother sprang to her feet and half-pulled the tablecloth off the table, followed by the coffee cup. She glared at Lise, and for once her voice was trembling:

'Don't you tell anyone he's out. Not a living soul, do you hear?'

58

PETER DROVE HOME from the meeting with the Vangs. As he drove, he tried to analyse his anger.

There was nothing at all wrong with having strong beliefs; he had to keep telling himself that. The mothers of the beleaguered teenagers were in that category: women with opinions. Women who fought for certain causes. Yes, they were also activists and yes, they were breaking the law. But it was not a law of nature that their children should therefore be persecuted by an avenging murderer. No one could have predicted that.

Even so, he was angry. He directed his anger where it belonged: at his own mother. Her actions had given him an Achilles heel, he was painfully aware of that. Parents failing their children made him angry. Full stop. And these parents had failed their teenage children. Not because they fought for their causes, but because they hadn't been attentive. They hadn't seen that their children were frightened and inadequately protected.

He turned off by Gjerrild and let the countryside filter in and soften him, lessening his anger until it became a weak undercurrent. Here were fields, a mink farm and pig farms. Here was the cliff and the Kattegat by the northern corner of Djursland, where tankers rode the waves. Here was everything that usually made him feel calm.

The lane wound its way towards the cliff and the cottage where his dog was waiting. He searched for the calm and the peace and the feeling of freedom, but it all seemed beyond reach, like mirages shimmering in the air.

He thought about Victor and Ea-Louise. He only hoped they

were with Magnus. Clever, capable Magnus, who was somewhere out there clinging to life by his fingertips. But for how long? How long until he also ended up on this madman's garrotte?

After Hasle he had driven to Skejby Hospital. There he had met a carbon copy of Ea-Louise's parents, in the singular, because Ketty Nimb was a single parent with two children. Victor had been gone for two days now. He had sent her a postcard. He had turned eighteen. You couldn't control them once they were of age, could you?

Peter had just returned to his house on the cliff and was about to switch off the engine and take the dog for a walk when his mobile rang.

'My name is Anders Klein. I'm the manager of the Brugsen supermarket in Fjellerup by the camp site . . .'

'Yes?'

'You put up a kind of missing person notice, about a boy called Magnus?'

'Have you seen him?'

'He was here yesterday. I'm fairly sure it was him.'

If he found Magnus, he might also be able to find Victor and Ea-Louise.

'Was he alone?'

'He was with a young woman.'

'You're sure there weren't three of them?'

There was a small pause, then the man said:

'They seemed very confused. They left behind a rucksack with some clothes in. I still have it.'

'OK. I'll be there in fifteen minutes.'

Most people would probably have preferred Fjellerup Beach on a beautiful summer's day with the sun baking the sand dunes.

Today wasn't one of those days. Today, the sand was airborne, helped on its way by a sharp northerly wind. The air was full of stinging drops of seawater and the lyme grass rose like a toupee from a bald pate. Peter was reminded of this image when he stepped inside the supermarket to meet Anders Klein as they had arranged. He was anything but *klein*, small, that is, and tufts of a blond comb-over clung to his egg-shaped head.

'They appeared at around four o'clock yesterday afternoon,' the Brugsen manager said. 'I was here on my own. There's not much business at this time of the year. They bought some packets of soup and milk.'

'Did they say anything?' Peter asked.

'Nothing. On the contrary, they were very quiet. They looked as if . . . Well, as if they didn't know quite what to do.'

'How did they pay?'

'Cash. He paid. The girl offered, but he insisted.'

'Anything else?'

The man handed Peter the rucksack. It was a small, blue Fjällräven model. A single glance told Peter it didn't belong to Magnus. Bella had said he had taken his scout rucksack with him. No matter how confused you were, you didn't take two rucksacks if you were hoping to survive in the wild. It made no sense. You could only carry one at a time.

A quick look at the contents of the rucksack told him that the clothes didn't belong to a girl.

Peter nodded to Anders Klein.

'And you're quite sure there wasn't a third person? On his own?'

'Yes, I'm quite sure. I would have remembered. As I said, not much happens at this time of year.'

Peter nodded by way of thanks as he left. When he reached his car, he drove down to the beach, let the dog out and gave him a jumper to sniff from the rucksack.

'Search, Kaj!'

The dog stood still for a moment as if he had no idea what to do. The wind was blowing from every direction. Sand and seawater mixed in the air. Peter knew it was a very slim chance, but it had to be tried.

'Search!'

Kaj regarded him, unconvinced. Then he padded first in one direction, then in another, until he suddenly seemed to make up his mind and move inland, up towards the dunes.

Peter followed. The dog grew increasingly agitated. Then he started to whine.

It crossed his mind that if they found what he thought they would find, a lot would change. He wouldn't be able to continue on his own. Not that he could, anyway. Who did he actually think he was, some kind of self-appointed avenger and protector?

Help us, Peter. You help yourself.

He hadn't helped anyone. On the contrary. If he could have persuaded Sister Beatrice to go to the police, things would have looked very different now.

The dog barked. From a distance, Peter could see sand being sprayed into the air and Kaj's tail swishing from side to side as if he was digging into a fox's earth.

'No, Kaj! That's enough!'

The movements stopped. Peter plodded up the dune. At first he thought it might be an animal, possibly a fleeing deer smashed to pulp by a car. But then he saw that the gory mess was a human being. Some protruding flesh turned out to be a hand. A foot was just a clump of blood. But the worst was the face: the nose was missing and a crater in one cheek was so deep that he could see the white cheekbone and half the teeth.

The dog looked anxiously at Peter and whined.

'Sit, Kaj.'

He crept close to Peter's left leg. Peter took out his mobile and entered Mark Bille Hansen's number.

Peter looked at his watch. It was four thirty. He sat down on the sand and waited. His mobile rang soon afterwards, but his first reaction was to ignore it. Bad news rarely came alone. But the ringing was insistent and he answered the phone to stop the noise.

'Peter.'

'Peter, Ida here.'

He had to turn the name over in his mind to remember who she was. His visit to the mink farm seemed like the distant past.

'My dad told me you came to see him.'

'Oh yes?'

His reply came slowly. He tried to pull himself together.

'How are you, Ida? I was sorry to hear about the brutal attack.'

'Oh, my dad's exaggerating. I'm all right. Listen. I have some information for you, or the police, or whoever needs to know. I don't want to go it alone any more.'

He couldn't take any more information. Or any more people who wanted him to do something that had nothing to do with him. Nonetheless, he said:

'OK. What have you got?'

He listened to how, through patience and ingenuity, she had managed to contact a group of women activists online and what she now knew about their forthcoming actions.

'And you're quite sure this isn't a hoax?'

'Quite sure.'

'They suspect you're a spy,' Peter said. 'You do know that, don't you?'

'Take it easy. My source is reliable.'

'But how . . .?'

Ida laughed modestly.

'Let's just say I'm good with computers. My boyfriend is an IT nerd.'

Ida the hacker. Peter had to shake his head to get the image to fit. But she sounded convincing. He hoped her tone had rubbed off on him a bit when soon afterwards he heard sirens and steeled himself to tell Mark Bille about the forthcoming raid.

59

'I HOPE THE intelligence from your spy is sound. Otherwise, you'll be in trouble.'

Mark delivered his rant and looked at his watch. It was midnight. He wished the moon would go in, but there it hung, pale and insistent. He hoped it wouldn't give away their positions, or those of the two other teams from Grenå police who were on duty on this windblown, icy November night. Even the cloud cover had failed them.

'I've got enough trouble as it is,' said the man next to him.

Mark nodded in the dusk. It was nine hours since he had arrived at Fjellerup and had found the body of Victor Nimb in the dunes and a taciturn Peter Boutrup and his dog. Now they were sitting in Mark's police car with the windows rolled down so that they could hear anyone coming. It was parked behind some bushes.

They sat for a while in silence. Then Peter asked:

'Had he been garrotted?'

Mark nodded.

'It looks like it.'

'Then the rest must have been a fox or a dog?'

'We presume so, but the autopsy will tell us.'

He turned to Peter. 'Your dog wouldn't have had time to do it, would it?'

Peter shook his head.

'No, he didn't touch the body. And he didn't have blood around his mouth, either.'

'Then it must have been a fox,' Mark concluded.

Once he had been called to a case where a dog was on its own with its dead owner. It was the most disfigured corpse he had ever seen, but the body in the dunes came a close second.

Peter Boutrup touched his arm.

'Listen.'

Mark heard the faint sound of a car approaching. Then another one. He spoke into the police radio.

'We have lift-off. Now remember. We need to catch them with tools in their hands and mink shit on their boots. Nobody move until I say so.'

An affirmative came back from the other two teams. Working with the owner of the mink farm – it was his second visitation by activists this year – they had put up 100-watt lamps at either end of the cages and concealed two further police vehicles on the property. Eight colleagues were ready to apprehend the black-clad activists.

The activists – if indeed it was them – drove carefully and without lights. Mark heard the engines being turned off about a hundred metres away. And then they heard something else: four thousand mink stirring anxiously inside their wire cages.

In the few seconds that passed, Mark thought back to the afternoon. Images flickered past his eyes: the dead boy in the dune. Boutrup and his dog keeping watch by the body, so that they could barely get to it. Anna Bagger's arrival, along with the CSOs and the pathologist, Sara Dreyer. Anna's questioning of Boutrup and his subsequent account of the network of women he suspected: activists who set mink free. A cause Mark had some sympathy for, but which possibly had a connection with the killings.

And that was why they had staged this ambush, hoping to catch the women, like cowboys ambushing a herd of cattle. Bit of a long shot, one might justifiably say. But they had nothing and needed even a minor breakthrough, which was why Anna Bagger had agreed to let them go ahead.

'In a way I understand them,' Mark said as they waited, listening for footsteps in the darkness. 'Life in a cage is no life at all.'

Peter Boutrup sighed out loud.

'But that's not what this is about.'

'So you say. But if they know there might be a connection between the killings and the mink, why didn't they call off tonight's raid?'

'Perhaps because they don't accept that there *is* a connection,' Peter said. 'Perhaps because it was too late to cancel. I imagine a raid like this takes careful planning.'

Or perhaps because the two things really did have absolutely nothing to do with each other, Mark thought, but instead he said:

'Here they come.'

They fell silent and listened. The footsteps were almost noiseless and they were approaching at speed. Mark wondered how many there were. On Henrik Hansen's mink farm they had released half of his six thousand mink and the cages had been opened with bolt cutters. That kind of thing took time. He guessed there were at least ten; twice as many as Peter Boutrup could name.

He froze. Peter yanked his arm. They were here. He could see the figures dressed in black now and prayed they wouldn't spot the cars. Then he heard the sound of bolt cutters going into action and cages creaking as they were forced open.

He looked at Peter. They nodded to each other. Then he whispered into the police radio on his jacket collar:

'OK. Olsen and Nyborg, go down to their cars.'

He looked at his watch. He let a minute pass to give the men time to reach the activists' cars and immobilise them so they could not be used for a quick getaway. There was no other form of transport in the countryside at this time of night. They would catch all the activists, of that he was sure. Then he took a deep breath and said:

'Remember, we don't want any casualties or fatalities, and no one draws a service pistol unless their life is in danger.'

He paused for a few seconds, then said:

'OK, switch on the lights.'

60

PETER SQUINTED INTO the sharp light that pierced the night within a millisecond and revealed the scene in front of them.

The whole thing was like a Theatre of the Absurd production in a foreign country. People dressed in black darted around trying to escape the spotlight and the police. Escaping mink ran between the cages, their eyes caught in the light. Mark was out of his car at once. Everywhere there was screaming and shouting, female voices mingling with the men's; some of those dressed in black were pushed to the ground between the cages; others resisted vigorously, yelling and kicking and biting to get free. Tools were hurled away in an attempt to dispose of forensic evidence.

Peter took another look around. He walked up and down the rows of cages with only one purpose. He would be able to recognise her, he was sure of it. Even if she wore camouflage clothing and had a balaclava over her head. He could find her with his eyes closed and that was why he had come. They had given him permission to be here. He had pleaded with them. It was his operation, and Bella was his. Out of nowhere came a blow to the stomach region and he was almost knocked over by a fleeing activist. He reeled and made a grab for the figure, but it sped off, away from the floodlights and into the darkness.

'Let's get out of here. That way,' he heard.

'Bloody cops. Knock them down,' someone called out.

Chaos still reigned. The activists were more militant than he had expected. He saw one of Mark's officers with a gash to his forehead and another lying on the ground being bludgeoned by a pair of bolt cutters in an activist's hands until she was overpowered by another officer.

'Get them into vehicles as quick as you can.'

It was Mark who was shouting. Then, suddenly, the light was out and darkness enveloped them.

'They've cut the power. Turn on the car headlights,' Mark shouted.

Confusion seemed total until the headlights lit up the scene somewhat less effectively.

'Fuck it!'

'Nick them!'

'Ruuun!'

The air was filled with voices, the sound of footsteps and orders. Some activists were still cutting wire. Then he spotted her. She stood there completely still, caught in a beam of light from Mark's car. Elfin and delicate and with her eyes darting round on all sides. She had a pair of bolt cutters in one hand, hanging down by her side. Her chest heaved and sank as if she had been running. Now she looked bewildered. He would have recognised her anywhere.

'Bella!'

She turned her face in his direction. A whole second passed with them just staring at each other. And then she ran, sprinting off with long, gravity-defying strides.

He burst into a run, but she was fast and soon out of sight until he saw her further ahead. She had no chance of getting away, but she was fired up with adrenaline and her legs were going like egg whisks.

'Bella, wait! Stop, damn you!'

But she didn't. He didn't know what she expected or hoped, but she was like a will o' the wisp, both existing and not existing at the same time. An elf maiden dressed in black with the ability to disappear and allow herself to be swallowed up by nature. My, he thought. My as she could have been. As she was when you peeled everything away. This was what My would have wanted to be: a defender of animals, a champion of the doomed. Somehow it made sense, and he saw the clear resemblance between mother and daughter.

Then he heard something a great deal more human. A stumble, a groan and sobbing. He went closer. She was lying in a ditch, looking up at him. There was defiance in her eyes, and for a moment he felt the shame of the hunter.

He hesitated for a second. Then he knelt down by the ditch and tentatively held out his hand to her.

'Come on, Bella. I'm not going to hurt you.'

She didn't move. She just stared at him, her body trembling.

'It's OK. I know you're doing this for the best of reasons.'

Then there was some movement. He felt her skin against his as she reached out her hand and he helped her up.

He got her into his car, which was parked further down the road. The raid appeared to be nearing its end. Mark seemed pleased.

'You can have her. I promise. We've got the others,' he said. 'Except Brask. She's too smart to get her hands dirty.'

'Anni Toftegaard?'

Mark shook his head.

'No, we haven't got her either. Nor Ulla Vang. But Ketty Nimb is here. Now I finally know why we couldn't find her and tell her Victor was dead.'

Mark shook his head and looked at Peter.

'You've been right so far. I wonder if you're right about all this having a connection with the killings?'

Peter looked over to his car, where Bella was sitting with her head resting against the window.

'We'll see. But there has to be a link.'

'An angry mink farmer goes berserk and kills activist children?'

Mark's voice sounded sceptical. Peter repeated what he had said.

'We'll see.'

61

KIR WAITED IN her car some distance from Jeanette's house.

Kasper Frandsen was inside. Yet again, she had followed him from Veggerslev. He had been there for two hours now and it was past midnight.

Her stomach was tied in knots. This time the children were at home. They were four and six. She felt like running up the garden path, kicking down the door and dragging the husband down to the police station before he could beat them up or worse.

But she had to be patient. She wanted to expose him as a killer, that was her plan. It all fitted. A sobbing Jeanette had told her he had a previous conviction for assault and one for rape. True, it was a long time ago now, but God only knew what crimes could have gone undetected in the meantime.

And then there was his presence at the harbour: an obvious opportunity for him to sabotage the fishing boat and to meet Nils, which had clearly triggered something in him. It didn't take much to set some people off. Dr Jekyll and Mr Hyde. Morten's description had been apt. Morten who, under duress, had promised to help her.

She needed his help with another matter, but she hadn't dared mention it yet. Off the coast of Læsø, forty-five metres down, the *Marie af Grenå* still lay at the bottom of the sea. A second look at the boat wouldn't do any harm. If she discovered the propeller had been sabotaged or that Kasper had tampered with some other vital element, that might be enough to convict him. But for that she needed a safe dive, a reliable diving partner and favourable weather conditions, and for the time being she was on sick leave and the mine divers had gone back to Kongsøre.

This was where she had imagined Morten could come into the picture. So far it was only an idea that was taking shape in her head, but it would be good to nail that bonehead Kasper Frandsen and to hand him over to Mark, from whom she had heard nothing. At least, she had thought, they had been on the same wavelength regarding the bones in the box, but now he seemed to be going solo.

Just as she was thinking that, the door to the house was opened and Kasper Frandsen stormed out with his fists clenched, shouting and waving them threateningly at the woman who quickly shut the door after him.

'You fucking bitch!' the street echoed. 'I hope you bloody choke on your own spittle!'

Kir looked up as he stomped over to his car, started it and pulled out with the headlights on full. For a moment she was caught in the beams as they swept across her and the red pickup, which wasn't exactly the most inconspicuous vehicle on the planet. She hoped he hadn't seen her.

She waited until he was out of sight, then she got out of the pickup, walked up the garden path and knocked softly on the door. Jeanette let her in, her hair and clothes a mess and her lips swollen from punches.

'That bastard. Come on, let me put some iodine on that.'

'Thank God the kids are asleep. I don't think they heard anything.'

Kir nodded. 'Yeah, right, and I'm the Queen of Sheba,' she muttered. Of course, the children had heard everything. They would be huddled up, hugging each other, until it was all over.

With a bit of help from Jeanette, Kir located the first-aid kit. She dabbed Jeanette's lips.

'I've got what you wanted,' Jeanette said after Kir had finished. 'I hid them while he was in the shower. He always has a shower. He says I'm gross and that he'll probably catch something off me. He calls me a slag.'

Kir watched Jeanette from a distance. She wondered what it would be like to be humiliated like that. It was unimaginable to her. She was a soldier, trained for battle, to defend herself and others. It was beyond her comprehension – even after Jeanette explained that otherwise he would take it out on the children – how anyone could submit to such brutal sexual violence and listen to the degrading, demeaning words that came out of the mouth of such a monster. Somewhere in the back of her mind, Morten's warning rang out: *Be very careful. Women like her can do a complete volte face. Before you know it, she's stabbing you in the back and defending the only person she knows: her husband.*

Perhaps Morten was right. What did she know? But evidence was still evidence and she intended to collect some.

Jeanette got up on wobbly legs and staggered into the bedroom. She returned with a bag which she handed to Kir.

Jeanette touched her throat.

'He loves it. He loves playing executioner and victim. It's what he lives for.'

Kir looked into the bag. It contained the neck brace and the handcuffs.

In a cold voice Jeanette said:

'There should be plenty of DNA on that. I hope he rots in hell.'

62

PETER HAD PLAYED out the scene countless times in his head, ever since he'd found the letter to the editor about fur farming and discovered what Gumbo's photographs meant. He had imagined himself sitting there asking the questions and her answering them. He had imagined himself ignoring her frailty and her femininity and her big eyes that asked questions and propelled him back to the years with My. He would put on his authoritarian voice and bark an *'Out with it, woman. It's time to tell me the truth, don't you think?'* And he had imagined her response: respect, even fear. He would see the dawning understanding in her eyes that she had been found out, and the realisation would make her put all her cards on the table, one by one.

He had waited for this moment, knowing full well that he couldn't have done it any sooner. She would have denied everything. Just as she had lied and deceived him ever since the day she had turned up with Miriam.

She couldn't deny everything now.

And yet it turned out to be so different from how he had imagined it.

He looked at her as she sat pressed up against the corner of his sofa. She was no longer the pushy woman who had driven over with a dream cake and stopped him on his way home to the cliff. She looked more like the woman huddling in the corner of the kitchen after Gumbo's visit. But she wasn't beaten. There was still a spark there. And some sexual tension as her eyes met his.

He shook his head.

'I don't know how the hell you do it.'

'Do what, Peter?'

Her voice was hoarse from screaming and shouting on the battle-field not so long before.

'Nothing.'

He had to gather his thoughts. He started tentatively. Slowly. Of course, she wasn't a killer, but then again, she wasn't entirely blame-less, was she?

'OK. Perhaps it's best if you just tell me what happened,' he said. 'What's going on, Bella? What are you mixed up in with Alice and the others?'

'The others?'

She sounded completely innocent. He pulled out a copy of the letter and handed it to her. While she looked at it, he counted out loud on his fingers.

'Alice Brask, you, Anni Toftegaard, Ketty Nimb, Ulla Vang.'

'Yes?'

'Tell me what you're up to.'

This time it was Bella's turn to sigh.

'Surely that's obvious. We have opinions and we're not afraid to back them up with action. We're against fur farming. You saw those poor creatures. Some of them have sores the size of five-krone coins.'

She stretched out a black-clad arm.

'You love nature, don't you? So you must hate the thought of animals caged up! You must hate cruelty to animals.'

'Of course. But I hate cruelty to human beings even more.'

He knew very well that he couldn't oppose her like this. Their action probably did have a point, but for him this was about some-thing else.

She opened her mouth to add something. He beat her to it.

'Melissa is dead. Nils is dead.'

'Nils drowned,' she said, sounding just as surprised as Ulla Vang had earlier. 'It was an accident.'

'You're blinkered, Bella. You see what you want to see and you hear what you want to hear. Nils was garrotted and placed in the wheelhouse of a boat, which then sank.'

She was genuinely shocked.

'That can't be true . . . But, that's awful.'

He looked at his watch.

'Twelve hours ago, I found the body of Ketty Nimb's son, Victor, in the dunes by Fjellerup Beach, where he had fled to join Magnus and Ea-Louise.'

'You did *what*?'

He ignored her question and carried on.

'Victor had also been garrotted.'

He leaned forward.

'Wake up, Bella! Your children have been living with threats and you knew nothing. They protected you, not the other way round, while you were busy running around with your gang and making enemies.'

He took a breath and went on while she stared at him blankly, as though someone had picked up a pair of bolt cutters, whacked her on the head and stunned her.

'And somewhere out there, enemy number one is in action, killing your children. Who is he, Bella? Trawl through your memory and he'll be there. It's someone you know. Someone who knows your children and the other women's children and who feels humiliated by something you did in good faith and with the best of intentions, but which was the cause of great anger. This is someone wreaking their revenge.'

She shook her head and held up her hands as if to avert further blows. Tears gushed from her eyes and her words came out in gasps.

'It's just a group of like-minded people. OK, so we release some mink and we spray paint on some fur coats, and yes, it's other people's property, but that doesn't make us killers!'

Privately, he had to agree with her. It didn't add up, and yet there was so much evidence to suggest that this had to be the reason.

'So what's really going on?'

'What do you mean?'

Her eyes were swimming in tears; they brimmed over and trickled down her cheeks. 'Magnus had just had enough. He's eighteen. He wanted a different life, so he took off. That's all there is to it . . .'

'You're living in a dream world, Bella. Gumbo said Magnus met Melissa. Melissa had received threats every year on her birthday. You yourself showed me a threatening letter you'd found in Magnus's drawer . . .'

He continued patiently:

'He and Melissa supported one another. And the other children of the five co-signatories.'

And who knows, he added to himself, perhaps there were more? There had certainly been more than five activists tonight.

She shook her head. He could see she was making an effort to compose herself and think clearly. He got up and found some milk in the fridge, mixed it with cocoa powder and heated it in a saucepan, to give her time to think.

When he came back and handed her the mug of hot cocoa, she clasped it with both hands and said:

'This can't be about animals. I refuse to believe that. It has to be something else. Something about us, yes. About our group. But not what you think.'

'Then what is it, Bella? What have you done that could turn one man into your children's killer?'

She put her lips to the mug and sipped the cocoa carefully, with knitted brows. She stared at him and sucked him into her professed innocence, and his dream from the other morning surfaced.

'That's exactly what I'm trying to remember, Peter.'

63

AARHUS CATHEDRAL WAS packed to the rafters, but despite the sombre occasion, far from everyone was wearing black.

In her blog, Alice Brask had asked people to wear bright colours to celebrate Melissa's short life. Many in the congregation had done as she requested. Most of them, in fact, except the nuns from the convent. They sat on two pews in their white habits with black mourning bands.

'We should have picked her up last night,' Mark said. 'We don't have the time to consider feelings.'

Next to him, Anna Bagger shook her head imperceptibly.

'She hasn't killed anyone.'

Mark wasn't so sure about that.

'She's a bloody nuisance and that business last night was clearly unlawful, and yes, she's the brains behind it,' Anna Bagger said. 'But she isn't a killer. And she has lost her daughter.'

'And now she's turning the funeral into a circus,' Mark whispered.

He was sure Melissa would have preferred a more low-key funeral at the convent church, but she was no longer around to express her wishes. And her mother was her next-of-kin and had somewhat more flamboyant taste than her daughter, of that Mark was sure.

That was why the white coffin was decorated with a garish display of flowers; and all around the cathedral there were scarlets, purples and oranges. And that was why most of the bouquets and wreaths – there were so many they hung or lay on every available surface – were orgies of colour. Meanwhile the bereaved mother, who was sitting with her closest family nearest the coffin, wore a trouser suit that matched the splurge of flowers. A young boy sat next to her, no more than ten years old. His face was closed and he was absent-mindedly dangling his feet and kicking. It was Melissa's younger brother.

In his hand Mark held a sheet of paper: the order of service. One had been placed on every single seat. It didn't look like anything Melissa would have chosen, either. There was a variety of items, probably from friends and acquaintances and the family. And all rounded off by a Kim Larsen song: *'Om lidt bli'r her stille'*. Soon all will be quiet. The lyrics were printed on the sheet because it wasn't in the hymn book. He read them: *'Fik du set det, du ville? Fik du hørt din melodi?'* Did you see what you wanted to see? Did you hear your tune?

He casually raised a hand to the tie he had put on out of respect for the occasion and loosened it slightly. The words buzzed around his head and penetrated a space he had sealed hermetically after his illness. Fear. Uncertainty. This constant accursed envy of the healthy. No, he hadn't yet seen everything he wanted to see. However, he had seen a lot of things he hadn't wanted to.

'We can't arrest her today,' Anna Bagger decided. 'But let's see if there's anything here that might prove useful for us. Keep your eyes peeled.'

Mark raised his eyes to the high ceiling. He needed sleep after last night's raid and the preliminary interviews. And if he couldn't have sleep, then action. He had wanted to drag Alice Brask out of bed that same night and make her face some tough questioning. But Anna Bagger had said no on compassionate grounds and of course she was right. They had to be patient. Meanwhile two young people were on the run from a madman with a garrotte, and God only knew how many more of them were out there. Teenagers in peril. Big kids who might never get to see the things *they* wanted to see.

The police only knew of Magnus and Ea-Louise, but there could be more. One glance across the sea of people in the cathedral was confirmation. Alice Brask had many friends and network connections.

The organ started. Mark felt he was about to choke. He started sweating all over and his palms got so wet they could barely hold the programme. Everyone sat very still, listening and waiting. It was like sitting in a bell jar. The room spun around and devils and angels from the frescoes traded places in front of his eyes. He got up, panting for breath, and tore off his tie.

'Where do you think you're going?' Anna Bagger hissed in a loud voice and tugged at his sleeve to make him sit down. 'People are looking. Sit down now, Mark.'

But he didn't care. He had to get out. He made his way along the pew, stepping on several toes and handbags and earning himself some glares in the process. He headed for the heavy cathedral door, threw himself against it and opened it to inhale fresh air, while behind him, he heard the congregation joining in a hymn. The only one he had recognised so far.

He leaned against the red-brick cathedral for a while, recovering. *'Sov sødt, barnlille! Lig roligt og stille,'* they sang inside. Sleep well, my little child! Lie calm and still. He looked around. There were still small clusters of people outside, of all ages, but most of them middle-aged. People who could be the parents of older teenagers.

Some of the teenagers had been receiving threats for years, just like Melissa. Ever since she was ten years old. That was what Boutrup had told him, and Sister Beatrice, her friend at the convent, had confirmed it. From that perspective, the mink raids were a more recent activity. The women the police had interrogated said they had started their actions after the famous letter to the editor Boutrup had copied, so in 2005. That was six years ago.

Mark drew the fresh air deep into his lungs. From the church he heard the words of the hymn again. Sleep, my little child! Lie calm and still now.

It wasn't until the cathedral bells started ringing, as the coffin was carried outside, that the bells in his own head set off:

Six years obviously wasn't enough if Melissa had been receiving threats since her tenth birthday. This meant it went back much further than the letter from 2005.

He started pacing up and down on the cobblestones. They had been idiots. This wasn't about animals or fur coats. It was about something completely different. It was about people.

He stood for a moment watching people walk across Bispetorv. Then he sat down on a bench and waited until the coffin had been carried to the hearse, followed by close family.

The whole congregation came afterwards. Some were probably heading home, but those who wanted to – he knew this from Alice Brask's blog – were welcome to join her at Skovmøllen Restaurant for coffee and cake.

He waited until he saw Anna Bagger slip out. And then, in the crowd, he spotted another figure he recognised. Small and round, her neck tucked well down below her coat collar, her eyes alert, studying the gathering just as he was doing.

For a moment it was as if those eyes met his, and they looked at each other for a fleeting second. But it was over so quickly that later he doubted whether it had happened at all.

64

LISE WERGE WISHED she hadn't seen the police officer and that he hadn't seen her. Looking into his eyes was like meeting someone who wanted to extract information from her. And right now she wasn't in any mood to give anything to anyone. Right now, *she* needed information. That was why she had gone to the funeral.

She had hoped to see Simon amongst the mourners, but also dreaded seeing him of course. It would be his style to show up at the murdered girl's funeral. Sitting there, soaking it all up: the mourners, the music; the thick atmosphere of death.

Simon had always been in love with death.

She pulled the collar of her coat around her ears to protect herself against the wind and prevent anyone from recognising her. She didn't want to be approached or questioned. What could she say? That she was scared her brother was responsible for the girl's death? That she had no idea where he was because her mother had kept him hidden? For however long it had been – she didn't know.

She trudged up Strøget with the gusting wind buffeting her in all directions. But she held firm as she always did and navigated her way through the crowds towards Salling car park, where she had left her car.

As she walked she cursed her family to hell and back. Had it not been for the ingrained loyalty with which she had been vaccinated at an early age, she would have broken with them long ago. Then the police officer could ask whatever he wanted. And she would tell him about the depravity that went all the way back to the days of the Cardinal and perhaps even further.

But she had stuck her head above the parapet only once before, and then it was because she thought it would be helpful. It hadn't been perceived as such, and it was one of the reasons she feared Simon.

She walked through the perfume department in Salling with the scents nearly choking her. She left the department store at Mister Minute, found the multi-storey car park and paid at the machine, but a tingle of unease began to spread through her. Had he gone to the funeral after all? Perhaps he had followed her. Was he about to put his arm around her neck and squeeze while no one was watching?

Her hands were shaking as she took the ticket. Nonsense, she told herself, rushing up the stairs to the second floor where she had left her car. Utter nonsense.

But when she was inside her car, she locked it. And it wasn't until she had driven through the exit and was in the street that she started to relax. She turned on the radio to drown out what was going on inside her head, but it couldn't stop the memories that came flooding back in a steady stream, like the Saturday traffic winding its way out of town.

She had always been scared of him, even though he had been her little brother. She could have loved him and worshipped him, but only one person had that privilege, and that was her mother.

A mother who couldn't see or didn't want to see that there was something very wrong with her adored son.

Involuntarily, Lise touched her neck as she drove and remembered things she didn't want to remember:

The basement in the Woodland Snail, one dark Sunday afternoon. Her and Lone and Simon and his friend, who had sneaked down the forbidden staircase while the adults were taking a nap after lunch. Simon had managed to open the trap door under the carpet, down to Grandpa's den. The game he wanted them to play, which involved her being strapped into Grandpa's strange chair.

'Come on, Sis. Sit down.'

His eyes had burned with excitement. Lone and the friend had stayed in the background. The authority in Simon's voice and his surprising physical strength when he pushed her down onto the hard wooden seat.

'You need to be punished. And I'm the one who's going to punish you.'

Lise blinked away the tears as she drove. She didn't know why she hadn't resisted. But that was how it was with Simon. His voice hypnotised her and probably also the two others. She hated him, but he could make her do anything he wanted.

She remembered the iron collar closing around her neck. She remembered the shackles closing around her wrists and ankles. She remembered Simon's voice.

'You're going to die now, Sis. You're stupid and ugly, and you're going to die. That's the law.'

How did he know what to do? She had asked herself that question so often. But perhaps it was just something that boys knew. Perhaps it was in their genes.

He knew how to kill her. He knew how to turn the clamp and tighten the iron collar so that the metal spike slowly began to bore its way into her neck. He knew all that and much more.

Driving towards Djursland, she remembered the sense of her own powerlessness and the world closing itself off from her. Her eyesight fading, seeing Lone standing there, very still, like a blurred, quivering mirage. Her arms and legs starting to twitch and her bladder opening and releasing hot fluid from beneath her.

Her hands shifted position on the steering wheel, which was clammy with her sweat. The traffic was slow but she was finally out of the city. She longed for her home, her small flat on the outskirts of Grenå. Nothing special, but it was hers and no one else's. She very rarely received guests, except her neighbour every now and then. She didn't let anyone in. Her security was the intercom downstairs and living on the third floor in a new block, which she told herself was safe. She had five chains on her door.

She couldn't remember what had happened next that day in the basement. But they had told her afterwards. The adults had woken up after their nap and wondered where the children were, because it was so quiet. It was her father who had thought to check the basement, and who had saved her and insisted that Simon had to be seen by a doctor. Simon was ill, he insisted. Mentally ill.

'That boy's dangerous,' she remembered him saying.

But nothing ever happened. Two months later her father fell ill and died. Simon was and would always be the apple of his mother's eye, and no one could touch him. Until the day when everything went wrong.

At last. She switched off the engine in the car park and carried out a visual check of the area as always, but saw nothing unusual. Would he come here?

Her heart was pounding as she unlocked the door to the stairwell and took the lift to the third floor. Her hands were shaking so much the keys were jangling in her hand as she unlocked the front door, both at the top and the bottom. Finally, she could open the door and shut it behind her. She breathed a sigh of relief, fumbled to put the security chains on and, for a moment, rested her forehead against the door.

Then a hand was placed on her shoulder and she felt cold steel against her throat.

'Welcome home, Sis,' Simon said.

65

'THINK HARDER. YOU must be able to remember something!'

Peter looked at Bella, who was wandering around her house touching different objects as if that could stimulate memories. She shook her head.

'I don't know what it could be.'

Then she returned to Magnus.

'I just know you'll find him, Peter. If anyone can find him, you can.'

To hell with them all. She had My's faith in him, the faith she should never have had. My had called him wise. And look where that had got her. Bella stood still in front of him. He felt like shaking her. Instead, he took her by the shoulders, led her to the kitchen and plonked her down on a chair. Her son, Christian, was sleeping over at a friend's house, she had told him. They were alone.

'Finding Magnus and Ea-Louise isn't enough,' he said. 'Although that alone might prove to be pretty hard. We need to get to the bottom of this. We need to go right back to the beginning.'

He looked at the posters in her kitchen, about furs and whales and animal transport.

'OK,' he said, trying to inject some enthusiasm into his voice. 'Begin at the beginning.'

They hadn't made much progress since last night. They had talked and talked and tried to narrow down the problem, narrow down the time to when something went wrong and the urge for revenge was born.

Then she had fallen asleep on his sofa, completely exhausted. And now, after she had been interviewed by the police, he had driven her home.

'Again,' she mumbled.

'How did you meet Alice Brask?'

'We were neighbours.'

'Year?'

She calculated.

'It was 1994. I was pregnant with Magnus.'

'And My?'

'My wasn't there.'

'Did Alice Brask ever meet My?'

'No.'

She shook her head vehemently.

'This has got nothing to do with My,' she said. 'It's impossible.'

'Nothing is impossible.'

Peter was thinking so hard his eyes blurred. The gnawing feeling had come back. Everything was connected. My was part of the story, he was convinced of it.

'OK. Then what? You had Magnus.'

'Yes, and Alice had Melissa soon afterwards.'

'What about a mothers' group?'

It was pure guesswork on his part. What did he know about becoming a parent?

'What about it?'

'Did you belong to something like that?'

She nodded.

'You and Alice. But none of the others? Not Anni Toftegaard? Not Ketty Nimb or Ulla Vang?'

'No.'

'What about other women? Any names?'

She shook her head.

'Ooh, Peter. This is a really long time ago.'

'Try.'

She pushed herself up from the chair.

'I'll have to check.'

He followed her into a study-cum-guest bedroom, where she pulled down some old ring binders from a shelf. She sent him a thin-lipped smile.

'From back in the days when they still used paper. These days everything is done online.'

She didn't find anything in the ring binders, but dug out a pile of old diaries from a box under the futon he guessed served as the guest bed.

Peter's hope soared. Diaries were treasure chests of gossip. In his experience, women wrote everything down.

Bella dusted off a white spiral diary from 1994 and flicked through it.

'We took turns to meet at each other's houses,' she said. 'Here.'

A date and a name followed by an address: Helene Sparre. Lystrupvej 5.

Peter found some paper and a pen and copied it down.

Meanwhile, Bella discovered another name: Isa Nielsen. Randersvej 334 in Lisbjerg.

Bella found a few more and he wrote them down as well. Maybe they could give him a lead. Maybe not. Peter would be lucky if he could track down these people.

'OK. And you and Alice belonged to that group?'

Bella nodded.

A network, he thought. Somehow this is all about a network. If it's not animal activists, then it's something else. It was like overlapping circles. Some women belonged to several groups, others to just a single one, perhaps the mothers' group. But what other groups had there been? That was what he needed to trace all the way back.

'What about the men?' he asked. 'Where do they figure in all this?'

She shrugged.

'You're a man. What do you think?'

He had never regarded himself as typical of his gender, but perhaps he was more ordinary than he had believed. He had never been a member of any group and had never wanted to be.

'Men watch football, drink beer together or play in a band,' Bella said.

'What did your husband do?'

The man who didn't want My. Who thought her autism was the result of a childhood vaccination. Peter loathed him with all his heart.

Bella looked blank. There was nothing to be gleaned from her face or her body language as she bent over the pile of diaries.

'Nothing,' she said.

'But he knew Alice Brask?'

'Yes.'

'Did they get on?'

He asked this, prompted by unashamedly primitive feelings of hatred.

'They agreed on lots of things,' Bella said, dodging the question.

'And you? Did you agree as well?'

'To a large extent.'

He sat down. He remembered the head teacher at the nursery saying Bella had had poor advisers. She might have been thinking about something that Bella's husband and Alice Brask had pressurised her into.

'I know they're private, but please may I borrow these diaries?'

She nodded.

'I'll call you if I have any questions.'

Another nod.

'Are you going to go now?'

Her voice had suddenly become very small.

'That was the plan.'

She leaned back and looked up at him. She seemed so vulnerable and naive that he believed her.

'Stay,' she said. 'Just a little bit longer.'

She stretched up on her toes. He saw tears rolling down her cheeks, then she gently placed her hand on his shoulder and, with a small step, closed the distance between them.

'Stay, Peter,' she whispered.

He could feel her heart beating and remembered the swallow he had held in his hand the other day. He wanted to resist, the way he had in his dream about her, but his body obeyed her and not him as her hand fluttered up to his face and stopped when her lips were pressing against his.

'Listen, Bella.'

He pushed her away in a friendly manner, but she quickly returned. He pushed her away again, but she had already pressed her body so close to his that it was impossible not to react.

'This isn't . . .'

Her lips opened and let him in. His whole body was pounding and he gave in and they collapsed onto the futon, she with her hands wandering down towards his zip and her fragile body glued to his.

It wasn't the first time in his life he'd had sex knowing he would regret it later. Nor was it likely to be the last, he thought, before he allowed himself to be swallowed up completely by skin and flesh in a cocktail seasoned with lust and profound scepticism.

Afterwards they lay panting and she refused to look at him. He grabbed her by the arm, hard, and made her look.

'What was that about?'

But he already knew. He had to be distracted. She didn't want him walking all over her guilty conscience.

'Nothing,' she muttered. 'You wanted it as well.'

He nodded.

'But it's not going to distract me, if that's what you're thinking.'

'Why would I think that?'

She spoke in an airy tone, a little girl's voice once more. He sat upright.

'What was the name of your doctor back then? You and Alice must have had the same GP.'

'Why? He was a silly old buffer.'

'Because I'm tapping in the dark here.'

Bella wrinkled her nose. He looked at her as she lay there, still naked, in front of him, small breasts and a thin shaved stripe. Not young but, in a strange way, ageless. Her eyes were close to his, dancing, even now, and he pulled a blanket over her.

'He's retired, thank God.'

She sat up, pulling the blanket right up to her neck in a sudden fit of modesty. 'He lived in Lystrup.'

'Name?'

'Poul Gerrick.'

'Why didn't you like him?'

In a detached way she gazed at the wall and then up at the ceiling.

'He never had any children of his own. What did he know about being a mother?'

66

WHAT WAS DONE was done, and he didn't do remorse. But after the session with Bella Peter promised himself there would be no repeat performances. He checked the notes he had made and drove to Lystrupvej 5. Helene Sparre, it transpired, didn't live there with her family any more and the new owners didn't know where the family had moved to.

He Googled her on his mobile and learned that she had moved to Højbjerg. However, he decided to make for Lisbjerg and visit Isa Nielsen.

He was in luck this time. Her husband opened the door – fortunately he didn't have a problem with letting Peter in – and called out to his wife, who was taking a shower.

'I'm taking Anton to football,' the husband said. 'So she's all yours. The big one is asleep. He was at a party last night.'

The big one. Peter thought that must be the child Isa had had when Bella had Magnus. What a long time ago this all was, it struck him. Would they be able to remember anything at all? And why would someone with a motive for revenge from way back wait for so many years before getting what he regarded as justice?

Isa's husband looked more like a marathon runner than a football player. He zipped up a sports bag on the dining table.

'Bella. Yes, I remember her. Nice girl, but very shy. Even so, we got to know the family a bit, of course.'

Isa Nielsen came in. She had thick chestnut hair reaching down to her shoulders and was as tall as a flagpole and as lean as her husband. She was also a bright woman. 'Yes, I heard about Melissa. Poor thing. She used to be such a lovely little girl.'

She winked at Peter.

'Not that her mother would allow that, of course. Alice dressed her as a boy. She went in for equality.'

'There's not much equality in that,' Peter ventured.

A quick smile flashed across Isa Nielsen's face.

'You'd never say that to Alice, or she'd bite your head off.'

'So even then she was . . . a woman of strong opinions.'

Isa shook her head at the thought.

'She was terrible.'

'You're the first person I've heard say that.'

Isa Nielsen laughed. Peter wouldn't call her beautiful, but her humour was infectious. Her mouth was big and looked as if it could swallow anything. As she laughed, her nose wrinkled and her eyes practically disappeared.

'If you keep digging, you'll probably discover that I'm not alone.'

She grew more serious.

'It's awful, of course. What happened to Melissa, I mean. She was the apple of Alice's eye. But Alice herself . . . My God, she was always trying to tell us what to do in the group.'

'And did she succeed?'

She wound a chestnut lock around a finger and was clearly giving the question due consideration.

'Remember, we were so young and naive. Alice was older than the rest of us, and she knew so much about . . .'

Isa's hand circled in the air. 'Well, about everything.'

'She blogs,' Peter said. 'Do you follow her?'

Another grin.

'No, I certainly do not. I don't need Alice telling me what to think.'

She added: 'And I never did.'

'But some did?'

'Not all of them, but some people.'

'And Bella?'

She rolled her eyes.

'Silly little Bella. She knew nothing about the world, except what that idiot of a husband told her.'

'Did Alice also tell her what to think?'

Isa nodded.

'The pair of them shaped Bella like you'd shape putty.'

Peter waited for more. It came after a toss of her head sent her flowing mane into a swirl.

'During the time we met – we hung around together for about four years – Bella turned into a passionate champion for everything Alice felt she ought to espouse. I still have my doubts as to whether she ever had an independent thought in her head.'

As though fearing that she might have crossed the line, she added:

'Please don't think I'm saying Bella was stupid. Far from it. She simply adapted. She survived in the waters her husband and Alice shared.'

'Her husband made her give up her first child. Did you know that?'

Isa nodded.

'She had some form of autism. Bella had her when she was very young.'

'Bella's husband reckoned her autism had developed after an MMR vaccination,' Peter said.

Isa's eyebrows shot up. She sat for a while as if ruminating on something.

'Oh, so that was why . . .'

'Why what?'

'He and Alice were as thick as thieves when it came to the MMR. Alice was vehemently against it, and I don't think Melissa was ever given that vaccination, even though the doctors recommended it.'

She added:

'And they still do.'

'And Magnus? Did he have it?'

Isa's head turned slowly from side to side.

'I don't know. I opted out of that debate. I wasn't going to trust Alice on science, even though there was conflicting information at the time.'

'When does a child have the vaccination?'

319

'The first is at the age of fifteen months. The booster is given at around the age of four, as far as I remember. At the time a British doctor was linking the vaccine to autism. As a result, many parents were reluctant to have their children immunised. Alice ran a campaign in the newspaper. This was before we were blessed with blogs and Facebook.'

She pulled a face.

'If we had known then how the Net would develop, some of us might have considered blowing it up.'

She must have seen the question in his eyes.

'I'm guessing you don't have kids?'

'Correct.'

She smiled. 'You should see mine. When they're not playing football or going to parties, they're on Twitter or Facebook and they don't live in the real world. Except when there's food on the table, of course. They're seventeen and fourteen and eat like horses.'

She paused briefly, then said:

'Now you're probably thinking I'm just as strident in my opinions as Alice.'

Peter got up.

'You're entitled to your opinions. Thank you for your time.'

When he got home, he took the dog for a short walk on the cliff and then started looking through Bella's diaries.

Isa Nielsen had been a great help. But she and the mothers' group had obviously lost touch with Bella and Alice before the point when the killer started seething with hatred.

The story about the vaccinations buzzed around his head. He considered calling Bella, then decided to check all the diaries first.

He read through 1994, 1995, 1996 and 1997 very carefully, but found no appointments for vaccinations.

Instead, he found something else. 'P-party, Alice's', he saw. And somewhere else. 'P-party, Anni Toftegaard'. And then the address of Nils's mother. And yet another one: 'P-party, Ulla Vang'. And then her address.

It looked as if Bella had met both Ulla and Anni via Alice and the first P-party.

What was a P-party?

He gave up trying to guess and picked up the phone to ring Bella, who sounded drowsy, as if he had woken her up.

'Did Magnus ever have the MMR jab?' he asked and was met with a deafening silence.

'Is that important?' she asked.

'Very. What's a P-party?'

He noted some resistance in her voice.

'There's no law against it.'

'Is it a pox party?'

'Yes, but . . .'

'How did it work?'

She launched into an explanation:

'When I was a child, everyone got childhood diseases as a matter of course. Rubella, German measles, chickenpox and mumps. You had them, and afterwards you were immune to them. But in the 1980s some boffins discovered a vaccine which protected children against all of them,' she said.

'My was one of the first children in Denmark to be vaccinated. It really was a revolution. But then some doctors thought they had discovered serious side effects, in the form of autism. There was something in the research to suggest a link.'

She hesitated.

'Some parents – the better informed ones – decided to opt out of the vaccination.'

'And instead they organised these so-called pox parties?'

He could hear her walking about, on bare feet. He repressed the memory of her skin on his and listened to her defence.

'It wasn't illegal, Peter. We just believed children should have as natural a life as possible . . . I couldn't risk the same thing happening to Magnus as had happened to My.'

This was not an area he had much experience of, he told himself. He didn't have any children. However, he didn't think for one second there was a link between the vaccination and autism and he was sure he had read that the theory had been disproved: there was no link. But in 1994 many people had believed there was. Bella had acted in what she thought was her children's best interests.

'Thank you,' he said at length. 'You've been a great help.'

Like so many before her, she had been well-intentioned, he thought. It must have been difficult, being bombarded by information that pulled you in every direction. But goodwill and best intentions were twins, and they had a habit of turning into disaster and tragedy. He was living proof of that.

She hesitated. He could hear her accelerated breathing.

'What just happened, Peter . . .'

'Forget it.'

'I know you regret it.'

He made no reply.

'I haven't had a man since my divorce,' she said. 'I just want to say thank you.'

Said by the Bella who had wanted a job with Miriam. His scepticism reared its head to warn him. Yet again the thought surfaced that she wasn't someone he could trust.

'Thank *you*,' he said and ended the call.

67

'THIS HAS NOTHING to do with animals,' Anna Bagger said. 'In that respect, last night's raid was a waste of time. We've got the activists and we've spoken to the respective mink farmers. Yes, it's illegal. And yes, it's irritating when somebody lets out your mink. But it doesn't give us our killer. We have to look elsewhere.'

She paced up and down for a little while. Then she pointed to the board where photographs of the key players were displayed. She rapped a knuckle on the photograph of Melissa's mother.

'Boutrup is right about the following: Alice Brask and her network is the target for our killer. So we need to go through everything Brask has written in the last eighteen years with a fine-tooth comb. We need to find every single person who could be the common denominator for these five mothers.'

'We have three dead teenagers and two missing ones. And there could be more we have yet to identify in the killer's spotlight. This is urgent. It's a race against time.'

This was after Melissa's funeral. They had wasted valuable time observing the crowd of mourners at the cathedral and later at Skovmøllen Restaurant. Mark and Anna had subsequently spent two hours questioning Alice Brask in a room at Aarhus Police Station. They had little to show for it except Brask's feigned politeness and detachment, and Mark had thought she seemed remarkably unconcerned about whether her friends' children were in danger or not. She had lost Melissa and no investigation, no matter how successful, could bring her back. Alice Brask denied having planned the mink farm operation and had stressed that the activists involved acted 'completely on their own and on their own initiative'. She regarded it as no more than a coincidence that some of them were co-signatories on the 2005 letter to the editor.

'We might move in the same circles,' she had said. 'We're people with opinions about what's happening in society. That's all we have in common. We don't see each other socially. We're not close friends. Every individual is responsible for his or her own actions.'

'We're still looking for a motive,' Anna Bagger said to her team. 'Revenge seems to be a strong candidate. The killings do not suggest an overtly sexual theme. And yet there is an element of sadism.'

'What about pure and utter evil?' Pia Thorsen suggested. 'Is that a possibility?'

'Mental health issues?' Martin Nielsen proposed. 'Paranoia. Maybe he sees the young people as some kind of threat.'

'There's no harm in checking with psychiatric hospitals and prisons about who is currently on release,' Anna Bagger said. 'But these crimes require great patience and considerable planning. I find it hard to believe that the killer could be a very sick person.'

'A psychopath,' Mark suggested.

'He definitely has a deviant personality of some kind,' Martin Nielsen said. 'But that doesn't necessarily make him insane.'

'Right, Martin,' Anna Bagger said. 'Perhaps you could look into that and possibly contact the relevant institutions . . . Mark, any news about the bones in the box?'

Mark nearly fell off his chair in surprise. It had been days since she'd last asked him about the old bones and he had deliberately stopped briefing her. But now she was desperate and willing to try anything.

In broad strokes, he attempted to summarise what he and Oluf Jensen had discovered, but for some reason he omitted to report back that he had seen Lise Werge outside the cathedral. He couldn't quite account for this himself. Perhaps he wasn't sure that it really was her. Or maybe the real reason was that he was still confused about the photographs Marianne Holme-Olsen had let him keep.

'So it's likely to be a Resistance man, someone killed right after the war?' Anna Bagger asked.

'Looks like it. We took a blood sample from a cousin on the maternal side, so we'll know soon. The widow gave us another important piece of information,' Mark said.

'Oh yes?'

'Her husband broke his right leg in an accident with a horse and cart. The fracture healed and it fits one of the bones in the box.'

'And the Cardinal, as he was known, could be the killer? Using a home-made garrotte?'

'Perhaps. But if the timeline is right, he had already disappeared when the murder was committed, so it's possible he isn't the killer after all,' Mark said. 'But yes, we believe he had a garrotte which he built himself. Someone could have used it.'

'All sounds a bit thin to me,' Anna Bagger remarked.

Mark couldn't deny that.

'Nevertheless,' Anna Bagger said. 'We can't ignore the fact that it was the same MO, both then and now. Let's take a closer look at the family, from a present frame of reference,' she added. 'Mark. Can I leave that one with you?'

Present frame of reference. It wasn't the first neologism she had used. Nor was it likely to be the last, Mark thought.

He nodded.

'I'll look into it.'

From the police station he drove straight to the nursing home.

He found his grandfather in his wheelchair in front of the lounge TV. At first glance it looked as if the old man had fallen asleep, but his head jerked when Mark gently placed his hand on his shoulder.

'I wasn't asleep,' Hans said, blinking.

'Of course not.'

He nodded towards the TV. A few other residents were sitting there, a couple with relatives who had come to visit. But it was a big lounge and they could easily talk undisturbed.

'That's an interesting programme. I always watch it.'

Mark glanced at the screen. He never watched television himself, but he recognised the grainy black-and-white images from the Second World War. How appropriate.

'It was a difficult time,' he said, pulling out a chair.

'The worst,' his grandfather answered.

Mark couldn't think of a better opportunity. He was dying to show him the three photographs he had in his pocket. He took them out.

'I spoke to Allan Holme-Olsen's widow,' he said and instantly noticed that the old man had pricked up his ears.

'Haven't you got bored with digging up the past yet?' Hans mumbled. 'It's so long ago.'

Mark nodded towards the television.

'As you said. It's interesting . . . love and war,' he added. 'It fascinates us all.'

His grandfather let out a dismissive snort, which sounded like an incomplete sneeze.

'You should be spending your time on those killings. The girl in the moat and all that.'

He was remarkably well informed, Mark had to give him that.

Mark placed the three photographs on the table.

'She let me borrow these.'

His grandfather impatiently wafted his hands around.

'I can't see anything without my glasses – not that I need to look at them anyway. I'm not interested in the past.'

'But you were just watching a film about the past.'

'That's different,' Hans grunted.

Mark offered to fetch his glasses, but the old man brushed aside his offer with a show of annoyance. Mark pointed at the photograph of the three friends.

'Why didn't you tell me you were in the Resistance, Grandad?'

The old man made no reply. He just sat staring, unseeing, at the photograph.

'After all, it's nothing to be ashamed of. You were regarded as heroes.'

'Heroes! Pah!' Hans spluttered. 'I had no need to be a hero.'

'But the war was over.'

The old man looked at Mark.

'For a police officer you're very naive.'

His grandfather pointed to the two other men.

'Allan Holme-Olsen. Bent Engelbreth.'

'What about them?'

'Well, what do you reckon?'

His grandfather hissed.

'I didn't want that picture to be taken. Bent's wife took it.'

His breathing sounded laboured.

'I got angry. I told her to give me the negative.'

He jabbed the photograph with his finger. 'That picture is the reason we fell out.'

He looked at Mark.

'They didn't understand that it was still too dangerous, that it would always be dangerous. We should have left it well alone. We should have slipped quietly back into society and taken our places in it and looked after our families.'

The relatives in the corner of the lounge were starting to turn around and send looks in their direction. Hans pointed at the two men, Allan and Bent, and spoke more quietly:

'Two months later they were both dead.'

'Two months after the end of the war?'

Hans nodded. His eyes were limpid as he looked at Mark.

'And I know who did it.'

68

Pox parties. MMR vaccines. Unconvinced parents who refused to have their children vaccinated.

What was the link with the killings?

Peter tried to assemble the pieces like a jigsaw puzzle. If he really was hot on the trail of something here, it had to be because their decision to reject the vaccinations had had consequences for others. For the killer.

Measles was one of the most infectious viruses in the world. He had read about it on the Net. Scientists hoped one day to completely eradicate the measles virus which claimed so many lives every year, especially in developing countries. A reluctance to use the MMR vaccine contributed to the fact that the virus still existed.

And some people not only refused to have their children vaccinated, the more proactive of them arranged pox parties. Whenever someone's child fell ill with measles or rubella the whole network was stirred into action. Parents could turn up with their children, as far as he had gathered, and expose them to infection so that they would develop antibodies against the disease in a 'natural' way.

The world's most infectious virus. Peter wasn't a doctor and didn't have a clue about such things, but if it was *that* infectious, was it really possible to contain the disease within the network? Didn't you risk giving measles to lots of other people?

Of course, most would be unaffected because they had been vaccinated or would have had the disease as children. But surely some people would be at risk, wouldn't they?

Peter was reminded of his visit to the nursery where the head teacher, Annelise McPherson, had hinted that Bella had had poor advisers. Was that what this was about? Had Bella's attitudes had consequences for other families?

It was a Sunday. The nursery would be shut, of course, so he would have to find another way to contact her.

He found her easily on Yellow Pages and thanked his good fortune that people were no longer content to be called plain old-fashioned Jensen or Petersen but preferred more exotic surnames.

She lived in Trige. Ian and Annelise McPherson, Directory Enquiries informed him. He could have chosen to ring them, but something told him it was better to meet face-to-face.

He started his car and drove to Aarhus.

Charm wasn't going to work. He realised as much when he rang the door of the 1980s house and a beefcake of a man appeared. He was wearing a vest and black jogging trousers and his muscles bulged like a professional wrestler's. Grizzled hair curled on his chest and had spread to other places.

'It's her day off. Come back during working hours,' the man said in accented Danish, rolling his r's and revealing his Caledonian roots.

'It's important.'

The man sized him up.

'It's also important to have time off.'

A voice called from inside the house.

'Who is it, Ian?'

She appeared behind him. Her hair was a mess and she wasn't wearing any make-up. Annelise McPherson looked at Peter, and he could see her sifting through her memories, one of which soon clicked into place.

'You again. Haven't you found him?'

She pushed up her hair. It was steel grey and shoulder-length. When he had seen her at the nursery, she'd had it pinned up.

'Magnus is still missing. Three teenagers are dead.'

He had to shock her; otherwise he would never get anywhere. *'Dead?'*

'Melissa Brask, Nils Toftegaard and Victor Nimb. They were all eighteen.'

'I knew Melissa, of course.'

Annelise shook her head. 'I've read about it. There's a whole page in the paper today about her funeral.'

She eyed him sceptically. The Scottish guard dog sent him a fierce stare.

'You said you were a friend of Bella's?'

'It's complicated. I knew Bella's older daughter.'

'Older . . . I didn't know she had a daughter.'

'Bella gave up on My. She had autism. According to Bella's husband, it was due to the MMR vaccine.'

Her eyes widened.

'My and I grew up at the same care home. Perhaps you've heard about Titan? Near Ry?'

'That awful place?'

Peter didn't like playing the Titan card, but it usually worked. Everyone had heard about the care home and the atrocities that had taken place there. And her face did indeed quickly change. She opened the door.

'You'd better come inside.'

The Scottish guard dog padded happily away and went somewhere else in the house. Annelise showed Peter into a living room with an open fireplace and exposed brick walls. Abstract art hung on the wall behind the sofas.

Peter asked his question before they had time to sit down.

'I've been wondering if you ever had a measles outbreak at the nursery.'

She took a log from a wicker basket, knelt down by the fireplace and put it on top of the others.

'And what if we did?' she said with her back to him. 'Do you think it has anything to do with what has happened?'

She wedged the log solidly in place, then sat for a while gazing at it as the fire took hold.

'I think so,' Peter said.

Annelise got up and sat on a leather stool near the fireplace. She scrutinised him as though trying yet again to figure him out. Who was he really? A murderer was at large somewhere out there. How could she know it wasn't him? Obvious doubt made her look away. Then she appeared to make up her mind. Her eyes were back on him.

'There was a measles outbreak,' she said.

'When?'

She counted on her fingers and furrowed her brow.

'It must've been in 1998.'

'What happened?'

'Some of the nursery children were carriers. It spread. Three children in the Under-Two unit went down with it.'

Of course. The nursery also had an Under-Two unit for the very youngest. Babies. Some of them too young to have had the MMR vaccine.

Annelise rubbed the side of her neck with one hand while resting the other on the leather stool.

'It was awful. People were very angry and frustrated. We were closed for two weeks.'

Her hand was now sliding up and down her throat, up and down, up and down, as if trying to smooth out the skin.

'But the worst was the children, of course. Two of them were very ill.'

'Then what happened?'

She shook her head.

'Actually, I don't know. We were never told. The sick children didn't return to our nursery. I think the council found other places for them . . .'

'But none of them died?'

'Not as far as I know. But you'll probably have to check with the local Health Authority. Or rather, don't bother; they won't tell you anything.'

She looked at him sternly.

'Medical records are confidential.'

She looked like someone who was wondering whether she had just broken the rules herself. But he had to ask one final question:

'Was it Magnus who brought the infection with him from his home?'

The wood in the fire crackled. Annelise McPherson picked up a poker and prodded the logs absent-mindedly.

'Or it could have been Melissa. Afterwards we learned that some mothers in the town had started having so-called pox parties. Children came from out of town to be infected. It was quite a set-up.'

He thought about Ketty Nimb and Ulla Vang and Anni Toftegaard. Whoever was looking for revenge must have got the list of all those involved in the group. Or found their names in some other way. Then again, that might not have proved to be all that difficult.

'And the ringleader was Alice Brask?'

Annelise stared into the flames once again. He could tell from her back that she didn't feel like replying, but in the end she did.

'This is something I've given a lot of thought, because you can spot it instantly in a group of nursery schoolchildren. They divide into Chiefs and Indians in a matter of seconds. And if there are too many Chiefs there's trouble. Among children, that's translated into pushing and shoving. Among adults . . .'

He knew the situation well. His upbringing had been marked by a pecking order. The managers of the care home were not the only ones with power and authority. Children, too, were recruited to keep the others in check.

'It's a fine line between that and bullying,' Annelise said.

'Are you saying that Bella and the others were bullied?'

She took her time to answer:

'I wouldn't call it bullying.'

She opened her palms.

'I would call it normal human behaviour. Nothing more, nothing less.'

'The rule of the mighty?'
She nodded.
'But might isn't necessarily right.'
She added: 'Isn't that what history tells us?'

69

Kir drove slowly past Grenå Police Station. Outside there were several cars. Mark's was there too. She had heard about the discovery of the boy's body in the dunes and the night raid on the mink farm. Peter Boutrup was also involved, and rumour had it that he had found the boy. Not for the first time, she imagined the two of them together, Mark and Peter. One who upheld the law and one who, on paper at least, broke it.

She drove from Vestre Skovvej towards the town, and on to the harbour. Roughly halfway she pulled over at the florist's, where she bought a bunch of carnations. Then she continued down to the harbour.

She thought about Morten. Everything was arranged for that evening. He and Kasper Frandsen would meet at the Bull's Eye at seven o'clock for a beer and a pizza. For old times' sake. She would easily have a couple of hours. Plenty of time.

The harbour was fairly busy for a Sunday afternoon. Sports sailors were tinkering with their dinghies and there was also activity on the fishing boats. It was cold, but the sun was shining and the Kattegat looked seductively like summer. The sea shimmered silver and mother-of-pearl and you couldn't tell from looking that the water temperature was only around 7° on the surface. Down below, it was much colder.

There was still considerable anger among the fishermen over SOK's decision to call off the rescue operation; she had read that in the paper. There were thinly veiled accusations of laziness and an indifference to human life because SOK hadn't considered it possible for the crew to survive for long in the rough sea. The gesture of sending divers down was small comfort. And when it turned out that there had been an extra man on board, the entire operation was regarded with huge scepticism.

Kir hadn't been to the harbour since. She had been brought up in this environment, but now she had absolutely no idea whether she was popular or unpopular with the fishermen after finding Nils's body and ending up in the pressure chamber. She hoped the former. Especially as she needed allies for her plan.

She parked the pickup by the harbour master's office. A small diving ship was moored at the first quay. She could see oxygen tanks and flippers of varying sizes scattered around the deck. It didn't look especially tidy.

She took the bunch of flowers and set off along the harbour.

She stopped at the empty berth where the *Marie af Grenå* had been moored. A couple of bouquets and a single wreath were placed against the railing. She placed her carnations next to the other flowers.

'So, are you on the mend, then?'

Svend Iversen, also known as Svend Skipper, was stacking crates on the deck of his old boat, which was tied up opposite the empty space.

'Absolutely,' Kir exaggerated.

'From what we heard it was quite a drama.'

'It wasn't as bad as it sounds.'

He looked unconvinced.

'You're still a bit pale round the gills, though.'

'Oh, you never get much of a tan in a diving suit.'

He grinned and rubbed his cheek.

'Fair point.'

He nodded towards the flowers.

'That was a real tragedy. Reckon the family will be allowed to bury them soon?'

This was always an issue whenever an unexplained death occurred. The bodies had to have a post-mortem and the cause of death had to be established before they were released to the next-of-kin.

'Soon, I hope,' she replied.

She walked round and leaned against a mooring post where Svend's boat, the *Karen Margrethe*, bobbed up and down in the water.

'What's the word amongst you lot?'

He shook his head and spat over the railings.

'Well, what do *you* reckon? SOK aren't exactly flavour of the month, as you probably know.'

She nodded.

'Has anyone thought about the boat?'

'What do you mean?'

'The *Marie*. She's in forty-five metres of water.'

'That's a bloody long way down. We'll never see her again.'

'Perhaps not. But doesn't anyone wonder why she sank?'

Svend took out a small box from the depths of his pocket, found a piece of chewing tobacco and popped it under his tongue. He narrowed his eyes for a moment and looked at her.

'There was a storm.'

'But you've been to sea in a storm and you didn't sink.'

'Yes, but . . .'

Kir straightened up.

'Then again, it's not something SOK are going to do anything about, is it? But if I were you, I'd be wondering why one of your own couldn't handle a storm.'

'Are you saying the boat . . .'

He shifted the chewing tobacco around inside his mouth.

'I'm not accusing anyone. But I'm a diver and I'm curious. If someone had a boat available and would sail me and a colleague out there, then I'd dive to see if I could find an explanation.'

She managed to deliver the offer in a suitably nonchalant fashion. She took a step forward.

'I'm sure Jens Bådsmand would want someone to take a closer look if anyone had tampered with his boat.'

Svend Skipper's eyes widened.

'Tampered with it? Do you really think so?'

Kir shrugged.

'Don't forget, there were three bodies down there, not two. The circumstances are already suspicious.'

He nodded slowly.

'You might be right about that. Perhaps someone ought to do it. Someone like you would have the location, wouldn't you?'

'Yes.'

'I'll speak to the lads.'

'Let me know what you decide.'

She patted the mooring post.

'He was a good man, Jens. A good father and a good fisherman.'

Svend sighed and turned over the chewing tobacco yet again.

'The best of the best. Hmm.'

He looked up at the clouds.

'Tomorrow's supposed to be fine.'

'I've got time,' she said. 'I'm on sick leave.'

He angled his head to one side. His mouth was churning away.

'Perhaps we should strike while the iron is hot.'

'Might be a good idea, Svend. Call me tomorrow morning if you and the others think we ought to do something about it.'

Her mobile rang as she was walking back to her car. It was Mark.

'Sorry. There's been a lot going on.'

'So I gather.'

Silence. She could never read him. Least of all over the telephone.

'I was wondering . . . Are you free tonight?'

'I have plans, Mark.'

'With Morten?'

She could hear his disappointment. And that he was working himself up into a lather. In a way, it *was* with Morten.

'Morten, yes.'

'OK,' he sulked. 'I hope you have a nice time.'

She smiled and knew he could hear it.

'You don't mean that.'

He clicked off.

70

THERE WAS STILL no Facebook message from Magnus. Peter switched off the computer, took the dog and went onto the cliff to let the fresh sea air clear his head.

After the walk he made a phone call. Then he got in his car and drove to the churchyard. It was quiet. The graves lay like small refuges in the afternoon sun, which had finally come out.

It felt like years, but it was only a few days since he had come here after Sister Beatrice had told him about the night of dead souls. He hadn't had any expectations. But, even so, he had secretly hoped for a meeting, he admitted to himself now. A meeting of the living and the dead.

His wish had been grotesquely fulfilled. He hadn't met My, but he had encountered an element of her in the shape of Bella. She had tugged at his sense of responsibility and broken down his defences. It troubled him that they'd had sex because that wasn't what he had wanted – least of all with her.

He heard a sound and turned around. Mark Bille was walking towards him. His footsteps seemed weary and his face haggard.

'Ulla Vang and Ketty Nimb have both made complaints about you.'

'I'm not surprised.'

'They say you behaved like a self-appointed police officer.'

'They're probably right.'

Mark gazed across the gravestones, but his eyes settled on Peter.

'We've abandoned your activist theory. There's no link between the killings and fur coats or animal raids.'

He shook his head. 'Last night's operation was a waste of time and resources.'

'Not entirely,' Peter objected. 'We know more now. Much more.'

As though they had made a joint decision to walk, they set off together. The gravel crunched beneath their feet, otherwise there was total silence.

'You're right,' Peter said. 'This isn't about fur. But it *is* about some of the women involved in the fur raids. They've known each other for a long time, from the days of their mothers' groups.'

Mark raised an eyebrow.

'You're looking for someone who has lost a child, or whose child is very sick. Someone who has reason to blame this network for the loss of their child. Their healthy child,' Peter added.

Mark shook his head as they walked.

'First you want us to think it's all about fur. Now all of a sudden it's something else.'

Peter explained patiently:

'The MMR vaccine. Does that mean anything to you?'

'Not off the cuff.'

Peter went into detail. Mark listened, but it was hard to know if he understood.

'It still sounds like conjecture to me,' Mark said afterwards. 'Yes, I can see that there might be a connection. But it could easily be about all sorts of other things.'

'The motive fits,' Peter said. 'You don't go out and kill people if someone releases your mink or vandalises your shop by tipping paint over your fur coats. You get angry. But you don't kill.'

He looked at Mark.

'Family is the strongest bond there is. The strongest motive for murder must be if someone kills your child.'

Frustrated, Mark threw up his hands.

'I can go along with that. So give us a name!'

'I can't. I haven't got one. You're the police. Contact the local Health Authority. Or get a warrant . . .'. Peter glanced sideways at Mark. 'That's not usually a problem for you.'

They had stopped their peregrinations around the cemetery paths. Peter's gaze drifted off.

'I should never have got involved in any of this,' he said.

'You probably had your reasons.'

Peter shot the other man a glance from the corner of his eye. For him, the police would always be a place you should never go. However. In another world, and at another time, the two of them might have been friends.

'So what are you going to do?' Mark asked.

'I don't know. But I can't drop this now.'

'You could always leave it to us.'

Peter couldn't suppress a smile.

'With everything I've just told you, you'll have plenty to do.'

His gaze swept randomly across the gravestones. Then it stopped abruptly, and at about the same time he heard Mark catch his breath.

It wasn't a grave. Nor was it a resting place for an urn. It was a memorial plate which had been sunk into the earth. Next to it, stuck into a purpose-made hole, was a fresh bouquet of flowers.

The plate was engraved with the following inscription:

Kurt Falk 1900–1945
RIP

But it was the wording beneath which held Peter's gaze:

'Viva la Muerte'

71

'Do you remember her, Sis? Isn't she beautiful?'

Lise Werge heard the voice from far away. She wanted to open her eyes but couldn't. Her body refused to obey. She remembered nothing. Didn't want to remember anything.

'Have a look. Now it's just the three of us. You and me. And her.'

One eye opened. The eyelid simply jumped before she could stop it. Simon. She had heard his voice. Now she could see him as well. He was sitting on the stiff-backed chair with a gleam in his eyes. He caressed the primitive, rectangular arm rests. He leaned back, pressing his neck against the iron.

'Haven't you missed her all these years?'

These years. They had passed and she had shut him out of her mind. Seventeen years. Back then, seventeen years would have seemed like an eternity, like enormous security. But now time had caught up with her. And here he was. This was what she had always feared.

'I'm cold.'

It was her mouth that had uttered the words. If she had known that it would betray her, she would not have opened it. He got up and kicked her in the ribs.

'There. That'll warm you up. There's nothing like feeling your own body.'

The pain sent waves through her and bile rose into her throat. Cold fear poured into every limb and goose pimples appeared on her skin. He grabbed her hair from the back. She felt something woollen pressing against her lips.

'Open up.'

She clenched her lips.

'Open your mouth or I'll use the knife on you again.'

Again? What had he done? She had no recollection. Had he cut her? Had he chopped off a finger or two, as he had always threatened to do? Suddenly she couldn't feel her body.

'This is your final warning, Sis.'

She couldn't. It was as if she had lockjaw. Then she felt the cold steel force its way in between her lips.

'The knife is your friend,' he whispered. 'It loves all your orifices.'

He twisted it and she tasted blood. She opened her mouth with a gasp, and the woollen sock – or whatever it was – was pushed in, filling her mouth and almost choking her.

He slid his hand up her thigh. The blade rasped against her nylon tights and blood flowed in narrow, ticklish streams and collected beneath her.

'All your orifices,' he whispered. 'Including this one.'

She froze, then shook her head frantically. The blade cut through her panties.

'Does it turn you on, Sis, being fucked by a kitchen knife? Is that the best you could do? Did nobody else want you?'

The steel cut into the flesh, or that was how it felt. She had no idea what was happening down there, but she expected the blade to penetrate her at any moment. The gag reflex took over. Spasms rolled upwards from the pit of her stomach.

He held up the knife once more.

'On the other hand,' he said. 'Ultimately, it's a question of choice.'

He stroked her hair with the steel. 'And of course the choice has already been made.'

She closed her eye. If she vomited, she would choke and he would do nothing to help her. Or would he? What had he just said? He had other plans for her. She knew she was going to die, but not in this way. She would die in the way he had decided. In a way he had probably been fantasising about all these years.

The effort involved in suppressing the spasms caused her to sweat profusely. For a brief moment she was grateful for the cold floor.

How had she ended up here? She had been in a state of terror ever since she'd heard from her mother that the doctors had let him out, but she had thought she was safe in her own home.

In fact, Lise had already known that he was out before her mother had confirmed it. As soon as she heard the story about the girl in the moat, she had known. Once the manner of her death had been made public. Not that anything had been said or written in so many words, but Lise could put two and two together: shackled with iron rings. Broken neck.

She didn't need to know any more.

But how had she ended up here?

Simon kicked her again.

'Now don't you go falling asleep on me, Sis. We've got work to do. We've got a game to play, haven't we? The game we never finished.'

He sat down again on the wooden chair that their grandfather had built.

'Ahh. This is very comfortable.'

He leaned back.

'Don't you remember, Sis?'

She blinked. The funeral. She had returned home after the funeral and he had been there. How did he get the keys? How had he got in?

Her mother, of course. Lise kept a spare key at her mother's house in case she locked herself out. She had never imagined that this would happen. And here she was. Her punishment had arrived. The punishment for being different. For going against the family. For that was what she had done. She had betrayed her family, that was how they saw it.

And now she was going to die.

Once upon a time she had thought she had reconciled herself to the idea of death, but now panic gripped her throat and she heard herself whimpering.

'Now you probably think Mum was in on this,' he said chattily. 'And in a way she was, in her own passive fashion.'

He grinned.

'Handy that she's such a heavy sleeper. I made sure she was in a really nice, deep sleep when I moved you in here.'

Sleeping pills. He had given their mother an overdose. And what about Lise herself? Somehow he must have got her into a car – her car? – and then driven her here.

She remembered fragments now. He had held a knife to her throat when she locked the door. She had tried to resist. Instinctively she had thrust a sharp heel behind her and hit him in the shin. The knife had slipped to the side, but not before it had cut her. Blood had spurted out, although it was only a surface wound. She had fled into the living room. He followed. She remembered him saying:

'Well done, Sis. Fight for your life.'

She remembered seeing the thrill of the chase in his eyes. She had screamed and shouted in desperation and thrown things at him. But it was a small flat. He had trapped her in a corner of the bedroom.

She didn't remember anything else. Perhaps that was just as well.

'You were so compliant, Sis, I almost got bored. I coaxed you down to the car. You walked next to me without any trouble at all.'

That was because you were holding me at knifepoint, she wanted to say; his words had reminded her of more. The drive, her behind the wheel and him holding the knife. The house, which was dark and deadly quiet apart from Alma's snoring in the bedroom. The staircase going down.

'Anyway. We're wasting time.'

He jumped off the chair.

'We'd better get started.'

He lifted her up. She discovered that she couldn't stand up.

'Oh, that's right. I think I broke your leg. Never mind, you're not going very far, Sis.'

He held her like a rag doll. She started to black out as blood from the cut ran down her leg and soaked into her tights and the taste of steel spread around her mouth. She could feel his muscles. He was strong. He had probably been working out all the time he had been incarcerated.

'Please sit down, Sis.'

He pushed her down onto the garrotte.

72

MARK LEFT THE cemetery with an uneasy feeling that the threads were coming together, not into a beautiful and logical pattern but something that looked more like the knot on a hangman's rope.

Viva la Muerte. Peter Boutrup had stopped in his tracks, just as Mark had at the sight of the memorial plate. Not because of the name – Peter obviously didn't recognise it. But because of the rest. The inscription. *Viva la Muerte.* Long live death. The motto of the Spanish Legion, Peter had told him, after which he had at last gone on to tell him about the rosary which Sister Beatrice had given him and which Mark had seen on the day they had searched Peter's house on the cliff.

Viva la Muerte. Nothing was buried under the plate. It was purely commemorative. Kurt Falk's body had never been found.

Lise Werge lived in an apartment block in the northern part of the town.

The area was quiet, curtains were closed and blinds were down, as if the buildings had also decided to heed the day of rest. He parked, located the entrance and rang the intercom, but there was no reply. Undeterred, he rang the neighbour's bell.

'Who is it?' a crisp voice asked.

'Mark Bille Hansen, Grenå Police. Please would you let me in?'

There was a pause. He could actually hear the woman hesitating.

'Who are you looking for?'

'Lise Werge.'

'She's not in.'

'Nevertheless, I'd still like access.'

'Has anything happened to her?'

How would I know? Now open that bloody door before something happens to you.

That was what he was thinking, but he said something else.

'Perhaps there's a caretaker I could contact?'

'He's not here. It's Sunday.'

He was about to make a further comment when help appeared in the shape of an old lady and a small dog, who let him enter in their wake. Both of them subjected him to a critical glare.

He felt ridiculous as he finally stood outside Lise Werge's front door and rang the bell. There was no response. The neighbour came out.

'She's not in.'

'Do you know where she is?'

'She was here yesterday.'

Mark tried the door. Nothing happened. Then he spotted the stain on the doorstep. And another one. He tracked an almost invisible pattern towards the lift. He had seen blood often enough to know what it was.

'Who's the caretaker?'

'His office is closed on Sundays.'

'I just need his name and address.'

At long last something happened. She shuffled inside her flat and returned with a business card, which she was happy enough to show him. Judging by the holes in the corners, it had been pinned to her noticeboard.

'Thank you. I promise you'll get it back.'

He took the lift down and found more bloodstains. By the exit he followed them out into the car park. He roused the caretaker – a man called Søren Alm – and enticed him away from the Sports Channel. Together they went upstairs to Lise's flat, and Søren Alm unlocked the door.

It took Mark two seconds to realise they were looking at a crime scene. There was blood on the carpet in the hallway, some of the furniture had been knocked over and a mirror had been smashed.

'Lise?'

He entered with caution and searched every room in the flat, counting at least three places where a physical assault had taken place and where there was a lot of blood. Not streams of it. Nothing to suggest an artery had been cut. But enough for him to call Anna Bagger to request assistance while he carefully explored the flat, taking care not to touch anything.

He was reminded of the day Lise Werge had arrived in her car at her mother's house. The family resemblance was striking. Why had she turned up at Melissa's funeral? Did she know the girl? Nothing in the investigation had suggested any sort of link between the two of them, so what was going on here?

Mark looked around. Lise Werge's home looked like a perfectly ordinary flat inhabited by a single woman of around fifty. The decor was fairly austere, yet had an obvious feminine touch, the clean lines and bright colours of the furniture. Very little in the way of knick-knacks. That didn't seem to be Lise Werge's style. Nor did she care much for family photographs, it seemed. The ones he found were, for some strange reason, back to front on the window sill. There were two of them. One of her children, he presumed, a boy around ten and a girl around twelve – although he had no idea about children's ages. Both had the same family features and the photograph looked as if it had been taken quite a few years ago. The other one was even older. It was of three children sitting on a bench. He took it and turned it round: 1972, it said. The boy sat in the middle, flanked by two girls, of which one had to be Lise aged twelve. She looked just like her own daughter when she was her age.

He heard someone clear their throat. The neighbour was standing by the living-room door.

'Stay where you are,' he said at once.

'You forgot to return my card.'

'Oh, right.'

She came closer, even though he had told her not to.

'What on earth has happened here?'

348

Mark ushered her outside. In his haste, he forgot he was still holding the photograph of the three siblings in his hand.

'Here you are.'

He rummaged around in his pocket and gave her back the caretaker's business card. She took it and nodded at the photograph.

'That's her brother and sister.'

'Do you know where I can find them?'

'Her sister's in prison. She killed her husband. She never talks about her brother.'

'Can you tell me her sister's name?'

'The surname's Byriel. First name Lone. She used to work at a solicitor's office before . . . it happened.'

'How long has Lise lived here?'

The woman pondered.

'Let me see. I moved here in 1999. Lise came six months after me. She must have moved in at the start of 2000.'

'And you're good friends?'

'Good neighbours,' she corrected him. 'We have a coffee every now and then. But we're not in each other's pockets . . . Lise values her privacy,' she added.

'Thank you,' Mark said and flashed a smile. 'You've been a great help.'

Reluctantly, she returned to her own flat, but Mark noticed that she had left her front door ajar.

Good neighbours, he thought. For over ten years. They had drunk coffee in each other's flats and Lise had told her about her sister in prison, but never mentioned her brother.

73

Kir's house stood in an enclosed field at the far end of the old summer-house area south of Grenå. It was from the 1960s, with black wood cladding and an asphalt roof. Her red pickup was parked outside.

Peter rang the bell, but it didn't work. One look at the property told the story of a house in charming decay. When something went wrong the response had obviously been: patch it up. Cracks and gaps in the rotting window frames had been filled with silicone, paint had been applied on the areas with the worst peeling, a loose gutter above the door had been tied up with a piece of string. Grey smoke poured out of the chimney.

'Kir?'

He knocked on the window. She came out.

'Did I wake you?'

She shook her head much too vigorously. Her hair was a mess of red curls and she looked bleary-eyed. She was wearing a grey track-suit and had sheepskin slippers on her feet. He couldn't help but smile.

'Come in.'

'I thought I would take a look at your house.'

However, that wasn't the real reason he was here.

'Coffee? Tea?'

She seemed flustered, possibly even nervous.

'I can come back another time, if this isn't convenient.'

'No, no, it's fine.'

In a neutral tone of voice she started telling him about the house, highlighting the improvements she had in mind.

'I've saved up thirty thousand kroner. I don't know how far that will go.'

'I can give you a quote, if you want.'

She did want. They sat for a while. The silence wasn't embarrassing, it felt cosy. The fire crackled in the wood-burning stove and the tea was hot. The house was cheap but nicely furnished, although she clearly wasn't a born nest-builder. Her background as a soldier could not be denied. It showed in the posters displayed on the walls and the objects lying on the window sills. Where other women might collect glass figurines and exotic plants, she had military and diving treasures, such as barnacle-covered knives and seashells as big as your hand, old cartridge shells and photographs of a life above and below water.

'*Viva la muerte*. Are you familiar with that expression?' he asked.

'Is it Spanish?'

'Long live death.'

She nodded.

'Why?'

'You told me about the garrotte. I thought there might be a connection.'

'With what?'

She looked confused.

'The Spanish Foreign Legion.'

He could see her mind working overtime from the way she narrowed her eyes and averted her face slightly. He grabbed the opportunity to tell her about the rosary and his meeting at the cemetery with Mark.

She nodded.

'I think he's checking out the family in connection with those bones in the box.'

'Kurt Falk's?'

'Yes, but I don't know any more than that.'

She got up and fetched something from her bookcase. It was a family photograph album.

'The Legion. I saw them marching once, in a Catholic procession in Malaga. They have strong links with the church.'

She opened it and he saw photographs of a procession of priests carrying Christ in agony on the cross through the streets, flanked by soldiers in green shirts and trousers with black braces. On their heads they wore 'chapiri' caps with red tassels.

'Their training is said to be the hardest in the world,' Kir said. 'I've heard live bullets are fired at their feet when they have to march or run, but that might be just a rumour. They call themselves *"novios de la muerte"*.'

She met his gaze.

'It means bridegrooms of death.'

He looked into her eyes, which were always so intense. He remembered what he had thought about her, that she didn't have an agenda. The question crossed his lips before he had time to think.

'Why did you become a soldier, Kir?'

He watched her struggling to come up with an answer which would satisfy them both.

'Because it's an honest trade,' she said at length, which was entirely in keeping with his view of her. 'Now, of course, there's just as much bullshit in the Armed Forces as in the rest of the world, but being a soldier is ultimately a simple choice for each individual: kill or be killed.'

'And the garrotte? How do you view that?'

She thought about it again.

'The garrotte isn't a weapon like the ones you use on the battlefield or in any other kind of combat. The garrotte is what the gallows once were in Denmark: the ultimate punishment. The sentence you got for committing the ultimate crime. Murder.'

'So there needs to be a trial?'

'Of some kind.'

'And then a verdict is pronounced.'

She nodded. She seemed to be on the point of adding something, but stopped herself when a car pulled up outside her house. She got to her feet and ran her palms down her thighs as though they were sweaty. Though he didn't know her very well, he could tell she wasn't her usual self.

He got up.

'Anyway, I'd better get going. Thanks for the tea. I'll sort out that quote for you.'

She nodded absent-mindedly and opened the door. Changing the guard, he thought, when a man she quite clearly knew appeared in the doorway. He was taller than Peter and stronger, like a bear. Square-jawed. The face was square too; hair short and blond like Peter's. He had a small scar near one eye and didn't seem terribly enthusiastic about bumping into another man on the front doorstep.

'Morten,' Kir said. 'This is Peter. He came to take a look at the house.'

Morten nodded.

'Hi.'

Peter nodded and turned to Kir.

'I'll get you that quote.'

There was something in her eyes he couldn't fathom and for a moment he was tempted to hang around until this Morten had finished his watch.

'Great. See you later.'

It sounded deliberately casual. He turned and caught a glimpse of Morten's broad back as he stepped inside the house just before Kir closed the door.

74

K<small>IR</small> <small>WAITED OUTSIDE</small> Kasper's house. Tension lay like a fine layer of sweat on her skin. She repressed the meeting with Peter. This was about now; now was what she was good at.

She had been in far more dangerous situations than this. She had hunted pirates. She had killed. She had handled firearms and done close combat. She wasn't scared. She was fired up.

While waiting, she took the time to analyse her own motives. With every fibre of her being, she wanted this man locked up and rendered harmless. Yes, she wanted to wipe that smug grin off his extremely irritating, evil face. He had maligned and humiliated her. But uppermost in her mind was her intention to stop him carrying out his dark deeds. She needed to make sure he wasn't in a position to kill innocent children any more.

She sat in her pickup parked some distance down the street from the grey bungalow. She was wearing camouflage clothing. It was getting dark and fortunately the moon was covered by clouds. A street lamp gave off a pale light, but apart from that the illumination was nothing to shout about.

The house seemed to be empty. There was only a single lamp lit above the front door, otherwise it was dark. Morten had picked Kasper up and they had gone into town together. Everything had worked out perfectly.

She carried only a few tools and a small, powerful halogen torch. Everything was in the pockets of her camouflage vest. A penknife in her trouser pocket was her only weapon.

Carefully she opened the car door and stepped out. Behind windows she could see figures milling around, and the smell of fried food was borne through the air by the breeze. Family Denmark was hungry tonight. No one cared what was happening in the street outside.

She darted around the back and found the rear entrance, hidden from view by the garage. The old Ruko lock was a cinch. A small click, a twist of the universal key and she was inside.

She softly closed the door behind her and located her torch in her pocket. It wasn't much bigger than a pen, but it sent a strong light into the nooks and crannies.

She was in a back hall. There was nothing here, apart from coats and boots, so she opened the next door and found herself in the heart of the house, which wasn't very big: a small, old-fashioned kitchen from the 1950s; a small living room with a corner sofa and a dining table and a desk in another corner. All very neat and devoid of interest.

Where was the garrotte? Where was the smoking gun she dreamed of presenting to Mark? What was she actually doing?

Determined, she continued to search. She went through drawers and cupboards and made sure she left everything looking untouched. But it was all dull, impersonal and predictable.

The house had no basement. So where could he hide his activities? The thought struck her that he might have a bolt-hole somewhere. A summer house, maybe, or a cottage in the forest, or another house he had access to.

Then she remembered the garage. She kept all her stuff in the garage. Kasper was a diver. Where did he store everything to do with his job?

She had just decided to examine the garage when she heard a car in the street outside. She quickly turned off her torch and held her breath, hoping it was someone visiting the neighbour, but it sounded ominously close. The engine was switched off. The car was right outside the bungalow.

She tiptoed into the living room. A figure was coming up the garden path. Was it Kasper? Perhaps his plans with Morten had fallen through. Kasper's temper could have flared up and led to a row.

The bell rang and her heart skipped a beat. She waited as the seconds passed. Then the bell rang again, followed by fists beating on the door. She heard a voice she recognised:

'Kasper? Open the door. Are you there?'

Frands. Kasper's brother. He shouted through the letterbox:

'We need to talk about the rent, Kasper!'

Then she heard a key being turned in the lock and the door opened with a creak. The light was turned on. In one single leap she was behind the door, just before he entered the living room and turned on the light there too. She heard his breathing close by and she could see him through the crack. He stood still for a moment, as if deciding what to do. Then he marched across to the desk she had just inspected. He pulled out the drawers, looking for something. Money, she guessed. Frands had obviously rented the house to his newly divorced brother.

If he turned around, he would see her. She couldn't run the risk. She took a deep breath, thanked the Lord the carpet had a thick pile and dashed into the passage.

'Kasper?'

He had heard her. She headed for the front door. She couldn't get there fast enough.

'What the . . . Come back!'

His roar followed her all the way into the street. She sprinted. Her legs went like pistons and she was grateful for her fitness and the poor street illumination. She tried to shake him off by darting in and out of the neighbouring gardens. His heavy footsteps followed. She came to a stop in a hedge deep in the residential area, where she curled up behind some bushes. She heard him poking around. Neighbours came out and turned on lights; voices buzzed angrily.

She waited. Nothing happened. Eventually the voices died down and the footsteps faded away. No police cars came hurtling down the street with their sirens blaring. No spotlights swept the area to catch the burglar. He had given up. Maybe he had a reason not to involve the police. Perhaps he was Kasper's sidekick.

She heard a car driving away and squatted on the damp ground for a while until she judged it was safe to emerge from her hideout.

He might come back, but she hadn't completed her mission yet. She tiptoed back, with several glances over her shoulder and her ears pricked. The house now lay in darkness. Frands's car was gone. She opened the door to the garage, which didn't look all that different to her own. Diving gear hung from pegs or lay neatly folded on shelves. There was no room for the car. It was in the carport.

She shone the halogen torch into every corner, but found only what she would have expected to find: wetsuits, drysuits, boxes of flippers and snorkels and weighted belts. All sorts of measuring devices – he appeared to be just as much of a gear nerd as she was – coils of rope, masks, a harpoon, various knives. Murder weapons, yes, if that was what your mind was set on, but no worse than what she had lying around.

On the surface they were just a diver's ordinary working tools. However, she was nothing if not dogged and she started searching with a grim determination. Every box was emptied and the contents put back in the same places. She felt every shelf. She turned diving suits inside out. Examined every last nook and cranny.

Nothing.

She was about to give up and leave the place without the evidence she had come for when she heard yet another car. This time it was Morten giving Kasper a lift home.

She had to get out. She looked around. She was loath to leave this place empty-handed. Then she spotted the shelf above the door. She hadn't got that far yet. There was a bundle up there. She reached up, grabbed it and a plastic bag fell out. She opened it. She found a roll of gaffer tape, a coil of rope and some black clothing: a black tracksuit and a pair of dark plimsolls, size 45. But there was also something else. She unfolded the triangular piece of cloth and turned it over this way and that, trying to work out what it was for. Then she found the holes. Two for the eyes, a wider one for the mouth. It was an executioner's hood.

With her heart in her mouth, she quickly stuffed the cloth into the bag, hearing Morten's car go off down the road and Kasper let himself into the house. Then she slipped out through the garage door and walked down the garden path. She reached the street at the same time as a light was turned on inside the house, and she strolled calmly back to her pickup.

75

MØGELKJÆR STATE PRISON lay near Juelsminde in beautiful surroundings. A few years ago the women's prison in Amdrup outside Odder had been closed and the women were transferred here. There were eight prisoners in the women's ward, and for some reason, Mark found it depressing. Perhaps he was sexist. But in his view certain combinations didn't work. It was just like food. You wouldn't put mayonnaise on a roast pork sandwich, nor would you serve herring with red cabbage. It was like that with women and prison. They didn't go together.

And yet here they were, the women criminals. And one of them was Lone Byriel, Lise Werge's sister.

He skimmed her papers and saw the attached photographs, one full face and one profile. Without make-up and with a blank expression, Lone Byriel looked just like any other woman in her late forties. But her story was very far from ordinary.

As he read the file, it was hard not to admire Lone Byriel's initiative. There was no doubt her marriage to Laust Byriel had not been a walk in the park. They had two – now adult – children together, but alcoholism and violence had entered the picture right from the start. Laust Byriel had two convictions for assault but had nevertheless managed to charm Lone into marrying him, and then the spiral of violence grew and the marriage took a nose-dive, hardly before it had begun. Lone had stayed for the sake of the children and taken the beatings. But one day when Laust was asleep in a comatose stupor on the sofa after a particularly violent episode, she had looked at him and made up her mind. In court, she had explained that killing him was her only way out. She knew he would stalk her and that she would be looking over her shoulder for the rest of her life if she merely walked out on him.

She worked in a solicitor's office and was perfectly aware of the punishment she could expect. But she had calculated that the children were old enough to take care of themselves and was hoping for a verdict of manslaughter rather than murder – in light of her husband's threats, which she had recorded on tape, and the photographs she had taken of herself after the worst beatings.

So it was premeditated, but also in self-defence, the day she placed a pillow over his face, took the sharpest kitchen knife she could find and plunged it into his chest over and over and over again.

As she had said in court:

'There was no room for half-measures.'

The judge was a woman and the jurors accepted her explanation. But she had to be punished, so she got five years in prison for manslaughter.

So far, she had served two and was likely to be released on probation within the next six months.

When the door opened and a woman entered, Mark was almost certain he had made a mistake and that he was at a board meeting in a major company. He recognised nothing of the woman in the photograph. Except, possibly, the short neck – which on her was in no way reminiscent of a tortoise – and the guarded eyes. Everything else was different. She was wearing a light grey skirt that reached just above her knees with a matching tailored jacket and a pink blouse, and she could have been Anna Bagger on one of her super-efficient days with immaculate make-up. High heels clicked rhythmically across the floor as they came towards him and she held out her hand like a world leader receiving a colleague on an official state visit.

'Grenå Police?' Lone Byriel said, raising her brows mockingly. 'It's not every day we have such distinguished visitors.'

Mark nodded to indicate they should sit down. There was nothing world-leader-like about the decor, which had institution written all over the functional furniture and the hard-wearing upholstery.

'I've come about your sister, Lise Werge.'

Mark noticed her eyes showed no signs of fear. There was only businesslike interest.

'What about Lise?'

'She's disappeared. We think she was attacked in her flat.'

'Oh, no.'

They were the right words, but they were not articulated in the right way.

'You don't seem surprised,' Mark said.

Lone drummed her long fingernails on her cheek and looked at him.

'That's because I'm not.'

Mark leaned forward.

'Care to tell me why?'

She sat considering her answer while she fiddled with the sleeve of her jacket.

'I might as well tell you. You're going to find out anyway.'

'Tell me what?'

'My brother. Our brother,' she corrected herself.

'I saw a photo of you as children in Lise's flat.'

She laughed.

'I'm surprised she has that on display. I wouldn't exactly say that she and Simon are close.'

'What can you tell me about Simon?'

She crossed her legs modestly and smoothed her skirt.

'I'm afraid you'll think we're a family of criminals when you hear this. But if I'm frank, Simon *is* different. He has what they call a borderline personality disorder. He's been locked up for the last seventeen years.'

Mark felt the adrenaline pump restless energy around his bloodstream. Seventeen years. He thought of the age of the teenage victims.

'Locked up for what?'

She flung out her hand. This time it resembled more a helpless gesture than anything else.

'He killed his heavily pregnant girlfriend. That's the short version,' she added.

'And the long one?'

'The long one is that she was infected with something nasty and that the child died inside her, and that triggered something in Simon.'

'How did she die?'

'You'd better check the files. I wasn't there.'

Mark thought about the genes going back to the Cardinal. It was as if this family had played by its own rules right from the start. The thought of some kind of moral inbreeding wasn't far away. Was it possible for an entire family to encapsulate itself and live according to its own laws?

'What about Lise?' he asked. 'Could Simon have abducted her?'

Lone pursed her lips and shook her head slightly from side to side as if to suggest that she wasn't sure about Lise and Simon.

'Possibly,' she said. 'He's unlikely to have forgotten that she told the truth in court.'

'And the truth was?'

Pause. She studied her nails.

'You'd better read up on that as well.'

He didn't know how to shock her into giving him more. She didn't seem like someone who had strong feelings for her brother or her sister. But perhaps she didn't have strong feelings in general. 'What's Lise like?'

Now she smiled. It was a cool, measured smile, like a dental assistant's or an indulgent consultant's. He'd met more of those than he cared to remember.

'Lise's just like the rest of us. Only she doesn't know it.'

'What's that supposed to mean?'

Her nails tapped on the table. Lone smiled, but only to herself.

'She loves to polish her little halo. But she's no better than the rest of us.'

'Does she visit you?'

'Oh yes. She loves it. She always brings me books.'

'When was she last here?'

'Only a couple of days ago.'

'Did she want anything in particular?'

Mark tried to circumvent the businesslike façade, but no matter which approach he took, he hit a brick wall. And now she was casually rubbing the corners of her mouth with a finger.

'The silly little creature was rattled by something she'd read in the newspaper. She wanted to know if I knew anything about it.'

'About what?'

'About the murder of that girl, of course. It happened close to Mum's house, and then the method . . .'

'What about it?'

She pursed her lips again and picked a piece of fluff off her skirt.

'Nothing. I told her to forget it.'

'Forget what?'

She looked at him with wide-open eyes.

'Forget that Simon might have anything to do with it, obviously.'

76

Poul Gerrick lived modestly in a newish terraced house in Lystrup.

The retired doctor who opened the door was an elderly gentleman in slippers with tousled morning hair. Peter introduced himself.

'How can I help you?'

'I live in Djursland. I was the last person to see Melissa Brask alive.'

The doctor nodded.

'Terrible tragedy. I knew her mother.'

'That's why I'm here,' Peter said. 'Because, years ago, you used to be the family's GP.'

Poul Gerrick frowned.

'Precisely, years ago. What's this all about?'

The tone was not one of hostility, only a friendly curiosity. Peter seized the moment.

'Childhood illnesses.'

'What about them?'

'I'm interested in the MMR vaccine and a measles outbreak which infected two babies at Elev Nursery many years ago.'

Poul Gerrick stood still for a couple of seconds, absorbedly staring at a point to the right of Peter. Then he said:

'Why would that old story have anything to do with Melissa?'

Peter explained.

'I believe Melissa's death was some kind of revenge for what happened back then.'

He looked at the elderly man and wondered if this was the point where he would slam the door in his face, or cite patient confidentiality as the reason he could not discuss his patients, living or dead. But instead, Poul Gerrick said:

'You'd better come inside.'

Peter followed him into a study with an old-fashioned gentleman's desk and a couple of narrow armchairs either side of a small round table. The shelves were packed with books and a glance revealed most of them to be about medicine.

Poul Gerrick invited Peter to sit down in an armchair. He sat down in the other.

He gestured with his hand.

'This is my den. If the world is against me – and this happens more and more often, even now, without any patients – I prefer to read my books here.'

'You make it sound as though patients were a chore.'

'Don't get me wrong. On the whole, helping my fellow human beings was a privilege.'

He looked at Peter, as if trying to assess whether he would understand what was about to come next.

'Only I discovered that not everyone wanted to be helped.'

'Such as Alice Brask and Bella Albertsen?'

The reaction was hesitant.

'You are of course aware that I have a duty of confidentiality.'

'I apologise.'

He could have bitten his tongue. They sat for a while in silence.

'Actually the police should be here rather than me,' Peter said eventually.

'Perhaps,' the doctor said. 'But, as it happens, you're here.'

Peter leaned forward in his chair.

'There's a killer out there. Killing young people. People whose mothers didn't have them vaccinated. They infected the killer's child. Does that make sense?'

Poul Gerrick stared at him. The movement of his lips suggested he was searching for the right words.

'What makes you think that was how it was?'

Peter carefully outlined the case. The doctor looked as if he understood. At last he nodded.

'You may be right. It sounds rather far-fetched, of course, but yes, something happened back then, which taken to extremes might conceivably have triggered a thirst for revenge.'

He shook his head, like someone who has given up trying to understand the world.

'I'm retired now and I can say whatever I like. No one ever really asked me about the specific circumstances.'

'I thought the local Health Authority was involved,' Peter said. 'I thought the whole thing was quite official back then.'

'They spoke to me for two seconds and closed the case in three. It was bad publicity for the council and there was a council election the following month. It never made it to the press.'

'But they closed the nursery?'

Poul Gerrick snorted.

'Renovation was the official reason. No one cared a jot about the truth.'

'I suppose nothing illegal had happened, had it?'

'Lots of things aren't illegal. But they can still be dangerous.'

'Did anyone die?'

Poul Gerrick shook his head slowly.

'But the actions of the parents who had started the spread of the infection were deeply irresponsible.'

Peter asked:

'So if no one died, then what did happen?'

The doctor crossed his arms and bobbed a slipper-clad foot up and down.

'In rare cases measles can lead to nasty complications. One of the children got encephalitis and another suffered permanent hearing damage.'

'What happened to those children?'

'The child with encephalitis developed very slowly and had permanent learning disabilities.'

'How bad?'

'At the time we assessed that she would never get beyond the mental age of a five-year-old. I don't know what happened later.

366

The parents eventually moved away. The other escaped with her mental faculties intact, fortunately, but lost hearing in both ears.'

'What were the names of the parents of the first child?'

'Do you seriously believe they're the ones killing other people's children now? After all these years?'

'I think it's a possibility. I think they feel they're punishing the parents by killing their children.'

The doctor looked unconvinced.

'But the girl didn't die. And why wait until now, after so many years?'

It was a question that had also occupied Peter.

'Caring for a disabled child is hard work,' he said. 'Perhaps the killer has been waiting, planning the murders all the years he was looking after his sick daughter.'

'You're suggesting she's dead now,' the doctor said.

Peter nodded.

'She might have died recently. But for the killer, she died many years ago. The way I see it, it's the only explanation for the seventeen-year delay.'

The doctor studied his hands in his lap. Then he raised his head.

'The father was absolutely distraught. As well as angry, obviously. The mother reacted differently. She retreated inside herself. They were divorced a couple of years later, that I do know.'

He looked at Peter.

'The parents agreed that the father would have custody.'

'Do you know where he lives now?'

The doctor shook his head.

'Would you at least give me his name?'

Time passed. Peter could see the contradictory feelings at work in Poul Gerrick's face: consideration for patient confidentiality and the Hippocratic oath and everything he had worked for and believed in. And consideration for the young lives that had been taken and those it might still be possible to save.

Finally, he nodded. He opened his mouth and closed it again several times, sighed, and looked out of the window before standing up and letting in the fresh air. He deliberated further, while inhaling and exhaling deeply. Then he turned to Peter and gave him what he had come for. Due process. Followed by a verdict.

On his way home Kir's words kept churning around in his head. He was convinced that this was what it was all about: one man who found it acceptable to appoint himself police, judge and – ultimately – executioner.

77

It was a beautiful day and the weather was perfect for a dive.

Kir stood by the gunwale and let the breeze catch her hair and lash her skin with salt. She listened to it and the steady chug-chug of the engine and could make out Skipper's figure in the wheelhouse, as seagulls followed them over the last stretch out of the harbour.

She studied Morten, who was by her side. He stood with an inscrutable expression on his face as he looked towards the coast. Here, in the clear light of day, she had a little twinge of doubt in her stomach. What were they actually doing?

They had both been high on adrenaline when they met at her house after the events of Saturday night. She had shown him what she had found and had finally managed to convince him, even though it had been an uphill struggle. Morten was a man who was prepared to give the accused the full benefit of the doubt, she sensed that plainly, and she respected him for it. But the bag with the executioner's hood and the other objects told their own story, even he had to admit that.

Kasper was guilty. And his brother Frands might be guilty too. Brothers working in concert had been seen before. Not least in Kir's own family, where her two brothers had stepped outside the law and plunged into the abyss together.

'But why?' Morten had continued to insist. 'Why would they do it? Kill teenagers like that . . .'

Kir had turned it over in her mind yet again, all too aware that her reply was influenced by her personal experiences.

'To demonstrate their power.'

Frands and Kasper were both macho types who liked to flex their muscles. Kasper beat his ex-wife and had made obscene suggestions to a female colleague. Frands had been condescending towards her, to put it mildly, while they were struggling with Melissa's body. She elaborated.

'To demonstrate the power they can't show in their everyday life when they have to work with others.'

Morten had taken a sip of his wine and said:

'And they get their kicks by showing up in the eye of the storm when the bodies are found?'

Kir nodded.

'It's been seen before.'

'But why teenagers?'

Again Kir had her answer ready.

'Jealousy, perhaps. Because they have a future.'

'And that is what has to be destroyed?'

'Something along those lines, I think.'

They had been sitting on her sofa. It was such a long time since she'd had a man in her bed. I could ask him to stay, she thought. I could have him tonight.

Nevertheless, she dismissed the thought. It was too complicated.

'Perhaps it's tied up with his divorce,' Morten had then suggested. 'And him not living with his children any more.'

Kir had heard and seen enough twisted motives to wallpaper an entire railway station. People did crazy, stupid, terrible things for reasons very few would understand. She was ready to buy his explanation.

'Kasper clearly has an urge to play executioner. Jeanette says so herself.'

'But then why doesn't he kill her and the kids?' said good-natured Morten, playing devil's advocate.

'Perhaps he will. Later,' Kir said after further reflection. 'When he's had enough practice.'

It had grown late and they had drunk some more wine. Morten had reckoned she should call Mark Bille immediately and brief him on this latest development in the case, but she held back. Partly because it didn't look good that she had broken the law to secure evidence. And partly because she knew perfectly well that even a bag with an executioner's hood, some rope and a roll of gaffer tape wasn't enough. More concrete evidence was needed.

Early the next morning Svend Skipper had called to say that he was up for a trip to Læsø if she was still on. He had talked to the other fishermen and everyone agreed it was worth taking advantage of the opportunity to dive down to have a look at the *Marie*.

'For everyone's sake,' as Svend had put it on the telephone. 'And the weather is perfect.'

And so here they were, on what was effectively their own diving ship. They had lugged their gear on board in next to no time, and she had given Svend the location of the *Marie* forty-five metres down. For extra security they had towed a rubber dinghy with an outboard motor, which they could dive from. It couldn't go wrong.

She gazed at the waves and the foam crests rising with calm regularity, as if on a conveyor belt. All of a sudden she couldn't rid herself of the notion that she had acted hastily. Yes, she had found a bag of circumstantial evidence, yes, Kasper was a violent, unpleasant man, and yes, there were grounds for taking a look at the boat on the sea bed. But she had no authority to back her up. She had exceeded her powers and ignored everything she had been trained to respect. She was in overdrive, pushed there by a frustrated love life and enforced idleness after her visit to the pressure chamber, she knew that. And with Morten standing so close to her she felt uneasy, but she was painfully aware that this wasn't his fault. The fault was entirely hers. *She* had got them into this mess. *She* had to try to finish this in the best possible way, preferably with useful evidence to show for it, then get it back to dry land and get Morten out of her life.

* * *

'Are we going down together?' Morten asked.

She had thought it through. There were pros and cons with every option because the reality was that they were embarking on an unauthorised dive, which would have horrified her colleagues in Kongsøre if they had known.

'I think you should stay up here,' she said. 'Be on standby with the line so you know if I'm in trouble.'

'OK.'

He was as compliant as always. She was the expert. She had much more training under her belt than he had. But she had also just been treated for nitrogen narcosis and was still on sick leave.

'Are you sure you don't want me to go down?' he offered as she had expected. 'I'd be happy to.'

She shook her head. They both knew that the offer was just for form's sake. He hadn't been trained to dive so deep or so quickly.

'I'll go down,' she said decisively.

'OK.'

He pushed himself away from the gunwale. 'Right, shall we get cracking?'

They rigged up the equipment. Kir turned all her attention to checking her instruments. Morten filled her diving tanks with compressed air from the compressor they had brought with them, mounted on the deckhouse.

Everything was done by the book. After sailing for an hour and a half, Skipper had found the location and they could see the small orange buoy with the rope attached to the sunken fishing boat. Kir got into her drysuit. Once again, she checked the air pressure and all the measuring devices. Everything was in order. Morten was on standby in full diving gear. They could communicate through the line using Morse code, and in an emergency, he was suitably equipped to jump straight in. The weather was as it should be.

She looked down into the water. On the surface it was a perfect diving day. She met Morten's gaze and he gave her a thumbs-up. Images flickered inside her mind from her last dive, when she had lost control. She pushed them aside. It wasn't going to happen this time. Everything would be all right. Why shouldn't it be?

She signalled to Morten and let herself fall backwards into the sea.

78

THE FACEBOOK MESSAGE shattered all of Peter's plans. It was clear and ultra-brief:

2 p.m. Grenå Cotton Mill, Magnus wrote.

Yes! His fist shot up in a gesture of victory. Kaj looked on in astonishment as Peter danced a jig.

He glanced at his watch. Shit! It was ten minutes past two. He quickly donned his jacket, thought about leaving the dog at home, then ended up taking him.

'Time to go, Kaj.'

He put on his boots and let the dog into the drive. The dog had proved useful before. Magnus was a young man who knew how to play hide and seek. Peter didn't expect major problems tracking him down since Magnus had given him the time and location, but you could never tell. For the same reason he made sure his gun was in place in the glove compartment. He was already running late. He hoped he wouldn't be *too* late, but the risk was there. What he would find inside the old mill if he was late didn't bear thinking about.

He started the car and drove much too fast to Gjerrild and onwards to Grenå, to the city centre and over a roundabout. After a kilometre, on his left, he passed the big Kvickly supermarket where Nils had worked before he had ended up being garrotted and later dumped at the bottom of the sea.

The mill stood opposite Kvickly. It was a derelict red-brick factory that hadn't been in use for a long time. A giant chimney reached high into the sky and most of the windows had been smashed. There was something oppressive about the place, big as it was. Peter had never been inside.

Why had Magnus chosen the mill of all places, so close to where Nils had worked? It didn't fit in with his strategy of living in shelters and camping outdoors. Perhaps he had been forced to change his plans since Ea-Louise had joined him. Or had the killer already captured Magnus and was the Facebook message not written by him at all? It was a possibility he couldn't afford to ignore.

He stuffed the gun in his inside pocket and grabbed a handful of ammunition, which he tipped into his jacket pocket where he always kept his Stanley knife. He looked at his watch. He was thirty minutes late.

He let the dog out and carefully made his way around the building. Kvickly was closed on Sunday afternoon, so the car park was deserted. There wasn't a soul to be seen, yet he soon had a sense he was being watched.

He began his circle to the right of the building. It was impossible to see in through the high-up windows and the inside of the factory lay in shadow. There was a fence all the way around the perimeter to keep out trespassers. But there were holes in the fence, probably made by bored local youngsters on a Friday evening. Peter sent the dog through one of the holes and followed after him. From there it wasn't far to a tumble-down gate which led into a yard that echoed with emptiness.

Once there had been a beating heart inside the factory, with workers from Grenå and the surrounding district operating the different types of loom and the boiler rooms. The chimney had spewed gigantic smoke plumes across the town and the sea, and the smoke was a sign that there was life and work to be had in the area.

Peter and Kaj crossed the yard and found a peeling green door, which wasn't locked. Carefully they stepped into the darkness and the somewhat cooler air, which smelled stale and fusty, mixed with the stench of oil. After an ante-room and a couple of offices they came into a large hall with iron pillars and pipes going up two floors.

Peter stopped and listened. No Magnus. Occasional drips from a leaking pipe pricked holes into the silence.

'Magnus?'

He shouted into the empty space. The echo rebounded off the walls and from under the iron staircase.

The reply came from nowhere.

Pee-ooww!

The bullet danced between the iron pipes and the metal steps. The shock spread through his body as he instinctively threw himself to the concrete floor, scraping his jacket as he did so. The first shot was quickly followed by two more:

Pee-ooww. Pee-ooww.

Whoever was shooting either missed the dog or he wasn't the intended target. Kaj crept behind him and lay flat on the ground at his master's command. Peter's brain went into overdrive as he tried to get his bearings and suss what was happening. He pulled out his gun and flicked off the safety catch. This was an ambush. He had walked into a trap and it wasn't Magnus who had set it.

He saw a shadow flit between the landings. Then another. There were two of them. At least. Judging by the noise, they were armed with powerful handguns.

This had nothing to do with Magnus or the killer. This was about Peter.

His thoughts were in a whirl. He wanted to kick himself for being so naive, but there was no time to be angry. He strained to get an overview of the situation. What weapons did he have? A small, fairly useless pistol and a Stanley knife in his pocket. And if he had to include absolutely everything: a killer dog, or at least on the face of it.

He would have to be resourceful.

'Where's Magnus?'

He hurled the question into the hall in the hope of opening communication. But the answer came in the form of yet another bullet, which ricocheted between the metal pillars, swirling up dust only a metre away from him, and the dog started to bristle and growl. Bollocks! He had thought this was all about finding Magnus, but Miriam and Bella were playing a different game. Or they were playing two games simultaneously. This was exactly what he had feared: they had other agendas. Outdoing each other to manipulate him. They had sold him to his enemies.

'Rico!' he called out. 'Can we do a deal?'

A long time passed. The silence resonated like the draught through the old factory building. Then came a hoarse voice:

'You haven't got anything to sell, Peter. Unless you're offering us your head on a platter in exchange for a bullet.'

'Grimme got what he deserved. It was an old feud,' Peter shouted. 'It had nothing to do with you.'

'You know I don't calculate in the way you do,' Rico said, sounding closer now. 'And Grimme wasn't your only victim.'

'Grimme or Grimme's henchmen. Same thing. And they would have loved to see the back of you – preferably with a bullet in it,' Peter answered. 'You've only benefited from Grimme's death. Think about it!'

'You're a dead man, Peter. We haven't forgotten Gumbo either.'

'Gumbo was small fry.'

'But he was *our* small fry.'

They stepped forward, one after the other. Peter heard the metal construction above him groan. There were three of them. They had the usual biker gang attributes: big, bulging bodies, probably pumped full of anabolic steroids and artificial muscle. They had strength and they had the upper hand. But in close combat they would be slow.

However, being slow wouldn't matter much if there were three against one, barring a miracle.

'I don't have any beef with you lot any more,' Peter said. 'There's no need for this.'

'I think you're forgetting that we have a beef with you,' Rico said in his falsetto voice, the result of excessive use of performance-enhancing drugs in the fitness centre.

'Don't go there,' Peter said. 'If you try anything, the whole police force will be down on you like a ton of bricks. And you know, it's one thing beating up a gang member, but quite another dealing with someone like me.'

He tilted his head back to see where the three of them were. But they had spread out above him. There was no point wasting bullets.

'Use your napper, Peter. That's why we're here today,' Rico sang in his falsetto. 'It won't be us who mash you to pulp in the blender. It'll be him. Your garrotte villain.'

They had planned it carefully, he had to admit. That was why he had to be tricked into going elsewhere. If they simply took him out in his house, the police would be after them in no time at all because they knew who Peter's enemies were. Now someone else would get the blame and they could walk free.

'How much, Rico? What's in it for Miriam and Bella?'

'Keep them out of this, Peter,' the answer rang out, above him now. He could make out a shadow on the wall. 'They're in a different league from you.'

He couldn't deny that. Their combined efforts to set him up were worthy of Machiavelli. Miriam was the brain, Bella the accomplice, as always. The Chief and the Indian.

He heard footsteps on the iron stairs. One by one, they came down with their weapons at the ready. The dog growled.

At least he had one advantage. They didn't expect him to come armed. He took aim.

Thwack!

The gun wasn't up to much, but he hit one of them in the groin, and the guy spun around on the bottom step.

Thwack!

Then a shot to the shoulder and the massive guy collapsed with a whimper.

One down. Two to go. The second biker had time to take aim. Pee-ooww!

Peter felt the bullet catch him in the side. He staggered and fell. The dog leapt up and stood whining over him. Rico called out:

'Throw your weapon over here. Nice and easy now.'

Peter looked up. There was a gun pointing at him on the end of Rico's outstretched arm.

'Fucking do it! Or I'll shoot your dog!'

79

MARK RACKED HIS brain.

Police officers and CSOs had searched the overgrown house in the forest without finding anything useful. They had discovered evidence in the attic that suggested someone had been living there recently, but of course old Alma had denied that Simon had been there. They had turned every piece of furniture and cupboard upside down, but now he was gone. Old Alma had made it quite clear that she was not best pleased.

'Treat us like a bunch of criminals, they do,' she had snorted, shifting her great weight across the kitchen. 'Come here thinking they can do whatever they like!'

They had brought a search warrant. From that point of view she didn't have a leg to stand on. Still, Mark had a sense she was hiding something. And he had a hunch that some object here would point him in the right direction and link the two cases: the old bones in the box and the new garrotte investigation.

He didn't know exactly what he was looking for. But there had to be something to do with the family and its bizarre history. A testament of some kind. A manifesto, perhaps. Or just a pile of photographs, letters or something that could shed light on the Cardinal and his descendants.

There was a suspicious absence of documents in the Woodland Snail. It was as if everything had been hoovered up or someone had taken a pile of paper and burned it in the garden outside.

He concluded he would have to look elsewhere, go back to Lisa's flat.

He thought about the family while driving to the apartment

379

blocks on the outskirts of Grenå. All the way back to the Cardinal. He hoped Lise was different, that she wasn't quite like the rest of her family.

He had read the seventeen-year-old files of the case against Simon. Lise had undoubtedly believed she was doing Simon a favour by describing him in court as mentally abnormal.

She had told the court of several threatening, dangerous episodes when she had feared for her own life or those of others with Simon around. She had described a specific incident in her childhood when Simon had forced her onto their grandfather's chair, shackled her and put an iron ring around her neck. Even though her sister and a friend had been present during the game. Neither of the children had apparently had the courage to intervene.

'He's not normal,' she had said in court. 'A normal person would never do this. And he's always been like that. I've always been scared of him.'

It had clearly taken guts to speak out. But Mark guessed that Lise had taken a gamble: if she didn't tell the truth, her life would continue to be in peril. If she was lucky, however, Simon would be locked up in an institution. It would give her breathing space. And that was what Lise Werge had had. A seventeen-year-long breathing space.

Her picture of a brother with a personality disorder hadn't been supported by her mother and sister, who presented Simon as a normal young man who'd had a breakdown when his heavily pregnant girlfriend fell ill and the child died in her womb. He had killed her by stabbing her in the stomach – and in the foetus – over and over and over again. Alma and Lone had no recollection of the childhood incident which Lise had described and both of them maintained she was distorting the truth.

'Lise has always had a lively imagination,' her mother said.

But eventually Lise's statement was backed up by a mental health assessment carried out by doctors and Simon was declared so dangerous that he had to be institutionalised. He was diagnosed as having a borderline personality disorder. He wouldn't be sent to a mental health hospital, nor would he be in an ordinary prison. He ended up at a facility for highly dangerous inmates.

Contrary to what Lise might have expected, Simon was not at all grateful for having avoided prison. It was as if being labelled with this diagnosis was a far worse punishment than an ordinary custodial sentence could ever be. He reacted with aggression.

'You're going to regret that, Sis!'

That was what he had shouted in court after the verdict had been pronounced. It was seventeen years ago now. Why no one had informed Lise about his release was beyond Mark's comprehension. However, this system was so fallible. Simon was regarded as harmless now, after all those years. And no one suspected that a harmless person would want to take revenge.

Mark got the caretaker to let him back into the block. Lise's flat was now a crime scene and the door had been sealed. The CSOs had been there with their various powders and tools that could reveal more blood traces, DNA material and fingerprints. They were looking for something, anything. If they couldn't find it in Alma's house, they might be able to find it here – in the home of the daughter who wasn't quite like the rest of her family.

Mark pushed open the door to the flat. Everything had been left as it was when he was here last, plus the CSOs' trademarks: the bloodstains on the floor were circled with chalk and there was pink powder on all the surfaces and handles where they had hoped to find fingerprints. The mess was the same. The mirror in the hallway was still cracked and the broken pieces lay spread across the floor. Lise's two framed family photographs were still standing with their backs to them.

Mark stopped for a moment in the middle of the living room. He tried thinking, not like a CSO, but like a detective looking for hidden treasure. If Lise had had cause to hide something, where would she have put it?

He started searching systematically, including the places where the CSOs had already been. Nothing.

Then he started thinking laterally. If there was something to be found, Lise might have hidden it in an obvious place, such as a folder or a case, or in a desk drawer – or she might have done the exact opposite and been very crafty.

He had checked all the cupboards and the space under the bed. He had squeezed the pillows and mattresses. He had turned her duvet, which still smelled of sleep, inside out. He had been through the bathroom cabinet, looked behind the cistern and even patted down the shower curtain. He had turned over every rug and knocked on the floor for hollow sounds. He had taken every picture off the wall and subjected them to the same scrutiny, without finding anything.

Now he was in the kitchen. It was small and horseshoe-shaped. The fridge was almost empty. The kitchen cupboards were easy to search because Lise didn't have much china. She appeared to live a simple, almost ascetic life.

Mark looked up. The ceiling was white plasterboard. He had dismantled the lamp, again to no avail. He had run his hand along the top of every cupboard. The oven! He opened it, but it was empty. He straightened up and his gaze travelled from wall to wall. Then it stopped.

The freezer.

There was a small freezer on top of the fridge, just big enough for a plastic container and a bag of bread rolls.

He opened it. And that was exactly what he found: two plastic boxes and two bags of bread.

He took out the two boxes. One contained the remains of something that could have been bolognese sauce. The other contained an exercise book.

He took it out carefully. It crackled with the cold, but the box had protected it and there was no ice on it. The handwriting was slanted, neat, bordering on punctilious. *Dictated by Alma. Written by Lone*, it said on the cover. Nothing else. He opened the first page, terrified that it would crumble into frosty powder. He read the first sentence and knew instantly that he had struck gold:

Some families have a talent for playing music. Others for baking or cooking or gardening. In our family we have a very special talent. We have a talent for killing.

80

KIR DIVED TOWARDS the bottom. At once she felt the cold sea enclose itself around her like an icy glove. As always, visibility was poor, but it was better than the day she was last here. She encountered fish and tiny particles on her way through the muddy, grey-blue water as she followed the rope down to the wreck.

Her body reacted by resisting. She was demanding a lot from it, she knew that. It was only a few days ago that it had protested so vigorously she had barely survived. *Now what?* it screamed when she pushed it on a run or lifted weights. *Leave me alone. Let me rest.*

She felt the pressure in her ears and her whole head, as if she was about to explode, but she continued downwards. She had to. This was about Jens Bådsmand, Simon and Nils. And their families. They had a right to know what had happened.

On reaching the wreck, she struggled to get her bearings at first. Which end was the stern and where was the bow? She swam into lines and hooks, and there were also remnants of the wreck protruding from the seabed. This was seriously dangerous, she knew, yet still she carried on.

She was round by the port side when she realised that something was wrong. It was as if she couldn't breathe properly. Even staying still in the water made her breathless. She tried to ignore it by concentrating on the hull of the boat, but then her heart started to race. She was hyperventilating, even though she was doing everything she could to calm herself down. What was happening to her? This was not good at all.

Her anxiety continued to grow. Perhaps the events of the last few days were getting on top of her: the near fatal dive and the nerve-racking evening when she had searched Kasper's house.

She could usually handle stress. She could usually talk herself down and get her pulse under control. But not this time. She was in deep shit here.

She stared through the muddy water to get a proper look at the boat and made a final attempt to finish the job when suddenly her eyes started flickering. It was like looking into a screen that was going blank.

I have to get up now. She signalled by pulling the line to Morten, but received no response. Good-natured, solid Morten, who had sat on her sofa trying to defend Kasper until it was obvious that he was beyond defending. Slow, steady Morten, who couldn't take the pace when they went running and invariably ended up making the coffee.

What the hell was he doing? Couldn't he feel her pulling the line? That had to be the explanation. She had almost no strength left now.

And still she kept fighting. She kicked her way up, knowing full well she risked bursting her lungs by ascending too quickly. What had gone wrong? She had checked her equipment as she always did. Morten had filled the oxygen tanks. They were both professionals.

She yanked the line once more, but felt all alone in the world. The sea was sucking the air and the life out of her. She tugged frantically at the line, but could feel her strength fading. Everything was dark. She couldn't make out the light above. The cold penetrated her bones and paralysed her.

She knew she was going to die.

81

PETER FELT THE freezing cold concrete beneath him. His thoughts throbbed in time with his pulse. Miriam and Bella had set him up. They were in cahoots. They had used Magnus's disappearance to bait the trap. What did they get out of it? Peace, would be his guess. Miriam and Lulu already lived at the mercy of the biker gang, and they owed them protection money. Bella would probably be let off her debt to Gumbo and she had paid Peter with sex that she had wanted more than he had. Shit. While he was getting a taste of concrete, Magnus was almost certainly safe and sound somewhere, he was fairly sure of that. After all, they wouldn't gamble with the boy's life, would they?

'Chuck your pistol over here,' Rico repeated. 'Now!'

The pain from his flesh wound went from being distant to unbearable. Peter gritted his teeth and picked up the gun with two fingers. Then he threw it with a clatter across the floor towards Rico's boot-clad feet, now firmly planted five metres away from him.

'Get up.'

He did as he was told, but nearly fainted from the effort. Kaj whimpered, crept forward to meet him and licked his hand. He wished he hadn't brought the dog. He wished he hadn't come.

Rico gestured with a hand to his henchman.

'Search him.'

The thug came over. The dog growled.

'Stupid mutt. Shut up!'

He directed a kick at Kaj. Peter saw what was going to happen. He also saw that he could do nothing to stop it.

'Sit, Kaj!'

But Kaj interpreted the kick as an attack on his owner. He rocked back on his haunches and leapt at the thug's throat.

'Nooo! Kaj!'

The weight of the dog hit the man in the chest and sent him tumbling to the floor. A shot sounded as Peter kicked the hand holding the weapon. Kaj landed on top of the thug with a yelp. Blood mixed with blood. Peter's anger gave him strength. He wanted to rip the heart out of the man who had shot his dog. But before he could react, two gigantic hands closed around his throat.

Rico's hands tightened from behind. The enormous thug on the floor had got up and was pointing his gun at him. Peter would be a dead man if he was hit again. He leaned back into Rico and lashed out with a boot at the thug, smashing it into his genital area. The gun flew out of his hands and he sank to his knees like a felled ox next to the dog.

Rico squeezed harder. Peter rounded his shoulders and pumped up his neck to resist the pressure. Rico tightened his grip still further. Peter's field of vision narrowed and went black. He reached behind him and found Rico's fingers. He broke them, one after the other, and heard the bones crack. Then he sent Rico reeling with an upper cut and a kick to the groin.

In the meantime, the third man had staggered to his feet. He was big and solid and the bullets from earlier had only had minimal impact. He rushed towards Peter like a huge ball of fat – a massive lump of meat with bulging muscles, a bull neck, a shaved head and typical biker tattoos up his throat.

Peter lunged forward and used one of the oldest tricks in the book: he sank his thumb into the man's eye and his other fingers into his ear. These were the most vulnerable spots because every-thing else was armour-plated with fat. The man's eyeball was almost out of the socket. He screamed and pulled at Peter's wrist. Then there was a movement from below. Rico was recovering and had risen to his knees. Peter kicked him in the face and he went down for a second time. The man with the wonky eyeball was hors de combat. He staggered around like a roaring, wounded animal. The thug with the smashed nuts was no use to anyone and Rico lay groaning with his face a bloody mess.

Peter hated himself. But he hated his enemies even more. Adrenaline was pumping around his body. He hadn't wanted the confrontation, but he said a silent thank you for the years in prison where he had learned to stand up for himself. Rather that than die. He picked up his gun, which Rico had dropped in the heat of battle.

He looked down at Rico, who sat leaning against an iron pillar, spitting out teeth and blood.

'Where's Magnus?'

Rico muttered something inaudible. Peter pointed the gun at him.

'Where is he?'

'F . . . kd . . . f . . . I . . . know,' the crater of blood said.

'Then who does?'

There was a pause. Rico's eyes burned with hatred and pain.

'Answer me!'

'M . . . m . . . MM . . . Mi . . . m . . .'

'Miriam?'

Rico nodded and gulped, his Adam's apple going up and down like a lift. His face was pulp. One eye was dangling from the socket, his nose was broken. A section of white jawbone lay exposed under fibres of flesh.

Peter pulled out his mobile and tapped in Miriam's number. When she answered, he said quickly:

'Hi, honey! One of your fans wants to ask you a question.'

Rico's broken fingers hung in the air, no good to anyone. Peter squatted down on his haunches and held the mobile to his ear.

'Ask her.'

'Mi . . . mmm . . .'

The injured man strained. His lips moved as if chewing every single letter. Peter could hear Miriam:

'Peter! Talk to me!'

Peter spoke.

'It's your friend, Rico. He's not feeling very well. But he wants to know where Magnus is.'

'. . . Magnus . . . Peter . . . It's not what you think . . .'

'I'm sure you're right. I bet it's much worse.'

Again, he held the phone to Rico's ear.

'I know it goes against the grain, but try telling the truth for once. If you can find your way around all your lies, that is,' he shouted.

Miriam's voice blasted out. She, too, was shouting.

'What have you done, Peter?'

'What do you think I've done? What I always do,' he shouted, still with the phone to Rico's ear. 'Where is he?'

'The convent,' she said, so quietly he could barely hear.

He pressed the mobile to his ear.

'Since when?'

He felt dizzy. They had been manipulating him all along, but how long had they been blatantly lying to him?

'Since yesterday. Magnus contacted Bella. He'd had enough of being on the run. Rico was pumping me and Lulu for money. They always want more . . . It was my idea to get Magnus to safety and keep you looking for him . . . That way we could also send the killer off on a wild goose chase . . . Peter, I know it looks as if . . .'

'The convent. Who with?'

She told him.

'We'll have to talk about this, Peter. Do you hear?'

Peter was well aware that Rico could shut down Miriam and Lulu's business with a snap of his fingers. Though less easily now. Grimme's successor must have put pressure on her after his henchmen had been humiliated that night on the cliff. And Miriam – as he had already guessed – had in turn persuaded Bella.

'What's there to talk about, my lovely? About how you had to save your own skin? About how you had to sacrifice a friend?'

Her protracted sigh wasn't convincing.

'I knew you would be all right, Peter . . . You always are,' said Miriam of the mobile, who wasn't the Miriam with whom he had once made love and with whom he had once been friends. 'I owed them . . .'

'Of course. Money matters more than your friends.'

He had to vent his anger, even though it was painful to talk.

'Perhaps you should start looking for another job and a new life, Miriam. And, while you're at it, get yourself some new friends.'

He pressed *Off*. Then he got up and looked down at the biker who had shot Kaj, leaving his ear hanging by a thread. He fished out the Stanley knife from his pocket, knelt down by the thug and held up the blade.

'Do you know what happens to people who hurt my dog?'

The biker stared hazily at him and shook his head.

'They get a taste of their own medicine. Do you understand? Unless they say they're sorry. And they really mean it.'

The thug groaned.

'Louder. I can't hear you.'

The groan rose in volume. Peter shook his head.

'I think there's a problem with my hearing. Here, let me show you . . . It won't hurt very much.'

He reached forward and grabbed the man by the ear. The Stanley knife flashed close to his skin. The man started to shake. Fear-induced sweat dripped from his forehead and into his eyes.

Peter swiftly sliced off the ear. Ssshhht. Blood flowed. The guy passed out. Peter slapped his face until he came round.

'Stay with me. I want you to see what happens next.'

The guy blinked several times. Peter threw the severed ear to the dog. Kaj didn't bat an eyelid. Not so much as a flared nostril to sniff the air for raw meat.

'Would you look at that. Not even the dog wants you!'

Peter left the man. He knelt down by his dog and felt a spasm of pain in his side. Kaj looked up at him and his mind was cast back to another day. Another life. He had loved Thor, his dog, the most beautiful Alsatian you could ever wish for. He had watched him bounding towards him when Hans Martin Krøll's bullet hit him. His legs had still been running towards Peter when he keeled over in the yard.

He shut down the memory and shovelled his arms under Kaj, who was whining in pain. Then he staggered to his car, still cradling his dog.

82

'YOU AGAIN, IS it?'

Old Alma hissed through the crack in the door at the Woodland Snail. The security chains remained in place.

'Are you going to let us in or do we have to let ourselves in?'

Mark had no patience. An old lady wasn't necessarily a good person or someone who needed protecting. Especially not this old lady.

The tortoise-eyes hid under heavy lids. They zoomed in first on him, then on Anna Bagger.

'Who's she?'

Mark introduced Anna.

'We've come to search the house again.'

Alma's eyes bristled with hostility.

'You won't find anything.'

'You may be right.'

Mark showed her the search warrant. 'But first we want to take another look at the basement.'

The hate-filled eyes directed themselves first at Mark, then Anna. The three CSOs and two detectives from Anna's team stayed in the background.

Mark was wondering if they would have to break down the door when the old woman started removing the chains, one by one. Ultra slowly.

The house seemed even murkier and less inviting than usual. It was as if the corners were darker and the electric light bulbs had less energy to emit the light required to see.

They entered the kitchen. She had been doing her crossword again. Her daughter was missing, her son was wanted and she was cold-blooded enough to be able to sit there scribbling down her guesses for 'repulsive', seven letters, and 'bog body', six. Mark was about to offer a couple of sarky suggestions as she hunched over the table and masticated a white-bread sandwich. But instead he pulled out a chair and sat down, while the team and Anna Bagger disappeared down into the basement of the house.

'The bones we found turned out to be those of a Resistance fighter called Allan Holme-Olsen,' Mark said, taking the liberty of exaggerating the forensic examiner's findings somewhat. The DNA result still wasn't available, but a preliminary marker showed a high probability.

Her reaction was unmistakeable and she didn't even make an effort to conceal it. She froze in mid-movement and stared hard at her jam sandwich.

'Who killed him, Alma?'

'How would I know?'

'Was he the man who killed your father?'

Her eyes burned. For a brief moment her neck slid out of the carapace.

'Two men came for him.'

'And one of them was Allan.'

She said nothing. She kept munching as if the jam sandwich was an enemy that had to be devoured.

'You were fifteen years old,' Mark said. 'You knew your father's methods. You knew about the garrotte.'

She stared blankly at him.

'I found the exercise book containing Lone's notes,' Mark explained. 'Lise had hidden it in her freezer.'

She sat for a long time without expression. Then she sneered:

'That stupid girl.'

'You killed Allan,' Mark stated. 'I don't know how you tricked him into coming here. But you did trick him. My guess is you had help. But that detail is missing from the exercise book.'

She looked at him in a moment of triumph.

'I did it all by myself,' she hissed. 'He was easy. I was fifteen and he liked young girls.'

'And then what?' Mark asked. 'How did his bones end up in a box at the bottom of Kalø Bay?'

Her mouth became a pinched thin line. Mark could hear the defiance humming in her amorphous body like the current in an electric fence.

'Who helped you? Was it Simon? My guess is you had the body lying in the basement for all those years until one day, Allan Holme-Olsen's family started getting suspicious. Perhaps they even visited you?'

The silence was eternal. Then she nodded.

'His son.'

'So you decided it was time to get rid of the bones?'

Again she sat in silence. He wasn't sure if she was keeping up. But then she suddenly picked up the pencil and scribbled a three-letter word in the crossword, down.

'It was in 1990. Lone was working as a supply teacher in those days. They were told the school was to merge with another school. Some of the equipment became surplus to requirement.'

'The box of bones from the biology lessons, for example?'

She shrugged her heavy shoulders and her neck disappeared temporarily.

'There were two boxes. It was easy.'

'So you disposed of the original contents of the box, took Holme-Olsen's skeleton and distributed it between the two boxes?'

She nodded.

'You numbered the bones to imitate the original contents?'

'It was so easy.'

'And then, you dropped the boxes into the hollow made by the elephant mine that had exploded in 1969? A place where no one was allowed to sail or fish?'

She made no reply. Mark could see she was squeezing the pencil. She forced yet another word down onto the page. He could guess the rest: Holme-Olsen's family had given up their search. The secrets were safe. Alma had won.

He looked at her. What would the consequences be for her now that she had been found out, an eighty-six-year-old woman? She was unlikely ever to go to jail. She had got away with it for all these years. And she would continue to get away with it. She could carry on eating her jam sandwiches and doing her crosswords.

He heard shouting from below, got up and went down to join the team working away in the basement.

They had pulled away the felt from the floor. Underneath there was a small trapdoor. Access to a basement under the basement – clever, Mark thought. The Cardinal had planned this den right from the start. Who would have guessed that the basement could have several levels?

The CSOs were working with the full range of their equipment to prevent any evidence being lost. They eased open the trapdoor. A damp smell of earth, rot and excrement met them. Mark stepped closer. There was a narrow ladder down. Someone shone a torch into the darkness.

'Oh, my God,' Anna Bagger exclaimed, covering her nose with her sleeve.

'Lise?'

Mark called down into the hole. There was no reply. He gripped the torch between his teeth and started climbing down into the depths. It was a long way. He counted twelve steps and the further down he went, the stronger the sensation that he was diving into an oxygen-deprived hell.

It was like a primitive dungeon. The room seemed to be L-shaped. It had an earthen floor, and the walls and ceiling were strengthened with thick beams. Chains and fixings had been mounted on the wall. There were hooks for various instruments of torture on a crossbeam. They hung there, old and rusty, and Mark could hear the silent screams that must have rung out between these walls.

The torchlight landed on the various decorations, one after the other. The flag stood out because it was spread across the middle of the wall. He recognised the symbols from Boutrup's rosary: the halberd, the crossbow and the gun – the Spanish Legion flag. Other objects surrounded it: old photographs of General Franco, uniforms hung on display, antique weapons and Christ in agony on a crucifix.

This was a collector's holy shrine and it reeked of death: *Viva la Muerte*. The motto was printed in blood-red letters on a yellow banner hanging above the flag.

Mark felt a chill penetrating the soles of his feet as he crossed the room with his head bowed. He shone the light further into the darkness and towards a corner where a high-backed chair was the only item of furniture. It stood with its back to the onlooker and the incumbent staring at the wall.

'Lise?'

Still no reply. He stepped closer. Anna Bagger and the chief CSO were right behind him.

Lise Werge was attached to the chair by an iron ring that fitted closely around her neck. The garrotte itself was simple: a tall piece of wood mounted on a hard horizontal plank to sit on. The whole construction rested on a wooden stand reminiscent of an oversized, old-fashioned Christmas tree support. Thick iron shackles were secured to her ankles. Her hands were gathered in her lap and also shackled. Mark was immediately reminded of Oluf Jensen's sketch. At the back of the wooden upright was a clamp. It could be tightened and the ring would strangle the victim as an iron spike bored into the neck from behind.

Lise Werge stared at him without seeing. Her mouth was half-open and caked with encrusted blood. Her eyes were dull. Anna Bagger felt for a pulse in her neck.

'It's weak,' she said.

Mark called for an ambulance. He had just finished the call when his phone rang. It was Peter Boutrup.

'I know who did it,' the voice said. 'And I know where Magnus and Ea-Louise are.'

'Take it easy,' Mark said. 'We're here.'

'Where?'

'We're here,' he repeated. 'We've found the garrotte.'

'Where?'

'The killer's name is Simon Falk Ørum. He was recently released after seventeen years in a mental institution.'

There was silence down the other end. Then Boutrup said:
'It's not him.'

Mark walked down to the far end of the dungeon while his
colleagues freed Lise Werge and placed her on a blanket ready for
the medics. No one was prepared to administer first aid. It was too
difficult to assess whether the garrotte had already done its work
and fractured her spine.

'Of course it's him,' he said and explained that they had found
Lise.

But Boutrup insisted.

'The man you're looking for is Morten Kold. He and his wife
lived in Elev in 1996 when Alice Brask and her followers boycotted
the MMR vaccine and triggered an outbreak of measles. Two babies
at the local nursery were infected. One child, a girl, was brain-
damaged. The girl died last year.'

'So you're saying there are two of them?'

'I don't know if they're working together. But perhaps they know
each other.'

'That seems unlikely,' Mark said. 'No family would share this
hell-hole with anyone else.'

He thought of the exercise book and the stories it contained. But
then he remembered something. Simon's file and the trial where
Lise had appeared as a witness. What had she said? Something about
an incident in her childhood?

His mind started buzzing. The witness statement. But Peter had
no patience.

'There must be two of them,' he said. 'I can believe that. If you're
with one of them, I need to find the other one. I have the address.
I'll go there now and call you once I get there.'

'Morten Kold? Who is he? I mean age, job, et cetera.'

'Forty-two years old. Former Falck diver, but now works as a
doorman at Club Summertime.'

The pieces fell into place. Kir's running partner. The sweat on
Mark's back froze and his tongue felt like a piece of leather. Between
sharp intakes of breath he told Peter.

'OK. I've met him,' Peter said. 'I know what he looks like.'

'They had a date last night,' Mark said. 'Christ almighty . . . If only I had known . . .'

'I'm on it,' Peter said. 'I'll find them.'

The medics moved Lise onto a stretcher. A doctor gave her an injection and spoke to her in an attempt to rouse her from her comatose state.

'Wake up, Lise,' the doctor said, patting her cheek. 'Talk to me.'

Time passed. Then Lise's eyes sprang open and she gave a loud gasp. The colour of her face changed from waxen to pink. She blinked.

'What's your surname, Lise?' the doctor asked.

'Werge,' she said in a rasping voice.

'Good. Listen to me. Have you been given any pills or injections of any kind?'

She moved her head slowly from side to side.

'Have you been given water? Food?'

'Water,' Lise said.

Mark intervened before the doctor had time to protest.

'Hello, Lise. My name is Mark Bille. We spoke at the nursing home. I initiated the search for you.'

The doctor glared at him. But Lise nodded.

'I have one very important question,' Mark said. 'In your brother's trial, you spoke of an incident in your childhood. You were shackled. To the garrotte, is that right? You never said so directly, but you spoke about a high-backed chair.'

She nodded. Mark carried on.

'There were four of you in the basement that day. You, Simon and Lone. Who was the fourth child?'

'Simon's friend,' she said.

'I must protest,' the doctor said. 'The patient is in no fit state to answer questions.'

Mark leaned over the stretcher.

'Can you remember the name of that friend?'

Lise's gaze brushed past the doctor, who had opened his mouth to voice another protest. She made a vague gesture in the air as if to signal it was OK.

'Morten.'

'Morten what?'

He didn't get a reply.

83

KIR'S HEAD WAS about to explode.

She couldn't open her eyes, but she registered the pain and the accompanying nausea. Together they were so overwhelming that she was tempted to let go and allow herself to be sucked into her own misery. Never to open her eyes again, simply to dive into the all-consuming black hole.

But something prevented her. Distracting thoughts flailed around and beat against the shell of the pain. Reluctantly, she opened her eyes. The black dots behind her eyelids became light, and she saw a flock of white cotton-wool animals gambolling against a background of blue. It took a moment for her to realise they were clouds chasing across the sky. It took even longer for her to be able to relate this moment to what had happened:

The fishing boat. Morten. Diving down to the wreck of the *Marie*. Problems with her air supply. Morten, who hadn't reacted to her tugs on the line. Her grim fight against the black dots in her eyes and the physical exhaustion. Then finally death, which had kissed and embraced her, and the sensation of letting go and allowing something bigger and stronger than her to take over.

Where was she now?

Her eyes started adjusting to the light and the breeze. A headache broke through into her consciousness, but she had to navigate around it. She tried to work out where she was. She could smell paint. Turned her face a fraction. The fishing boat. The deck. She was lying on the deck. Alone. Where were Skipper and Morten?

Her throat was dry. She wanted to touch her body to check if she was in one piece, but she couldn't move her arms. Realised that her hands were tied behind her back and that something had been forced into her mouth. But she couldn't work out why anyone would have done it, or indeed who. Whenever a fragment of a thought attempted to emerge, it disappeared into an inner sea of lethargy.

She continued to lie there, staring into the sky, recovering – how long she didn't know.

What on earth was going on? Why would anyone want to do this to her? She wasn't at war. She wasn't hunting pirates in Africa. She was in quiet, peaceful Denmark.

So who?

It boiled down to two options. There were only two other people on board. Her brain slowly turned over their names. She had known Skipper since she was a child. Morten . . .

Morten! Could it be him? Could that really be true?

It took her a while to grasp the truth. Meanwhile the clouds drifted across the sky above her. Time passed as calmly and inexorably as the waves she could hear splashing against the hull.

She could have kicked herself. She had been wrong. All her instincts, all her antennae had been pointing in the wrong direction. It was her own fault. There was no one she could blame. She had been stupid enough to believe he was a good-natured, lumbering giant. The reality, however, was quite different.

But why? What could be his motive for wanting to kill her?

She scraped her cheek against the painted deck, which smelled of fish and the sea. Slowly reconstructing the past, she went all the way back to the start, but still she couldn't make it add up. She calculated. It was eight years since they had met for the first time. At a fitness centre in Grenå. They discovered they had a shared interest in diving. He had been working as a Falck diver. She was dreaming about training as a mine diver. He was divorced now, but he had a child, a seven-year-old girl, she never got to meet. She had the impression the child had some kind of disability.

It had only ever been an innocent flirtation. When she moved to Kongsøre, their paths went different ways. Then one evening, not so long ago, she had seen him in the doorway at Club Summertime, obviously working as a doorman. She had been out with a female friend. That was roughly a week before Melissa was found in the moat. They had talked about meeting up for dinner and resuming their friendship. She had been a little vague because she was still pining for Mark. But when Mark gave her the cold shoulder that day at the moat, she had been going to ring Morten when she was interrupted by the pathologist calling her about the bones in the box. Then she and Mark had agreed a truce, and she finally called Morten and arranged to go for a run with him because she wanted to pump him for information about his colleague, Kasper Frandsen. That was the day Mark turned up and interrupted their breakfast with his hissy fit.

She had used Morten to get information about Kasper and to irritate Mark. But Morten had also used her. Through her he had gained snippets of information about the investigation. Whatever his role in this case – and for the moment she couldn't see what it was – he would have regarded it as useful.

And now she was lying here. Through her own fault. She was a soldier, she was a professional and yet she had let her judgement become clouded by other issues.

The deck reverberated with the sound of approaching footsteps and she saw the tips of his shoes right by her nose. He prodded her with his foot. She peered up at him. He looked even bigger from below, but she was not afraid. She was angry, mostly at herself.

'My big heart got the better of me,' he said. 'Your grave was meant to be down below where you would have been eaten by the fishes, but I couldn't really come to terms with that.'

She tried to say something, but her mumbles were stifled by the rag in her mouth. He bent down and took it out.

'It's not as if anyone can hear you anyway.'

'The compressor,' she said, suddenly joining the dots. 'You filled my diving tanks on the deckhouse.'

'You should have noticed,' he said. 'But you were too busy playing with all your sophisticated gear. Some mine diver you are, hah!'

He snorted with contempt. 'You lot are so besotted with your fancy equipment that you don't see what's going on around you.'

'You let the compressor suck exhaust fumes in from the funnel,' she said as more dots joined. 'You deliberately let me inhale exhaust fumes!'

The thought was chilling. She looked at him with fresh eyes. She had dived down forty-five metres with her tanks filled with CO_2 and CO, gases with no taste or colour, which had nearly killed her. That had been his plan. To kill her. Yet he had fished her out. Why? Was this her one chance?

'Where's Skipper?' she asked.

'He'll be busy in the wheelhouse until we're a couple of miles off shore. Then he won't be busy any more, and the two of us will take the dinghy.'

'Why, Morten? What's all this about?'

He stared vacantly into the air.

'You'll never be able to understand.'

'Try me.'

He shook his head.

'I don't need a therapist, but I can tell you this much: it was a good idea to throw suspicion on Kasper. A great move, I'll grant you that.'

'And you helped by planting evidence in his garage.'

He executed a small bow, as if accepting applause.

'I aim to please.'

'But why me?'

'You'd have worked it out sooner or later. You were all fired up with your talk about the garrotte and the bones in the box. Like a terrier, you were.'

'Worked what out?'

He gazed across the sea.

'Forget it.'

But as long as she didn't know what was really going on, she had no chance of finding a way out.

'The garrotte? That was you? Is that what Kurt Falk used?'

He pursed his lips as if giving weighty consideration to the question.

'Yes and no.'

'What does that mean?'

He squatted down and studied her closely, as if to record every one of her movements.

'I was just a friend of the family, I suppose you could say. No one ever really noticed me.'

'But you noticed them?'

He nodded.

'I went to school with Simon. Alma's son.'

'Alma . . .'

'Kurt Falk's daughter. She's old now.'

'And there really is a garrotte?'

She had never quite believed it. An ordinary Danish family with a killing machine in their home.

He nodded.

'I saw it when I visited Simon and I've never forgotten it. The simplicity of the construction. It was so straightforward. For years I toyed with the idea of building my own, just for the fun of it. And then one day I found I needed one . . .'

His voice was swallowed up by the breeze.

'Why?'

But clearly, he wasn't ready to tell her.

'What's going to happen to me?'

He shrugged.

'You'll get to meet my good friend, the high-backed chair.'

He left her lying on the deck. She tried to crawl up and look over the railings to see where they were, but it was impossible, so instead she checked the position of the sun in the sky. They were sailing due west. Heading back to Grenå. The afternoon was drawing in and soon they would be in darkness.

After about an hour – she followed the length of the shadows and the angle of the sun's rays – the engine cut out and all she could hear was the waves lapping against the side of the boat and the screeching of the seagulls. They were near land.

He came back. With a gun, which he pointed at her. He also had a knife. Without saying a word, he cut the ropes. She struggled to her feet. Everything started spinning and her head felt like it was bursting, but the worst was almost the dryness in her mouth. He pushed her towards the ladder. Down in the water, the dinghy was waiting. Her brain was working at fever pitch exploring possible escape routes, but for now her only option was to do what he demanded and hope that an opportunity would present itself later. She teetered down the ladder on wobbly legs and into the dinghy. He followed. She wanted to ask about Skipper, but knew there was no point. Either he was dead or rendered harmless in some other way. She hoped for the latter.

Morten let her do all the work. She started the small outboard motor. It wasn't far to the shore. She could see the beach, it wasn't far from her summer house. This was all planned, she realised with a jolt. There would be no mistakes. Whatever he was up to, it was an operation that he had planned down to the last detail.

She steered the dinghy towards the beach until it hit a sandbank. He gestured for them to wade ashore through the water. On a November day like this there wouldn't be a soul on the beach. No strangers she could alert.

He jammed the gun into her back as they waded through the shallow water and found a path which led them to the road. A hundred metres ahead there was a green Toyota. *Salon Lotte*, it said on the side in looping gold letters.

He tied her hands behind her back again, stuffed a rag into her mouth and blindfolded her. Then he pressed the remote to open the car and forced her into the boot. The darkness around her, after he banged the boot shut, was total. Then she heard the door on the passenger side open and felt the car sink on its suspension as he got in. He slammed the door on the driver's side and started the car with a roar.

84

Kir's summer house was empty. Peter checked the garage. He didn't know her very well, but it looked as if some diving equipment was missing from the pegs on the wall. She was a dedicated diver. She had probably just gone out for a dive. Mark could stop worrying.

He drove on. A quick call to the Summertime Club had informed him that Morten Kold lived in a flat in Nørregade. But he wasn't at home.

'He moved in a month ago,' said the caretaker, whom Peter found in the laundry room in the basement where freshly washed clothes wafted the scent of detergent through the building. Peter pretended to be Morten's cousin. Luckily he'd had a spare jacket in the van, so he could cover up the bloodstain on his shirt.

'After his daughter died, you know,' the caretaker said. 'He's selling his house because he can't bear to live there any more.'

Peter nodded and tried to show sympathy.

'It must've been a terrible time. I've been living abroad for the past ten years, so I haven't kept up.'

'Morten was distraught.'

'Remind me again where the house is?'

'Somewhere in Ørum.'

'Do you know him?'

The caretaker nodded. He turned on the tap and water gushed into the deep sink, but it didn't drain properly. He bent over the sink with a red plunger and started pumping.

'But not well,' he said, with his sleeves rolled up and the plunger held in two hands. 'He was in the year above me at school. But I did hear he'd got divorced. And then his daughter died. Don't forget, this is a small town.'

'Do you know where I can find him?'

'It's Sunday,' the caretaker said. 'So he's probably not working.'

'At the club?'

The caretaker nodded. 'But he has a day job as well . . . As a gardener or something like that. I don't know where . . .'

The caretaker pumped away and some black sludge came back up. 'You've got to take what you can get to make ends meet.'

'What about his family?' Peter asked, hoping the question was broad enough not to rouse the man's suspicion.

'There's his sister. She owns a couple of hairdressing salons. My wife goes to the one in Glesborg.'

'Nice girl, as I remember. Where's the other salon?'

'In Ramten, I believe.'

Peter thanked him and made to leave. Then the caretaker said:

'I saw him carrying some equipment to his car earlier. He used to be a Falck diver, you know, so perhaps he was going diving . . .'

Peter turned his van around and drove down to the harbour. It was late in the afternoon now and the sun was shining on the harbour from a low angle. He saw activity near the fishing boats where several fishermen were hosing down or mopping their decks. He had spoken to one of the fishermen previously on another matter.

'I was very sorry to hear about the accident,' he said tentatively to the man on the deck, who recognised him and raised a hand to his cap by way of greeting.

'Yes, it's a terrible story,' the fisherman said.

'I'm looking for a former Falck diver,' Peter said. 'His name's Morten Kold.'

'A big, broad fella?'

Peter nodded. It had to be the same Morten he had met at Kir's.

'He's got a scar over one eye,' Peter said.

'That's the one. They went out in Svend Skipper's boat to look for that wreck out by Læsø. But we haven't heard from them since and we can't make contact with them.'

'Who's the they?'

Peter's premonition was confirmed when the fisherman said:

'It was Kir Røjel's idea, as I understand it.'

Peter was aware that everyone at the harbour knew Kir.

'She brought along a helper,' the fisherman said. 'The fella you mentioned. Morten. They wanted to see if the *Marie* had been scuttled deliberately.'

Peter turned over the information in his mind. Kir was at sea with Morten as her helper and an old fisherman as the skipper. He didn't like the sound of it. Nor did he like it that they had lost contact. He gave the fisherman his mobile number.

'Please call me if you hear anything. It's important.'

The fisherman nodded and stuffed the number in the pocket at the front of his overalls.

'It'll be dark soon,' the fisherman said, voicing what Peter was mulling over. 'They should have been back long ago.'

'Perhaps you should contact SOK?' Peter suggested.

The man spat out a gobbet of saliva. 'They don't give a toss about us.'

Peter phoned Mark Bille and outlined the situation. The policeman sounded composed, but Peter could clearly hear the underlying tension in his voice.

'I'll get a patrol boat sent out,' Mark said. 'What will you do?'

'I'll try to track down the sister and her hairdressing salons.'

'But if they're at sea . . .'

'If Morten is the killer, he must have a place where he keeps the garrotte. He needs to return home to complete his work.'

'Complete?'

'This is about a trial,' Peter said. 'He sees himself as judge, jury and . . .'

'Executioner?'

Peter hesitated.

'Executioner, yes.'

'And Kir?'

'She got in the way of his plans. She risks being dragged into them and being judged.'

'What about the skipper?'

'Morten's not interested in him,' Peter said.

'But his boat isn't there.'

'Not in Grenå, no. But perhaps it's somewhere else.'

'Have you been to his flat?' Mark asked.

Peter smiled through the pain from the superficial gunshot wound in his side. He had patched it up as best he could with a bandage from the first aid box he kept in his car.

'I can't just wave around search warrants, you know. That's what we've got the police for.'

There was a tiny pause. Then Mark said:

'OK. We'll take a look at it. Perhaps it'll give us a clue as to where to go next.'

They hung up. Peter got in behind the wheel of his van and pulled a face as the pain shot through his body. He didn't have the time to feel pain. Morten had to be found before he killed any more people. And what about Kir? If she knew anything, and the evidence suggested she did, she was in mortal danger right now. The very idea that someone might hurt her caused him to squeeze the steering wheel. He reversed and turned the car around with the image of her at the petrol station with the nozzle in her hand and a gleam in the corner of her eye. There were so many options and loose ends that it was almost hopeless. The house in Ørum. The sister's salons. The club. He decided that the salons would be easier to find. They would be closed, but there had to be neighbours he could ask.

He had almost got as far as Ramten when his mobile rang. It was the fisherman from the harbour:

'Something's not right. Skipper's boat is drifting in the wind three miles offshore. One of the lads from here has gone alongside.'

'Does that mean there's no one on board?'

'There's certainly no one steering the ship.'

Peter hit the accelerator.

85

MORTEN KOLD'S FLAT looked barely inhabited. It was attractive and had been painted recently, but he had yet to put anything up on the walls, and in terms of furniture, there was only the basics: in the bedroom a bed, in the living room a sofa, a coffee table and a television in the corner. Flat-pack bookcases waiting to be assembled lay in a pile on the floor. A desk had been put up, but a place had yet to be found for it, so it stood all forlorn by the sofa.

Mark and Anna Bagger and two CSOs walked carefully around the limited space wearing blue plastic shoe covers and latex gloves.

'Not much of a home,' Anna commented as she glanced at the unopened removal crates in the hallway, living room and bedroom.

'He probably has other things on his mind,' Mark said. 'We need to take a look at those crates.'

Anna told the CSOs to search the crates. She had her sceptical face on; Mark could tell from the way she moved about stiffly and her pursed lips. Everything told him she regarded Simon as the prime suspect, and that they should be looking for him rather than wasting their time on an old school friend of his. She had already deployed a lot of manpower on the search for Simon and involved several other police forces. Anna Bagger's money was clearly on him.

But now they were here. They checked every cupboard and kitchen drawer, but found nothing. They also searched the desk drawer: again, nothing. So far, the flat was devoid of anything that could link Morten Kold with the murders of Melissa and Victor or the old Spanish execution method.

Suddenly an exclamation came from one of the two CSOs going through the removal crates.

'What's up?'

Mark stepped across the bookcases to see what the man had found.

'This looks a little odd,' said the CSO, who was holding up a blue cardboard folder like the ones they sold in *Bog og Idé*, the stationery shop.

Mark took the folder and examined its contents, but saw only a mass of lines and numbers. It took a moment before he realised what they were: drawings of a building, as if an architect had been involved, with the measurements and angles of each room.

'What is it?' Anna Bagger asked.

Mark showed her. She looked at the drawings and flicked through them. There were some close-ups of specific details. And in several places circles had been drawn with a pen rather than a pencil, like a black marker.

'Look here.'

The other CSO handed her another folder from a removal crate.

'Melissa,' he said.

In it was a series of photographs printed on specialist paper. Melissa could clearly be seen moving across the convent yard in her light habit, apparently unaware that she was being photographed. But there were also other, older photographs. Melissa on her bicycle with her school satchel on her back. Victor and the other teenagers. Grainy photographs taken without their knowledge.

Anna Bagger shook her head.

'Sick bastard. He's been stalking them for years, it would appear.'

She looked up.

'We need a detailed profile of him. Where did he grow up? Where does his family live? Where might he go? Who the hell is he?'

She pointed at the architect's drawing. 'And find someone who can make sense of this.'

She scratched the paper with a fingernail.

'That's where he is.'

86

KIR STRUGGLED TO find her bearings. They had been under way for some time. Not so much as a crack of light seeped into the boot where she was lying, in a foetal position with her knees tucked under her chin. The silence was as complete as if she had been buried in a deep grave.

She tried to reconstruct the journey from the beach until now. Probably fifteen minutes had passed. He drove the car first through Grenå – she had heard the engines of other cars and knew they had stopped at traffic lights a couple of times – and then to the other side of the town, where he accelerated and the car went round several bends and up and down gentle hills. The boot smelled of hairspray, which made her think of her mother.

A moment ago, the car had almost come to a standstill, then turned sharply as if it was being slowly manoeuvred through an archway and into a courtyard. To her it felt as if they were driving over cobblestones, or at least a surface that wasn't tarmac.

And now they had come to a complete halt. She listened attentively. Almost total silence. Apart from the creaking sounds in the car as it cooled down after the engine had been turned off. A gentle breeze rustling the trees and the odd raindrop that landed on the stony ground or the car with a hollow clunk.

The boot was opened and Morten pushed his great shovels of hands underneath her and scooped her up. They couldn't be in a public place, she thought. It must be dark now, anyway, but even so. They were in the countryside. Unobserved. At the back of a warehouse, a farm or some other isolated place. Somewhere he felt in charge and at home.

She was quickly carried down some steps. A heavy door groaned on iron hinges and she was taken into a room which smelled stale and mouldy. From here, they went down several more steps and the fresh air went from her nostrils and was replaced with a stuffy atmosphere, as if they were in an underground cavern. But the ground here was a stone floor. She could tell from his footsteps as he carried her.

For a while she was deposited on the freezing cold floor while she heard him fiddling with something in a corner. Then he picked her up and she could feel herself being sat down on a hard seat. He made some adjustments and she felt cold metal around her legs and neck. Then he took the blindfold from her eyes without saying a word. She knew why. He had something to show her. And what she saw would frighten the life out of her.

She was sitting on a garrotte. Her arms were attached to arm rests and her legs were enclosed in iron cuffs. The iron ring closed around her neck.

And then something different and completely unforeseen happened. He started to rig something else up. It took time and he was very careful, and she heard him muttering to himself. She followed his every move. All the time, she knew what he would do next before he actually did it. She started trembling as he pushed an object under her bottom.

He bent over her and with his lips touching her ear – she could smell his breath – he whispered:

'You'll have to excuse me. I have another, more urgent matter to attend to. Now don't you go bombing off again.'

He turned the clamp. The iron ring tightened around her neck, and she felt herself being strangled as the sharp steel spike bored into her neck. Coloured dots danced in front of her eyes. She couldn't move a millimetre.

She listened in the darkness for his footsteps, which receded down a corridor to her left. She strained to follow how far he went, but it was impossible. Instead, she heard another sound. Tick tock, tick tock. In her imagination it soon grew into a deafening noise and filled the whole room.

The ticking was the bomb he had attached to the garrotte and to her.

87

THE FRONT OF the salon looked like something from the 1950s. A sign saying *Salon Lotte* hung above the door, and in the sole shop window, on a bed of distressed velvet, there was a display of faded photographs of women with elaborate hairstyles, along with a variety of hair products in a range of colours: shampoos, conditioners, mousses and other essentials. The opening hours printed on the door told him the salon was closed on Sundays, but Peter could hear voices inside and he knocked.

A middle-aged woman opened. She had short, raven-black hair, which looked dyed. Her skin had spent the day in a tanning salon and her bust bulged in a tight black T-shirt. Everything about her looked artificial, except for the green eyes that observed Peter with curiosity.

'Come on in. I'll only be a minute.'

Peter entered. A woman sat in the hairdressing chair. The black-haired woman picked up her scissors and resumed her work, holding a lock of hair and cutting it off. Blond hair fell to the ground, where there was already a huge pile.

Peter sat down next to a young girl with black roots beneath her long, butter-coloured hair. Obviously a VAT-free haircut on an official day of rest was so desirable that you had to queue.

'You don't look like you need a trim,' the hairdresser, whom he took to be Lotte, commented over her shoulder.

'I'm looking for Morten Kold. I believe you're his sister.'

She turned around with the scissors in her hand. She was about to say something when there was another knock on the door.

'Hang on.'

She went to open it and a man of around Peter's own age entered.

Lotte motioned for Peter to get up and guided the new arrival into the chair where waiting customers were sitting.

'Why didn't you say?'

She winked at Peter. He recognised flirting when he saw it.

'You didn't ask.'

She smiled and resumed her cutting.

'I don't know where Morten is. But I hope he turns up soon because he borrowed my car yesterday and he still has it.'

'Doesn't he have his own car?'

'He said it was in the garage.'

Peter decided to play up to the flirting she had started.

'Nice place you have here. Perhaps I should consider getting myself a Sunday haircut.'

He ran his hand over his short hair. 'I mean, when it's had time to grow a bit. I last had it cut two weeks ago.'

'Where?'

'In Grenå.'

She looked at him in the mirror. He saw the glint in her eyes.

'I can do a better job. And probably cheaper.'

'I'm sure you can.'

She sent him a smirk, still via the mirror, while the scissors snipped off a few more strands of hair.

'I can give you my card.'

She took one from a pile on the counter and handed it to him.

'I imagine you do the whole family, don't you? Your own family, I mean.'

She giggled.

'All of them.'

He took a guess:

'I bet Morten is one of those people who just wants a number three?'

She made a half-turn.

'Takes me two minutes. He has no patience. I've no idea why he's always so busy.'

Peter said in a friendly voice:

'Perhaps it's best to keep busy, given what's happened to him.'

She put down the scissors and ran her fingers through the client's hair, which was still damp. He saw her sad expression reflected in the mirror.

'Of course. Losing Liv hit him hard. It was hard for all of us.'

In a flash, Peter understood the anger that could consume a man whose child had been subjected to what Liv had had to go through. How would Peter himself have reacted? He couldn't know, but he imagined it would be hard to suppress the hatred and desire for revenge. And yes, it would be tempting to want to give those responsible a taste of their own medicine so they would know what it was like to lose the most precious thing in the world. It wasn't a nice thought, and he wasn't proud of it. But it would have crossed his mind, he had no doubt.

'Where do I start looking, if I want to find Morten?'

Lotte shrugged.

'He's in the process of selling his house, so he probably won't be there. Have you tried the flat in Grenå?'

'I've just come from there.'

She mulled over the question.

'Morten is the type to go missing and suddenly reappear. We've learned to live with that in our family.'

'Ever since he was little?'

She nodded, took a hairdryer and started drying the customer's new haircut. She shouted over the noise:

'He always found somewhere to hide. It was bloody irritating, especially when we had just been told to do the washing-up.'

She added: 'And there are plenty of places to hide out here in the country.'

A hunch made Peter dig deeper:

'Don't tell me you're a local girl? I thought I detected a touch of Copenhagen in your accent.'

She clearly enjoyed being associated with the big city and life in the fast lane.

'I lived there with my husband for seven years. But I come from the provinces.'

She puffed up the client's hair.

'Out by St Mary's, in fact.'

Peter held his breath. She smiled.

'Our dad was the gatekeeper there,' said Lotte, now with her back to him while she let the hairdryer shape the client's hair. 'We lived in the gatekeeper's lodge when we were kids.'

Peter released the air between compressed lips. The convent. Beatrice. Magnus and Ea-Louise. Inside, he was like a sack that had been tied at the top with all the events of the last few weeks. Miriam and Bella. Simon and Morten. Old bones and fresh bodies. He hoped there wouldn't be any more.

He nodded to thank the hairdresser and held up her business card as he waved.

'I'll pop back some time.'

He took her smile with him as he disappeared out of the door.

88

'AND YOU'RE QUITE sure?' Anna Bagger asked.

In the meantime, it had grown dark. They were sitting in Mark's car, all three of them, outside the entrance to the convent beneath the tall trees. Mark passed on the question, with a glance at Peter, who was sitting at the back. Anna Bagger sent the man on the back seat a sceptical glare via the rear-view mirror. In front of them, in one of the police's big vans, eight officers from the Armed Response Unit wearing visors and carrying specialist weapons awaited orders.

'There are no guarantees,' Peter said. 'But yes. He must know these buildings inside out.'

Mark was convinced Peter was right.

'It fits with the drawings. We scanned them and emailed them to a local architect. He thinks they're drawings of the crypt beneath the old chapel.'

Peter nodded. Mark knew they were on the same wavelength. It made sense. The chapel was no longer in use. It must be possible to come and go unseen, especially if you knew the area well.

'Everything leads back to the convent,' Mark said, now primarily addressing Anna. 'It fits with the discovery of Melissa, his first murder victim. Afterwards he grew more audacious with increasingly spectacular crime scenes.'

'So the garrotte is somewhere inside the convent?' Anna Bagger asked.

Mark nodded.

'Peter's right. This guy knows his way around. He's studied this place, recently as well as in the past.'

Peter briefly met Anna Bagger's gaze in the rear-view mirror. He wasn't a huge fan of hers, but at that moment he could feel the responsibility that weighed on her shoulders.

'Poor Melissa,' she said. 'She didn't know it, but by moving out here she walked straight into a trap.'

'Perhaps it wasn't such a coincidence,' Mark said. 'He could have manipulated her in some way, we just haven't found out how.'

'On the Net?'

'For example. The IT department hasn't finished with her computer yet. They might have been in contact through some chat room, where he pretended to be someone else. Perhaps Melissa asked for advice.'

Anna Bagger smiled thinly.

'Something like this: I'm a young woman who just wants to be left alone. Where can I go?'

Mark nodded.

'Melissa might have thought she was talking to another young woman.'

'And then that woman said: I once spent a year in a convent. I can recommend it?'

'Something along those lines,' Mark said. 'He must have made contact with her somehow. Just like he stalked all of them, for years. They were his hobby. It kept him alive.'

Anna Bagger wrapped her arms around her chest and gave a shiver, as though she were cold.

'What does the drawing say? How about access?'

'There are two ways into the chapel.'

Mark unfolded the drawing and pointed. 'And once we're inside, there are two doors with steps leading down to the crypt.'

He shone the narrow, precise beam of his torch on the map.

'We need to cover both routes, of course. I suggest half the Armed Response Unit go through this door, with us . . .' he pointed, 'and the rest stay on standby outside the other door.'

'Sounds good to me,' Anna said. 'I'll negotiate, if there's anything to negotiate.'

All great theory, of course. But if Morten had Kir and she wasn't already dead, he might threaten to kill her. They might have to persuade him to give her up.

'OK,' Mark said to his boss. 'Shall we go?'

Anna Bagger gave the order to the head of the Armed Response Unit to move carefully through the terrain towards the target. Then she opened the car door and turned around to Peter in the back.

'Thanks for the tip-off. You can go now.'

Big words, coming from her. Mark heard Peter mutter some remark before he opened the car door and left, as if he couldn't wait to put distance between them. At the back of his mind, though, Mark knew the carpenter had no plans to go home to his cliff. He was in much too deep for that. But Mark said nothing; he just watched Peter walk away until he was swallowed up by the darkness.

The convent was located on a plot the size of six football pitches. The old chapel was situated roughly in the centre. They moved towards the target, through the convent gate, over the moat, and across the cobbled convent courtyard to the other side. It was like a computer game, Mark thought. Soldiers in the darkness. When you knew they were there and you were trying to be quiet, the rustling sounded like a reverberating echo as they deployed into their positions.

When they reached the chapel, they saw the *Salon Lotte* car parked discreetly under some foliage, close to the forest. Anna Bagger touched the bonnet.

'Cold,' she said.

Mark put his hand on the wing and the cold went through him. The air temperature was around 3°, he guessed. How long would a car stay warm? How long had Morten been here, alone with Kir?

They found the two entrances and split up in silence. After some time he heard Anna Bagger's voice in the darkness:

'Right, we're going in.'

89

PETER STOOD AT the door to the church, which was about one hundred metres from the old convent. The church was a part of the new convent building, where the nuns lived. It was very quiet, but nevertheless he sensed there was life inside.

He stopped for a fraction of a second to reflect that here he was, about to interrupt a sacred time of divine grace and shock people out of their rituals. It felt like bursting a beautiful soap bubble, but it couldn't be helped. Then he stepped forward and opened the door to the church. Inside, wax candles flickered down the aisle and four nuns were kneeling by the altar. He recognised the small, round figure on the far right and set off up the aisle. She knelt there praying for the forgiveness of man's sins, and thereby also his. He briefly considered the irony of the situation. Because while she was praying, while she had her life at the convent, she had indirectly pushed him into the arms of his enemies and was perhaps at this very moment exposing Magnus and Ea-Louise to danger. Nothing was ever simple in this world. What on the surface appeared to be good could turn out to have the opposite effect. What appeared to be an evil act could turn out to be good.

He knew they would hear his footsteps, but no one turned around. He sensed that prayer books were being clutched and eyes were being pressed shut to maintain concentration and shut out the real world.

He dropped to his knees next to her, not caring about the chaos he brought with him. His side was throbbing where the shot had nicked him and his whole body ached after the fight with Rico and his men at the old mill. He thought about Kaj, whom he had left at the vet's. Kaj's eyes had followed him, loyal and patient, as he left, and Peter had felt like a traitor. Anger was now raging inside him, spreading to his hands, which he rested on the brass rail in front of them. He could see and feel they were trembling and he had to restrain himself from grabbing Sister Beatrice by the shoulders and shaking the truth out of her.

Instead, he whispered next to her hood:

'Where are they?'

He saw her reaction: she shut her eyes tight and likewise her mouth. She tried to conceal her face by lowering her bowed head towards her folded hands.

'You've used me.'

He said it aloud this time. The other nuns shifted uneasily.

Beatrice gathered up her habit, got to her feet and left the altar without a word and started walking down the aisle. He followed her.

When they reached the porch, he saw that her cheeks were flushed.

'They're in a safe place, Peter. We agreed it was better this way.'

'We?'

'Magnus,' she said. 'And his mother and her friend.'

Miriam, Peter thought. The nun and the whore. Together they had cooked up a dish consisting of outright lies and lies of omission – all in a good cause.

'So Magnus is no longer on the run through fields and woods with his rucksack?'

He said it so aggressively that she flinched.

'He and his mother contacted me yesterday. Melissa had told him about me and said he could trust me. They thought he and Ea-Louise would be safe here.'

Beatrice sent Peter a pleading look.

'I couldn't say no. For Melissa's sake. So I agreed to hide them.'

'But they made it look as if he was still drifting from place to place?'

'It seemed logical to distract the killer's attention in that way,' Beatrice said. Miriam couldn't have put it better herself.

'And me? I was just a pawn in your game. A naive, trusting man whose job it was to keep looking for Magnus and so lead the murderer in the wrong direction.'

'I never asked you to look for Magnus.'

He rolled his eyes towards the ceiling.

'But you knew what Bella and Miriam were up to. The three of you concocted the whole thing together.'

'Not until yesterday,' she said. 'I didn't know Magnus had run away when you and I talked about Melissa.'

He put his face close to hers, hating her innocence and her purity. She was just another do-gooder. A champion of good intentions, who trailed catastrophe in her wake. He'd had enough of goodness. Better an honest villain than a dishonest angel, he thought. Better a prison than a convent.

'Now you just listen to me, Beatrice,' he said, and made every word count. 'The news is that Magnus's mother and Miriam, her friend, had an agenda. You in your naivety and blind trust didn't know that. Their idea was to force me into the spotlight so that my enemies could get at me. But, oh no, you don't want to soil your hands with that story, do you? You only lied with the best of intentions, didn't you? For Magnus and out of love for Melissa . . .'

She flinched again. He could see she was confused and frightened. He reined himself in.

'Well, never mind about all that,' he sighed. 'Tell me where they are, Magnus and Ea-Louise. They may not be as safe here as you think.'

'I'll take you there.'

She produced a key from the depths of her pocket.

'They're locked in, are they?'

'It's for their own good. Follow me.'

There were tunnels everywhere underneath the old convent and she knew them like the back of her hand. There were rooms for tools and storage; there were stone walls and floors so ancient they had to be a part of the original convent. It was dark and dank and smelled of humus and mould and insects rustling in the corners.

'Here.'

They had walked for a long time and criss-crossed the crypts along narrow tunnels, lit only by a small lamp she had brought with her. He thought about his mobile, which could light up the dark. He also thought about his gun, which he had stuck into the lining of his trousers, and the Stanley knife he had used to cut off the biker's ear. Still, he felt unarmed. He knew only too well that weapons weren't always enough.

She knocked on a door, but there was no sound. Pressing her ear to the thick wooden door, she listened, then looked at him anxiously and held up the key. He pulled out his gun and saw the shock in her eyes. But it receded. She inserted the key into the lock and turned, but it didn't catch. She tried the door. It wasn't locked and there was light on the other side. Peter tried to stop her, but it was too late and she pushed open the door.

90

Mark couldn't see a thing. They had gone down into the chapel and had found one of the two routes to the crypt. Now they were standing at the very bottom of a shaft and were enveloped in darkness.

As he kicked the door open with a boot, the leader of the Armed Response Unit shouted:

'This is the police! We're armed!'

Mark gripped the handle of his service weapon. The door opened and they tumbled inside. The first armed officers screamed and shouted as they secured the room. Mark and Anna followed. A powerful cone of light cut through the darkness. Then he heard a sound and his cry got no further than his throat. It was the sound of a human being, a muffled, suppressed grunt from someone who was prevented from speaking.

'Kir!'

He called out her name and got an answer in the form of a long, drawn-out warning. Then he saw her, caught like an animal in a trap on the high-backed chair, a copy of the one in the basement at the Woodland Snail. But there was no sign of Morten. He must have known the end was near and they would be looking for him and Kir. He had devised this as a kind of endgame.

Mark barely had time to blink. Everything happened at a frightening speed. The room was filled with the noise of the officers and Anna Bagger, who walked towards the garrotte with her arms outstretched while offering words of reassurance.

'We'll get you out, don't worry.'

But then the warning cry came again, and Kir's eyes jerked from side to side and he saw what the others had not yet seen.

'Watch out!'

He had never used his lungs like this – it felt as if they would explode into atoms. His words reverberated around the room. Anna Bagger froze for a millisecond, but it was enough. 'There's a bomb!'

Total silence. Anna Bagger retreated.

'Clear the room!' she yelled. 'Call the bomb squad.'

Damn her. Mark stepped forward. She tried to order him away.

'Out, Mark. This isn't our department.'

He ignored her. He approached the garrotte, carefully reached out his hand and said to Kir:

'I'm going to take the gag out of your mouth, OK?'

Kir nodded. The iron ring around her neck was tight. He could see she was close to fainting. He did what he had said he would do. She moved her lips, but only a dry sound came out.

'Take it easy now,' he said.

She smiled wanly.

'I'm afraid Batman was busy. And Superman has been eating kryptonite again . . . You're stuck with me.'

She chuckled. Or croaked. He realised she had to hold her head up high and press it against the back of the chair in order not to be strangled.

'What do you know about bombs?' she wheezed.

'Not a lot,' he admitted. 'But you know plenty. We'll have to help each other.'

Meanwhile Anna Bagger herded the Armed Response Unit out of the crypt.

'Check the time,' Kir said in her distorted voice, trying to look out of the corner of her eyes. 'There might be a timer.'

He searched, but couldn't find anything.

'OK,' she said. 'That makes sense. He's made it motion-sensitive. If you get me out of the garrotte, and I stand up, it'll go bang.'

He gulped. His throat was dry and his hands were shaking.

'Well, at least there's no time pressure,' Kir said.

She closed her eyes. Her face twitched. They both knew she was

425

lying. She couldn't keep her head up for much longer. The moment she passed out, the bomb would be triggered.

'It's true I don't know anything about bombs,' Mark said, feeling the sweat running. 'But I'm good with my fingers. My guitar teacher always said so.'

She smiled.

'There's only one small problem: I'm sitting on the detonator and three sticks of dynamite.'

91

'Drop your gun.'

The man had a weapon pointed at the two teenagers trussed up in the corner. Peter dropped his gun with a clunk.

'Kick it over here. Hands above your head.'

Peter held his hands in the air and kicked. Morten picked up the gun and stuck it in the lining of his trousers, still keeping his own gun pointed at Magnus and Ea-Louise. The small scar by his eye throbbed. Peter remembered what Beatrice had told him: that Melissa had jabbed her keys into his face.

'We should never believe we can keep things to ourselves,' he said. 'I've known this place since before you were born.'

He nodded towards Sister Beatrice. Peter had pushed her behind him. She didn't say anything.

The man with the gun now pointed it straight at them. He was leaning against the wall. A naked light bulb shone from the ceiling. The room measured roughly ten square metres and was like an old-fashioned pantry. There were bags of potatoes in nets, wooden crates of apples and oranges, pumpkins, beetroot and leeks. On the shelves there were what looked like jars of marmalade and syrup from the convent garden. In the corner on the cold floor the two teenagers sat back to back. Two skinny, freezing teenagers. Peter could hear their teeth chattering and almost see their bodies shivering.

'Your sister sends her love.'

Instinct told him that talking was the way forward.

'Who the hell do you think you are?'

'We met at Kir's. My name's Peter.'

'I know who you are, smart arse. You're the one who's been rushing about like a bull in a fucking china shop.'

'Was it you who took my rosary that day on the cliff?'

'It was *my* rosary. I found it in the Cardinal's basement many years ago.'

The gun wavered nervously.

'Don't anyone move. Or they'll get it!'

Again Morten pointed the pistol at the two teenagers. They cowered in fear.

'Easy now,' Peter said. 'We're not going to do anything.'

Sister Beatrice stood as still as a column, but he could sense her distress. He held her arm, mostly to reassure her, but also to tell her to stay where she was. She wriggled free.

'Where's Kir?'

Morten grinned.

'She's dynamite, that Kir. Fancy her, do you?'

Peter's heart pounded.

'She's a friend.'

'*She's a friend*,' Morten mimicked. 'Anyway, right now your so-called friend is sitting on the famous chair with a bomb up her jacksie.'

'Where? In the crypt?'

'Wouldn't you like to know?'

Peter searched for a way to pump him, but decided to change the subject. He hoped the others would find Kir. He hoped she was alive and he would see her flaming-red hair and dimples once more.

'Simon,' he said. 'You used him.'

'Of course I used him.'

'You knew he would be suspected of killing Melissa.'

'Doh! The garrotte's second nature in that family.'

'You waited for him to be let out before you started on your spree.'

Morten smiled.

'I'm not a complete idiot. The timing was perfect. Everyone's entitled to a bit of luck if your daughter is going to die anyway.'

'How much did he know? Did you help each other? Did you

help him with his sister, and he returned the favour with Melissa and the others?'

The bitterness was there, despite the smile.

'Simon knows nothing,' Morten said. 'He might suspect something, but he's too busy taking his revenge on Lise. He doesn't care what I get up to. I just had to provide him with a place to stay.'

'Where?'

'My house, obviously. It's on the market.'

There was a moment of silence. Then Morten continued as if he wanted to justify himself:

'Do you have any children?'

Peter shook his head.

'Then you won't understand.'

'Probably not.'

Morten leaned back against the wall again. The gun moved between the teenagers and Peter and Beatrice in a never-ending circle.

'You think it's your job to give them security and a good life. You think it's within your power.'

The words came out between gritted teeth.

'You have to protect your children from constant danger.'

He blinked.

'And you're happy to do it. Because you love them deeply, as you've never loved before. But then one day something happens you have no control over. Your child gets sick. Almost dies. And afterwards she's not the same child. The same daughter.'

The gun was shaking. His body shook with it. This could end in tragedy, Peter thought.

'Her name was Liv,' Morten said with death in his eyes. 'My daughter's name was Life. But after the infection there was no more life left in her eyes.'

Peter didn't know which was worse: a father who loved or a mother who didn't. He had no wish to be in a situation which mirrored his own life in reverse.

Morten turned to Beatrice.

'You,' he sneered. 'You couldn't keep a secret if you tried. You make so much noise when you walk that the devil can hear you in hell.'

'Was that how you found your way here?' Beatrice asked in a nervous voice.

He sent her a single, hostile nod.

'All I had to do was follow you. Dead easy. I knew they were here.'

The body next to Peter was convulsed in sobs. Panic took hold of Peter, but he suppressed it. They were in it up to their necks here.

'I did it for Melissa,' Beatrice wept. 'But I got it all wrong. All of this is my fault.'

Peter pushed her back, but she rushed forward.

'I'm sorry, Magnus,' she wept. 'Please forgive me.'

'Beatrice!'

Peter shouted, but she didn't seem to hear him. She ran to the two children as if to embrace them. Morten raised his arm with the gun.

'Help them, Peter.'

They were her last words, then Morten fired and she collapsed on the stone floor. Her habit settled around her like a punctured balloon. Peter went for Morten while he was still watching in amazement. He used his head as a battering ram and launched himself at the man with the gun. The arm holding the weapon slammed into the wall and metal scraped against stone. Peter kneed the man in the groin and knocked him off balance. The gun went off and fired into the ceiling, raining dust and stone down on them. In the noise and the confusion, Peter pulled the Stanley knife from his boot. Morten grabbed Peter round the neck and tried to throttle him, but let go when Peter stabbed him in the throat. He gurgled and the gun fell to the floor with a clunk. Peter picked it up and quickly pulled his own gun from the lining of Morten's trousers. But there was no resistance left in Morten. He slowly slid down the stone wall and slumped to the floor. Peter watched as Morten's life ebbed away with the blood spurting from his neck in a thick jet.

'I hope it was worth it,' Peter said.

The other man met his gaze. His breathing was shallow. Then his eyes closed and a smile spread across his face before his last sigh extinguished that too.

92

THEY WERE ALONE in the crypt. The Armed Response Unit and Anna Bagger had left. It was up to them. Mark knew they might die. This was a huge risk.

'OK,' Kir said. 'Now listen to me.'

'I'm listening.'

'Good. A bomb consists of three things: a power source, a circuit with a switch – which sets off the bomb – and a detonator. Are you with me?'

'I'm with you.'

'The safest option is to find the power source. Usually that's a battery.'

'OK.'

'If you can't find a power source, you can go for the circuit, the switches or the detonator.'

He said nothing for fear that his voice would quiver.

'I think he hid the power source on me,' she said. 'He rummaged around my clothes. He stuck something down the back under my jacket. And, as I said, I'm sitting on the detonator and the main charge. Approximately six hundred grammes of dynamite by my calculations.'

She closed her eyes briefly and opened them again.

'As Morten left, I could hear a clock ticking. It stopped after two minutes and has been silent ever since.'

'OK. What does that mean?' he asked.

'He was afraid to connect the switch while he was still here. So he equipped the bomb with a small clock. I think that was the sound I heard. So the clock activated the bomb two minutes after he had left.'

'How . . .'

He was about to ask her how, but she had already moved on. He saw moisture on her upper lip. She was starting to shake. Time was running out.

'I want you to examine very carefully where he placed it on me,' she croaked. 'Don't worry. I'm not embarrassed.'

He opened her jacket.

'It's in your lap,' he said.

'Perfect. What is it?'

'An egg timer.'

It looked like a crazy Heath Robinson device. There were two nails glued to it and a length of cable had been soldered to the nails. He described it.

'That's the switch,' she said. 'Don't touch it. Where do the cables go?'

'One goes under your bum.'

He took a closer look. 'And there are two cables sticking out of your trousers. I can't follow the second cable.'

She nodded. He heard her gulp and she seemed to be swaying slightly.

'Are you OK?'

It was a stupid question. She nodded.

'Never better.'

But now he could see her eyes were really starting to cloud over. He grabbed her and held her against the upright of the garrotte. Her eyes rolled back, revealing the whites.

'Stay with me, Kir,' he said.

'Give me a good reason,' she mumbled.

'I'm not one. I'm impotent.'

Her eyes rolled down and stared at him. He quickly continued.

'You deserve better. A better man than me.'

She smiled.

'Thanks. At least that's an explanation.'

She seemed to pull herself together by sheer force of will. She moistened her lips.

433

'OK. We'll hurry but slowly. It's too risky to tamper with the circuit,' she explained. 'I don't know how he assembled it. We need to remove the detonator near the explosives, so only the detonator will go off. With me?'

'Yes.'

'Don't want it going off while I'm sitting on it,' she said.

Mark ventured a smile.

'Right, so what do I do?'

'Put your hand under my bum. Find the detonator. It's probably the size of half a pencil. There will be two cables in one end.'

Carefully he slipped his hand under her camouflage trousers. His fingers quickly found what they were looking for.

'I've got it.'

'Check. Is there more than one cable?'

Warily, he felt around, centimetre by centimetre.

'Just one.'

'Good. Very, very carefully, remove the detonator. If it goes off, you might lose your hand, OK?'

'OK.'

His hands were trembling. He hoped she couldn't see.

'Easy does it. Pull the detonator away.'

Sweat was pouring down his neck and off his forehead into his eyes. They misted up. His heart was pounding like a piston as he, very, very carefully, slid the pencil out of the marzipan-like dynamite a millimetre at a time. He had always imagined he would see his life flashing by in a situation like this. But in his head he only had room for her and him. The rest flickered like a defective TV screen.

'Done!'

She swayed again.

'Kir!'

'OK,' she said in a thick voice and her eyes rolled around in their sockets. 'Put the detonator as far from the explosives as you can. As you pull me out, that will be the only thing to explode. Take off your bulletproof vest and place it on top of the detonator and put your foot on top so that it won't slide off.'

He did as she said and mouthed a silent thank you to the head of the Armed Response Unit who had insisted on him wearing the vest when he – like some rootin'-tootin' cowboy – blurted it wasn't necessary.

'And then get me out of this fucking chair.'

He set to work with his foot resting on the detonator under the vest. First, he freed her legs. Then her arms, and finally, he removed the ring around her neck. She blinked lethargically, but then visibly braced herself.

'Right, here we go. When you pull me off, the switch underneath me will complete the circuit and your detonator will go bang. Have you got that? You might end up with a sore foot. Press down hard on the vest.'

'Understood. I've got you. On the count of three?'

'On the count of three.'

He grabbed her under the arms.

'One.'

'Two.'

'Three.'

He pulled her off the garrotte. At the same time he heard the bang and felt a small explosion under his foot. He lost his balance as he was propelled backwards with Kir in his arms. They landed on the floor, she on top of him.

A few seconds passed. She lay limp in his arms. She mumbled:

'Just friends then?'

He sensed the relief.

'Just friends,' he said, and stroked her hair.

'Good friends?'

'None better.'

Epilogue

23 April
Gjerrild Cliff

PETER READ THE invitation once more and then he stuffed it in his pocket.

'Stay, Kaj.'

He tried to call the dog. But the hare was proving more interesting, and soon the chase was on across the pale green shoots on the cliff top field, precisely where a farmer's horses had once refused to plough, or at least that's what people in Gjerrild said. No carrots or whips could get the working horses back in front of the plough. However, it transpired that the horses knew best. They sensed a landslide was imminent. And, sure enough, half of the farmer's field vanished into the sea, part of where the plough would normally have been working. This was the area now known as Gjerrild Cliff.

The dog raced in vain after the hare across the field where now there was no sign of a horse-drawn plough. However, there was a team of forensic anthropologists with their assistants in white coveralls that billowed like parachutes in the fierce wind.

Peter took this as an opportunity to walk along the field boundary to collect his dog and have a few words with Mark Bille, who had arrived in a police car. He too stood on the cliff, windblown, his black hair whirling around him, staring at what the forensic anthropologists had unearthed.

'Ever find your leak in the force?' Peter asked.

It was cold. He stuffed his hands in his pocket and touched the envelope.

'Nope.'

The wind took extra hold of the policeman's hair as if to underline the fact that the untrustworthy officer's name was still blowing in the wind. Peter wasn't surprised.

'Is it true what they say?'

'What do they say?' Mark asked.

'That those are the Cardinal's bones?'

Mark looked at the bones that had been laid out on a tarpaulin. The forensic anthropologists had reconstituted the skeleton, which appeared to be intact.

'At least the information about there being a dead man here on the cliff turned out to be correct.'

'Reliable source?'

Mark nodded. The whole of Djursland knew that his grandfather had confessed to killing the Cardinal, before dying from pneumonia earlier that spring. It was a murder which had been committed in the turmoil after the war: the Resistance fighters' revenge on Kurt Falk, the traitor who had made a fortune out of collaborating with the occupying Nazis.

'Fairly reliable,' Mark said.

'How did he die?'

Mark pointed to the skull and Peter saw the bullet hole at the back. An execution. Mark's grandfather must have been as cold as ice.

Mark flashed a half-smile. 'And you're still sure you had nothing to do with that incident at the old mill?'

The envelope rustled in Peter's pocket as he scrunched it up. He stared down at the Cardinal's bones. In one hundred years all of this would be forgotten. That included these old bones and the invitation from his mother and sister. A summer party. A seventy-fifth birthday. One of them was turning twenty-five, the other fifty. Had the time arrived when he could no longer hide out here in his chosen exile?

He looked at Mark and shrugged.

'Of course. I don't know anything about that.'

He thought of another dead person, one lying in the cemetery. My. Bella had relinquished any authority over her daughter's earthly remains and Peter was content. It was a kind of pact he had entered into with her and Miriam. Winter was over and spring had arrived, and he had reckoned it was time to make his peace. It had taken him this long – five months – to reflect on the women in his life. Eventually he had given up. There was no logic to it.

When he had gone to visit Beatrice in hospital, the others had also been there: Bella and Miriam and the abbess. Together, they had made the ward reek with their sickly-sweet, sticky flowers, like a Turkish whorehouse, and how they could have so much to talk about was beyond him. Non-stop yackety-yackety-yak. So much for silent, contemplative nuns. He had carefully placed the rosary he had found in Morten's pocket on Beatrice's bedside table and made a quick getaway.

'Here, Kaj!'

The dog slunk back, hare-less and embarrassed. Peter brought his conversation with Mark Bille to an end. But before he drove over to Kir in the twilight and the promise of a fish supper, he stopped by the cemetery and the dog accompanied him down the narrow paths. As usual, he hadn't brought a candle or a wreath or flowers. Nevertheless, he squatted down, stroked the stone and did some weeding while Kaj roamed around and chewed the odd flower or two.

Peter didn't say anything. He couldn't find the words, but felt a little like the horse that had bridled at ploughing the farmer's field. Something was stirring inside him. It was as if a gust of wind had blown past him and touched his cheek. Then – somewhere out of the corner of his eye – he thought he saw a fleeting figure in a coat several sizes too large, her mousy brown hair flapping in the breeze.

Even the dog appeared to see her. He stopped in the middle of a flower bed, tipped his head back and emitted a mournful howl, as if to call her back.

Time passed, possibly only a few seconds, then an icy blast tore at his clothing and flattened the dog's ears and the moment was gone.

Peter got up. The dog followed him as he walked back to his car. Hoping against hope, he glanced back over his shoulder, but whatever it was they had just seen had . . . gone with the wind.

About Elsebeth Egholm

Author photograph © Sanne Berg

Elsebeth Egholm is a former journalist who is now the bestselling Danish 'Queen of Crime'. Her books have been bestsellers in Germany, France, Sweden, Italy and Norway. In 2011, she published *Three Dog Night* which was the start of a new series introducing ex-convict Peter Boutrup and was an instant bestseller. This is the second in the series.